D0791042

Praise for Crystal Jordan and *Carnal Desires*

"World building is truly an art, and Crystal Jordan has created not just one, but multiple complex worlds in which to set her erotic romances. Each story is more fascinating than the one before. There are books you read and those very special ones you devour. . . . *Carnal Desires* is definitely one of the latter. Utterly spellbinding, with magnetic plots and luscious romances that will stay with you long after the story ends. This is definitely an author to watch. More importantly, these are definitely stories you don't want to miss."

Kate Douglas, author of *Wolf Tales*

Books by Crystal Jordan

CARNAL DESIRES

ON THE PROWL

SEXY BEAST V
(with Kate Douglas and Vonna Harper)

Published by Kensington Publishing Corporation

ON THE PROWL

CRYSTAL JORDAN

ROUND LAKE AREA
LIBRARY
906 HART ROAD
ROUND LAKE, IL 60073
(847) 546-7060

APHRODISIA

KENSINGTON BOOKS

http://www.kensingtonbooks.com

APHRODISIA BOOKS are published by

Kensington Publishing Corp.
119 West 40th Street
New York, NY 10018

Copyright © 2009 by Crystal Jordan

All rights reserved. No part of this book may be reproduced in any form or by any means without the prior written consent of the Publisher, excepting brief quotes used in reviews.

All Kensington Titles, Imprints, and Distributed Lines are available at special quantity discounts for bulk purchases for sales promotions, premiums, fund-raising, and educational or institutional use.

Special book excerpts or customized printings can also be created to fit specific needs. For details, write or phone the office of the Kensington special sales manager: Kensington Publishing Corp., 119 West 40th Street, New York, NY 10018, attn: Special Sales Department, Phone: 1-800-221-2647.

Aphrodisia and the A logo Reg. U.S. Pat & TM Off

ISBN-13: 978-0-7582-2900-7
ISBN-10: 0-7582-2900-3

First Kensington Trade Paperback Printing: May 2009

10 9 8 7 6 5 4 3 2 1

Printed in the United States of America

Acknowledgments

A smart woman will always thank her best friend first. Or at least a woman who has a strong sense of self-preservation. I do my level best to fall into at least one of those categories at all times, so this one is for Michal.

There are those rare and splendiferous people who go the extra mile and help you clean up the utter crap that is the first (or ninth) rough draft. They deserve all the love I can muster and, at the very least, a nod on my Acknowledgments page. In the perfectly random order I prefer, they are Loribelle Hunt, R.G. Alexander, Eden Bradley, Lillian Feisty, Jennifer Leeland, Dayna Hart, Karen Erickson, Robin L. Rotham, Gwen Hayes, Red Garnier, Gemma Halliday, Imogen Howson, Bethany Morgan, and Jennifer Bianco.

I'm instituting a moment of silence for the profound awesomeness that is Jax Cassidy and Kristen Painter, wonderful women, superb talents, and founders of my lifeline, Romance Divas.

My Grams deserves to be thanked for being The Grams. Accept no substitute.

As ever, deepest thanks go to Agent Awesome Sauce, a.k.a. Lucienne Diver, and John Scognamiglio.

Contents

Claim Me

I

Antonio watched the men circle his mate from atop a building far above the alley they'd cornered her in. A few nimble leaps brought him to the end of the shadowed corridor. He jerked his clothes off and dropped them as he ran, shifted into his Panther form to let his black fur blend into the night, and stalked the men as they had stalked her.

The predators became the prey.

He ran his tongue down a long fang, anticipation and rage boiling hot in his veins. They would pay for scaring her. God and all the saints couldn't save them if they harmed her.

It had taken two days to track her scent after he'd sensed her in the city. And now he'd found her. Nothing compared to the ice that froze the blood in his veins when he heard her first scream, the terror of seeing men hunt her. Yes, these men would beg for his mercy before the night was through. A growl rumbled from his chest as he moved down the alley, his claws clicking on the pavement.

When one of the men grabbed for her, a roar ripped from his throat. Everyone froze, turning in slow motion to stare at the newcomer. A Panther. He bared his teeth and watched the man closest to him turn ghostly pale. He could smell their fear, taste the tang of it on his tongue, and he took a small amount of satisfaction in that.

This close, even his rage couldn't cloud the fact that the men weren't human. They were Panthers, like him. Worse, they were from his Pride. The Ruiz brothers—Marcos, Juan, and Roberto. His own people, under his rule. Why would they hunt a Panther female? If she belonged to another Pride and was visiting his territory, then her Pride leader would hold him responsible for any harm his people caused her. Not to mention she was his mate and he would shred them alive for hunting her in the first place.

She screamed, and the frozen tableau broke into chaos. Antonio lunged forward, slicing his claws into Roberto's calf. He went down with a spray of blood and saliva, squealing and clutching his leg.

Antonio leaped over the fallen man to sprint forward, intent on reaching his mate. Juan shifted to Panther form, hissing a warning, but it meant nothing to Antonio. They were past the point of warnings. A single leap forward and the two of them clashed in midair, claws and fangs tearing into each other. Antonio slashed across the young Panther's face and he rolled away with a whimper, his black fur matted with dark crimson blood.

Antonio's tail whipped around as he sprang for Marcos. The man tried to climb the wall, but he had no more chance of escape than Antonio's mate had. Antonio dragged him down to the ground, his fangs digging into the man's jeans. Both front paws planted on the younger man's chest, making him wheeze, and Antonio shoved his face into Marcos's. A growl vibrated his vocal cords, and what little blood was left in the man's face fled. His bloodshot eyes went wide with horror.

His mate's soft cry reached Antonio's ears, jerking him back from the edge of feral. He shuddered, fighting the instincts of his Panther nature. He turned toward her, wanting to comfort her and soothe her fear.

But she wasn't looking at him—she snarled at Juan, bracing her back against the wall as she hissed deep in her throat. A purr rumbled his chest at her courage.

Marcos took the opportunity to speak. "Please, sir. Listen to me. She doesn't deserve protection. She's a—"

A roar ripped free from Antonio's throat as he transformed into his human form. He hoisted the shorter man up by his T-shirt until they were nose to nose. "*Silence!* The three of you will be in my study when I return to the mansion. Is that clear?"

"But how long until—"

"Obey me. You won't enjoy the consequences if you don't. But I will." He dropped Marcos to his feet. The younger man scrambled away and ran. His brothers had already disappeared.

He turned back to his mate. "Are you all right?"

"Yes. You?" She shoved her dark hair out of her face, her fingers sifting through the streaks of blond that shot through the long strands. He soaked in the details of her, taking in every curve of her face and body. Her chocolate-brown eyes searched him and they went wide when she saw the straining erection jutting between his thighs. Shifting back had left him naked. A wry smile pulled at his lips. He was going to have to figure out where he'd dropped his clothes and hope some vagrant didn't steal them before he got there. For the moment, he focused on his mate.

She sucked in a quick breath when he took a step toward her. Swaying on her feet, she stared at him for long moments. The silence stretched to a fine breaking point. She shook her head, pressing the heel of her hand to her forehead. "It can't be."

She'd finally sensed it—that they were mates.

"Oh, but it can be. It is." Stalking forward, he backed her up against the brick wall. His nostrils flared to catch her sweet scent, the one he would become addicted to. He had no doubt she had the same adrenaline humming through her as he did, and it morphed into something hotter, more carnal. Anger and fear still pumped through his system. His shaking fingers fisted at his sides. His eyes narrowed at her and a dart of excitement flashed through her gaze. The delicate smell of her wetness filled his nostrils. It was heady. She swallowed, her lids dropping to half-mast.

She released a breathy laugh, and naked want shone in her gaze. "I don't believe it. We can't be mates."

"Let me prove it to you," he growled. His hands wrapped around her waist, lifting her against the rough brick. Her legs curved around his flanks, she arched against him, and made him snarl with his need. She drove him wild. Jerking her dress up, he found her naked underneath. Perfect. He pushed forward, his hips fitting into the cradle of hers. The blunt tip of his cock rubbed over her slick folds. Her gaze flashed with the same desire that burned in his veins. "Your name. Tell me your name."

Her little pink tongue darted out to slide along her lips. "Solana."

She whimpered, tightening her legs about him. He groaned, but held back from plunging his dick into the snug fit of her damp pussy. Barely. "Yes or no, Solana?"

Her hands reached for him, fingers burying into his hair. Choking on a breath, she arched her hips toward the press of his cock. "Yes."

He thrust hard and deep. She screamed, the slick muscles of her pussy clenching around his dick. He groaned, hammering his hips forward. Her back arched, and she shuddered around him. He held on to his control by the tips of his fingers as her orgasm fisted her sex around his cock again and again. She was so responsive, so amazing. He kept pushing into her until her moans caressed his ears and she moved with him toward another orgasm. A tear leaked down her cheek and she hissed softly. Her head rolled against the brick wall, and her eyes slid closed. He wanted her gaze on him, wanted to see her come apart in his arms. "Look at me, Solana."

She moaned, but didn't obey him, so he seated himself as deep as he possibly could, and stopped moving. Her brown eyes flared open. "Don't stop."

"I won't." He withdrew halfway and plunged back in, starting a slow, hard rhythm. She whimpered, clamping her knees on his hips, but she kept her gaze locked with his. Passion flushed her face, made her dark chocolate eyes shine. She was so beautiful—the most beautiful woman he'd ever seen. His mate. A grin curved his lips. "Tell me you want me."

A deep blush raced up her cheeks, her fingers tightening in his hair. She glanced away. "I'm doing it with you in an alley. Do you really have any doubts?"

He smiled down at her. "Ah, but I want to hear you say it."

Clamping her pussy around his cock, she pulled a groan from him. A hot, purely female smile flashed across her face as she locked her gaze with his. "I want you. I want you to fuck me hard and fast."

He choked on a breath and gave her what she asked for. The scent of her, the damp feel of her around his thrusting cock drove him right to the edge of his control. His fangs extended and he knew his eyes had turned the deep gold of a Panther's as he held himself back from shifting. The sound of her demanding he fuck her harder made his head feel as though it were going to explode. And if he was lucky, he might get fifty more years of this with her. A purr tangled with a groan in his throat. "You make me crazy."

"*I* make *you* crazy? Do I need to mention we're in an *alley* again?" She laughed, and it made the soft skin of her belly quiver against his. His breath hissed out.

He rotated his hips against her, and she shivered. The urge to finish the mating swamped him. To bite her. To make her his forever. Mate.

"No mating. No biting." She pressed her lips to his before he could take what he wanted. Her tongue twined with his, and their kiss was as harsh and demanding as their coupling had been.

He drove into her soft, willing body until she strained against him, until all he could think about was the orgasm just beyond his grasp. Fire crawled over his skin, settling deep inside him. The muscles in his belly tightened as the need to come overtook him. When she pulled her mouth free, her cries of passion rang in his ears, spurring him on. She twisted in his arms, sobbing as her pussy milked the length of his cock. A harsh groan burst from his throat as he froze, every muscle in his body locking as he jetted deep inside her.

They clung to each other in the aftermath of orgasm, their breathing nothing more than rasps of air. The instinct to finish the mating still clawed at him, but he forced himself to ignore it, to savor the feel of her in his arms. His mate. Unclaimed, but his.

She stirred against him, pushing at his shoulders. They both groaned when he pulled out of her. Her muscles clenched around his dick in one last spasm, and he fought the urge to shove back into her, to thrust his cock deep and sink his fangs in her flesh until she knew she could never be parted from him.

Dropping her feet to the ground, she slid out of his embrace and stepped away from him. She smoothed her dress down around her thighs, not looking at him. "I don't even know your name."

"Antonio." He stepped in front of her, silently demanding she acknowledge him, what they had experienced together this wild night. "I am Antonio Cruz."

"Cruz?" The color leeched from her lovely face. "Esteban Cruz's heir?"

Arching a brow at her reaction to his name, he shook his head. "Not heir. My father died last month."

"Ah." Her shoulders drew into a tense line. Obviously, his father had made no friend with this woman. "I'm afraid I don't keep up with Pride politics."

"You weren't at the loyalty ceremony. I would have remembered you." He might not have been able to resist taking her then and there. His cock swelled again.

Her arms folded protectively around her waist. "I'm not a member of your Pride."

"Which one, then?" Once they were mated, she would have to leave her current Pride to join his. Unless she was a Pride leader herself. Then, well, things would get complicated. But the only Pride in the world with a female leader right now was in Australia ... and she was well into her fifties. Definitely not his mate.

"None of them." She lifted one shoulder and let it drop.

"No Panther is without a Pride." It just wasn't done. They found strength in numbers. Without the Prides, they had to hide who they were from everyone, and in cat form were the prey to any human with a gun.

"This one is." She turned away, ghosting down the alley.

"Wait." He took a step after her, confusion flooding him at this new turn of events. "Why?"

She didn't turn around, just paused for the briefest of moments. "Why no Pride? I was part of your father's Pride, but I left when I came of age." Bitterness edged her soft voice. "Or I was invited to leave."

He had no doubts about his father's ruthlessness and need to control everything and everyone around him—including his heir—but the more members a Pride had, the more prestige for the Pride. Bigger was better. "My father wouldn't do that."

"Even to a non-shifter?"

His mouth opened and then snapped closed as shock rocked through him. He watched her slip away, disappearing into the cool mist of the San Francisco night.

"*Dios mio.*" Nausea fisted his gut. A non-shifter. A Panther shifter unable to change forms. They were second-class citizens in the Prides, treated as nothing. Less that nothing, depending on the Pride leader's attitude toward them. So much of what made a Panther a Panther remained a mystery, including what made a non-shifter unable to change forms. Some of the older, more superstitious Panthers thought non-shifters were a curse upon a Pride.

Scientists believed that panthers were any large cat that was black, usually a genetic mutation of a leopard or jaguar. The average human thought panthers were a separate species all to themselves. The average human was much closer to the truth than they knew. While leopards and jaguars *could* be all black, a true Panther was a shape-shifter able to transform between animal and human forms. Some thought it was a demonic curse, others thought it was a blessing from a benevolent god. The truth of their magic had been lost long ago. Now it didn't matter why—they just needed to survive.

Contrary to popular legend, a wereanimal's bite wouldn't turn someone in to a shape-shifter. If only it were so simple to keep the population alive. Panthers had to breed in their animal form, and humans couldn't be turned into Panthers. Survival was a constant struggle. It might be easier if they could breed without being mated, but they couldn't. Panther children were rare and highly prized. That the Cruz family had *four* children was almost unheard-of among the Prides. If anything, one or two was much more normal.

The Ruiz family was another with exceptionally high breeding rates—and the Ruiz boys' actions toward his mate made sudden, sickening sense. She must have come and gone in his Pride while he'd been fostering in South America. With his very conservative father as a Pride leader, he didn't even want to imagine what she must have been through. And what more would she have to go through now that he had discovered what she was to him?

He swallowed. His mate couldn't shift, couldn't have children. And he was the Pride leader. God help him.

What the hell was he going to do?

2

Wh23hat the hell was she going to do?

Solana raced through the streets of the city, letting the fog disguise the fact that her movements were far too fast for a human. The bitter irony of it clawed through her. If humans knew what she was, they'd recoil from her as though she were a monster—because she was a shape-shifter. Her own kind recoiled from her as though her inability to shift was contagious. Not shifter enough to be Panther, too shifter to be human.

Either way she had to hide. As a teenager, she and her father had concealed her non-shifter status for as long as possible. And after she left, she'd always had to hide that she saw too much, smelled too much, heard too much. Sensed too much because she had the extra abilities of a Panther. Except one. The only one that really mattered.

And her mate was the new Pride leader. *No. Please, no.* Why couldn't he have been a human? Someone who wouldn't care that she wasn't whole. Deformed. Broken.

Slamming inside her condo, she whipped the door closed behind her and locked it. Her breath heaved out in painful pants, a stitch lancing into her side. She clamped each hand over the opposite elbow and hunched forward at the waist for long moments. The couch was a few steps away, but it felt like miles. Exhaustion swamped her, pulling at her very bones. It was all too much—the attack, Antonio. Adrenaline had pumped through her veins and now that the rush had passed, she crashed hard. Collapsing onto the sofa, she shivered, her teeth chattering together.

Sheer, unadulterated terror had ripped through her when she'd smelled the three Panther males and known they'd followed her after she got off work at the bar that night. No good had ever come of her interactions with other Panthers, not since it became apparent that she was . . . different.

Panther children didn't gain the ability to shift until they reached puberty. The rush of hormones that caused maturity in human children also unleashed the feral animal inside Panthers. Thankfully, it also meant Panthers were old enough to understand what could happen to them if they shifted at the wrong time, in front of the wrong people. In front of humans. Small children couldn't be trusted with their secrets.

Her father had claimed she was a late bloomer for as long he could, but by the time she turned sixteen it was more than apparent that she simply wasn't going to be able to shift. Ever.

That's when her existence had become a living nightmare. They'd moved from the Pride in Europe to Australia and finally to America, trying to pretend that no one ever saw her shift because they'd just missed it. An elaborate façade that her father had grown weary of. Unwilling to deal with a deformed daughter, he'd left her in San Francisco—at the mercy of the North American Pride leader.

She pulled back from the ugly memories, the realization of what a freak of nature she was. She no longer allowed herself to feel the self-pity she once had. On a good day, she felt . . . nothing. But now she experienced an unfamiliar rush of sympathy for Antonio. He hadn't asked for this any more than she had. She doubted a man groomed to be a Pride leader had ever known the kind of rejection that would prepare him for denying himself his mate, and she knew what a bitter pill it was to swallow the first time. And the second. But it got easier with time. Less painful the more emotional distance one gained.

Today it was hard to maintain that distance, hard to pretend it all didn't matter. That finding her mate and not being able to claim him didn't hurt like hell. Her eyes burned with tears she hadn't shed in over a decade. Her hands trembled and she clenched her fingers into fists. She swallowed and pulled in a deep breath.

Don't lose control. It was a lesson she'd learned long ago. Never ever lose control. It was a weakness she couldn't afford. She wrapped her arms around herself, hugging the emotions tight, locking them within herself as she forced her limbs to stop shaking, as she contained herself behind a protective wall. It had saved her so many times, that wall. When Esteban found out what she was—or rather what she wasn't, he'd condoned every slight, every mistreatment, every cruelty visited on her. She was nothing to him, taking food from his Pride members' mouths. She couldn't contribute, couldn't give back.

No babies. Not ever. It was the cruelest slight. After all she'd lost, all she'd never have. To never feel a child grow within her. She laid a palm to her flat belly. Never.

Shaking herself, she drew up straight. She'd accepted that long ago. Meeting her mate didn't change that. He was just one more thing she couldn't have. No sane leader would allow her into his Pride, let alone *mate* with her.

She closed her eyes and leaned back against the couch, sighing as she forced her muscles to relax one by one. What a crazy day. Night. Whatever. Her mind spun with exhaustion and the memory of her mate's hands on her skin. She'd always heard sex was more intense with a mate, but had never dreamed she'd ever know for herself.

A shudder ran through her when she recalled how his fingers had bitten into her hips, how the rough brick had rasped against her skin while his long cock had thrust into her. Heat rushed through her, and her nipples drew tight to chafe against the bodice of her dress.

Even with the carnal instincts of the Panther people, she'd never gone so far so fast, never let her guard down enough, lost control enough. And God, she'd fucked a man in an *alley*. A flush burned her cheeks, and excitement she shouldn't let herself feel fluttered in her belly. But she couldn't deny that her flesh still tingled where his lips had touched. Goose bumps broke over her arms, making her shiver.

She gritted her teeth, trying to ignore the sudden rush of fire that streaked through her. Nothing had ever felt as good as when he'd touched her, a man she'd just met. What would closer acquaintance do for that intrinsic bond? If not for her non-shifter status, she might be able to find out. As it was, she would have to live on the memory. And it would need to last for a long, long time.

Her nipples grew harder at the thought of her mate and she cupped her hands around her breasts, flicking her nails over the sensitive crests. Her torso arched and her body burned for his touch. She wanted the feel of his thrusting cock inside her once more. Hot juices flooded her pussy and she couldn't bite back a moan. It echoed loudly in her empty condo. There was no one here but her, no one to see if she indulged herself in a moment of fantasy.

Dropping one hand, she let her fingers brush over the top of her thigh. "Antonio," she breathed.

Her knees parted, and a rush of longing whipped through her. The craving her body had for her mate wouldn't be denied, but she couldn't go to him, so she'd have to feed it the only way she could. Her fingers pushed the hem of her dress up until she reached her pussy. The lips were slick under her hand and she pressed forward until she circled her hardened clit.

A whimper slipped from her throat as her movements grew wilder. The muscles in her thighs tensed when she flicked a nail over her clitoris. Closing her eyes, she let herself flow into the sensations. She stroked herself, picturing his hands on her, his cock moving within her until her walls clamped tight on his flesh and she screamed. The fantasy was too good, too real.

Moisture slipped in slow beads down the insides her legs. She wanted Antonio here with her so much. "*Yes.* Oh, God. Yes."

She plunged her fingers deep into her pussy, the heat of her own body shocking her. Shuddering, she tried to rein herself in, to not let herself go too far with this. She couldn't lose herself to the pleasure of it. Gritting her teeth, she distanced herself from the emotions that wanted to reach for Antonio. Sexual enjoyment? Yes. Emotions? No. They were too dangerous. Too exposing.

Working her fingers into her channel, she pushed herself hard and fast toward orgasm. Her body trembled, gooseflesh rippling over her skin. Her breath panted out, her heart racing. The walls of her pussy flexed around her thrusting fingers and still she moved faster. She was so close, her body quivered on the very edge. Angling her fingertips up, she flicked over her most sensitive spot. It was enough to make every muscle lock in her body as her pussy clenched over and over again. Tingles slid over her flesh in intense waves, but still not as intense as when Antonio touched her. The mere thought of him sent shockwaves through her and her sex pulsed around her fingers again.

"No," she whispered. She couldn't let herself dwell on him, on what could never be.

She jerked upright, slipped her hand free of her body, rested her forearms on her knees, and dropped her head forward to catch her breath.

"This is crazy." The silence of her home mocked her. She was always alone. What would it be like to have a mate beside her always?

It didn't matter. The look of appalled shock on his face was enough to tell her what he'd thought of what she was. A non-mate for a non-shifter. She'd never fit into his world.

A smile twisted her lips. No, she wasn't going to do anything more than fantasize occasionally about how hot it had been with him. As much as her body craved more of his rough possession, it was an addiction she couldn't allow herself to develop. It would only cause them both pain.

And the last thing she wanted was more pain—she wasn't stupid enough to set herself up that way. To let even a small amount of her control over her life slip away. She'd worked too long and hard to give it up now.

She could never see him again. Ever.

Antonio entered the Pacific Heights mansion that housed his Pride. Their den. All Pride members lived here. They could shift on the property safely—the walls and bushes that surrounded the house hid them from prying human eyes. Even then, it wasn't enough space to stretch into a full sprint. The Pride had large expanses of property in the Sierra Nevada mountain range for those who wanted to get away and really run.

Panthers were creatures of the night, and the hard rhythm of rock music pierced the air as he walked inside. Felines twined with human bodies on the antique furniture, and each watched his progress with a cool stare, nodding as he passed.

He swept along the gritty elegance of the halls, not pausing until he reached the adjoining suites of his twin brothers. Shoving the door wide, he stepped inside to see a woman arched in pleasure between them, screaming out as she reached orgasm. The twins ran their hands over her body, one in front, one behind as they worked inside her. Each man groaned and shuddered as they came in unison. That was the way of the twins—always together, always sharing everything, including their women. From the whispered rumors that abounded in the Pride, there were few women who complained about having them both; instead, the two were sought after as lovers. Tonight's woman seemed to have enjoyed herself.

Seeing them after fifteen years had come as something of a shock. Gone were the chubby young boys, replaced by the tall, muscular men who liked their sports extreme and their women wild. Their cavalier attitude didn't quite manage to cover the wicked intelligence that made them lawyers who looked after the Pride's legal affairs—even at their relatively young age of twenty-five, he wouldn't trust the duty to anyone else.

Panting for breath, the three lovers collapsed to the bed, their limbs intertwined. One of the twins patted the woman's ass and she gave a short, husky laugh.

Antonio snorted, waving away the scent of sex that permeated the air. "Ricardo. Diego."

The Panther female blanched at the sight of him, scrambling to her feet and trying to cover her nudity with too-small palms. "Sir, I—"

He jerked his chin toward the door. "Get out. I need to speak to my brothers."

The woman shoved herself into her clothes and darted past him to leave.

Diego pushed his shaggy dark hair out of his face, arching a sardonic brow. "Did you need something, Antonio?"

"A non-shifter named Solana. What do you know about her?"

"Solana." Ric's forehead furrowed in thought. "Unusual name. Solana *Perez*, I believe. I recall her vaguely—we were very young, but it was a scandal of some kind. She and her father joined us a month or so after you left for Rio de Janeiro. If I remember correctly, her father abandoned her here. Father forced her to leave when he found out what she was, of course."

"There is no *of course*," an angry hiss laced Antonio's voice.
Ric arched an eyebrow. "There was with Father. You know
that."

Folding his hands behind his back, Antonio forced himself
not to pace out his agitation. "She couldn't have been more
than a child."

"Why the sudden interest?" Diego tilted his head, feline curiosity in his gaze.

Antonio wasn't about to tell them the truth—he could barely
wrap his own mind around it, let alone try to explain how the
wonder of finding his mate had ended in a horrifying realization. "I found members of the Pride harassing her tonight."

"Who?" Diego leaned forward.

"Roberto, Juan, and Marcos Ruiz." Antonio bared his teeth
in a smile. "I'll deal with them personally."

Ric nodded. "Those three have always been bullies, and Father allowed it to keep their grandparents appeased."

"Not to mention he was shagging their mother on the side."
Diego stretched, snagged a pair of jeans off the floor, and stepped
into them.

"Well, yes. There's that, too." Ric flicked a glance at Antonio,
gauging his reaction to that bit of information.

He rubbed a hand over the back of his neck. Damn it, he
didn't like surprises. Not that he was shocked by his father's
ruthlessness, but it was his duty to know everything that went
on with his Pride. His father had drilled that duty into him from
the moment he was born. It was always his destiny to lead. But,
then, he and his father had rarely agreed on how that duty
should be executed. It was why he'd been sent to apprentice in
South America and hadn't been allowed back until after his father
died. Most heirs apprenticed as Second to another Pride leader
for the sake of alliance and greater experience, but not for fifteen years.

As heir, Antonio was the only one who could truly oppose

his father. Had he garnered enough support, he could have forced his father to step down as leader and retire early. But Esteban was a traditionalist to his core; he didn't have the inclination to listen to a son with more . . . progressive views. The same views that his mother had espoused before she died.

Thus his exile. What Esteban had tolerated when his mate was alive had died with her. There was no reasoning with him after that, no cajoling, just cold, hard duty. It was what had eventually driven his sister Andrea away from the Pride. She now made her way in human society as a model.

It was a pity the twins were too young to remember what the Pride had been like before. They were too young to remember much of their mother at all. A shame. Much of her outlook had influenced his own. She'd been outspoken, forthright, and fair. A much better leader than his father had ever been. Destiny had favored their Pride when it made her Esteban's mate.

She'd been as courageous as his own mate had been this evening. A small smile kicked up the side of his mouth. He had a feeling his mother would have liked Solana immensely—nonshifter or not.

He shook himself out of his reverie to find the twins staring at him, both completely dressed now and waiting for some kind of response. He sighed. "Use your contacts to look into what she's been doing since Father cast her out. I want to know everything."

"Of course. Our inquiry will be discreet." Ric nodded to emphasize his comment. "We'll have a file on your desk by tomorrow."

Dipping his head in dismissal, Antonio took a step backward. "See that you do."

"Antonio?" Diego lifted a staying hand. "What the hell's going on?"

Antonio arched a brow, still unwilling to give away anything more than he already had.

The younger man narrowed his dark eyes, the sharp, discerning gaze of a practicing attorney peering out of his baby brother's face. It was unnerving—and exactly why he trusted them to protect the Pride. Ric spoke up, "All this for a non-shifter who has been taking care of herself for over a decade? And frankly, brother, you reek of sex."

"If the two of you have something to say, get it said."

Diego snorted. "What Ric is too polite to ask is: is an outcast non-shifter playing a part in Pride politics because she's giving you a bit of trim? That would be . . . unwise as a new Pride leader."

"Your concern is touching."

"Don't take it as an insult, brother. We don't want to see anything happen to you. We have as much interest in seeing you succeed as you do." His lips quirked up. "Without you, they might make us run things. No more 'boarding or surfing for us, just paperwork and being boring and dutiful."

"Boring. Thanks, that's really nice." Antonio rubbed the back of his neck and tried not to smile. Diego always had a way with words.

He lifted a broad shoulder in a nonchalant shrug. "You know what I mean, bro. We don't want your life. We like ours."

Antonio sighed, the weight of all that had happened this evening threatening to crush him. *Madre de Dios,* he was tired. "Nothing lasts forever."

Ric leaned against the end of the four-poster bed and crossed his arms, his gaze sharp and assessing. "Planning on leaving us, Antonio?"

"Planning? Not at the moment." He grinned. "I was thinking more about how the two of you intend to keep your lives just as you want them when you meet your mates."

"I'm sure mine will like a little free fall. I have a nice destiny waiting for me." A cocky grin bloomed on Diego's face. "And so does she."

"We'll see, won't we?" Antonio snorted, wondering how his

certainty of his own bright future had gone up in smoke so quickly. Shit, what a nightmare. Frustration at his inability to fix this situation boiled in his veins. He tamped it down. A Pride leader didn't get the luxury of giving in to his frustration. His personal problems couldn't become an issue for anyone else.

Ric shoved Diego's shoulder. "Nah. Yours is going to be all stodgy and dull. A ball and chain that'll sink you right off your wakeboard."

Taking a breath, Antonio forced himself to pay attention and drag himself away from thoughts of Solana. "If you even have mates."

"It's not so bad, bro." Diego forked his fingers through his hair. "Without a mate we just keep all the ladies happy, not just one."

Antonio rolled his eyes. "Try not to break any hearts. Trample on too many and I'll put a crimp in your love life."

Flicking a glance at his twin, Ric gave a sheepish grin. "Maybe we should test drive a few more humans."

"Coupla snow bunnies look mighty good right now." Diego let a playful leer form on his face and moved his hands through the air to outline the shape of a woman's figure. "Remember that little blonde up in Tahoe?"

Antonio turned to exit the room, leaving his brothers to their usual banter. He rubbed a hand over his hair, still reeling over the information Ric had given him about Solana's membership in the Pride. But in the end, it didn't matter what he knew about her. As Pride leader, it would be the height of folly to think he could ever mate with her. The Pride would never accept her, and if he wasn't around to handle an issue, she would be the leader. That was how Prides worked. If they accepted him, they had to accept his mate and vice versa. A package deal. Unless he never mated.

A non-shifter. The words kicked him in the gut, made him bend over and grip his knees.

No. Please, by all that was holy, no.

"Antonio."

He straightened to see the contained countenance of his Second. He'd brought Miguel Montoya with him from Brazil. The man had been his best friend and closest ally since the moment he arrived to serve the South American Pride leader.

The man's long hair was pulled back in his usual queue, but Antonio could smell the scent of sex on him. Had everyone in this Pride gotten laid tonight? He hiked his brow at his Second. "Sampling the wares of my Pride?"

"No. A human."

He grinned. "Interesting choice."

"Not at all. I sought a . . . compatible personality, not a species." The fact that Miguel was dressed to go out meant that he'd probably been at one of the local fetish clubs. He lifted a shoulder in a shrug. "She wasn't my mate, after all."

At the word *mate,* Antonio winced.

"Something's wrong." Miguel's nostril's flared as he inhaled sharply. "A woman. Her scent is . . . different."

"I don't want to talk about it."

"Right, then." Letting the topic go, Miguel lifted his shoulder in a shrug. "Why are the Ruiz boys waiting in your study?"

Antonio's jaw locked and he bared his teeth in a smile. "I need to speak to them."

Miguel caught his shoulder before he could pass, stepping in front of him. "Antonio. I don't know what happened, but you're a new leader and the boys are from a powerful family in this Pride. Stop. Think. Tell me what happened."

"Get out of my way." Antonio stepped to the side, intending to move around his friend.

Miguel made himself a wall, tightened his hand on Antonio's shoulder, and didn't allow him to pass. "As your Second, I should be aware of what's going on so I can watch your back."

He snarled at the other man, his fangs sliding out. He'd

never been so close to punching his best friend in the decade and a half they'd known each other. "They attacked my mate."

Miguel's hand dropped, his brows arching almost to his hairline. "Why?"

"Because she's a non-shifter." The truth of that hit him again, and his fangs retracted.

If Miguel was surprised by the announcement, it didn't show on his face. His lip lifted in a curl of distaste. "Bigots."

Antonio nodded his gratitude. It was rare that Miguel made so blatant a negative statement. "The twins worry she'll cause problems with Pride politics—"

"That's their job, to worry about you and the Pride. For the moment, let's return to the Ruiz cubs."

He smiled, with teeth. "Yes, let's."

Miguel motioned with his hand, and Antonio fell into step beside him as they walked down the hall toward the stairs. "Let me handle them."

"What?"

"Diego and Ric are right about her clouding your judgment." Miguel gave a matter-of-fact shrug. "She's your mate—how could she not?"

Damn Miguel for always being so reasonable. It was why he made such a good Second. And why Antonio wanted to put a fist in his face. "They aren't privy to that detail."

"You'll tell them when you're ready, I'm sure." They paused at the top of the stairs, Miguel subtly blocking Antonio's path and lifting his brow.

Renewed rage bubbled in his veins. A muscle flexed in his jaw as he tried to reason with himself. His fists clenched at his sides, duty warring with the anger and fear he'd experienced when he watched them hunt his mate. Duty won out. "Fine. Handle it. But make sure they understand that no matter how bad they get it from you, if they *ever* go near her again, I will rip them limb from limb."

"Count on it."

He lifted his fingers to pinch the bridge of his nose. "What the hell am I going to do, Miguel? She's a non-shifter. I'm a Pride leader."

Miguel sighed. "Shit."

"Yeah."

"Despite whatever your own political leanings are—and even those of the rest of your family—the controlling families in this Pride are those who were loyal to your very conservative father." He took on the flat tone of someone delivering very bad news.

"They wouldn't accept her as my mate." Antonio nodded. This wasn't something he hadn't thought of himself, but some desperate part of himself wanted to hear his Second say he could somehow manage to make this work. That there was an angle he hadn't thought of yet. There had to be something.

"No."

"I know that." Damn it. He turned away, fighting with the instincts that roared inside him to track her down and mark her. She was *his*. And yet he could never claim her. Oh, God. How could this be? What cruel destiny would do this to a man? Anger whipped through him again, and the muscles in his shoulders went rigid.

"What are you going to do?"

His jaw clenched. Would the craving for her ever end? Would he fight it every day of his life? He barked out a bitter laugh and looked over his shoulder at his Second. "If I were smart? I'd never go near her again."

Miguel shook his head. "Good luck with that."

Forcing his feet to carry him toward the master suite, Antonio walked away. If he stayed, he'd give in to the temptation to take his frustrations out on the three stooges.

A smile tilted his lips. Given Miguel's predilection for whips and chains in the bedroom, Antonio knew his Second was very *creative* when it came to punishment. He had no doubt the boys would suffer for their actions toward his mate. It did little to alleviate the tension racing through his body, the need to pummel someone with his fists. Three particular someones.

He snapped the door open to his rooms and shut it behind him. He froze in place, his hand still on the doorknob. Someone was in his bathroom. The water ran in his shower. Drawing a deep breath, he smelled his sometimes-lover, Carmen.

"Shit." Just what he needed tonight. Lacing his hands behind his neck, he dropped his head back.

He let his arms fall and stepped toward the bathroom as Carmen stepped out of the doorway nude. He groaned . . . and not with the kind of longing she would be accustomed to. The last thing he wanted to deal with tonight was a jealous female, and there was little he could do to stop it. Best to get it over with quickly.

Pulling in a deep breath, he picked up the silk robe she'd draped across his leather sofa to hold it out to her. Her brows lifted, but she accepted the garment. "Are we taking this outside?"

"No. I'm afraid we're not taking this anywhere." He reached out to place a gentle hand on her shoulder, but she jerked back, the robe slipping from her fingers.

Her nostrils flared, cold anger filling her gaze. Her fangs bared a bit, offended feline mixed with spurned woman. "There's someone else, isn't there? I can smell her on you."

He sighed. "You knew this couldn't be permanent, Carmen. We aren't mates."

"Until then, I thought we'd—"

"We both know you've found your mate. You just don't want to admit he's human."

Fear trickled into her gaze. "I can't have a human mate. I— I'd be no better than a non-shifter. I wouldn't be able to breed. I'd be cast out."

"Not by me." He understood her terror, though. Mating to

a human *would* make her status in any Pride equal to that of a non-shifter. No better than his mate. Even as a Pride leader he wasn't immune to the dangers of being exiled—the worst fate for any Panther. One Solana had had visited upon her just for being unable to breed. He fought a wince at the thought. No Panther wanted to live outside the protection of the Pride ... outside the circle of people like them. The alternative was living a lie—never telling anyone what they truly were.

People who couldn't add to the Panther population were cast out as not contributing to the most important mission of the Pride: do not go extinct. It was an ugly prospect, watching the last of their kind dwindle to nothing. Still, was breeding the only function that helped a Pride? He didn't think so, but he knew he was in the minority there.

Carmen's lips compressed. "Would the rest of the Pride ever accept it? I doubt it."

"You don't get to decide who your mate is." Didn't he know that for the truth? He found it interesting that she didn't ask how he knew who her mate was, but the sooner he got her out of his rooms, the better for both of them. Exhaustion crashed over him, and he wanted nothing more than to be left in peace. If he could encourage one of his Pride members to possess what he couldn't have himself, then it was his duty to do so. To lead. He met Carmen's gaze. "Track him down, Carmen. Don't let him slip away."

"He lives in Seattle."

Antonio tilted forward, letting a small smile pull at his lips. "Then what are you waiting for? I'm not stopping you."

Stepping forward, she brushed her mouth over his lightly, a farewell kiss. She threw herself into his arms, pressing herself to him in a tight hug before she released him and moved back.

He watched her slip her robe on in silence and walk out of his life, her hips swaying in the kind of soft invitation that he'd pursued when he arrived back in San Francisco. But he had to accept that a woman who had heated his blood on many a night now left him cold. Her touch did nothing for him, and his stomach clenched at the thought of fucking any woman besides Solana.

As much as he knew he shouldn't go near her, he didn't think any woman would satisfy him now except his mate. Damning himself for his weakness, he knew he'd track her down again.

A quick flick of his fingers and the lock engaged on his door when Carmen left. He flipped the light off and collapsed on his bed.

With any luck, sleep would bring him some peace and he wouldn't dream of Solana's touch.

3

A quick knock sounded on Antonio's office door before it opened enough to let Ric's head pop through. "Antonio? Do you have a moment?"

He nodded and dropped his pen on the wide oak desk. "Come in. What can I do for you?"

"I have that file for you on the non-shifter female." The younger man dropped a manila folder on his desk and clasped his hands behind his back, standing at attention.

Antonio held back a wince. How many times had he stood in just such a way in front of this desk, waiting for the Pride leader to flay him alive for speaking his mind?

"Sit down, Ric." He waved his brother into a deep leather chair in front of the fireplace and moved to join him in the matching chair. "Tell me what's on your mind."

"It's about the woman."

"Something in her file disturbs you?" He did his best to hide the intense curiosity he had about his mate. What would he find in her paperwork?

"No. Other than the fact that she's a non-shifter, she has a clean record and seems to be what humans consider an up-standing citizen."

"Good."

"What I—we—want to know is why does it matter? Diego thinks she means a bit more to you than an easy lay. I have to agree with him." Ric's shoulders shifted uncomfortably in his suit coat, the fabric rustling against the leather chair. "We may not know each other that well because you've been gone so long, but no newly minted Pride leader in his right mind would tangle with an outcast without a reason. From everything we know or have heard about you in the last decade, you're as sane as they come."

"How deeply did you look into my background?" Antonio folded his hand behind his head and settled back in his seat.

His brother examined the carved mantelpiece as though he'd never seen it before. He cleared his throat. "Just the basics . . . so we could get a good idea of what you've been up to."

Antonio couldn't blame them. He'd had them researched thoroughly after his father died. It was how he knew about their legal expertise, their loyalty to the Pride. He'd expect no less of them. They were Esteban's sons, after all. All three of them had learned paranoia and distrust at their father's knee.

He didn't even want to imagine what his sister had learned from their father.

How much could he trust the twins? How much was he willing to trust them? As far as he and Miguel had been able to discern, they had no declared allies within the Pride, but what about subtler ties? He hadn't been here long enough to know. He closed his eyes for a moment and took a leap of faith. He refused to live with the deep fears his father had had, especially after his mother had died. If he couldn't trust his family, he doubted he could trust anyone in this Pride. "She's my mate."

"Holy shit."

He opened his eyes to see a shocked expression on Ric's face. "Yeah."

"Well, that changes everything." Ric leaned onto the arm of the chair.

"Does it?"

He lifted a brow, real surprise flashing across his face. "You don't think so?"

"No. Yes." Antonio ran a tired hand across his forehead. How many times had he run this around and around in his mind? "Hell, I don't know. I want it to, but how can a Pride leader claim a non-shifter mate? How can it even work? She can't mark me if she can't change."

"And she can't have children."

He pulled in a deep breath. "There is that."

"I'm sorry." The younger man hitched his right ankle onto his left knee. "What will you do?"

"I wish I knew." Antonio had decided to track her down again, but then what? There was no way he could mate with her if he wanted to remain Pride leader, was there?

He didn't agree with the reigning opinion that non-shifters were second-class simply because they couldn't breed, because they were *different.* But that didn't mean he could convince his Pride members to agree with him. And his life was to be spent serving his people. They gave him loyalty and obedience and he worked to keep the Pride lucrative and safe from the prying eyes of humans. It was a system that had worked for the Prides for as far back as their historical records stretched. But the mutually cooperative arrangement could be a double-edged sword. If they didn't accept him or his mate, then his effectiveness as a leader was nonexistent.

Find her and explore a sexual relationship with her? Yes.

Mate with her? No.

Solana wore her usual uniform to work, skin-tight white tank top with the bar's name emblazoned in red letters on the front, curve-hugging blue jeans, and well-worn cowboy boots. No way in hell was she wearing another dress like she had last night. She stomped down on the memory and focused on her work.

Her gaze swept the crowd at the bar she owned in the Mission District. The former owner had let her buy out his interest when he retired five years ago—he'd taken a chance on hiring her as a bartender when she was twenty-one and she'd worked her ass off to make sure he never regretted it.

She'd renamed the bar Cat Scratch Fever as a nod to her background—one her clientele would never know about—and made it a whole new club when she took over. The revenue showed her ideas worked. She'd kept the run-down honky-tonk feel to it, but now all her bartenders were women and they danced and sang on the long wooden bar to keep the crowd entertained.

Men loved it, and they paid out the nose for their drinks to see it. No strippers—she didn't run that kind of place. Just pretty girls who put on a hell of a show, but they were bartenders first. She didn't care how gorgeous they were or what kind of show-manship they could bring to the bar. If they couldn't make a decent drink, they wouldn't get hired.

The night was in full swing when she arrived. She always took the late shift so she could close up—and because she was naturally nocturnal. All Panthers were. Even if she couldn't shift, she had all the extra senses and foibles of other Panthers.

"Solana!" One of her girls, Michelle, shouted a greeting as she swung behind the bar.

She smiled and nodded as she got right to work. Her hands went automatically to the right bottles, setting glasses on the bar. Pouring, shaking, serving. It was as natural to her as breathing after so many years working there.

One of her bouncers, an enormous man named Lee, motioned her over to the end of the bar. She cashed out the tab she was working on and joined him. "What's up?"

"Ted called in sick."

She groaned. "Shit."

"I can work a double."

"You sure?" She lifted her brows. "You've got a new kid at home."

His big laugh boomed over the crowd. "I've got a new kid at home, so I can always use the extra cash."

She patted his shoulder. "Thanks, Lee."

"Any time, Solana. You know that." His teeth flashed in a quick grin before he turned to go back to watching the door.

"Yeah, I do know," she called after him. And she'd never be able to express how grateful she was that her people were loyal to a fault and treated her like family.

But she knew it was all an illusion, so she appreciated it while it lasted. If these people knew what she was, they'd run as far and as fast in the other direction as their very human legs could carry them. Not that they'd ever find out. It was the one rule of the Prides that no one could break. Ever.

Even an outcast like her wouldn't dream of it. It would get her killed. And not in the harassing way that the jokers from the other night could handle. No, it would be cold, quiet, and efficient. Probably a professional assassin.

She tossed her long hair over her shoulder and merged back into the ebb and flow of the girls behind the bar. At her nod, Rachel grabbed a microphone to belt out a country song and Lisa hopped up with her to dance along the bar. The crowd rushed the bar to get closer, and Solana grabbed a bottle of top-shelf tequila so men could buy body shots off of Lisa's lithe torso. When Rachel was done, they'd be yanking shot glasses of expensive liquor out of her impressive cleavage.

It was all so familiar—just as it had been for the last decade. A little wild, a lot wicked. She made her money off other people's thrills, their forbidden desires. Just a little tease, a taste of naughty, and they could go back to their normal lives.

But everything felt off tonight, different. *She* felt different, off balance. Antonio. She should never have had sex with him, but nothing had ever been so right. It was the way things should be between mates, or so she'd heard. Too bad it wouldn't work out. She was what she was and he was what he was. The ache in her chest, the weight pressing down on her was one she'd just have to learn to live with.

Time. She could only hope it would get better with time. She'd shake this tearing need inside her to go to him, find him, and let him claim her as his mate. To sink her fangs into him and claim him as *hers*. Only it would never be because she had no fangs—only shifters who could change forms had fangs. Still, it didn't make the instinctual urges stop.

"Are you dancing tonight, Solana?" One of her regulars leaned over the bar to grin at her.

She pulled herself back from her musings and gave him an answering smile. "Don't I always?"

Her heart skipped a beat when she thought about hopping up on the scuffed wooden bar and dancing out her frustrations and fears. It was the only real relief she'd get from all of this. Anticipation hummed through her veins and her smile widened. Maybe she would get up there twice tonight. She loved to dance, and she never failed to get the crowd on their feet cheering . . . and buying drinks.

How could she fight it when something she longed to do was also great for business?

Twenty minutes later, she stood on the bar, the hard, pounding rhythm of the rock song filling her body. And she moved, twisting in perfect time to the beat. Hips grinding, her muscles flowed as she danced. It was the only time she felt like she was one with the Panther within her, as though she became the feral cat when the music played. It made her wanton. Wild.

Executing three neat flips along the length of the solid wood bar, she sank into a crouch and tossed her long hair back over her shoulder. A wicked smile played over her lips. She heard the vague roar of the crowd in front of her, but they didn't matter. All that mattered was the dance and how it made her *feel*. It was the only time she allowed it, and she reveled in it.

Her arms flung out as she hit her knees and spun so she faced the mirror that lined the entire wall behind the bar. Wild. Yes, that was a good word for her now. But she had no time to think about it. The song picked up speed and so did she, leaping to her feet and slamming her boots down on the wood surface. Her hips swiveled, rolling her body in a sensuous undulation. Hands slipping over her curves, she parted her legs and arched in blatant invitation. A cat in heat. The music crested, and a part of her screamed in protest that she'd have to lock herself away again. She threw her head back and moaned, the noise drowned out by the slamming throb of sound that ended the song.

And then she caught his scent. Antonio.

Rolling her head around on her shoulder, her gaze went right to him in the sea of cheering people. He stood off to the side, arms crossed, and enough heat in his eyes to dampen her pussy and send fire racing through her veins. His dark gaze slid over her like a caress, brought the wildness inside her roaring back to life. She clenched her fists and tried to beat it back, but the instincts were too ingrained to fight. Anger whipped through her at her inability to maintain her calm. Why was he here? He had to know they couldn't be anything to each other. How dare he invade *her* space? Planting her palms on the bar, she swung her legs over the side, hit the floor hard, and strode toward him.

"Solana." Her name rolled of his tongue, the sound of it making her pause and reminding her how amazing his hands felt on her skin. Her jaw clenched. She was angry he was here, the desire shouldn't mean anything. Damn it. Her nostrils flared.

She jerked her chin toward her office door. "Come with me."

He said nothing, just followed her in silence. The heat from his body enveloped her from behind. She shut the door behind them, and he crowded her against the wood surface. His fingers sifted through her hair, sliding it away from her face as he spoke softly in her ear.

"That was so sexual, it was almost indecent." She felt him smile as his lips brushed over the skin of her neck. "I want you to dance for me. Privately."

She shook her head, sliding sideways to step away from the press of his body, walk behind her desk, and brace her hands on the battered surface. "That's my work, Antonio. I don't bring it home with me."

"For me."

A thrill went down her spine at the thought of being so untamed with him. For him. But she tamped down on it. Would she be able to pull back when the song ended? Or would she lose herself, her control, as she'd seen her mother do? Disgust roiled in her belly. No. She couldn't dance for him. Only for herself. She shook her head again. "Sorry, no."

"Maybe someday."

"Nope. Never." It was too tempting, and she couldn't let herself give in. It was a slippery slope to a deeper connection that neither of them could afford. Everything that had happened between them so far had shown her just how tenuous her control was around him. She wasn't tempting fate . . . it had never been kind to her. "Besides, there is no someday for us, is there?"

Regret shone in his dark gaze as he approached her desk. "No. There's not. There's only right now."

His fingers traced over the back of her hand and up to circle her wrist. Her gaze met his and that same recognition she'd felt in the alley last night hit her again. Mate. Her breath stopped. Every sense focused on him, his masculine scent, his midnight hair and eyes, the flush of lust that ran under his copper skin, the slightly rough texture of his fingertips.

A whimper caught in her throat and she reached for him. He was around the desk before she could blink, hauling her body flush against his. His mouth slammed down over hers, his tongue stroking between her lips. She moaned, mating her mouth to his and nipping at his lower lip. Heat sparked in her belly and whipped through her body like a wildfire. Her nipples peaked so hard they ached. She wanted his hands there, his mouth.

His fingertips slipped under the hem of her tank top to graze the skin at the small of her back. She swallowed, a shiver running through her. He pulled back to tug her shirt over her head. The ends of her hair tickled against her back when it slid free. His big hand closed over her breast, chafing the nipple through her bra.

"Oh, Jesus." She threw her head back and arched her torso toward his touch.

A soft chuckle rumbled from his chest before he dipped forward to brush his lips over the pulse point in her throat. His tongue flicked out to glide up the side of her neck until he sucked her earlobe into his mouth. She shivered again, her fingers digging into his broad shoulders. "More."

"I'll give you more. Don't worry." He flicked his fingers over the front clasp of her bra, and the cups peeled back to bare her to the cool air of her office. A small smile formed on his face as he took her in, his dark gaze flickering to Panther gold and back again as it slid over her naked flesh. Gooseflesh rippled in the wake of his gaze, and she wanted to scream with her need to go faster. His palms cupped her shoulders, moving down her chest to stroke over her breasts. Her back bowed, instinct driving her to seek the addicting heat of his touch.

He bent forward, taking her nipple between his teeth. He swirled his tongue around the tip, sucking it deep before he nipped at it again. She cried out and buried her fingers in his hair, tugging him closer. "Oh, *fuck.*"

Laughing, he pulled back to look her in the face. "That comes next, actually."

She snorted, but it ended with a squeal when he curved his hands around her hips and hauled her away from the desk. "What are you doing?"

"Exactly what you asked for." He spun her to face the desk, and his hands wrapped around her from behind, moving down to skim over the hem of her jeans. He popped open the top button and eased the zipper down.

Excitement flooded her system. Yes, she wanted him to touch her there . . . and everywhere else. The feel of his hands was the most amazing thing she'd ever experienced. His fingers slipped into her jeans and under the lace of her panties. The muscles in her legs shook so badly she had to lean forward and set her hands on the desk to brace herself.

When he brushed through her curls to stroke her clit, her breath stopped. Every sense she had focused on that one point of contact. Fire licked in her veins, made her shudder and bite back a moan. Her eyes drifted closed to enjoy the sensations rushing through her.

She choked when his fingers filled her, stretching the walls of her hot channel. "Antonio. I—"

"You?" He pushed in short strokes inside of her, sent her concentration reeling. The muscles in her belly tightened, her breath panting out. Every movement of his fingers made pleasure streak along her nerves and pushed her closer to orgasm. He flicked his thumb over her clit. "Solana . . . answer me."

"W-what?"

He chuckled, the sound just a little smug. "Nothing."

Her eyes snapped open when he withdrew. Desperation whipped through her, her body shrieking for more. She arched, but was trapped between her desk and the wall of muscle behind her. Her voice came out a harsh rasp, "Don't stop, damn it."

"Demanding, aren't you?" His arms banded around her torso, holding her in place.

A growl erupted from her throat and she wriggled against him. His erection pressed to the small of her back, but it couldn't help ease the ache that flamed in her pussy. "I'm demanding when the occasion warrants it. And this one does. Finish what you started."

"What do you think I'm doing? Hold still." His hands urged her forward to bend over the desk, and then slid around to cup her ass.

Pressing back into his palms, she moaned. "Hurry. Up."

He hooked his fingers into her belt loops and pulled her pants and underwear halfway down her thighs. His palms cupped her bare ass, the heat a contrast with the cool air in her office. God, she didn't know how much more she could take. She needed to come so badly, the feeling swamped her. Fire and ice raced over her skin. "I want you inside me."

"*Dios mio,* yes." He dipped between her ass cheeks, swirling around the pucker of her anus. Her breath stopped and her nails dug into the wooden desk beneath her. His fingers moved down to part her slick lips. The head of his cock rubbed against the sensitive tissue of her pussy and it was all she could do not to scream.

He entered her with short, hard thrusts. In this position, with her legs shackled by her jeans, it was an incredibly tight fit. She whimpered low in her throat. The feeling bordered on pain, but at this point, she'd do *anything* to assuage the need ripping through her system. The pain bled into all the other sensations spinning through her, a dark, twisting pleasure that maddened her.

Sweat beaded across her forehead, and her arms shook where they braced against the desk. She pushed back against him on his next thrust, seating him deep inside her. They both groaned.

His fingers clenched on her hips. "You feel so amazing, Solana."

He pulled back to thrust into her pussy with slow, deliberate movements. The edge of the desk bit into her thighs with each hard push. She closed her eyes, shaking with the sensations that threatened to overwhelm her. It terrified her, but she needed it. God help her. She couldn't do anything other than move with him, reaching for the climax that taunted her.

"I want more, Antonio. I want . . ." Was that wispy soft voice hers? But his cock withdrew and he rotated his hips to change the angle of penetration. All thought slid away, and her breath shuddered out. "Oh God, I want."

More. The heat in her body threatened to burn her from the inside out. Their bodies slapped together with each hard thrust and she could hear the ragged catch in his breath as they moved. Sweat slipped down her face in rivulets and her muscles burned. She clamped her walls around him. Tight.

"*Mierda.*" He groaned, his claws extending to rake up the outsides of her hips. Her body jerked as this new sensation piled on top of the others. He hissed loudly, his hips bucked hard one last time, and he seated himself inside her as deeply as possible as he came.

The hot feel of his fluid filling her was enough to shove her over the edge into orgasm. Her pussy flexed around him in rhythmic pulses. "*Antonio.*"

Her arms gave out and she collapsed to the desk, pressing her forehead to wood worn smooth from years of use. A small smile curved her lips. She doubted it had ever been put to this particular use before though. Would she ever be able to work in this room again without remembering tonight?

Long moments passed before her breathing and heart rate slowed to normal. As the sweat dried on her skin, she swallowed and closed her eyes. What the hell had she just done? Again? It had felt so right, so perfect. And it was all wrong, a lie that her instincts and body wouldn't stop telling her. She couldn't have this man, not permanently . . . and she shouldn't want him temporarily.

How had she let this happen? He may have shown up, but she'd reached for him, wanted him to touch her. She kicked herself, damning herself for her weakness and lack of self-restraint.

A hard knock sounded on the door, and Lee's voice came through. "Solana, you okay in there? Rachel sent me to check on you."

"I'm fine. Tell everyone I'll be right out." She slid away from the desk—and Antonio—to pull on her pants and refasten them. She walked toward the door, pausing to stuff herself back into her shirt and bra. "We shouldn't do this again."

"You're right. Damn it." He sighed. "We'll get in too deep. It was just . . . too good to resist."

She glanced back over her shoulder, drinking in one last look at him. "Good-bye, Antonio."

"Good-bye, Solana. It's been a pleasure." His Adam's apple bobbed when he swallowed. "I just wish . . ."

"Yeah." But no one knew better than she did that wishes were rarely granted. Not to someone like her. "I have to get back to work."

"Then I won't keep you from it." He adjusted his clothes, tucking his T-shirt into his jeans. "I know how important and consuming a job can be."

Their gazes locked and for a moment there was a connection, an understanding, that was beyond the physical one they'd explored so far. It shook her that they might have something in common. She hadn't expected it. They were so different. "This place . . . it defines me in a lot of ways, who I am, who I want to be."

"I know exactly what you mean." A smile curved the corner of his mouth.

Nodding, she forced herself to turn back around and walk away from the desire to stay and talk to him. She couldn't give in to the need to know all of him. A sigh slid past her lips, the bite of regret and all that could never be piercing her. Sighing, she stepped away from the Panther and back into the human world she inhabited.

A world he wasn't a part of any more than she was a part of his.

4

"The Ruiz woman wants to see you." The tight edge to Diego's voice was unusual. He was the more laid back and friendly of the twins.

Antonio's eyebrows lifted. "What's going on?"

"Apparently, it's not for me to know. I've been instructed to tell you she demands a private meeting."

"Private?" He couldn't hold back a snort. "I think the whole Pride could tell what this is about."

"Indeed." A muscle ticked in the younger man's jaw.

"Deny her polite request for a private meeting. If she'd like to speak with me, she can do it in front of my advisors. Get Ric and Miguel in here."

A wicked smile curved his brother's lips and he sketched a courtly bow. "As the Pride leader desires."

He chuckled. "I'm going to remind you of that the next time you disagree with me on something."

"It's my job to advise you, sir." Diego shoved his hair out of his face as he straightened.

"Go on."

"I'll be back with reinforcements."

Within moments, the side door to his office swung open and Miguel entered with Ric following close behind. Ric offered a tight grin. Apparently, Diego wasn't the only one to have a run-in with Lucia Ruiz.

Diego's voice echoed through the heavy wooden door. "I'll show you in, ma'am."

Antonio fought a grin, picturing the look on Lucia's face at being called *ma'am*. She'd been unpleasant to deal with when he was a boy, and he couldn't imagine how insufferable she'd become with the influence of being the Pride leader's favored mistress.

Her blue eyes widened when she saw Miguel and Ric, and then narrowed to angry slits as Diego shut the door and joined his twin behind the desk to flank Antonio's chair. Miguel propped his hip against the side of the desk and folded his arms. They no doubt made an intimidating picture, which was exactly what Antonio had hoped for. "Sit down, Lucia. Would you like a drink?"

She offered up a forced smile. "Sir, I'd asked to speak with you alone about a rather delicate matter. This is most unexpected."

"No, you want to complain about the treatment of your sons. That does not require privacy, and if this is an issue that affects the entire Pride, my advisors will be present. Sit down." He inclined his head to indicate she take a chair in front of his desk.

A flush mottled her smooth cheeks, and she plopped into one of the chairs. Her voice came out stiff and clipped. "Your . . . Second saw fit to—"

"Miguel acted on my orders in regard to your sons. What else may I help you with?"

Her nostrils flared. "We all know what this is about. Your

mistress left and suddenly there's this ridiculous proclamation that none of us can associate with your little non-shifter."

"You have no desire to *associate* with Solana . . . therefore, you may not harass her either. I will not have attention brought to the Pride for your narrow-minded prejudice." He shrugged, lifting a brow. "As for Carmen, she has her own concerns to deal with that have nothing to do with her former relationship with me."

"Don't think I can't tell this has nothing to do with protecting the Pride." The older woman's hands clenched on the arms of the chair. "That little misfit will never belong to this Pride again."

"That's not for you to say."

"Ha." She snorted. "You can't pass her off as a real Panther. Your father got rid of her, as he should have."

"My father is dead, Lucia. I am the new Pride leader." He flicked an invisible piece of lint off his sleeve.

She jerked to her feet and slapped her palm on the desk blotter in front of him. Her eyes flashed to gold for a moment, her claws extending. "I won't stand for you dragging this Pride down for a non-shifter."

He leaned forward, placing his hands flat against the surface of his desk. His voice went deadly soft. "Are you presuming to tell me how to run this Pride, Lucia?"

"N-no, sir." She sank back into her chair.

"Then hear me. Solana is not your concern." Nor would he ever allow this woman near his mate. He struggled to keep his tone calm. "I would suggest learning to keep your sons in line if you wish to remain in this Pride."

Her face blanched, making her look far older than her years. "The Ruiz family has been in this Pride since it began."

"Times have changed, *ma'am.*" He leaned back and steepled his fingers under his chin. "I suggest that the Ruiz family do the same or it will find itself severely out of favor in North America. Do I make myself clear?"

"Perfectly."

"Good. You are dismissed."

She rose stiffly and turned to exit the room.

"Well. That was interesting." Diego sighed and relaxed from his almost military stance beside him.

Ric wandered off toward a cabinet in the corner. "I think we all need a drink."

His twin smiled and dropped into a chair. "Hell, yes. Good thinking, bro."

"This is going to shake the Pride up a bit." Miguel sat down in the seat Lucia had vacated and let out a groan.

Antonio shrugged. He understood the possible consequences of his actions, but he also understood what would happen if he allowed the Ruizes too much leeway. "Perhaps it's time for a bit of shaking. I'm not my father, and this is as good a time as any to make sure the Pride knows it."

Diego hesitated before he sat forward in his chair. "They'll accept a change of the guards and the . . . policy changes that go with that, but that doesn't mean they'll accept her."

Antonio didn't need his brother to explain which *her* he was referring to. Solana. "I know that, Diego."

"Are you sure about that?"

"She's his mate, Diego." Ric handed a drink to his twin. "Can we really deny any man his mate?"

"A Pride leader doesn't get the kind of latitude that might be granted to lower ranking people. You'd think it would be the other way around, but it's not." Diego frowned at Ric. "Antonio is held to a higher standard and you know it."

He made a face, and settled into the seat beside Miguel's.

Antonio sighed. "Solana is my concern, not yours or anyone else's in this Pride. I know I can't have her. She knows that as well. Don't worry."

Ric's face pulled into an unhappy frown. "I'm sorry."

"I know." Picking up a pen to twirl it between his fingers, Antonio cleared his throat. "I'm sure you all have work to do, so I'll let you get back to it. Sorry for the interruption."

"That's what we're here for." Diego set his empty glass down, motioning for his twin to follow him out.

"Thanks." Antonio nodded in appreciation. No matter how long they'd been apart it was good to know his brothers had grown into loyal men he could respect. He sighed. "Miguel. A moment, please."

"You want me to keep Solana under surveillance in case the Ruiz family decides to remove the current thorn in their side permanently." Miguel stood, shoving his fingers into his pockets as he moved to leave.

"Yeah." Antonio threw his pen down when the door closed behind his Second and rubbed the back of his neck. "Shit."

For probably the first time in his life, he had no idea what the hell to do. He'd never run up against a problem he couldn't get over or around . . . and if that failed, he couldn't flatten. But nothing was going to solve this. The Prides worked the way they worked. It would take more than one Pride leader to change the attitude that had carried through hundreds of years.

But every instinct inside him urged him to claim her as his mate. It clawed at him, and he doubted he'd ever escape it. A part of him didn't want to, and that was the most dangerous part of all.

Instinct warred with duty, and he knew that duty should win. But a fundamental part of what made a Panther a Panther was the instincts within each of them. It's what gave them their senses, their ability to shift. It was the magic inside them.

And there wasn't a damn thing he could do about it. He dropped his head into his hands, rubbing tired eyes. He shouldn't see her again. He wanted her too much. A casual relationship with her was foolhardy, the temptation to mark her too strong.

But, dear God, he needed her. The dark longing twisted in his gut. Nothing had ever felt as good, as right, as perfect as sinking his cock inside her willing body. The sleek, wet sheath had fisted around him so tight he'd had to fight not to come the second he'd entered her.

There was no hope for it, no help for him. For either of them. Anger whipped through him again at the injustice of it all. Fate, other Panthers, his own birthright. Everything had conspired against his mating.

He was meant to spend his life . . . alone. The string of casual lovers he'd had in the past held no appeal. He wanted Solana. Only Solana. Forever. His chest tightened at the thought of her, so brave and beautiful. Bold, with a streak of wildness she tried to tame. So many layers he wanted to pull back. So much he wanted to know. The dossier the twins had put together only scraped the surface. He needed to know everything, all of her.

And feeding that need would be a mistake. He should never touch her again, but he had to know she was safe. This little spat with Lucia wouldn't be the last. She'd never have the influence with him that she'd had with his father. He had no doubt she'd challenge his authority until she either accepted his leadership or left the Pride. As much as he needed to keep his population up, he couldn't imagine being upset to see her go. He pinched the bridge of his nose and leaned back in his chair. His problem would come if Lucia managed to convince other families to leave with her.

The phone buzzed on his desk and he reached to press the COMM button. "Yes?"

Ric's voice came through. "Have you had a chance to look over those documents I left for you?"

"Yeah, I'll be over in a minute." He pushed away from his desk, shoving back his personal problems to deal with the task at hand—running a Panther Pride.

On his way out the door, he made a mental note to check in

on the arrangements Miguel was making for Solana's security. She wouldn't thank him for having her watched, but he'd risk her ire if it meant she was safe. It was as much his duty to protect his mate as it was to protect the members of his Pride.

Even if he could never claim her.

The weekend rolled into the work week, and it had been three days since she'd seen Antonio. Not since Friday night. Solana kicked herself for even noticing, but the hours seemed to stretch into centuries, her body rebelling at his absence. She didn't even know him. How could it matter so soon? She'd never heard of such a craving between mates *before* they'd marked each other. She'd scented him several times over the last few days as she'd gone to work and home again, watching her but never approaching. She didn't know what she would do if he came near.

A tremor wracked her body as she fought down the urge to go to him, to be with him. Her sex clenched at the memory of his touch, and she went hot and damp. Her nipples hardened to rub against her lace bra. The rasp of sensation made her bite her lower lip. Jesus, she needed to get a grip or this was going to drive her insane. Perpetual horniness was unacceptable—she simply wouldn't have it.

Someone was coming up the stairs of her building. She could hear the creak of each step. Hanging out on the landing in front of her door, all hot, sweaty, and panting was the perfect impression to make on her human neighbors. They'd have her shipped off to the nice men in white coats. *Get. A. Grip. Solana.*

Tightening her shaking fingers around her house key, she shoved it into the lock and turned it to let herself in. She pulled in a deep, steadying breath. And then whipped around just as Antonio topped the stairs.

"You followed me." She narrowed her eyes to slits, glaring at him as though he were to blame for how much her sex ached to be filled by him. "What are you doing here? You shouldn't be here."

"I wanted to make sure no one bothered you. I had to—had to see for myself." He sighed, looking frustrated, pissed off, and a little dangerous.

"So I have you stalking me now instead of them." She forced herself to turn back around and open the door. If she didn't get away from him soon, she might jump him and beg him to fuck her again. Even though she hadn't masturbated since that first night, her dreams had been so filled with lustful fantasies about him that she'd awoken crying out in orgasm more than once.

"It isn't like that and you know it."

"Maybe we have a different perspective on things." She opened the door and stepped through, glancing over her shoulder at him. She had to get him to leave, but her voice failed her a moment. Fire licked through her, heating her pussy. She was so wet, so desperate for him and only him. It was all she could do to keep her legs from collapsing underneath her. "Since your father made me an outcast, any interaction with other Panthers is . . . unwelcome to me now. That includes with you, Pride leader or no."

He arched a brow and crossed his arms over his broad chest. "You didn't seem so reluctant to *interact* with me last week. In an alley *and* in your office."

"Sex is something I enjoy as much as the next woman." She let her shoulder lift in a nonchalant shrug.

A muscle ticked in his jaw and he took a step toward her. She scrambled back. Please, please don't let him touch her. Her casual act would crumble into nothing and she'd be lost. She had to hold on to what they really were to each other. Not just mates, but Pride leader and non-shifter. He kept pace with her, taking a step forward for every one she took back until he was in her living room and locking the door behind them. "Solana, I didn't come here to fight with you."

She swallowed hard, set her keys and purse down on the coffee table, and shed her jacket. "No, you came here because you knew that I knew you were following me."

Footsteps sounded on her hardwood floor before his heat enveloped her. He blew out a breath. "I didn't want you to think I was stalking you or intending to upset you. I just . . . wanted to make sure you were all right."

"As you can see, I'm fine." She scuttled away from him and into the kitchen.

"I've forbidden the Pride from harassing you. If anyone does again, I expect you to contact me."

She tossed him an incredulous glance. "Um, no."

"No?" The stunned look on his face was almost laughable. Had no one ever told him no before? Probably no woman had. She wrinkled her nose and barely held back an angry hiss at the thought of him with another female.

She shook her head at him. "I've managed just fine on my own for almost a decade. These aren't the first to think I'm fair game. I'm not asking the Pride leader for help. I never have before and I don't intend to start now."

"I'm also your . . ."

He ground to a halt, a pained look on his face. The relish she felt when she finished his sentence wasn't kind, but it was all wrapped in the bitterness that had edged her life for so long. "Mate? Can't bring yourself to say it, can you?"

"Solana—"

"Please go." She ran the tips of her fingers over the granite countertops and swallowed the old pain. A sigh slipped from her lips. "There's nothing either of us can say or do to change the way the Prides operate. I understand that this has put you in an unfortunate situation and I'm sorry."

He set his hand on the counter next to hers. "This is hardly your fault."

"You're one of the only to ever think so." She stared at their hands. His were large, strong, and tanned. Hers a bit paler, smaller, and delicate in comparison. She wanted his hands on her. She had to make him go, she needed him to stay and fill the emptiness inside her.

A sad smile tilted his lips, a man torn between duty and destiny. "Non-shifters are born that way. No one knows why they can't change form."

"Yes, that's me. A freak of nature. Maybe they should put me in some kind of special exotic zoo." A laugh slipped out of her and she stepped away from the counter, away from the temptation he presented just by being here. But that's all he could be, a physical temptation. If she didn't allow her heart to be involved, maybe she could give in . . . just a little. Couldn't she?

His dark brows drew together in a frown. "This isn't funny."

"To you, maybe. I've lived with this for a long, long time. There have been those who suggested something not far from what I just said."

A hiss ripped from him and anger flashed over his face. "That's disgusting."

"Thank you. I wholeheartedly agree."

"God, you were *eighteen* and Panthers aren't raised to be out on their own. What did you do? How did you survive?"

Her shoulder lifted in a shrug. "Waiting tables, parking cars as a valet at a country club, answering phones as a secretary for an accounting office. That's where I learned a hell of a lot about what the books should look like for a successful business. When I turned twenty-one, I hired on at the bar. Then I bought out the owner when he retired. That's the whole story."

"I've read your dossier, Solana. Those are dates and facts." He ran a hand over the back of his neck. "It doesn't tell me shit about how many of those nights you went without food or heat. How often did you struggle to make ends meet?"

"Quite often. But not anymore." Her heart tripped at the

thought of him worrying about her, even in retrospect. She knew he'd have her checked out, and it didn't bother her. She shook her head. Who had ever really worried about her since her dad had left her? No one. The humans she worked with were good to her, but they didn't know her deepest secrets. Their friendship was a double-edged sword. But Antonio knew . . . and some part of him was beginning to *care*. It thrilled her. It terrified her. God, she was so mixed up. This thing between them was going to drive her insane.

"Not anymore." He sighed. "You've done . . . incredibly well for yourself. Without sounding condescending, I'm very proud of all you've accomplished with so little to help you."

"Thank you." It didn't warm her that he was proud of her. It didn't matter, damn it. It didn't. Her jaw clenched and she turned away from him and all the chaos and confusion he sent rippling through her. She reached into the fridge to stop herself from reaching for him and pulled out a bottle of merlot from Pahlmeyer—her favorite winery in the Napa Valley. It was her last bottle, so she'd have to make a day trip out there soon. She fished a glass out of the cabinet and hesitated before she closed the door. "Would you like some wine?"

"Yes." No hesitation, no doubt. She had a feeling it was how he lived his life. Precise and decisive.

She liked those qualities in people, in men. She liked everything she'd seen of him so far. A sigh slid from her throat. Of course she liked everything about him—he was her mate. If only he wasn't who and what he was. If only *she* wasn't who and what she was.

Pouring the two glasses, she left his on the counter and stepped away. She wasn't about to hand it to him and risk him touching her. Sipping her wine, she turned to find him watching her. Gooseflesh rippled down her arms and she shivered. "Stop."

"I can't. Do you think I would be here if I had a choice?"

She huffed out a laugh and closed her eyes. "No, neither of us would be here if we had a choice. Destiny is a total bitch."

"I couldn't agree more." The clink of his glass hitting the counter reached her ears a moment before the heat of his big body closed around her.

"We shouldn't. It will only make it worse for us." But she didn't pull away, didn't open her eyes. She wanted him too much. The fire within her rose to a fever pitch with his nearness, shrieking for him to touch, to take, to claim.

His breath brushed over her cheek when he spoke. "I know."

"Nothing can come of this." She finally met his gaze, resignation flooding her. It was nothing less than the truth. As much as her body needed him, she couldn't let her emotions become entangled. She had to keep as much of herself as possible tightly guarded. That was the key to being safe here—he could only touch her body. God, yes. She wanted that. "*Nothing* can come of this."

Pain filled his ebony eyes, roughened his silky voice. "I know."

Her palm came up to cup his strong jaw, and he leaned into her touch. The same soul-deep recognition of a mate that pulled at her reflected back in his gaze. "Antonio."

"I crave you, my mate." There was no joy in his tone, just the agony that she felt as well.

Tears she hadn't allowed herself to shed in ten long years misted her vision. She blinked them away, tucking her pain deep inside where it couldn't steal her control, couldn't rob her of this moment with a man made just for her. This would cause them both pain, but she knew pain and she accepted that there was no escaping the pain of this cruel new twist fate had visited on her. No, she wouldn't think of that, she would treasure this tiny measure of time when he was hers. Her mate, her lover, the focus of her world. Just for this moment. "Kiss me."

"Yes." He swooped forward and pressed his lips to hers.

This time, she didn't just let herself be taken. This time, she took. Her arms wrapped around his neck, her tongue shoving into his mouth to twine with his. He grunted, tightened his arms around her waist, and kissed her back with greedy enthusiasm.

Heat raced through her system and her breath sped until she was panting. Their hands were everywhere, they couldn't get enough. His palm cupped her breast, his thumb chafing her nipple. She moaned into his mouth, sliding her hand down the sloping muscles of his chest, the soft cotton of his shirt warmed by his skin. Her fingers bumped over his belt and down to stroke his long dick through his pants.

His breath hissed out as she curled her hand as far around him as his slacks would allow. Her fingers slid up and down, and his cock grew harder and thicker.

She broke her mouth away from his. "I want you inside me."

Lust pulled his skin tight across his sharp cheekbones, and his expression grew savage. "I won't be gentle."

"Neither will I." She could see his extended fangs with every bellowing breath. That she could drive him to the edge of his endurance made her feel powerful, female, feline, made heat and longing and too many other emotions she couldn't afford to examine race through her.

Later she would deal with the consequences of her actions. Right now was for him. And for her. She pulled her T-shirt over her head and reached behind her to pop open the fastenings on her bra. She slid it off and handed it to him.

A feral smile curved his lips, baring his sharp fangs. His pupils dilated as he took her in. He dropped her bra to the floor and jerked his shirt over his head. "If you don't want me to take you on the floor, I suggest you move that pretty little ass into the bedroom."

She spun, putting an extra swing in her hips because she

knew he watched. Her thighs brushed together with each step and the friction only increased the burn between her legs. She was so wet, so ready. Rounding the corner in the hall, she stepped into her bedroom. The deep red duvet and pillows lay neatly on the bed. That wouldn't last long.

She smiled, glancing back over her shoulder at him. He stood in her doorway and toed his shoes and socks off. His pants followed behind, and then he was gloriously naked. Smooth tanned flesh stretched taut over heavy muscles. Her gaze skimmed down his long body and settled on his cock. It stood in a rigid arc that curved to just under his navel. He moved to stand beside her next to the bed.

Dipping forward, she flicked her tongue over the flat brown disc of his nipple. It hardened under her lips. He started, growling out a soft warning. "Solana, I—"

Her foot hooked behind him, and she planted her hands on his chest, pushing. He tripped and fell backward onto the bed. His short bark of laughter was cut off as he bounced against the mattress. He rolled and settled against the pillows, the corners of his sensual mouth curling upward. "Well, you have me where you want me. Now, what?"

"I think you can guess."

He ran his tongue down a long fang. "Show me."

"No mating. Just sex."

"Show me," he demanded again, but a chuckle rumbled from him, and his fangs retracted.

Nodding, she quickly shed her boots, socks, and jeans. She couldn't wait. She wanted him now. Her knee slid onto the bed, and she threw her other leg over his lean hips, mounting him.

She curled her hand around his cock, pumped him through her fingers for a moment, and then rubbed the bulbous crest against her swollen lips, teasing them both. He drew in a sharp breath, his palms lifting to cup her ass and draw her forward to press harder against her. It felt so amazing. She couldn't stand it.

Holding his gaze with hers, she sank down on his dick. The walls of her pussy squeezed around him, her sex clenching at the exquisite burn of it. Heat and pleasure twisted deep within her, made her nipples peak tight and sweat bead on her skin. His big hand closed over her breast, stroking the tip until she couldn't hold back a moan. Tingles rippled over her arms and legs.

She tensed her thighs, pushing up and lowering herself onto his cock. Wetness slipped down the insides of her legs, she was so turned on. The scent of it, of him and her and their passion, filled her nostrils. Urgency spurred her on, made her movements quicken. The springs in the mattress squeaked under their weight. Her muscles tightened and shook as she rode him harder and faster.

Both of his hands now dug into her hips, and she could feel his claws scoring her skin. The pressure of his fingers guided her movements up and down, sliding her up the length of his cock, and pulling her until she was seated firmly. He filled her so completely, the stretch of it was . . . divine.

"I love how you feel around me, Solana." His groan reverberated off the walls of her bedroom, his eyes burning to pure gold. "I love . . . I love . . ."

Love. The one thing she could never have from him. Grief mixed with longing so intense it burned inside her. She threw her head back, screaming as he rotated his pelvis until he hit her just so, and then arched his hips beneath her. She closed her eyes and the world shattered around her.

Starbursts exploded behind her eyelids, and she shuddered over and over again. Sensations tangled with emotions. They ricocheted through her, too many to be contained. His big body bowed between her thighs, lifting her with him as he came hard inside her. The sound of their panting breaths was all that filled the room. Her heart rate slowed, the sweat cooling on her skin.

She collapsed onto his broad chest, curling into him. The aftermath of all she'd felt and all she'd denied herself swept her under, and a dreamless sleep claimed her.

Time became fluid, elastic. She felt herself rising into wakefulness, but fought it. Something was different, but she didn't remember what. She felt too good to question it. Yes, just sleep and sweet dreams. That's all she wanted. One moment she was sliding back into unconsciousness, the next her eyes snapped open. "Antonio."

"Hmm?" He yawned, his dark eyes opening to meet hers.

They lay facing each other as the last rays of sunshine were fading from the sky, the golden light bursting through her curtains to bathe his face. God, he was beautiful, amazing. Her heart clenched.

She'd been such a fool to think she could touch him and only let her body be involved. He was her mate. Everything inside her was made to fit him perfectly. To want him. To love him.

He was everything she'd ever wanted. Strong. Caring. He didn't even seem to mind that she couldn't shift. He just . . . wanted her. The sweetness that flooded her made it impossible to breathe.

She stared at him, drinking him in. It would be so easy to fall for him. She *wanted* to fall. But no matter how strong and caring he was, he couldn't afford to catch her. Not and keep the Pride. So, she would fall alone. Because she was terrified she'd already come too far not to fall at all. Her finger traced his eyebrows and down his nose.

His eyes closed tight. "This is too good, Solana. Too *right*. How can we deny this?"

"We have to." She felt a sad smile curve her lips. "You know that."

Jerking upright, he shoved a hand through his hair. "Damn it, why? We can find a way."

"The only way is if—"

He glanced back at her. "Is if I weren't Pride leader any-more."

"And that's not possible." She shook her head. No way in hell would she let him give that up for her. They both knew the second most powerful family in the Pride were the Ruizes. If he stepped down, and none of his immediate family stepped up, that horrible family would make a bid for leadership. "It's *not* possible."

He pinched his eyes closed again. "No. But, God, I wish it were. If my sister or one of the twins were willing—"

"But they aren't, are they? Andrea ran away from your father's rule a long time ago and hasn't been back. Only you'd know what the twins were willing to do, and you've just said they wouldn't. So, you can't step down. If there's no clear successor, think about what will happen to the Pride. Look at what happened to the African Pride."

Throwing aside the covers, he stood to pace the length of her bedroom. She took a moment to admire the fluid movements, the tightly controlled grace. He growled, frustration in his every step. "There are no Panthers in Africa, because . . ."

"Because the leader died with no sons, no siblings, no heirs . . . and the resulting power struggle destroyed the Pride." She drew up her legs and rested her chin on her knees. "You can't let that happen here. I'm not worth civil war. *We* aren't worth that."

He rounded on her. "Why are you so concerned about the Pride? They threw you out."

"I get why, though." She lifted a placating hand. "It sucks, but it happened. The only reason humans didn't find out about our kind is because Africa as a continent has such a violent past. But, here? Humans would notice if that many people ended up dead or if there were that many panther sightings in the city. If we're *lucky*, they'd put it down to gang violence or cult activity. We can't take that risk."

"I know. Damn it, I *know*." A great weight seemed to settle on his shoulders and she watched them bow. She wanted to rid him of his burden, but she couldn't. He looked back at her, stubborn determination filling his black gaze. "There has to be a way. We're destined to be together. Do you know how precious that is?"

"Yes, but not every destiny can be fulfilled. Not every destiny ends happily." She jerked to her feet, grabbed some clothes out of her dresser, and turned for the door. Rage whipped through her, made her hands fist in her clothing until her knuckles ached. She set her jaw, struggling for calm. "This isn't a fairy tale, Antonio. And I refuse to pretend as though I'm living in one. If you can't accept what we are to each other, then we shouldn't see each other again. I told you before, *nothing can come of this.*"

"Solana—"

She forced her voice to remain steady and level. *"No.* Don't do this to me, Antonio. I can't. I just can't hope. There's no solution to this situation where we all win. You, me, the Pride. Something's got to give . . . and we both know it's going to be us." She spun around to dart into the living room, and she heard him stalk after her. "I have to get to Cat Scratch Fever. I have work and I'm sure you do, too. Good-bye."

He said nothing in return, but she felt his gaze burning into her back as she hastily dressed and sped out of her apartment.

5

Things couldn't go on like this. It had been weeks and he was slowly going insane. His fists balled at his sides. They'd been having the same argument over and over again. He couldn't force her and he couldn't have her. Not really. Not fully. Not the way fate had intended. Frustration gnawed at him. He'd finally given up on work tonight and paced the width of her living room, waiting for her to get home from the bar. Miguel would escort her—the two of them had grown to like each other in the last few weeks. Which only angered Antonio more. Were he in his best friend's position, he could mate with her and just walk away from his responsibilities.

Everyone in the Pride was walking on eggshells around him, wary of his foul temper. For once in his life, he didn't give a damn. For once in his life, he resented the hell out of what being born first demanded of him. His mate. His life.

He understood all the reasons he couldn't claim her, and if he didn't, she was more than happy to explain them to him. Again. He snarled and flung himself into a chair. He didn't like losing control this way. He didn't like how far this had pushed him, how frayed his temper was.

Sucking in a deep breath, he pushed away his anger. That wasn't what he wanted to give his mate. He wanted to treasure her, but openly. As she deserved. He sighed, leaning forward to drop his face into his hands. Such a tangled mess they were in. He could extricate himself, but he'd leave his soul behind. It belonged to her now. He'd stay as long as she would let him, no matter how much it pained them both. He'd done many things he didn't want to in his life—left his home and everyone he loved to go to South America, remained there for far too long in order to keep peace with his father and in his Pride. But this. This he wasn't strong enough to do. He couldn't leave her.

So he sat back and waited for her to return, determined not to fight with her. To just . . . cherish his time with her, no matter how fleeting.

She froze when she walked through her front door and saw him in her condo. "I won't even ask how you got in here."

"That's probably for the best."

"Look, I've had a shitty day. Two of my girls are out with the flu, I've worked double shifts for the last three days, and a customer tried to carry six shots of Jack Daniels back to his table but ended up dumping them down the front of my shirt so I smell like a distillery. I am really, *really* not in the mood to deal with you tonight." Her voice broke slightly and she cleared her throat, looking angry and embarrassed at once.

"Sounds like you need a shower and a massage."

Her mouth snapped shut and she blinked, surprise flickering across her face. "I—"

"Have you eaten?"

"No." Wariness filtered through her chocolate-brown gaze.

He smiled, just to throw her off further. It was high time he had control of this situation again. "There's a great Thai place I know of that delivers twenty-four hours a day. You like Pad Thai?"

She nodded silently and continued to stare at him as though he'd grown two heads.

"What?" Innocence oozed from his tone, and he gave her a grin to match. "We don't have to argue all the time."

Her gaze narrowed and she folded her arms across those lovely breasts of hers. He wanted to suck them into his mouth until she moaned. Her chin jutted. "We shouldn't even be seeing each other at all. How many times do I have to say it? This isn't going to end well."

"You're right. And I don't care." He rose from his chair and held his hand out for her, palm up, in offering. By now he knew she'd resist because she craved control and feared its loss. Someday he hoped she'd tell him why. But she was stubborn . . . and he was even more so. He'd wait her out—she would give in. She always did, because she wanted what he wanted and they both knew it.

She hesitated for the briefest of moments, a smile tucking into the corner of her lips. "Touching you is always a mistake."

"We do tend to combust, don't we?" He let a challenge fill his eyes and arched an eyebrow. "Scared?"

"Yes," she said, and placed her hand in his.

He tugged her forward, rested his forehead against hers, and looked deep into her eyes to see the fear and weariness. "I'm sorry you've had a bad day."

She sighed, her eyes drifting closed. Her hands pressed to his chest. "I'm glad you're here."

"Me, too." Pushing his fingers into her hair, he tugged it free of its loose ponytail. He tilted his head to brush his lips over hers. She stood on tiptoe, licking his lower lip. He shuddered, but forced himself to keep it light and worshipful. He wanted to savor her tonight.

He stepped back and turned her by the shoulders toward the bathroom. "I believe I promised you a shower, dinner, and a rubdown."

Instead of walking forward, she moved back and pressed her back to his front. His erection rested against the curve of her ass. Cupping her hips in his hands, he spoke in her ear. "You wish to push me, do you?"

"Right over the edge, lover."

"We'll see about that." The scent of her hair, her skin, filled his nostrils. He wanted her. Heat fisted in his gut, and every instinct inside him screamed for him to take her, to mark her as his. His fangs slid forward to prick his tongue, and he was grateful she faced away from him. Clenching his teeth, he forced his instincts down. He couldn't claim her. He could only cherish her for whatever time fate blessed them with—no matter how short that was. His fangs retracted and he slid his tongue from the base of her neck to her ear, sucking the lobe into his mouth.

She moaned, arching back into him, rubbing herself against him. "Please, Antonio."

"I'm going to make you moan tonight, Solana. Over and over again. But not just yet." He placed his hand on the small of her back, pushing her into the bathroom.

Wrapping his hands around her trim waist, he lifted her onto the counter next to the sink. Her knees bracketed his hips, cradling his cock at the juncture of her thighs. He gritted his teeth against the feel of her soft curves. *Madre de Dios*, it was sweet having her in his arms. Despite what he'd said, he didn't think he could wait to have her.

He bent her back over his arm and sucked her nipple through her dark gray T-shirt, humming in the back of his throat. "Mm. Whiskey."

A laugh startled out of her, and she lifted a hand to cover her mouth. The fingers of her other hand clenched in his hair, pulling him closer.

Grinning down at her, he brushed the tips of his fingers under her shirt and over her midriff. "You have a lovely laugh."

The corners of her eyes crinkled. "Thank you."

He tugged her shirt over her head, and her brunette curls tumbled down her shoulders and back. He leaned away to stare at her for a moment. She wasn't wearing a bra, and her pale golden skin contrasted with her tight, dusky nipples. Passion flushed her high cheekbones, and her chocolate eyes were dark and hooded. "You are so damn beautiful."

"You're not bad yourself." A slow, hot smile spread over her face. "Now, hurry up."

"As you wish." He smiled. "Lift your ass."

She laughed again, leaning back on her hands to leverage her hips up so he could pull off her jeans and boots. Then she pushed him back, her Panther strength catching him off guard. He caught himself and straightened. "What—"

"Strip. I want to see you naked." She slid off the counter, reached into the shower, and flicked the dials until water and steam hissed out of the spigot.

He swallowed, his gaze glued to her ass as she bent forward over the tub. A shudder ran through him, and he jerked his T-shirt and jeans off, kicking his shoes away. She glanced over her shoulder, a wicked little smile that heated his blood playing over her lips. "Coming?"

"As often as possible."

She chuckled and walked into the spray. If someone pressed a loaded gun to his head, he doubted he'd have been able to stop himself from following her. He shoved the shower curtain aside and stepped in behind her. Bubbles from the shampoo she was rinsing out of her hair and beads of water rolled down her skin. He wanted to trace the path of one over her flesh and taste the salty sweetness of her.

For the moment, he contented himself with reaching for the soap and working up a lather between his palms. Water ran over his body, misted his face, and created an erotic seal when he pressed his body to hers. "You feel so good, Solana."

"I love it when you touch me." Twisting her torso, she turned her head to kiss him. One hand reached back to fist in his hair. Their lips played together, their tongues dancing. Her teeth nipped at his upper lip before she sucked his lower lip into her mouth, dragging her teeth over his flesh. His heart hammered in his chest, beads of sweat and water blending to slip down his skin.

Gliding his soapy hands up her torso, he cupped her breasts and pinched the taut nipples. Hard. Her mouth broke away to cry out. "Antonio, please. *More.* Oh, my God. Please."

"You'll have more. But we have to make sure you're clean, don't we?"

She huffed out a laugh, grabbing one of his hands to push it down her body and between her thighs. "Very clean. Don't miss a spot."

"I won't." He plunged into her slick heat, flicking his fingertips over her hard clit. Her muscles jerked and she arched into his touch, her hand locking around his wrist as she moved with his stroking fingers. He paused for a moment to heighten her excitement. "Is this the right spot?"

She moaned, her head rolling against his shoulder. Her breath choked when he pushed deeper, into her hot channel. "Or how about this one?"

"*Yes.*" Her hips moved in fast, hard snaps, matching his rhythm. "Oh. Yes."

She clenched the fingers she had in his hair, her body twisting as her movements became frantic, her breath exploding out in hot little pants. Her wetness slipped down his fingers as he pushed inside her, rubbing against the slick walls of her pussy. "Come for me."

He angled his fingers deep inside her and every muscle in her body went rigid before her sex convulsed around him.

"*Antonio.*" Her nails bit into his wrist, raking up his forearm. She shivered, slumping back against him.

Spinning her, he pushed her against the tiled shower wall. Her dark eyes were still hazed with passion. She braced her hands on his shoulders as he dropped to his knees. "Wha-what are you doing?

"I have to taste you." He hooked one of her thighs over his arm, pulling her wide open for him.

She gasped when his lips touched her. "Oh, well. Don't let me stop you."

Hot water beat down on them, rolling down his body. It added to the sensations rocketing through him. The feel of her, the taste of her, he let himself soak it all in. Her smoky taste rolled over his tongue as he licked inside her. His fingers trailed from her slick sex to her tight anus, letting her own wetness ease his entrance. She mewed softly, twisting in his arms, moving her hips to the rhythm his mouth and fingers set for her. Her cries told him how close she was to orgasm. A few more moments and she'd come against his tongue.

He stopped.

"No!" Outrage flashed over her face when he rose to his feet. "Don't stop. Don't—"

He kissed her, knowing she'd taste herself on his lips. He slid his fingers around her body and over her ass, parting her cheeks to dip between them.

She shuddered, tearing her mouth from his. "Antonio."

"I'm going to fuck you here." His fingers circled her anus to stimulate her and press into her tight hole again. Her breath caught and her hands braced on the slick tiles of the wall behind her.

"Yes. Please, Antonio."

He wrapped her legs around his waist, lifting her high to position the head of his cock against her ass. He pressed in slowly, gritting his teeth against the sensation of her stretching around him.

"*Madre de Dios.*" He groaned when he was seated to the hilt inside her.

Her fingers curled over his shoulders, a bit of the wildness she always denied flashing in her gaze. He knew it scared her that he could push her even as far as he did. What would it be like to have all of that untamed woman in his arms? He intended to find out someday . . . for now, he'd take this.

"Do you want more, Solana?"

"Always." Her thighs gripped him tight and she arched into him.

He pulled his dick halfway out before sliding back in, letting her muscles adjust. She was so tight, so hot. Her hands pulled at him, impatient, demanding. He increased his pace, giving them both what they wanted.

They moved together, the water rolling over their skin, creating a sensual friction between their bodies. His dick slid in and out of her anus, the muscles dragging at his hard flesh. And all the while, he watched her face, the intensity, the pleasure, the wicked little smile that played across her lips.

"This is so good." Her head rolled against the tiles and her body bowed toward him, rubbing her hard nipples against his chest.

"You are so damn beautiful." Possession, sweetness, and some fierce emotion he couldn't name banded around his chest, threatening to choke him. His skin felt too tight for his body, and any moment he was going to explode. He thrust his cock deep into her soft body again and again, needing to come inside her.

Her nails bit into his skin, her thighs locked around his hips, and her torso arched hard. "*Antonio.*"

The muscles in her anus clamped down on his dick as she cried out in orgasm. He had no choice but to follow her, and he slammed in deep as he jetted his seed into her ass. A harsh shudder wracked his body, his fangs erupted from his gums, and a Panther's roar ripped from his throat. He buried his face in her shoulder, and reality returned with a sharp slap as he forced himself *not* to bite her. He reached out and turned off the water, cradling her close. He knew that each time he had her could be the last because she wasn't truly his. Not now, perhaps not ever.

He stepped out of the shower, bundled her in a soft towel, and swept her into his arms to carry her to her room. Depositing her on the side of the mattress, he kissed her lightly. "Now for dinner."

Scooping up the bedside phone, he punched in the number of his favorite Thai place and placed their delivery order. He turned back to face Solana when he was done. "It should be here in about forty-five minutes."

"Okay. Thanks." Her stomach rumbled and she slapped a hand over it. "I haven't eaten today."

"I'm not going to say how bad that is for you."

Her shoulder lifted in a shrug. "At least now it's by choice."

He winced.

Her lovely face blanched. "I—I didn't mean for that to make you feel bad."

"It kills me that my family had a hand in your deprivation." He shook his head, regret for not being here to save her then searing him. Things might have been so different if he had found her before he'd become Pride leader. But, then, where would his Pride be? Would his sister have cared that she should be next in line? Would his father have trained her to be a good leader? Duty. Honor. Instinct. Nothing made sense any more. He shook his head. "I've never done without in my life."

"I'm glad. I wouldn't wish those times on anyone, especially not my mate."

He leaned forward to stroke her hair away from her face. "I love hearing you say those words."

"Don't." Her lips quivered, emotion she never would have allowed him to see a few weeks before cracking through the surface. He was reaching her, and he treasured the measures of trust she gave him. Whether she realized what she was doing or not. She swallowed and met his gaze. "Don't say those things. I can't stand it and then have you leave me the way everyone else has."

Pain lanced his chest at her words. Was that how she'd come to see their time together after they'd parted? If he couldn't find a solution? "Solana, I—"

She turned her head aside and swallowed. When she looked back at him, her face was a composed mask. The muscles in her shoulders drew into taut lines. "I'm sorry. You've been so good to me. I didn't mean to—"

"You didn't do anything wrong." He stooped down in front of her, opening his mouth to say something to make it better, but there was nothing to be said. No matter how much he might wish things were different, he couldn't make it so. Brushing her hair out of her eyes, he pressed a kiss to her forehead. "Lie down. I still owe you a massage."

"Okay." Relief flooded her face that he wasn't going to push the issue. She closed her eyes, nodded, and turned to crawl onto the mattress. Settling facedown on the pillow, she propped her chin on her folded hands.

He tugged the towel open where she had it tucked together at her side. Working his fingers into the tension that ran through her muscles, he felt her flesh warm under his hands. She sighed softly, arching into him when he ran his palms over her shoulders and down her back. He loved how responsive she was to his touch. "How does that feel?"

"Amazing." She hummed in the back of her throat, turning her head so she could glance back at him. A little smile curved her lips.

Her tension melted away, her muscles softening under the

stroke of his fingers. Even though this was supposed to be a nonsexual act, he found himself growing hard. Just touching her was enough. He gritted his teeth and resisted the urge to move lower and cup his hands over the globes of her ass. Later, he promised himself. He'd have more of her later. Right now she needed to relax and unwind . . . and eat something.

He glanced at the clock on the bedside table, noting the passage of time. The delivery should be there any minute. As if on cue, the doorbell rang. He bent forward and kissed her shoulder. "I'll get that. You stay here."

"I couldn't move if you paid me." She hugged the pillow and snuggled in.

He leveraged himself off the bed and walked across the hall into the bathroom. Snagging his pants off the floor to pull them on, he fished out his wallet on his way to the front door. He paid the delivery guy and tipped him generously.

Hooking the plastic bags over his fingers, he swung around to head back into the her room. "Dinnertime."

"Mmm." She yawned and stirred in bed.

"Come on, honey. I have some amazing Asian cuisine here to tempt your palate." He pulled the white cardboard tubs out of the bag and set them on the side table while he fished out two sets of chopsticks.

Chuckling softly, she tucked the sheet under her armpits, sat up in bed, and pushed her damp hair away from her face. "Okay, but I was half asleep, so this better be some orgasmic Thai food."

He ran the tip of the chopsticks down her ribs before he scissored them to pinch the top of her thigh. She squeaked and laughed, plucking them out of his hands. He winked at her. "If it isn't, I promise to make it up to you with other kinds of orgasm."

She froze while reaching for the Pad Thai, her eyes crinkling at the corners as she looked at him. "I can always lie about the food just to get those other kinds of orgasms, you know."

He laughed. "Eat your dinner, woman."

"All right, but you better make good on that," she grumbled, wriggling to get comfortable.

He watched her as she ate, taking her in. God, but he loved her. The realization should have shocked him, but it didn't. It felt . . . right. It had been building for weeks now. She wasn't perfect, but perfect for him. And she would never forgive him if he told her how he felt. That was the damnable shame of it.

She paused with the chopsticks halfway to her mouth. "What?"

"Nothing. Just enjoying the view." He winked at her, keeping his expression playful.

Her nose wrinkled and she resumed her meal. Would it get easier, this constant pain and pressure in his chest? This jangling of instinct and desire? He doubted it. He didn't even want it to fade, because it meant he'd lost her, lost this connection that fed his soul.

Loving her was something he could never regret, no matter what else might happen between them. But it made him that much more determined to have her, to keep her. Something would present itself, if he schooled himself to patience. It had to. He couldn't live without her anymore.

6

"You should get some sleep." Antonio's voice rumbled in her ear.

Solana fought a yawn, setting her empty container of Thai food on the bedside table. He didn't need to tell her twice. She had been on her feet working her ass off for days straight, and she was beyond exhausted. Every muscle in her body was loose and warm. God, she felt good. She collapsed in the bed and as soon as her eyes closed, sleep dragged her under. A sigh eased past her lips.

But a nightmare awaited her, one so familiar it was burned into the back of her eyelids. One that never lost its horror because it was no dream, but a memory. The worst moment of her life.

The day her mother died.

She gazed out of ten-year-old eyes, staring at the scene that played out before her, small and helpless next to the adults. She whimpered, struggling against the pull of the nightmare. No. She didn't want to see this again. Didn't want to face it. But the terror had her in its grip and wasn't about to let her go.

Her mother and father had quarreled. Again. They lived in Spain at the time, part of the Barcelona Pride. A Panther scream had ripped from her mother's throat. She slashed at Father with her claws, halfway between human and cat form. Tears leaked down her cheeks.

Father tried to reason, his voice low, his tone patronizing. Solana hated it when he talked to her that way. Her mother hated it more. It just made it worse. Her mother screeched, her face flushing bright red. Her hair hung in dark strings down her back, making her look wild and crazed.

Solana had never been so terrified in her whole life. Nausea crawled through her belly, made her hands and legs shake. Her knees turned to jelly and she was glad she squatted on the floor under the table in their suite.

Why didn't anyone come in and stop them? Sometimes the Pride leader or his Second came. Someone had to come. This was worse than she'd ever seen them and she was scared. So scared. She curled tighter into herself, rocking and whimpering softly. She tried to be quiet. Father didn't like it when she was too loud.

"I hate you!" Spittle flew from her mother's mouth as she screamed.

"You're useless. I wash my hands of you." Father waved her away as though she were no more significant than a bother-some fly.

Spinning around, her mother raced from the room, still halfway between animal and human form. Sobs ripped from her throat. Where was she going? She was supposed to stay in the suite when she was this upset.

Solana scrambled to her feet and ran after her. "Mama! Wait, Mama!"

"Solana, stay where you are." The command in her father's tone brooked no argument, but she didn't turn around.

For the first time in her life, she disobeyed him. Her mother was so upset. She needed to make sure nothing bad happened to her. Her father wouldn't do it.

She heard footsteps pounding behind her as she darted through the front door of the mansion and out into the street. Horror streaked through her as she watched her mother change form in broad daylight.

Humans shrieked and leaped back as she ran down the sidewalks. Solana's short legs burned as she struggled to keep up. "Mama!"

The Pride leader would be so angry. No one was allowed to change into a Panther in front of people. Not ever. Her chest squeezed and all she could hear was her heart pounding in her ears and her panting breath. Tears filled her eyes, blinding her as she ran. Only her sense of smell told her which way her mother had gone. Lights flashed in her vision and she swiped at her eyes to clear the tears away. Sirens and lights from police cars were in front of her. Men in uniforms surrounded her naked mother, still half changed.

They shouted at her, but her mother didn't seem to hear them. She struggled against their hold on her arms when they grabbed her. Spinning, she threw two of them over the hood of their car.

Other cops raised their guns and fired at her like she was a rabid animal.

Solana cried out and her father's hand clamped over her mouth as he raced up behind her. "Contain yourself, Solana."

And she did. She knew in that moment that she'd never lose it the way her mother had, endanger herself and everyone she loved by letting her control slip. Some door had closed within her that day, locked and barricaded.

Her mother choked, blood gurgling from the corner of her mouth to pool around her. She reached out, an entreaty in the fading light in her eyes.

Then there was nothing left of her mother except a body

that reeked of death; the smell of it choked her, made bile claw its way up her throat until she gagged on it.

Solana bolted upright, a low cry ripping from deep within her. Cold sweat ran in rivulets down her face. Rough shudders wracked her body.

"Solana."

"I'm here now," she whispered, her voice harsh from screams that had made her throat raw.

Antonio stroked her sweaty hair back. "What happened?"

Embarrassment flooded her that she'd freaked out that much in front of him, even in her sleep. She shrugged and looked away. "Nothing. Just a nightmare. I'm fine."

His arms closed around her, holding her tight, protecting her from the past. She wished it could last. Tears welled in her eyes and she blinked them back.

She should pull away. Letting herself depend on him for even a short amount of time would only end in *more* pain for them both. His broad hand stroked up and down her back, comforting, soothing, and warm. Against her will, a slow purr soughed from her throat. The cat half of her wanted to trust him, to be his and only his. The logical woman knew better, but her body relaxed into feline languor.

"Tell me."

She licked her lips, her eyes sliding to half-mast. "Mmm?"

"About your dream. Tell me."

A tiny warning flickered in her mind. "I shouldn't."

"Please?"

So she did. The story jerked out in fits and starts. She'd never told anyone about it before, or about how often the nightmare haunted her. Her parents were an example of everything that could go wrong with a mating. Destiny could give a Panther a mate, but that didn't mean they didn't have to work on a relationship, learn to compromise, and *bend* to find some balance with each other. Even with the extra help of their magic, mating didn't guarantee Panthers had good marriages. It gave her one more reason not to trust in what was developing with Antonio.

Look what mating had done to her parents. It had stolen her mother's soul, her life.

And yet . . . it had been so long since she'd been able to reach out to anyone. She was selfish enough to take advantage of what he offered. *For as long as it lasted.* Those words had gotten her through the last few weeks, when she'd been unable to push him away. They'd reached a stalemate in their arguments. He still hoped for a solution, she knew, but she couldn't afford the luxury of hope. She burrowed deeper into his embrace as she reached the end of her story, her memory. The last day of her childhood.

"I'm so sorry." He kissed her forehead, his hands still stroking her skin. Heat fluttered in her belly, spreading through her body in lapping waves of warmth.

She pushed away from him, forcing herself to sit up and flick the hair away from her face. "It happened a long time ago."

"It still affects you." His fingertips trailed up and down her arm.

A sigh slipped past her lips. "The past is what shapes everyone, isn't it? I'm no different. In that regard anyway."

"Your uniqueness fascinates me." He lay back against her pillows, folding his hands behind his head and offering up a wicked smile.

"You're the only Panther to ever think so."

His brow arched. "You've never been with another Panther?"

"One." A flush of shame flooded her cheeks. "I found out the next morning he'd lost a bet."

His eyes narrowed to dangerous slits, his nostrils flaring as he pulled in a sharp breath. "Who was he?"

"It doesn't matter." She looked away.

He sat up, wrapping his fingers around her biceps. "It does to me."

"It shouldn't."

"Solana." A warning sounded in his tone, but she ignored it. Her life was what it was, belonging to no one. Not Panthers and not humans. She couldn't change it, and she refused to beat her head against that brick wall again. It didn't make her happy to always be on the outside looking in, but she'd accepted it.

He would as well, in time.

For now, a diversion seemed in order. She let a smile unfurl on her lips. Wariness replaced the rising ire on his handsome face. Smart man. It was just her poor luck she found intelligence attractive. Her grin widened.

Reaching out, she brushed her fingertips over his muscular thigh. His breath hissed out, his fingers dropping to ball in the loose sheets. "I know what you're doing."

"Let me." Her fingers closed around his cock, which was now fully erect. God, he was huge. Leaning forward, she flicked her tongue over the bulbous head. "Let me distract you, Antonio."

"*Fuck.*" He let go of the sheets and tangled his fingers in her hair, tugging her closer.

She chuckled. "How did you put it? *That comes next.*"

Sliding her tongue from the base of his cock to the crest, she pulled the tip of it into her mouth. One hand cupped the soft sacs between his legs while the other circled the base of his cock, squeezing lightly as she drew on the hard length. His fingers tightened in her hair, then relaxed and slid away to let her proceed as she saw fit. She smiled against his hot flesh, humming her approval. The vibration along his dick made him growl.

She loved it, loved the power that holding him in her hands and mouth gave her over him. That a man as contained as Antonio would slide right over the edge into feral from what she could do to him. Her legs clenched together at just the thought. God, it was such a turn-on.

Pulling him as deep into her mouth as she could, she worked her hand in tandem movements along the length of his dick. He groaned, the muscles in his thighs flexing and relaxing with every glide of her tongue.

Her nipples hardened and she shuddered when his hand stroked down her back and between the globes of her ass. His finger dipped into her from behind, sliding over the slick folds of her sex. She whimpered when his finger slid deep within her soaking channel, thrusting in time with her movements. Heat spiraled tight inside her, and she moaned on his cock.

Her muscles fisted on his fingers, and liquid heat rolled through her in dizzying waves. She closed her eyes, and the smell of him, the taste of him, the addicting feel of him, overwhelmed her senses. She craved him so much, every passing minute only made the need burn hotter inside her. She sucked him so far into her mouth, her throat contracted on the head of his cock.

His hands closed over her shoulders and he flipped her onto her back. She arched against him when he came down on top of her, roughly shoving her thighs apart. "I was having fun."

He growled low in his throat, baring his fangs as his ebony eyes flashed to the pale gold of a Panther. His nails extended to claws and scraped lightly down her sides to score her hips. She shivered, her nipples tightening.

A flutter of excitement whipped through her—that she could push him to the point of feral, of shifting, made her feel more powerful than she ever had in her life. Wrapping her legs around his lean flanks, she angled her hips up to his, opened herself for his penetration.

"Solana," his voice had gone deeper, rougher than his usual smooth tone.

The head of his cock probed at her slick opening. She curled her hands over his shoulders, digging her nails into his flesh.

Need raced through her, made her pulse race and her breathing speed up. "Please, Antonio. I want you."

A shudder wracked his big body. "I won't be gentle. I'm sorry."

Her fingers slid into his hair, pulling him down so she could kiss him. She ran her tongue down his fangs before plunging into his mouth. His hips slammed forward, burying his cock to the hilt inside her. He stretched her wide, and if she hadn't been so wet, he might have hurt her. As it was, he just excited her more. She loved his wildness, it was a luxury she never allowed herself.

She reveled at holding all that unleashed wildness in her arms. Just for tonight. His tongue mated with hers in a rhythm that mimicked the hard thrust of his dick within her.

He ripped his mouth away from her, threw his head back and roared. Her breath caught at the sight of him. He was so beautiful. Orgasm caught her by surprise, fisting her sex around his cock. Flames danced across her skin, the vortex of ecstasy sweeping her under. She cried out, her torso arching so hard, she lifted him with her. He braced his hands on either side of her on the mattress, still rock hard and thrusting within her.

The musky scent of sex and sweat permeated the room, the sheer carnality dragging at her. She raked her fingernails down his chest, pinching his flat nipples. "Come for me, Antonio."

A sound somewhere between a hiss and a snarl slipped from his throat. His body went rigid over her before his hot fluid filled her. Her pussy clenched in a small aftershock of orgasm, and she shivered, letting the pleasure slide through her. She stroked a hand down his strong back, relaxing into the bed.

Pulling his still semi-hard dick out of her pussy, he leveraged himself off of her and rolled to lie beside her. He tugged her into his arms and heaved a contented sigh. "I'm going to have to leave here soon. I have an early meeting today with an emissary from the Australian Pride."

She rose up onto her elbow to look down at him. He was so comfortable with who and what he was. If he'd ever questioned his destiny to rule the Pride, he didn't show it. He was so whole, complete . . . beautiful. If he stayed with her, would she ruin that for him—as she had ruined her father's life? He hadn't asked for a non-shifter daughter any more than Antonio had asked for a non-shifter mate.

In the end, she would lose him the way she'd lost her father . . . he would grow to resent what she could never be, but unlike her father, he could never abandon her because they would be bound together forever, *mated*. A small, selfish part of her craved the connection that would give her. Someone she could never lose, who could never leave her.

And in the process, she would ruin his life, rip him away from the destiny that was his, that *should* be his. Pride leader.

She sighed, turning her face away. She couldn't look at him— it hurt too much, knowing she would lose him. She had to, or there was a very real possibility that people would suffer and die on a level she could barely comprehend. And he would blame himself for it even if he never took a life himself; she understood him well enough now to know that.

She loved him too much to let that happen. So she had to leave him, sever this tie that grew stronger and sweeter every time they touched.

7

He couldn't find her. Antonio made another loop around Cat Scratch Fever, weaving in and out of the packed crowd in search of Solana. She was nearby—he could smell her, but he couldn't find her. He waved to Lisa and Rachel, who were putting on a show on the bar. Lisa wiggled her fingers at him and Rachel winked. He'd made a point to get to know all of her employees—the only family she could claim. Perhaps it was his way of making it more difficult for her to leave him, ingratiating himself into her world.

He crooked a finger at Michelle, who was serving drinks to a table full of frat boys. "Hey, have you seen Solana?"

She smacked a kiss on his cheek. "Hey, handsome. She left out the back about five minutes ago. Said she wasn't feeling well. She looked stressed, poor baby. You go take good care of her, okay? Call us if you need anything."

"Will do." He turned for the rear of the bar, nodding to the bouncer, Lee, on his way out.

He found her sitting on the hood of his Porsche, head down, hands clasped between her knees. Her dark curls tumbled around her shoulders and he paused for a moment to take in how gorgeous she was. When she looked up at him, what he saw in her eyes made his heart stop. Something was very, very wrong.

She licked her lips, and her voice came out a soft rasp. "We can't go on like this."

"I know." He closed his eyes for a moment, dread fisting in his gut. He'd known this was coming, it had been building since that first night. But he couldn't let her go. He refused. She was *his*, damn it. "I want to mate with you, Solana."

She shook her head and her hair flew around her shoulders in a cloud. "No. I'll take everything from you, and I can never give you children."

"Either way, I'll have no children." Pain lanced his chest at the thought, something she'd dealt with for years. "Why can't I have you beside me?"

"Because it isn't just you, is it?" A sad bitterness filled those chocolate eyes. "You're the Pride leader. They don't *want* me by your side. My presence would be offensive to them."

Anger slammed into him, and his fingers clenched into fists. Two strides brought him to her side and he hissed in her face. "Don't say that. Don't talk about *my mate* that way."

"It's the truth." She glared at him, her chin slanting at a stubborn angle.

He folded his arms. "I'm stepping down as the Pride leader. If they can't accept you, then they'll never really accept me. You're my mate. Mine. And I'm yours. This is destiny. Being Pride leader is nothing more than being born first."

Shock flashed across her face, but she covered it quickly and that enraged him even more, that she always kept herself aloof. There was always a part of her he couldn't touch.

"Being born first is destiny, too." She scooted off the car to stand in front of him and lifted her palms to press against his chest. "You can't mate with me and you can't step down, Antonio. The Pride needs you."

"And I need you, so the Pride needs you, too. Why can't you try? Mate with me. If they truly can't change, can't accept, then I will step down. In the meantime, I'll recall my sister." He clasped his hands around her wrists, trying to compel her to listen to him, to believe as much as he did.

She jerked her hands away from him, using a good deal of her Panther strength to do so. The incredulous look on her face clearly questioned his sanity. "Andrea won't thank you for calling her back. Even in the short time I lived with this Pride, she made it clear she hated your father."

"Do you?"

She sighed, glancing away. "I . . . want to. But would any other Pride leader have reacted differently? I don't think so. It's why my father moved us around so much—because I was too young and idealistic to really understand what would happen to us."

"I'm not like that. A loyal Pride member is a rare commodity, and breeding isn't the only use one can have to the Panther people." He reached for her and she turned aside to avoid him. He could feel her slipping away, and terror and anger made his voice harsher than he'd intended. "I would never have forced a non-shifter out of the Pride. There are too few of us as it is. It's not right. I'm just . . . not like that."

"No. You're not, but that doesn't change anything. I am a non-shifter. I'll never be good enough for a Pride leader's mate." She shrank into herself, wrapping her arms around her waist.

"You were made for me."

Her face flushed an angry red, and she stood up on tiptoe to snarl in his face. "Will you just *hear* me? It's *not* your decision to make, Antonio. I don't belong in your Pride or any other, and especially not to rule. I'm not even a real Panther."

"Damn it, Solana." His fist slammed into the hood of his car, making the metal groan and cave in.

She hissed at him. "I was born this way. It's not something I chose."

"I'm not angry at you." His knuckles hit the car again and the boom made her jump. "Actually, I am angry with you. Not for being a non-shifter, but for thinking you deserve this."

She heaved an exasperated sigh. "I told you, I don't think I deserve it. I just think it makes sense that people who can't breed aren't as valued as people who can. We have to keep the population up."

Reining in his temper as much as he could, he tried to reason with her. Again. "That kind of *sense* is what leads to abuse of power and throwing people out of Prides like they're garbage. That makes sense to you?"

"Stop it, Antonio. I can't change what I am and I can't change what happened." Anger lit her eyes, making them flash. "If I can find some peace with it, who the hell do you think you are to try and take that away from me? Oh, wait. You're the *Pride leader.*"

"You think I'm saying this to hurt you?" Could she really believe that of him? He shook his head, incredulity flickering through him.

"It's working." She bit her lower lip, her gaze hitting the ground as her fury sucked away.

"Why can't you just—"

"Be normal? Be someone you could mate with?" Her chocolate eyes met his and he watched them shutter, watched her try and pretend this didn't matter. "I can't, and I never will be able to. So, do us both a favor and leave."

He shook his head. "Solana."

One eyebrow arched and her jaw tilted to the side. "What? What, Antonio? This is a lose-lose situation. We can't win. Why won't you accept that?"

He narrowed his gaze down at her, crossing his arms and

propping a hip against his mangled car. "Why are you so eager to accept it? You are so afraid of getting hurt, you're not even willing to take a risk. I see that you're just accepting defeat the way you always have."

Her hands fisted in his shirt and she shook him. Her expression intensified, her nostrils flaring and her mouth working for a moment before words came out. "You don't know what you're talking about—you've *never* had to live with people who thought you were less than nothing. Even if you didn't get along with your father, you always had the power and influence of an heir. You have no idea what this is like."

And that was when he completely lost it. A part of him stood back and lifted his eyebrow at himself, but the rest of him shot up off the car to get right in her face, saying things he never would have imagined saying to his mate. The woman he loved more than life itself. But that woman was also worth fighting for, if only she could see it. If only he could *make* her see it. "Then why do you stay? If being near other Panthers reminds you of how inferior you are, then why are you still in San Francisco? Why didn't you just leave and never come back?" He flung his arms out, and bent even closer to her, until their noses were almost touching. "You have all of North America to play in—the Prides live together. Hell, pick a city anywhere in the world where there's no den and you're set.

"But you didn't, did you?" He straightened, shaking his head. "You stayed here because it's where your father left you. Did you think he was coming back? You keep saying you accept what you are, but deep down you want the people who abandoned you to accept you, don't you? The Pride, your father. I accept you, Solana. Why won't you reach out and take that with me?"

She shook her head, a tear leaking from the corner of her eye. "I can't . . . you don't . . ."

Spinning, she ran as fast as her legs would carry her. He grabbed for her. And missed.

Racing around the building, Solana stepped in front of one of her inebriated customers to jump into his taxi.

"Hey!" he yelled, but she paid him no heed.

She thrust a $100 bill at the cab driver. "Get me to the corner of Green and Scott Street as fast as you can."

"Yes, ma'am." The man planted his foot on the gas pedal so hard it threw her back against the seat as they pulled away from the curb.

She hugged herself tight, keeping all the demons chasing her at bay. Don't think about it and it wasn't there. Don't give in. Don't lose control. Just . . . don't.

About a block away from her condo, they came to an abrupt stop. Solana looked up to see flashing blue and red police lights. The cabbie looked back at her through the rearview mirror. "There's a wreck, ma'am."

"I'll walk from here." She slid out of the backseat and slammed the car door behind her.

She walked, her feet taking her up the steep hill toward home without direction from her mind. Alone, all the emotions she'd tucked away came rushing back. The anguish, the anger. All of it. She tripped over her own feet on the sidewalk, stumbling to catch herself. Her breath choked out. It wasn't true. Antonio was wrong about her. He didn't know her. Just because he was her mate didn't mean he knew her better than she knew herself. She knew who she was, what she wanted. He was just angry that she didn't want him. Her mind whispered at what a lie that was, but she squelched it.

How could he say things like that to her? She wasn't so desperate for acceptance. It made her sound pathetic. She'd lived for years without anyone's approval. He had no right to judge

her. So what if she stayed in San Francisco? It didn't mean anything, did it?

No. Not a thing. Right?

And damn him for making her question herself more than
she already did. Just because she had a firm grasp on reality and
disagreed with him didn't make her wrong. She knew the limits
of being a non-shifter. Pressing her lips together to stop their
quivering, she darted across the street toward her home.

A hand reached out of the dark and slammed her against the
wall outside her condominium building. Her breath whooshed
out, but her eyes locked with those of a deranged man. His hair
was dirty and lank, his eyes glazed with madness, and his breath
stank of cheap vodka. One of his hands bracketed her neck,
making it difficult to breathe. Her fingers rose to bite into his
forearm, but she couldn't escape his grip. What terrified her the
most was that she knew this man. Roberto Ruiz—one of the
Panthers who'd chased her the night she met Antonio. Icy fear
trickled in her blood and sweat beaded across her forehead.

He bared his fangs at her. "It's your fault. My family is being
punished because of you, the leader's new whore."

She coughed, pulling in a breath. "I didn't do anything to
you."

"Just your being born and breathing air is an insult to every
Panther." A sneer lifted his lips.

"I don't live among the Panthers. I'm an outcast." She fought
him, struggling for air, for life. Her nails raked at his flesh, anywhere she could reach. Her muscles burned, and sweat slid
down her face to make her shirt stick to her body.

He shook her like a rag doll. "But you're leading the Pride
leader around by the cock, aren't you, bitch?"

Hardly. She fought a hysterical laugh at anyone leading
Antonio anywhere. The two of them hadn't agreed on anything
from the moment they met. "You think he'll thank you for
this? You think you won't just get into more trouble? You and

your whole family? Just let me go and I won't say a word. Walk away now."

"It's too late for that." His fingers flexed around her neck. "Now you're going to regret ever being born."

"Too late for that, too," she wheezed. She was going to die. And the last words she'd ever spoken to the only person who'd ever truly cared for her had been words of anger and rejection. She'd never even told him she loved him. Too late for apologies, for self-loathing. Too damn late for any of it.

Spots flashed before her eyes. The world faded to darkness, and as much as she struggled, his grip only tightened. A gurgling breath was the last thing she heard.

She jolted back to consciousness when Roberto dropped her suddenly. Landing on her feet, she let herself lean back against the wall and slip down until her butt hit the sidewalk. Her head felt too heavy to hold up, and she drooped down to let her forehead rest upon her knees.

A roar echoed over the street and she rolled her head on her neck to see Antonio hauling Roberto away from her to slam him against the wall. She saw Miguel just beyond her mate, rage contorting his normally composed face.

Antonio's fangs were bared as a Panther's scream ripped free again. His eyes had gone gold in change, the feral beast more in control than the man. He slammed his fist into the younger Panther's face and body, his claws shredding his clothing and flesh to ribbons. Blood splashed over the pavement and the coppery stench of it filled her nose. Roberto tried to fight back, but his blows seemed to bounce off of Antonio like they were nothing. The boy was no match for a Pride leader defending his mate.

Miguel grabbed Antonio's arm, ripping him away from Roberto before he killed him.

"You dare to stop me?" Antonio roared in his Second's face.

Miguel didn't back down, shoving Antonio toward her. "See to your mate. She needs you now more than the Ruiz boy does."

Her mate staggered, turning to look for her. His pupils were dilated, dominating his dark irises.

"Antonio." Her lips formed his name, but no sound emerged. She swayed in place, even while sitting. Her throat burned and she couldn't draw a full breath. She choked and sputtered, but coughing only made the agony increase.

His hand hit the wall behind her head and he knelt down beside her. He cradled her face in his palms. "Solana."

She started to shake, every muscle in her body clenching and jerking. Her stomach heaved, but her throat was too swollen to let her vomit. She couldn't breathe, but the panic that should have overtaken her didn't come.

From a distance, she heard Antonio speak. "You need to sleep, Solana."

Yes, she needed sleep. It was how Panthers regenerated. Catnaps. They healed no faster than humans until they slept. Then the ancient magic that made them more than mortal took over, mended their bodies. They'd only have a handful of years more than humans in life, but it would be in amazing good health.

The world slid away into nothing. Death or sleep, she wasn't sure. Her thoughts went fuzzy, muddy. She blinked up at him, trying to focus through the darkness. A tiny part of her was relieved that she got to see him one last time. Her body went cold and then numb. And she knew nothing more.

8

Jolting awake, Solana glanced around, uncertain of where she was. She was naked beneath soft sheets, and she clutched the fabric to her breasts. The room was all dark colors and masculine leather. It smelled of Antonio. And beyond that was the scent of many, many Panthers.

Oh, God. She was in the Pride's den.

She jerked upright, cupping her hands around her throat. It didn't hurt, but the splashes of violent memories came foaming back. Scattered pieces, nothing concrete. Roberto. Miguel. Antonio.

And there he was, stepping out of a door to her left and wrapped in a towel. Steam curled around his big body. His gaze went straight to her and warmed. "You're awake. Are you feeling better?"

She nodded. "How long did I sleep?"

"About eighteen and a quarter hours. Not that I was counting." He dropped the towel and slid into bed beside her. His hand brushed over her hair, twining in the long curls.

Her palm lifted to cup his jaw and she said what she should have told him long ago. "I love you."

His eyes flashed with dark fire, and he pulled her to his muscled body. His cock rode against the soft curve of her lower belly. "I love you, too, Solana."

"I needed you to know that." She dropped her grip on the sheet, wrapped her arms around him, and pressed her body to his. "I love you more than anything, but I won't mate with you."

"But you'll love me now, mate."

His lips covered hers, smothering any response she might have made. He licked inside her mouth, mating his tongue to hers. She hummed in the back of her throat, melting against him. Tingles raced over her flesh, made her shiver. Her sensitive nipples hardened as they rubbed the rougher skin of his chest. He bit her lip lightly, sucking it into his mouth. She moaned when he pulled back, swaying toward him.

He held her tight for a moment, pressed his forehead to hers, and closed his eyes. "Seeing him with his hands around your neck—"

Stroking her fingers through his soft hair, she sighed, regret piercing her. "I know. I love you. I'm so sorry."

"Not yet, but you will be." He flipped her over his knee, one hand holding her wrists firmly at the small of her back. His other hand came down on her ass with a sharp crack. Her breath seized, shock ripping through her. Wicked pleasure followed on the heels of her surprise. No man had ever done this to her.

She bucked against him. "Antonio!"

He spanked her again and again, agony and ecstasy tumbling over each other until she couldn't tell one from the next. She whimpered, her nipples chafing against the crisp hair on his thigh. Her back arched when his palm swept under the curve of her buttocks, the sting of his hard hand hitting her flesh making her jump. She sobbed on a helpless moan. Something hot and wild screamed inside her, fighting to break free. She twisted in his arms, jerking at his grip, but he was far stronger than she. Flames licked over her skin where he smacked her. "Never. Run away. From me. Again. Solana."

Wetness flooded her pussy, making her ache with want. "I need you, Antonio. Please."

As quickly as it had begun, it stopped. He lifted her and tossed her back onto the bed. The sheets felt rough against her burning backside, but she didn't care—it was just one more sensation adding to all the wildness whipping through her. Excitement and pleasure had pushed her too far. She reached for Antonio, but he'd plucked up a pillow and jerked off the case. He ripped it into strips and used it to bind her wrists to the headboard.

She tugged against the ties, arching herself toward him in offering. "Please."

He jerked her thighs apart, sliding between her legs. He plunged his cock deep into her pussy, and her body bowed. She hooked her heels under his ass, pulling him closer. He thrust into her, hard and fast, but it wasn't enough. She burned, her body craving him more deeply than she ever had.

Each time she lifted her hips, the stinging in her ass twinged. Her sex clenched at the reminder of his spanking. "Fuck me hard, Antonio. I need you. Faster. Please, faster, harder."

"No."

"*No?*" Outrage spun within her, and desperation gripped her tight. Her hips twisted on the sheets and they chafed her backside. She gasped for breath, too many sensations rocketing through her.

"No. I'm going to go slow. I'm going to drive you wild, make you beg for more." He smiled, mocking her with his control.

Control. God, she had none left. Her body burned with a craving she couldn't quench. She needed him to touch her, fuck her. Now. God, now. "I'll beg now. Please, please, please. Antonio, *please.*"

He shook his head.

She sobbed out a breath, something deep within her ripping loose, a dam breaking, a wall crumbling. A Panther's scream, high, wild, and feral exploded from her throat. It was too much, she couldn't contain herself.

Throwing her head back, she twisted beneath him. She jerked at the ties that bound her and they shredded, the fabric no match for her Panther strength. She wrapped her arms around him, moving under him with untamed abandon. Her nails raked down his back. She grabbed his ass, trying to urge him to go faster, deeper.

His hips bucked against hers, a harsh groan ripping from him. He rotated his pelvis against her, taunting her with deeper contact. "Solana. My Solana."

"Yes," she choked. "Yours. Antonio, please. No more teasing."

His eyes squeezed closed, a pained smile crossing his lips, baring his fangs for the briefest of moments. "I can't deny you."

She burned for him, hotter than she'd ever been before. She needed him, *craved* him. Oh, God. She could smell her own wetness mixed with his richer, more masculine scent. Heated sweat sealed them together with each thrust, and she shuddered with the hard impact. She had no thoughts left, just the driving need for orgasm. "More, more, *more.*"

"Yes." He rolled his hips against her, changing the angle of his penetration. It was too much. She screamed, her sex clenching tight around his cock. Her nails dug into his back as she clutched him closer.

Tears leaked from the corners of her eyes to slip down her cheeks. But there was no release for her, no surcease. It went on forever. He moved over her, in her, his cock gliding against the tight, slick walls of her pussy. It built and built until it reached a peak. Surely it would break, she would shatter as she needed to.

But he froze, embedded deep within her, his dick stretching her wide. "Not yet. Not yet. I want more from you."

She sobbed a denial, her body quaking with the fever pitch of feral lust. "Everything I am is yours."

"No, but it will be. You will be. Trust me."

"I do." She loved him, trusted him, craved him. And this might be the last time she ever touched him. Roberto had only solidified her opinion—being with her would only ruin her mate. She couldn't do it—she loved him too much. So she moved against him, wanting to savor every second. Her hips snapped up to meet his, but his big hands held her down. She sobbed, desperate need driving her.

His lips closed over her nipple and he dragged his sharp fangs over the tight crest.

Pain wrapped around her soul, clawing at her. Never again. She'd never have him again. Choking out a breath, her body bowed and she convulsed around him. She flew higher than she'd ever been before, sheer ecstasy racing through her veins. Her lips closed over his shoulder, nipping and sucking on the salty heat of his skin. The taste of him burst over her tongue, drowning her in the carnality of *him*.

His cock jutted into her in quick, sharp thrusts. Her arms wrapped around him tightly, her hips pressing into his as they rode out the orgasm as long as possible. It was a never-ending free fall, tingles skipping over her flesh. "I love you, Antonio. Love you, love you, *love you*."

"*Dios mio*, Solana. You drive me wild."

"Yes." She loved him wild, loved him controlled, loved him more than she'd ever imagined loving another person in her life.

A rough chuckle was her answer. "You're perfect for me, you know that?"

Yes, she knew. She couldn't form the words though. It hurt too much. Tears swamped her vision, and her body still shuddered from orgasm.

Stroking a hand through her hair, he panted for breath. Then he went rigid against her and jerked back, his fingers running all over her body, pulling away the remains of the bonds around her wrists. "Are you all right?"

She frowned, wondering what had gone wrong in the last five seconds. Concern cut through some of the afterglow of sex. "Yes. What's the matter?"

He blinked down at her, some strange light dawning in his eyes. "Blood."

"What?" She looked around to see the sheets and her hands splattered with crimson. "Oh, my God. Is this from Roberto?"

Had she scratched the younger Panther during their struggle? She didn't remember any of it clearly. Why hadn't she noticed her hands before? She'd touched Antonio this way? Her stomach clenched.

Antonio twisted beside her to look in a tall mirror across the room, but he seemed more excited than upset. Confusion swamped her. What was going on?

The double doors to his suite slammed back and an older woman marched in, fury stamped across her face. Solana fought a moan as she tugged the bloodied sheets up to cover her nudity. Lucia Ruiz—she had a few more wrinkles than when Solana lived with the Pride, but she'd know the nasty bitch anywhere. Now it would begin. Knowing her, loving her, would ruin Antonio. She blinked back the tears that flooded her eyes. She wouldn't let the mother of men who'd hurt her see her weep.

The woman's eyes locked on Solana. "*You*. This is all—"

"The Ruiz family's fault." Antonio stood, blocking Lucia's path. Solana didn't wait to see what else transpired. She gathered the sheets around her and darted for the bathroom. She heard Antonio snarl. "Your son disobeyed a command from his

Pride leader. The rest of your family stood behind his actions and showed no contrition for his disloyalty. Therefore, the Ruizes have been banished, cast out. Find another Pride to take you in if you can, but your treasonous acts will be made public in the Panther world. Get out."

Banished? He'd cast out a powerful family in his Pride? Would the rest of the Pride stand for it? Too many questions took flight in her mind. Everything she knew about Pride politics, Panther history, and her personal concern for Antonio warred with each other for dominance in her thoughts.

A T-shirt and a pair of Antonio's shorts had been discarded on the vanity, so she washed the blood off her hands in the sink and put them on. Antonio and Lucia roared and hissed at each other the whole time, but then the noise suddenly ceased and a door slammed.

Peeking out, she saw the room was empty. She tied the drawstring on Antonio's oversized shorts and stepped through the suite and out into the hall. She needed to find him, needed to say good-bye. Roberto was one of many and she knew it. If this kept going, it would happen again and again until Antonio had no Pride left to lead. One way or another, being with her would rob him of his real destiny. And she would never be able to live with herself.

He was right about why she'd remained in San Francisco, right about so much. But not their mating. If she stayed, he'd have to exile all his Pride in order to keep her. And she wouldn't stand for it. She had to leave the city, find somewhere else to start over. Maybe make Cat Scratch Fever a chain. It was an empty prospect, but she held on to it like the lifeline it was.

"Is that her? The non-shifter?" A flurry of whispers reached her ears as she walked through the halls and down the stairs of the mansion. It was just as she remembered. "Why did Solana come back? What does the Pride leader want with her?"

A flush crept up her face, burning her cheeks like fire. It was one more harsh reminder of why she could never mate with Antonio. Being around him clouded reality, but now she remembered exactly what Pride life had been like after the truth came out about her. Her gaze hit the ground.

All her old insecurities returned in a rush, and the inadequacy she'd felt every single day of her life when she was among this Pride made her want to crumble. Instead she pulled back, her spine snapping straight. She raised her chin and narrowed her gaze at the whispering felines. Silence reigned as she reached the bottom of the stairs. It seemed the whole Pride had gathered in the foyer, and Antonio stood at the foot of the steps waiting for her. Thankfully, he'd put some clothes on since he'd left his room.

"Come with me, Solana." His hand closed around her elbow, pulling her out the door, around the side of the house, and away from the members of his Pride. Her bare feet tickled against the damp green grass in the yard. He sat her on a small cement bench set against the west side of the mansion. Flowers bloomed around her in wild abandon, but she focused on the man who paced in front of her.

"Why am I here, Antonio? You could have taken me to my condo instead of bringing me here. Were you hoping they'd change their minds just because a few years have gone by?" She shook her head, her hair brushing against her bare knees as she sat forward. "They remember. They know what I am."

"That's just it." He stopped his restless pacing and jerked around to face her, suppressed emotions simmering in his dark gaze. "I don't think you're a non-shifter. I think you just *haven't* ever shifted before."

Nothing he could have said would have shocked her more, and the anger that exploded through her caught her off guard. Why couldn't he accept? How many more ways could he have it thrust in his face that they couldn't be together? "Stop it, Antonio. Just *stop.*"

"No." He whipped his shirt over his head, revealing long claw marks with traces of blood in them. The kind of scratches a female Panther would give her lover.

Her heart seized. "It can't—I—"

Twisting his head around to meet her gaze, he snarled, "I swear to God, if you claim I've been with another woman in the last five minutes in order to deny what I'm telling you, I'll take you over my knee again."

"Promises, promises." She tried to force a smile to curve her lips and failed.

"I'm not teasing."

"I know." Even if she wanted to say he'd let some other female touch him, a thought that made fury roil inside her, she knew it wasn't true. She'd have been able to smell the woman on his flesh. All she smelled was the erotic combination of their wild coupling. "Antonio, I—"

Marco Ruiz rounded the corner just then. The evil delight that crossed his face said he was about to torment her. It slid away to ashen terror when he spotted Antonio. He backpedaled only to run into Miguel's broad chest. Antonio's Second grabbed the younger man up by the scruff of the neck and hauled him back the way they had come.

"Forgive our intrusion, sir. I'm just helping the Ruizes pack for their departure. Excuse us." He dipped his head. "Solana."

She swallowed, a million horrifying memories of just such incidences rushing through her mind. Not just the Ruizes, but many, many others. Only there had been no Antonio or Miguel to save her then. No protection. Nausea twisted her belly and she jerked to her feet. "You should never have brought me here."

"This is where you belong, with me."

She closed her eyes, sucking in a sharp breath. "We've already been through this."

"Yes. And if you were a non-shifter, then I might have some

reason to agree with you." He laughed and her gaze snapped up to meet his. He grinned, looking more confident and relaxed than she'd ever seen him. "Even then, I wanted to mate with you. You know that."

"It's not a good idea."

He folded his arms, still smiling. "It's a moot point. You aren't a non-shifter."

"I am." She shook her head. Getting carried away during sex didn't make her able to shift forms. It was a fluke. He was grasping at straws. She'd tried too long and too hard to let herself believe now—the failure would destroy her.

"Your eyes went gold, Solana. You clawed my back. The beginning stages of *shifting forms*. Why haven't you ever let go enough to shift all the way?"

Her jaw clenched, angry at him all over again. Did he honestly think he could snap his fingers and change what she was? "You don't know what you're talking about. Do you know how many years I *tried* to shift and couldn't't? This is insane, Antonio. Just accept the truth."

"I think you're the one in denial, not me."

The bubbling rage turned into sudden tears. She was going insane, every mooring she'd ever had ripped away. A tear fell and she brushed it away. So many years of pent-up frustration and he wanted to stomp on all her insecurities in the place where her worst nightmares had come true. This Pride, in this house, with these Panthers. "You're just like them. You can't accept me as I am."

His chin jutted at a stubborn angle. "I accept you completely and you know it. I want you as you are, my mate, shifter or not."

"Just. Like. Them."

She spun around, not wanting him to see the helpless tears. Inside she was crumbling, shattering into a million pieces. She tried to hold on to herself, to gather the shreds of her being back together, but Antonio was there, his arms wrapped around her from behind, the hard muscles of his body pressed to her back.

"Let go, Solana."

"I can't. I shouldn't. I *can't.*" She struggled against him, but the friction only drove her wild with the lust she'd never been able to control around him.

His palm slid under the waist of her borrowed shorts, his fingers delving into her pussy. Her breath hissed out, and she arched. Her thoughts scattered, instinct and boiling anticipation taking over.

"Let go, my love." His breath brush against her ear, made her shiver and drop her chin, her hair sweeping forward into her face. Still she tugged at his arms, trying to wriggle away while he slid his fingers in and out of her tight, damp sex. Terror and excitement fisted within her.

"Antonio," she sobbed.

His lips opened over the back of her neck, sinking his fangs into her flesh. Marking her as his mate. She shattered, lost. Her pussy flexed again and again, clenching around his thrusting fingers.

The world went dark and she collapsed to the grass. She pressed her cheek to the ground, panting for breath. Her body didn't even feel like her own, shivers still wracking her limbs in the aftermath.

She opened her eyes to see forelegs covered in short black fur. Antonio must have changed into his animal form. She wrinkled her nose and rolled to her feet. The forelegs moved with her and she tripped, landing awkwardly on her side again. She looked down at herself. Fur. Ebony tufts of it covered her body. Her cat body. Wonder and disbelief flooded her. She whipped her head around to look at her mate.

A huge black Panther lay sprawled across the bench where Antonio had been. He stared at her, gold eyes intent on her face.

He ran his tongue down a long fang, almost a smile. He rose, stalking her. A predator.

Instinct rippled through her. Mate. Predator. Hunted. She shot to her feet, claws digging into the soft earth as she sprinted away. He gave chase and she knew he would catch her, but not yet. Not yet. Freer than she'd ever been, she raced ahead, her legs stretching before her as she rounded the side of the mansion. Other Panthers turned to stare at them as they passed, but she ignored the stunned looks on their faces.

The only thing that mattered now was her mate. He had given this to her, pushed her to be her true self. She loved him so much. She leaped over a hedge, skidding to a stop as she reached the edge of the property.

And then he was upon her. Claiming her as she had always fantasized. Perfect.

Twenty-four hours later and Antonio was still grinning. The twins had harassed him endlessly. Even Miguel had commented on it. What could he say? Life was good sometimes.

Especially when Solana was waiting for him in his suite after they both finished work. He wasn't foolish enough to think they didn't have a great deal of work ahead of them—the Pride politics had been thrown into chaos with a former outcast coming out on top as a new ruler. But they'd work it out. There was nothing he wanted more than her by his side . . . in life and in the Pride. It was as simple and as complicated as that.

She stood in the middle of the room when he walked in, wearing a white knee-length coat that set off her dark hair and tanned skin. He shut the door behind him, leaned back against it, and folded his arms. "Damn, you're beautiful."

"Thank you." She grinned, the corners of her eyes crinkling. "Make yourself at home."

"Don't mind if I do." He pulled off his T-shirt, wadded it in a ball, and tossed it across the room toward the laundry basket.

Sinking onto the sofa, he groaned and let his muscles relax. He smiled at her, drinking in the sight of her here, in his house, in his private quarters. "I missed you tonight, my mate."

"Mate. Hmm." She tilted her head coquettishly. "I don't know if that's quite right."

He narrowed his eyes at her. "You bear my mark."

"But you don't bear mine." She arched her brows. "It's not done yet."

"Then let's finish it now."

She tossed the silky length of her hair over her shoulder and turned away from him. "I have a gift for you."

He laid his arms along the back of the leather couch and tilted his head at her, wondering what game she played now. He smiled. No doubt he would enjoy playing it with her. "A gift. I like the way that sounds. And where will you *gift* me with your mate mark?"

She grinned at him over her shoulder as she fiddled with the controls on his stereo system. The rough wail of a saxophone filled the room. "Mating isn't the gift."

"Then it can wait. Come here."

She shook her head at him, kicking off her shoes. Her slim fingers tugged at the belt to her long coat and she let it slither to the ground. He choked when he saw she was naked beneath. His cock went hard in an instant, straining against the fly of his jeans. "If I had known you weren't wearing anything under that—"

"Shh." She lifted her arms above her head, twining them in intricate patterns to the beat of the music. Her eyes closed, and her body twisted into the erotic dance. The tips of her fingers slipped over her bare flesh, the throb of sound picking up speed. And so did she. She became the music, all harsh bass and slamming drums.

His fingers bit into the leather as he stared at her, mesmerized. He'd never been so aroused in his life. Only Solana could do this to him. He could smell her heat, how the sensuality of her movements had taken hold of her. She was wet for him. He groaned low in his throat.

Her eyes opened, shimmering from dark chocolate to pale gold. Woman and Panther. Both danced for him, called to him. And still he did not pounce. He waited for her to come to him, knowing she gifted him with far more than a simple dance. No, this was his true mate, the woman who embraced both sides of her nature. And drove him wild in the process. God, he loved her.

"*Dios mio,* Solana."

Her hips undulated as she glided across the smooth wooden floor toward him. Her hands braced on his shoulders, and she threw her head back, arching her lithe body.

She slipped her knee beside his thigh, mounting him in one smooth motion. Rolling her head forward, she flashed a hot smile that made his mouth dry. Now her fingers danced over his skin, down his chest. Every muscle in his body went rigid when her fingers ran over the length of his fly, toying with his hard cock through the fabric of his jeans. She eased the zipper down until his erection sprang into her palms. His hips jerked, thrusting into her touch. He gritted his teeth as she seated herself on his dick, sliding him into her slick heat.

"*Te amo,* Antonio. *Te amo.*" Her voice was a breathless whisper in his ear.

He tilted his head back, baring his throat to her. He wanted her to claim him as he had claimed her, wanted to begin their life together.

Her gaze burned to pure, incandescent gold and her fangs slid forward as she leaned in to flick her tongue across his jugular. His heartbeat roared in his ears, and he had to fist his fingers to keep from reaching for her. She grinned against his skin. "Touch me, please."

He cupped his hands around her hips, loving the silky texture of her skin. Dipping his head forward, he caught her nipple between his teeth. Her breathing hitched. Sucking her nipple as deep into his mouth as possible, he worked his tongue over her beaded flesh. A moan slid from her throat, the sound a kiss to his ears.

Her scent filled his nostrils, the musky smell of her wetness a sweet aphrodisiac. The muscles in her thighs clenched on his hips as she moved on him. Her slick flesh hugged his cock and he ground his teeth together to keep from coming. He wanted to savor her. Pulling her down to the base of his dick, he rolled his hips. She cried out, letting her head fall back as she arched her body against him. Through it all, her eyes had remained the brilliant gold that signaled Panther change. She was there with him, wild and untamed. Her nails raked up his arms, turning to claws to bite into his flesh when she reached his shoulders.

As they moved together faster and faster, the creak of the leather couch beneath them and the slap of flesh filled the room. Her tongue slid along his collarbone until her lips closed over the base of his neck. She sucked his flesh, and he could feel the prick of her fangs. His cock throbbed inside her. He'd never wanted anything more than he wanted her to bite him right now. His woman. The perfect match for him. His mate.

"I love you, Solana." His fingers clenched into her hips, his breathing ragged and harsh.

She sank the sharp points of her teeth into his throat as he ground his pelvis into hers. He threw his head back and roared. His body locked in a hard line and he jetted his come inside her. The hot walls of her pussy fisted around his cock, milking his length. He shuddered hard, wrapping his arms tight around her and sealing their bodies together.

Her breath cooled the sweat on his skin as she panted. His muscles shook in the aftermath of the most intense orgasm he'd ever had. He closed his eyes, sliding his hand down her long curls. The warm satin of her hair wrapped around his fingers.

His chest was tight with the amazing gratitude of holding her in his arms, of having her here in his house. Thank God. Thank *God.* He loved her so much. Only in his wildest dream had he imagined that they might be together and not have to leave the city to get away from the main enclave of the Pride.

Contentment like he'd never experienced before sank into his soul. Nothing could compare to this feeling. To having her here, to having her whole and warm in his arms, to having her finally admit that they belonged together, "I love you."

"I love you, too." She pulled back to look him in the eye, resting her forehead against his. For once her gaze was open, letting him see all that she felt, all that she was. His. And he was hers.

Just as they'd always been destined to be.

TAKE ME

I

God help her. Andrea pinched her eyes closed, praying that her flight would never end, that she'd never have to go back home. Her heart raced and she tightened her fingers around the strap of her leather purse so hard she snapped it in half. Shit. Her stomach clenched.

She glanced around to make sure no one had noticed and shoved her bag onto the floor, tucking in the broken strap. She smoothed a hand down her khaki skirt and crossed her sandaled feet, trying to act casual. A woman as slender as she was shouldn't have the upper body strength to break a thick piece of leather—but then again, she wasn't just a woman. She was a Panther. And if she didn't get ahold of herself, she'd be a shapeshifter in a boatload of trouble with her Pride members. She swallowed and shut her eyes again, taking deep, calming breaths.

The smell of so many humans packed into such a small space was giving her a headache. Their energy hummed around her, vibrating against her nerves. Of course, in the mood she was in, just about anything would be enough to wind her tighter. God, she needed a drink. And if she didn't need all her wits about her when she came face to face with her family, she'd be sucking down the little bottles of booze the flight attendant had offered her.

"Ms. Cruz?" A light male voice sounded to her right.

She jolted and opened her eyes to see a slender man in his mid-twenties crouching in the airplane's aisle next to her seat. "Yes?"

He beamed. "I thought that was you."

Arching a brow, she pushed away her anxiety and tried to hide a grin. It wasn't often that she was recognized anymore. She'd quit modeling almost four years ago to start her own clothing company, Pantheras Designs. "What can I do for you?"

"I just wanted to say that I love your new men's line." He rolled his wide blue eyes dramatically. "My boyfriend and I spend way too much buying your clothes."

She chuckled quietly, relieved that he wasn't going to make a lame attempt at hitting on her like men who'd spent their teen years staring at glossy photos of her in a bikini. "I'm flattered. Thank you."

He gave her a sheepish smile. "My boyfriend will never believe I met you. Would you mind taking a picture with me?"

"Not at all." Anything that distracted her from the dread that coiled tighter and tighter inside her with every passing moment.

"I have a camera phone." The young man pulled out a cell phone and flicked it open to push a few buttons. Turning on his heels he leaned back toward her and lifted the phone to just above his face and tilted it down. She angled her head so that she was next to him, conscious after so many years in front of a camera of just how to position her body, her neck, her face to show off her features best. He snapped the picture and then flipped the phone around so he could see the image. "This is awesome. You look phenomenal."

"Thank you." Her gaze slid over the picture. Yep, she still had it. She grinned.

"Excuse me, but you can't have that phone turned on while we're in the air." A flight attendant hurried up to the first-class cabin to scold the young man.

He flushed a dark red, jerked to his feet, and fumbled to close his cell. "Oh, right. I'm sorry."

Andrea caught his wrist before he scurried back to his seat. He looked down at her, embarrassment reflecting in his blue eyes. She squeezed his arm. "It was very nice meeting you. You made my day."

"Thanks for the picture." Huffing a laugh, he stuffed his phone into his pocket. "I bet you have somewhere glamorous to go tonight, so I doubt this could make your day."

"Trust me, it could." She smiled and let him go. The kid had no idea. But, then, most humans couldn't guess at the life she led. Secrets, lies, and hiding her true nature were something she'd done every day for the last fourteen years. No human could ever know about her kind, so since she'd left the Pride at eighteen, it was the rare occasion that she'd been able to let her feral side loose and change forms.

She'd stayed away as long as possible, avoiding her brother's summons by claiming she had contractual obligations to fulfill before she could return to San Francisco.

Eighteen more months of freedom.

But her brother and his mate, Solana, were having their first child and she was required to take a loyalty oath to the new heir of the North American Panther Pride. There was no more escape for her. She knew once she returned, her brother would never let her leave again. A low moan caught in her throat. That was the last thing she wanted—to be trapped forever, a showpiece for her Pride and nothing more. They'd parade her around to all the other Prides until she found her mate and then the only point to her life would be to breed.

It still blew her mind that her brother had mated to Solana Perez—a former outcast from their Pride. When Andrea had last seen her, Solana was a non-shifter. A Panther who couldn't assume animal form. Such people were second-class citizens in the Panther Prides because only in Panther form could their kind breed, and the population was so scarce that they had to consciously work on making sure enough children were born each generation. Or they would die out. Extinction was an ugly prospect for everyone.

While Andrea could understand why non-shifters were seen as "less than" she disagreed with the idea that breeding was the most important function a person could perform. Her father had believed it though—his archaic attitudes had caused so many arguments between them that she'd given up ever co-existing peacefully with him and left to make her way in the human world when she came of age. She hadn't seen her brother since she was sixteen and he was a cocky twenty-year-old on his way to serve as the South American Panther Pride leader's second in command. Would he be as conservative—as stifling—as their father?

Nausea pitched in her stomach. She wanted to tell herself it was the mild turbulence as the plane circled to land at SFO, but she knew it was a lie.

Time seemed to speed, blurring as it whipped past. The next thing she knew, she was standing by the luggage carousel to collect her bag. There it was. She reached for the handle when a large male hand curved around her and lifted it for her.

"Andrea Cruz?" His breath moved the hair at the back of her neck.

A ripple of awareness went up her spine at the controlled voice behind her. She had to see the man attached to it. Some instinct went off in her head as she spun to face him. Her nipples tightened, thrusting against her lace bra. Gooseflesh broke down her arms, and her skin flushed with heat. Her pussy dampened, clenching with the ache of sudden want.

And then she knew.

Mate.

"Who are you?" Her voice came out a harsher demand than she'd intended, but the foundations of her world had just crumbled beneath her. She had to tilt her head back to meet his gaze. Unusual for a woman as tall as she was. He was gorgeous, eyes richer than dark chocolate and long ebony hair secured at the nape of his neck. Her fingers itched to rip the tie away and bury themselves in the long strands. Would they be rough silk or satin soft? She wanted to know with a desperation that scared her.

His brows lifted and he almost smiled. Almost. "I'm your brother's Second, Miguel Montoya."

Second. The shock of that announcement, the horrifying memories of her father's Second and what he'd done to her, made her stomach lurch. Oh, Christ. What the hell was she doing here? Every muscle in her body screamed at her to run, to get away from all the changes ripping through her life. She jolted when he took her elbow, and a frisson of heat she didn't want to feel slithered through her body.

"This way." His grip was gentle, but she doubted she'd be able to escape unless he wanted her to. She felt herded while he ushered her out to a waiting limousine.

Her senses reeled, panic and passion spinning through her so fast she couldn't keep up. His scent filled her nostrils, his fingers rasped against her skin, and the power of it threatened to drag her under. He gave her bag to the driver and handed her down into the open door. The leather creaked under her as she slid across the wide seat.

A gasp jerked from her when he sat beside her, plastering her against his side from shoulder to thigh. He shut the door behind him, shutting the rest of the world away to cocoon them inside the limo. Her gaze snapped to his, awareness flashing through his brown eyes. He knew. He sensed it as well. Mates.

Her body heated to a boiling point, need sharper than she'd ever experienced slicing through her. Her instincts drew her to him like a moth to flame . . . and she wanted to be burned.

"Andrea."

A shudder ran through her at the sound of her name on his lips. His hand curved over her leg just above her bare knee. Her fingers clamped around his wrist, stilling his movement. "We can't."

"I want you." His gaze locked with hers, refusing to let her deny what was happening. They flickered to a deep gold, the color of a Panther, of change.

It was too much to resist.

She eased her grip on his wrist, sliding it up her thigh. His fingers stroked over her skin, drawing circles on the inside of her leg. Her pussy was so wet she could feel her panties dampen with her own moisture. This was absolute madness, her mind tried to raise a protest. Her hormones didn't care. She needed to be filled.

Easing his hand under her skirt, he pressed his fingers against the lace of her panties. A whimper escaped her throat. She lifted her leg and hooked it over his thigh to open herself as much as possible in the confines of the khaki, giving him as much access as she could. He stroked her through the lace, using it to stimulate her clit. It rasped against her sensitive tissue and she moaned. His finger slipped under her panties to thrust inside her slick channel with one harsh push. Her eyes flared wide, her hips lifting as pleasure and pain shot through her at the shock of his invasion. *"Miguel."*

"Shh. You can take me." He used the opportunity to push her skirt up to her waist and bare her to his gaze. He added a second finger and then a third, widening her. She gasped. He moved inside her in slow, hard strokes. He wasn't gentle and she didn't want him to be.

She reached out to touch him, slipping her fingers through

his hair until it fell loose around his shoulders. Somehow it made him look more dangerous. A predator. And that made her the prey. She shivered, struggling to hold on to her sanity. "We shouldn't do this."

"Oh, yes. We should." His gaze never left her, watching, controlled. She moaned a protest when his fingers withdrew from her pussy, left her empty and aching. He lifted his hand to his mouth, slowly licking her wetness from each long digit. "Come here."

She dove for him, melding her mouth with his. He thrust his tongue into her mouth, harsh and demanding, and she could taste her own wetness. Excitement spiraled tight within her. She nipped at his lower lip, suckling its fullness. His arm slid behind her back, pulling her toward him. He curved his hand under her knee, lifting her until she straddled his lap and faced away from him. The rigid length of his cock pressed against her ass. She wanted him inside her, and she arched to rub herself against him.

He reached around her and with two sharp tugs, he ripped her panties off and tossed them on the floor of the limo. The coolness of the air conditioning rushed over her heated flesh, the contrast making her shudder. She heard the low rasp of his zipper sliding down and it sounded loud in the close confines of the car.

The head of his dick nudged her pussy, sliding against her swollen lips. She tilted her hips to make it easy for him to push inside her. His hands guided her descent as she eased down onto his cock.

He was so big. Her fangs slid forward as the pain twisted inside. Now she knew why he'd stretched her channel with his fingers. She breathed out of her nose as he filled her to the limit. Her nails turned to claws, biting into his wrists. She whimpered, but he held her in place, forcing her to adjust to his size. "I—I can't—"

"You can." His deep voice caressed her ears, his bellowing breath moving the short hairs at the base of her neck. Everything about him turned her on, made her hotter.

"Oh. My. God."

He chuckled, the sound vibrating against her back. His palms slid up her belly, raising her camisole top over her head. The short strands of her hair swung against her cheek as he let the shirt drop to the seat beside her. He cupped her breasts from behind, pulling her back until the buttons on his shirt scored her spine.

Their breathing sounded harsh to her ears. Want, sharp and hot, whipped through her. More. Nothing had ever felt so right. Her pussy fisted around his dick, and her hips twisted. The deep friction made her moan. "I need to move."

"Then move." He rolled her nipples between his fingers, plucking at their stiff tips. She gasped at the intense pleasure. Reaching over her shoulder, she buried her fingers in his hair and rotated so she could kiss him again. His lips were soft, but his tongue was hard and demanding as it twined with hers. He twisted her nipples to the point of pain and wetness flooded her pussy. "*Move,* Andrea."

The muscles in her thighs flexed as she lifted herself. Her slick flesh dragged against his cock, and he groaned. She sank down, taking all of him again. The stretch was incredible—the sweet burn of it whipping through her. Her muscles shook with the intensity of it and everything inside her craved it. Him. Her senses went wild with their deep, unutterable recognition of *him.* On her next downward push, he lifted into her, changing the angle of his penetration.

It was too much, too good. Her belly tightened, the drive for orgasm overtaking her. *Yes.* All she wanted was more of this— from him. His thrusts picked up pace and she stayed with him, moving faster and faster. Her head fell back over his shoulder and she choked on a moan. She was so very close . . . just a little more. Her body bowed with the intensity of her need. Tears burned her eyes, clung to her lashes before they spilled down her cheeks.

"Ask me to mark you." His tongue slid up the side of her neck, his breath cooling the moisture on her skin when he spoke. Her fingers clenched in his hair as their hips slammed together, animal instinct driving them. He rotated his hips against her, grinding into her. His fangs pricked against her skin. "Ask me."

"I can't," she sobbed. A warning went off in her head, pulling her back from the edge. Her movements stilled as too many sensations overwhelmed her, her heart and mind and body all demanding different things. The muscles in her thighs locked, and she shook under the onslaught of her warring needs. His arm wrapped around her waist, forcing her down onto the base of his cock. Her breath shuddered out.

He sucked her earlobe into his mouth, his dark hair spilling over her shoulder to tickle her sensitized nipples. She shivered. One of his fingers slid around, stroking her clit. She cried out, desperate to move again, but his arm still held her down, held her in place. She twisted, needing the deeper friction.

Her heart hammered so loudly she could hear it in her ears, and everything slowed down until she could feel each beat, each breath. All her senses focused on one need, one craving. Miguel. Only Miguel. Heat rolled through her in gathering waves until she couldn't hold them back. Her body bowed toward him in offering, her sex clenching around his cock so tight he groaned. "Come for me, Andrea. Now."

"Miguel, Miguel, *Miguel.*" She chanted his name, holding on to the one thing that felt solid as her entire sense of self burned away. The fire built and built until she screamed. And then it exploded inside her.

His hips snapped up in short, hard thrusts as he buried his cock inside her. Then he froze, his head buried in her neck as he hissed low in his throat. A deep shudder wracked his body and his come pumped into her.

Collapsing back against him, she wrapped her arms around her torso. His hands turned over to clasp with hers, fingers twining. Tears still leaked from the corners of her eyes. "Miguel."

"Yes?"

But she had no idea what to say. She was shaken by the intensity of their connection. There was so much to say, and she had no idea where to begin. Coming down from the thrill of orgasm, of her first time with her mate, made the terror return. What had she done? What had she been thinking to sleep with her brother's Second, no matter what he was to her? She hadn't thought, that was the simple answer.

His palms cupped her hips, lifting her free of his body to set her beside him. The inner drag against his semi-hard cock made her shudder and want to reach for him once more. "We're here."

Panic exploded in her veins and she scrambled for her clothes. Jerking her top over her head, she shoved her hands through her short hair to give it some semblance of order. She scooped her panties off the floor, stuffed them into her purse, and winced when she saw the broken leather strap. So not her best day.

"Where's my other shoe?" She straightened the wedge heel sandal on her right foot, but her left was bare.

He leaned sideways toward her and pulled her shoe from behind his hip and handed it to her. He zipped up his slacks and smoothed his dress shirt. Tugging on his cuffs, he lifted his arms. Deep scratches scored the parts of his wrists that she could see. "Want to kiss it and make it better?"

She snorted. As if kissing it would make it better. Panthers had to sleep in order to kick-start the magic that would heal them. He'd be fine after a catnap.

"Welcome home, Andrea."

"This isn't my home." She didn't look at him. Instead, she dug a hand mirror out of her purse and refreshed her lip gloss.

Anxiety knotted her belly again. No matter what had happened with Miguel, she still did not relish returning to a life that had stifled her. Here she'd always be Esteban Cruz's daughter, Antonio Cruz's sister. She'd be the big sister of the Cruz twins, Diego and Ricardo. She'd be . . . no one on her own. Just a part of the group when she'd spent over a decade standing out from the crowd as a model.

"Andrea." Miguel's hand closed around her wrist, stilling her movements. "Look at me."

His voice brooked no argument, which just pissed her off. Anger twisted with the panic rolling through her. She hated being ordered around—she'd gotten too much of that from her father. She jerked her arm away from him. "Don't tell me what to do."

She could feel his surprise, but she refused to let herself care. Mate or not, he wasn't going to help her get through the meeting with her family. Nothing could make this easier.

The end of her freedom.

Miguel followed his mate into Antonio's study in silence. Nervous energy rolled off her in waves, and it set every protective instinct inside him on high alert. What could cause such a reaction from her? As far as he knew, the only problem she had had here was with her father, and he had died almost two years ago. Her family had accepted him completely when he'd followed Antonio from South America to serve as Second. The Cruzes were all good people, and in many ways he was far closer to them than he had ever been to his own family. He shut down thoughts of his dysfunctional familial relations and focused on Andrea.

He set his hand between her shoulder blades, feeling her muscles tense and flex against his palm. He moved his fingers down to her waist, pushing her forward when she froze in front of the people spread in a semicircle around the room. Then he watched a mask slide over her beautiful features, and he saw her years as a model come forward.

Frustration made his hands clench. Hiding herself from her family was not the way to rejoin the Pride. He was torn between wanting to protect his mate from something that upset her and helping a family that had earned a permanent place in his heart. He watched her give Antonio a short, stiff hug before bending forward to embrace a very pregnant Solana. Antonio's eyes cut to him, narrowing. Diego and Ric also glanced at Miguel as Andrea moved toward them. He gave a quick shake of his head, indicating they not mention that they could smell him all over their sister.

"Later," he mouthed. He'd have to explain that Andrea was his mate or he'd end up in a very awkward situation with his best friend.

The other men nodded and Ric stepped forward to scoop Andrea off her feet. She squealed with laughter when Diego swooped in to steal her away from his twin and swing her in a circle. He planted a loud kiss on her cheek. "Welcome home, big sister."

"Thank you." Her face tightened and she turned to the side a bit, glancing up to meet Miguel's gaze. He saw the quiet panic, the flash of trapped anger before it was gone again. He wanted to strip her of that mask and discover what hid beneath . . . why returning to a Pride he loved disturbed her so much.

He'd wanted to comfort her in the limo, but perhaps it was too soon for that. If she thought she was going to pretend they weren't mates, that she hadn't screamed in his arms, then she'd have to think again or she'd find herself bent over his lap and spanked for her resistance. His cock swelled at the thought of her slim body bared and spread before him. A small smile curved his lips. His fingers flexed, wanting to touch her again.

Soon. Soon he'd have her just as he wanted her. The way she'd reacted to the small amount of pain she'd experienced in the limo, the scent of her wetness flooding his nostrils as her pussy hugged his cock, made him even more certain that they were well matched sexually. Anticipation hummed in his veins.

He pulled in a deep breath, caging the Panther inside him. For now, he'd let her cope with her homecoming and help where he could. Tonight, she was his.

Walking over to the bar, he poured drinks for everyone and handed them around. He grinned at Solana and gave her a chilled glass of seltzer water. "Sorry, no alcohol for you."

"I know. It sucks having a bar, you know?" She tossed her long dark hair over her shoulder. "I own all the booze and not a drop of it is for me."

He stepped over to Andrea, offering her a finger of Scotch. She accepted it, her hand clenching the glass until it groaned. He stroked his palm over the small of her back and leaned in to speak in her ear. "They aren't going to eat you." He let his nails curl into claws and scraped under the edge of her top. "That's my job."

She choked on the sip of alcohol she'd taken, her gaze snapping to him. A startled grin crossed her lips and it made her glow. God, she was beautiful. No wonder she'd been such a successful model. She shook her head at him and turned back to Solana. "You own a bar?"

"Cat Scratch Fever over in the Mission District."

A bitter little smile twisted her mouth. "No doubt the Pride leader forced you to turn the business over when you rejoined the fold."

"Over my dead body." Solana grinned, her cheeks dimpling. She leaned back against Antonio, and his arms engulfed her. "Cat Scratch is mine. I turn a percentage of the revenue over to the Pride—but I live and eat here, so it's only fair."

"I would never ask my mate to give up her career. Besides, it would be foolish to force a successful manager to step down from a profitable business. More money is always a good thing."

Antonio rested his chin on top of her head, cuddling her closer. Both their hands rested against her burgeoning belly.

It had been so good to see his friend find his mate, but it made Miguel want it, too. That closeness with another person, children, a woman who belonged to him and him alone. He'd never thought to have such a thing. As with all Panthers, if they reached thirty and hadn't found their mate, they were sent to all the other Prides to meet every other unmated Panther. Miguel had gone over ten years ago and found no one.

And now he'd discovered his mate in the least likely of places. So, there was a deep awe that banded around his chest, but also an uncertainty because he'd been so sure he didn't have a mate. He let his hand drift in soothing circles over the small of Andrea's back. She relaxed a bit and leaned into him, pressing herself to his side as she sipped her drink and let the conversation flow around her. She didn't say much, but the awkwardness had left the room and he was grateful for that.

He and the Cruz men had worked very hard to restructure the Pride after Esteban had died and Antonio took over. None of them wanted any tension with Andrea's return. They wanted her to be folded back into the Pride quietly, without a ripple in the power structure. He'd come with Antonio to serve as this Pride's second in command . . . and he'd done his best to be of use. But being Second only lasted a few years, so he knew he'd be going back to his own Pride in Brazil soon.

As his oldest friend, he knew Antonio wanted to keep him here, but that was a poor political choice. Panthers had predestined mates, so there were no arranged marriages to create alliances. The Prides had always used their Seconds as a way to influence other Prides and create those alliances. Though the time for arranged marriages had passed even among humans, the Second system worked well enough that no one thought to get rid of it.

He hoped Andrea learned to love it here as much as he did because there was no way Antonio could let her leave again. It would cause too many issues in the Pride. Until Antonio's heir was born, she was the heir to the Pride as second oldest. It left them in political limbo to not have her as a *present*, loyal supporter of her brother. Perhaps people might think they could use her as a pawn to overthrow Antonio.

And she was his mate. He couldn't leave the Prides the way she had. His life was with Panthers. He blinked when Andrea nudged him with her shoulder and he snapped back to attention. "Yes?"

She arched a brow. "Diego asked when your meeting with the Asian delegate was tomorrow."

"Ah." He glanced at the smirking twin. It wasn't often that they caught him off guard, so he had no doubt they'd relish this occasion. "Midnight."

Like most cats, Panthers were naturally nocturnal, so their days began after sundown.

Diego nodded, but his mocking grin didn't fade. "Are we ready to eat? I'm starving."

"You think with your stomach, bro." Ric shoved his twin's shoulder.

As irresponsible as the twins appeared on the surface with their shaggy hair and love of extreme sports, they worked as hard as they played. They served as the Pride's legal counsel and everything he'd seen from them impressed the hell out of him. On top of that, he liked them . . . they were good men, much like their older brother.

Antonio offered his elbow to Solana. "Shall we?"

She grinned and tucked her hand in the crook of her mate's arm. Everyone else fell into step behind them. They rounded the corner into the dining room when Solana stumbled and doubled over with a hand pressed to her belly. She moaned and Antonio caught her before she hit her knees, every ounce of blood draining from both their faces.

The room erupted in chaos, but for Miguel time slowed down. He simply reacted, strode into the hall, and picked up a phone. He dialed the suite number for the physician he'd recruited from the European Pride a month before. When the man picked up the phone, Miguel snapped out, "Get to the dining room. Solana collapsed."

His heart pounded loudly in his ears, his fingers clenching into fists. Walking back into the room, he forced his voice to remain even. "The doctor will be down in a moment."

"Thank you," Antonio said as he held Solana tighter, running his hands over his mate's body.

God help them all if something was wrong with her. She, like the twins, had become his friend in the time he'd known her. She was Antonio's balance and he couldn't imagine what would become of the man without her. He prayed harder than he ever had before that this was a minor issue with her pregnancy. He watched the panic and terror washing over his friend's expression . . . reflecting to a lesser degree on the twins' and even Andrea's face.

He reached for her and she stepped into his arms. Her breath shuddered out against his neck. "Oh, God. What am I doing here?"

"What you have to." He kissed her forehead, hugging her close. He savored the feel of her against him and pulled her out of the doorway when the doctor barreled in. He had the situation in hand within seconds and Solana was moved to the master suite.

Andrea jolted when her cell phone rang. She pulled it out and stared at it blankly for a moment before she looked up at him. "I—I have to take this call."

"Then take it in my office. You'll have privacy in there." He pushed her in the direction of the Second's office. She froze for a moment and something dark flashed through her gaze. Before he could decide what it was, her face went blank, she spun toward his office, and she had the phone pressed to her ear before she'd gone three steps.

The twins burned off their restless energy by pacing the length of the main hall, waiting for word from the physician. A murmur sounded behind him and he turned to see several Panthers hovering in the hall. He smoothed his face into one that exuded approachability and confidence. They all offered a tentative smile and he motioned them into the large kitchen that serviced the entire Pride. He soothed fears and reassured them all that nothing serious was wrong, hoping like hell that he wasn't lying, that Solana was fine.

Since there was little he could do for his friends now, he focused on making sure the Pride remained calm. Later he would deal with the tension running through him. This brought back so many unwanted memories of his family, his sister. That Solana had been abandoned and neglected by her father when everyone thought her a non-shifter had always made Miguel especially protective of her—not that the fiercely independent Panther female appreciated it.

He also couldn't help but draw parallels between her and his own sister, and in many ways Solana had filled the hole Nina's death had left in his heart. He balled his fists tight. God, please let Solana be all right. He couldn't lose someone else he loved. Not like this.

2

Andrea shut the door to her suite behind her and collapsed against the carved wood. She closed her eyes and sighed. What a hellish day. She pulled in a deep breath, and then her eyes snapped open at what she smelled in the room with her. Or rather, *who* she smelled. Her head jerked to the side to see Miguel sitting against her headboard.

"Hello." He crossed his legs at the ankle, his feet bare. He still wore his trousers, but his dress shirt was open at the throat.

She blinked. "Um . . . I'm sorry, I thought I was in the same room as I was when I lived here."

"You are."

"Then . . . what are you doing here?"

He arched a dark brow, a grin quirking at the corners of his lips. "Waiting for you. How was your phone call?"

"Long. How is Solana?"

"Braxton Hicks contractions. She's fine now, but the doctor is going to keep an eye on her." A flicker of emotion passed over his calm expression, but it was gone before she could identify it.

"I'm glad." She pulled in a deep breath. "If she . . . if she went into labor now, would she and the baby be okay?"

"I asked the same thing. She'd be about three weeks early, but the doctor seems to think so. She'll be fine." His deep voice was reassuring—but who was he trying to reassure? Her or himself?

"Thank you for telling me." She nodded to the door, letting him know he could go.

He crossed his arms, something dangerous flashing in his gaze and she was immediately wary. This man was more than met the eye. Everyone she'd spoken to seemed to think he was quiet, even sweet. None of them recognized the air of competence that surrounded him . . . or that he had clearly handled them when they found out something was wrong with the Pride leader's mate. The man was good. And much more dangerous than he looked. She had no idea how the Pride didn't see this, but if Antonio had any brains at all he was using it to his advantage. She huffed out a breath—everything about Miguel terrified her.

"This has been an insane day. I'd like to sleep now."

"Are we going to talk about it?"

"About what?" But she knew what he was referring to and she didn't want to have that discussion. So much of what had happened lately had been taken out of her hands. It was too much like with her father. No control. No say.

"Are you really going to take that tack?"

Her chin jutted and she folded her arms. "I don't know what you're talking about."

"Yes, you do." His voice lowered to a growl, sexual and possessive. "My mate."

A hiss sputtered out of her throat, and she strode forward from the door until she stood beside the bed. "We aren't mated, and I am not *yours.*"

"Yet." He rose to his feet before her, towering over her and forcing her to look up at him. That he was this close to her reminded her exactly how good it had been between them. Heat rippled through her, loosening some muscles and tightening others. Readying her for his possession. Her body recognized what her mind wanted to fight.

Her nostrils flared in annoyance at her weakness. He was as arrogant as every Panther male she'd ever met, even if he disguised it better than most. He certainly didn't seem to need to hide it from her. "Perhaps not ever. You're not going to force me."

His head tilted, lowering until his eyes were level with hers and their lips almost brushed. Her breath caught, longing so deep she couldn't contain it clawing through her. She wanted him to kiss her, wanted his lips on hers, his hands on her skin again. The slightest smile curled the corners of his mouth. "I've never forced a woman in my life. I'll have you willing, stripped, and begging me for more. We both know you'll enjoy it."

Liquid heat exploded in her veins as she pictured what he described. To be helpless beneath him, to let him fuck her any way he wanted. Could he take her where she needed to go? Where no man had taken her before? She squelched the thought. A snarl pulled from her throat. She'd put aside that part of herself the day she'd left this Pride. Shoving a finger into his chest, she hissed, "Look, just because I fucked around with you in the limo doesn't mean you know me or what I want. Don't make assumptions."

"I didn't. My only assumption was that you're a reasonably intelligent woman. Am I wrong?"

"Don't be an ass."

"An ass?" He moved so fast it was almost a blur. He snapped his hand around her wrist, spun her forward to bend her over the bed, caught her other wrist, and pressed her face to the mattress. His free palm pushed her skirt up to her waist to expose her nudity and cupped the cheek of her backside. "I quite like your ass, Andrea."

Her breath froze, her excitement exploding into heat that arrowed between her thighs. His shirt landed on the bed in front of her face and she heard the quick rasp of his zipper before the soft thud of his trousers hitting the floor. The heat of his skin branded the back of her thighs. Moisture slicked her pussy and her inner muscles throbbed. Her legs shook and she jerked at her hands, but he held her in place.

She couldn't escape.

Anticipation unlike any she'd ever known made her heart trip before it raced in her chest. His palm moved from her ass to slide between the cheeks and dip into her wet sex. His breath hissed out. "So hot. And all mine."

Any retort she might have made died on a scream when he knelt behind her and flicked his tongue against her hard clit. "Oh, my God."

He chuckled, and the sound vibrated her clit. She couldn't hold back a helpless moan. Tugging at her manacled wrists proved futile. She closed her eyes when he moved to suckle her pussy lips, nipping at the swollen tissue. One of his long fingers dipped into her sex, working inside her damp channel. She could smell her own wetness . . . could sense his contained excitement. It made her burn hotter until she trembled with the force of her feelings.

Trailing his fingertips from her sex to her anus, he swirled them around the tight pucker. Her own moisture eased his passage when he pushed into her. One digit, then two, entered her ass.

"Miguel," she breathed.

A low growl against her pussy was his only response. His tongue and teeth and fingers worked her in tandem, building her excitement to a boiling point. She was so close to coming, it taunted her. Then his fingers withdrew and his tongue slid up until it reached her anus. Every muscle in her body locked, shock making her breath catch. His hot, wet tongue pressed inside her ass, thrusting, licking, in a slow rhythm.

It was so wicked, so forbidden. She writhed against the bed, her hips pushing back into his mouth. "Oh, oh, *oh.*"

He hummed against her ass and she choked. The sensation was unlike anything she'd ever experienced. Her pussy clenched, orgasm shimmering just on the edge of her consciousness. A high, desperate sound burst from her throat when he rose to his feet, his mouth leaving her.

"No," she moaned. Her wrists twisted in his hand. God, she needed to come. She'd go insane if he didn't give her what she craved.

His thighs crowded between her legs, his hands pressing her more firmly to the mattress. The head of his cock pushed against her anus. She arched her torso, shoving her hips back.

"Andrea." The low rumble of his voice held a warning. But she was beyond warnings. Her breath puffed out in little gasps against the bed, her need coiling inside her until she had to lock her jaw to keep from screaming, from begging.

He thrust forward, entering her inch by slow inch. A ripple of sensation bordering on pain crawled up her spine as his hard cock stretched her. She shuddered, her eyes flaring wide. He groaned when he was fully seated in her ass. He pulled back slightly and then pushed in again, building up speed. Her hardened nipples chafed against the smooth silk covering on her bed as they moved together. The man held her captive in her own room. Her sex throbbed in response to that thought.

Then he stopped, his cock embedded deep in her tight anus. She whimpered. God, what would he do to her now? How could he just *stop?* His hand smoothed over her ass cheek and as full as she was, she could feel the caress inside and out. A moan jerked from her.

His palm lifted and cracked down on her butt, leaving a hot sting behind. She froze beneath him, dark pleasure coiling in her belly. A few moments passed before his hand came down against her upper thigh. She swallowed, every sense she had focusing on the agony and ecstasy that wound through her with each strike of his hard palm. She began to move again, arching as best she could into the blows. More, more, *more*. She wanted it, she needed it.

Switching hands, he kept her wrists locked against the small of her back. She sobbed on a desperate breath as he continued to spank her. Sweet pain echoed in her pussy every time his hand slapped her ass. Wetness slid down the insides of her thighs. She needed to *move*, but his hand and hard cock and heavy weight leaning against her held her pinioned in place. She could barely wriggle. His loose hair fell forward to tickle her back. One more sensation piling on top of all the others. It was too much, too good.

She opened her mouth to demand he stop, to scream, to plead, but no sound emerged. Pleasure fiercer than any she'd ever known held her tight it its grip. It was wrong to like what he was doing to her so much, but she couldn't stop it. Her fangs slid out of her gums, and she was closer to feral, to shifting forms, than she ever had been in any sexual encounter before.

"Come for me." His deep voice was a command, and she couldn't help but obey.

He spanked her over and over as orgasm tore through her system. Each smack made her pussy throb. She shuddered as heat built higher and faster until it coalesced into an implosion that made her entire body clench in reaction. She shattered into a million pieces, her sex fisting on emptiness, her anus tightening around his cock. They both groaned. It went on forever, it ended too soon. Tingles raced over her skin in waves each time her pussy flexed.

A low roar ripped from his throat and he finally began to

thrust again. His dick pistoned in and out of her ass. He let go of her wrists to grip her hips in his big hands. The deep lure of ecstasy dragged at her again, made her move with him when she thought she'd die of exhaustion. It didn't matter. Her body wanted more. Always, always more.

Her orgasm built faster this time, rocketing through her body. His belly slapped against her sore ass, sending throbs of wicked sensation shooting inside her. Her fingers clenched into the bedspread, her claws punching forward to slice through the material. She hissed, the low sub-vocal sound of a wildcat.

Reaching around her, his fingers rolled over her clit in quick, rough caresses. Her back bowed hard. "I'm coming. I'm coming, Miguel."

"Yes!" His hips slammed forward until he froze, his dick buried deep in her anus. Her muscles fisted around the length of his cock in rhythmic pulses. She closed her eyes as she felt his hot come flood her. A shiver ran over her skin. Her lungs burned as she gasped for breath, the scent of sex and *him* filling her nostrils.

Her pussy clenched in an aftershock of orgasm before she collapsed against the bed. She went limp as the events of the day replayed themselves behind her closed lids. It was all too much, and her mind refused to take in more. He was still inside her when sleep crashed over her, pulling her under. She sighed and the world faded away.

Miguel awoke wrapped around his mate's body. A deep contentment settled over him, and he couldn't help the grin that formed on his mouth. He brushed his lips against her temple, inhaling the intoxicating scent of her. The short length of her dark hair clung to his beard stubble and he smoothed it back as he eased away from her to sit on the edge of the bed. He buried his face in his hands, rubbing his eyes.

It had been better than he'd even imagined with her. He'd

gone further than he intended to, letting the primal urges inside him take over as he'd worked her with his hands and mouth. His cock filled just recalling the sweet feel of her clenching tight around him. Lust curled in his gut.

Shuddering, he forced himself to stand and walk to the door. If he stayed, he'd wake her up and fuck her until they were both spent. Again. His lips quirked up. It wasn't a bad idea, but he had a meeting with the Asian delegation soon. He should have been up and started his workday hours before.

Gathering his discarded shirt and slacks, he slapped out the wrinkles as best he could and pulled them on. He doubted he had time to change before the meeting. Damn it. He slid into the shoes he'd left by the door the night before. Stepping out of Andrea's room, he came face to fist with Antonio.

"She's my sister, Miguel. You're my best friend *and* my Second. I know the kind of shit you're into, and I'm fine with it, but she's *my sister.* I can't emphasize the sister thing enough. And if you're messing around with her and it blows up, then she might leave before the loyalty ceremony. That can't happen and you know it." He shook his head. "I . . . This is insane. What the hell are you doing?"

"She's my mate."

Antonio rocked back on his heels, his eyebrows arching. "Wh-what?"

"Mate." Miguel nodded, meeting the other man's gaze so that he knew this was serious. "We sensed it in the limo before we got here. And you know what happened after that."

"I could smell it, yeah." His friend huffed out a breath.

He ran a hand over the back of his neck. "Who couldn't? It's one of the serious downsides of being a Panther—can't get away with anything."

"Tell me about it." A grin creased Antonio's lips. He'd had a hard time keeping his mate secreted away from the Pride. She'd been a non-shifter outcast at the time and wanted nothing to do with the Pride ever again. Difficult for a Pride leader to have such a mate, but things had turned out well in the end.

Miguel could only hope for such a happy ending. Having a mate didn't mean that things went smoothly. Relationships had to be built and nurtured. The depth of connection with a mate only made it more intense, more imperative to compromise and fit together seamlessly.

An uncomfortable expression crossed his friend's face and Miguel almost smiled, knowing exactly what was coming. Antonio groaned. "Look, I'm not talking about the whips and chains, but . . . don't hurt her. She's my—"

"Sister." This time, Miguel didn't bother to hide the grin, but it fell away and he lifted his palms. "I know. I know what you mean as well. And she's my mate, so rest assured that I would never hurt her on purpose."

"Man, I don't want to know that my sister is into your shit." Antonio groaned and glanced away, letting his head drop back. "Damn, Miguel."

"I'd say I was sorry, but your sister is hot." He laughed, clapping his friend on the shoulder.

Antonio's head came back up and he glared. "I could kill you, you know."

Miguel arched a brow, smirking. "You could try . . . sir."

Rolling his eyes, Antonio shook his head. "We have a meeting. It's not like you to be late, so I thought you might need a reminder. Apparently, you needed someone to pry you from Andrea's bed."

"I was on my way." Miguel thrust his hands into his pockets, hunching a shoulder to indicate they move toward the stairs that would lead down to the conference room.

"The meeting started twenty minutes ago."

Had he really missed a meeting? Not once in his entire life could he recall being late to anything. He was always in control, always meticulous. Always punctual. He'd slept like the dead, curled around his mate. The feel of her skin, the scent of her . . . he hadn't wanted to move. Feline lassitude had sapped at his will to budge an inch and time had slid away. He wasn't certain how he would deal with this. A mate deserved a man who would bend, make changes for them, but his work had always been the most important thing, ensuring the success of his Pride. His fists balled in his pants pockets. *"Mierda."*

"Yeah." Antonio chuckled, reaching over to muss Miguel's long hair. He jerked away and snarled a warning. His friend just laughed outright. "It's pretty damn entertaining to see you running around like a chicken with its head cut off."

"Which head? Because this cat messed with our sister. More than once." Diego topped the stairs and crossed his arms, an unusually intense expression on his face.

Miguel lifted his hands in supplication. "Your sister, my mate."

With the twins' unpredictable nature, it was difficult to tell what their reaction would be. It was just as probable that they'd congratulate him on getting laid—whether it was with their sister or not—as it was that they'd jump him and do their collective best to beat him to death.

From the way Diego went rigid, that frown still furrowing his brows, Miguel let his hands fall loose at his sides and braced himself for attack. This could get ugly. He'd hate to have to hand the young cub's ass to him, but he would if he had to. And it wasn't as though violence would change the truth. Andrea belonged to him—whether she knew it yet or not.

A wicked smile creased Diego's lips and his hands snapped out to grab Miguel and yank him into a bear hug. "Sweet."

"I—what?" His brows lifted and he gingerly patted the other man on the back. What the hell had just happened?

"Well, this means you're gonna be part of the family, bro.

Officially and shit." The younger man looped an arm around Miguel's neck and faced Antonio. "Can we keep him? Can we, huh, huh? Pleeease?"

The Pride leader heaved an exasperated sigh. "I'm going to kill you."

Miguel shoved Diego away, flicking Antonio a glance. "How the hell did you get such an annoying brother?"

"I feel the love." Diego scoffed and straightened his French silk cuffs. "Come on, let's get this meeting over with so I can ditch the monkey suit."

The three of them jogged down the stairs and Ric poked his head out of the study door. "How long are you guys going to leave me in here alone? You know I hate dealing with these guys."

"Bro, Miguel is Andrea's mate." Diego decided to forgo the last few steps to vault over the banister and land lightly on the hardwood floor below.

"Awesome. Now get your asses in here." Ric withdrew back into the room and they followed him through the study and into the conference room where their guests waited.

Miguel's mind cleared and focused on the task at hand. Mate or no mate, he had work to do. When he was done, he'd figure out how best to proceed with courting her. The thought of his mate sent a wave of lust spiraling through him.

Anticipation was a sweet thing. Andrea was here and his for the taking until the new heir was born. She couldn't escape him, couldn't run away from this *thing* that was developing between them. It was an excellent prospect. A smile curled his lips. He couldn't wait to proceed.

Andrea hunched over a sketch pad in her suite that evening. She'd set up a mobile office in the sitting room—laptop, fax machine, scanner, printer, and her cell phone. All she needed to run her business, shipped to her courtesy of her assistant in New York.

Now, she let the creativity flow from her and onto the paper. Her world narrowed down to this, every concern and problem melting away to nothing. She was showing a new collection in Bryant Park at New York Fashion Week in a few months and she needed to complete the details. It all rolled through her head—colors, fabrics, cuts, style. Her business was about staying ahead of the curve. And she loved that challenge. A smile curved her lips as she worked. A flourish here, a straight line there. Yes, that was almost perfect.

She sat back, only then noticing the crick in her neck, the cramping in her fingers. But she didn't feel the effects of her wild night. The magic inside her had healed any mark Miguel might have left on her body. The memory was burned into her mind though. She doubted she'd ever forget the intense pleasure, or the guilt that hounded her now. She pushed aside the feeling. It could never happen again. That was final.

Stretching her arms over her head, she looked over her drawings and nodded. "Not bad."

"It's beautiful, actually."

Screaming, she leaped to her feet. Fear pumped through her veins, made her heart hammer in her chest, and her claws and fangs extend. Her chair tumbled back and away as she rounded on her surprise guest. Hissing a low warning, she knew her eyes had gone gold with change.

"Whoa." Miguel stood from where he'd leaned a hip against the back of a settee, lifting his hands in surrender. "I'm sorry I startled you."

When was the last time anyone had snuck up on her without every instinct inside her shrieking of a threat? And did she even want to consider what it meant that her instincts *didn't* consider him a threat? Instead, they clamored with the same message they'd given her the moment they'd met. Mate. His scent filled her nostrils, dragging out the memories of yesterday again. In the limo, in her bedroom. She shuddered, retracting her claws with effort. Her heart still raced, but not with fear.

She took a deep breath and turned aside to tidy her desk. A paper fluttered to the floor and Miguel picked it up to hand it to her. Glancing down, he saw the official letterhead for her company. The logo showed a panther poised to attack, the words Pantheras Designs scrolled above its back. He set it on the desk, tapping a long finger against the image. "Pantheras?"

"It's the genus name for all large cat species, tigers, leopards, jaguars." Her shoulder lifted in a shrug, and she looked up to meet his gaze. "I thought it suited."

He nodded, the cool composure she'd noticed about him yesterday evident on his face. "I can understand why."

A smile curled her lips and she brushed her hair away from her eyes. "I was often told I had a feline grace on the runway."

That startled a chuckle out of him and the sound warmed her, even though she knew it shouldn't. They needed to talk about what had happened between them. About what couldn't be allowed to happen between them. She swallowed.

Memories of the last Second she had let dominate her raced through her mind, over her body, and she went rigid. Every muscle in her body strung tight. He'd thrown her down, tied her up. Shame slithered over her spine at how she'd enjoyed it. And then he'd hurt her. She'd enjoyed that too, the pleasure that ripped through her along with the pain.

And then . . . then he'd gone too far and the pain hadn't been pleasurable. Then it had been about degradation and not mutual enjoyment. She'd struggled and screamed, used her Panther strength to rip herself free from the bindings, but her strength was nothing to his. And he'd laughed at her, mocking her. He'd used his fangs and claws to tear into her very human flesh until she bled. Until it had made her weak with blood loss.

There wasn't much she remembered after that, just that she had managed to escape and flee to her rooms. Passing out, she'd awoken the next day healed by the magic inside her. A part of her hadn't been sure she'd wake up at all.

As ashamed as she'd been, she found the courage to tell her father and he hadn't believed her. Her own father had believed his Second when he said Andrea exaggerated, that she was too inexperienced to understand the feral nature of Panthers. That she'd been more than willing and was now embarrassed by her own appetites.

Just enough truth to bury her.

She'd packed her bags and left that day. Nothing she could have said could make up for the fact that her parent—someone who should have defended her no matter what—had hung her out to dry when she told him she'd been abused. That was the end. She couldn't remain in the Pride after that.

And she'd never let anyone take control during sex again either. She'd cut that part of herself away. The weak part of her soul that craved pleasing other people. She was in charge of her body, her mind. Miguel needed to understand that. "I'm glad you stopped by, actually."

A quiet grin lightened his handsome face. "Are you? Good."

"Don't look too pleased. I need to talk to you about what happened . . . last night."

The grin turned wicked and his gaze slid over her body. She felt it like a possessive caress against her skin and she responded. Her nipples tightened, her sex dampening. She clenched her thighs together, but it did little to ease the empty ache between them. An ache she had a feeling only he could assuage now. The thought of another man touching her made her skin crawl. She cleared her throat and met his gaze. "It can't happen again."

He blinked, confusion flashing in his dark eyes for a moment. "Make love? But, we're mates, Andrea. Surely, you can't expect that we'll—"

"Not the sex part. That was . . . I mean . . . I want that part to happen again. If you're willing, of course." A blush heated her cheeks. How the hell was she supposed to say this?

"I'm willing." He took a step toward her, obviously intending to show her just how willing he was. Right now. Fire exploded in her belly and her sex contracted with want.

She held up her hand, tripping back a step and almost sprawling on her ass when she ran into her overturned chair. This was not going the way she'd planned. "I meant the hitting. You can't hit me again."

He froze in place as a mask settled over his features. If she'd thought him difficult to read before, now it was impossible. Not a single movement or flicker of expression crossed his face. He'd gone dangerously still. "You didn't protest at the time. I thought we both enjoyed ourselves."

"I—I did. I mean, I didn't." She swallowed, the blood leeching out of her face. "You didn't do anything I wasn't willing to do, so don't think that I'm saying that. It's—it's wrong for people to do that, and I'm just not into that kind of thing."

Liar. But the way he flinched and went pale stilled her tongue. He pulled in a deep breath, his eyes shuttered, and his voice was a harsh rasp of sound. "From what I could tell each time we fucked each other, you need pain with your pleasure. There's nothing wrong with that."

"It's sick and twisted and wrong." She shoved her fingers through her hair. He had to understand. He had to see that she was right. If he tried to do that again . . . Shame and longing slid through her. God, she was so fucked in the head. Hadn't she learned what could happen? Men couldn't be trusted to protect a woman, let alone respect her when she was vulnerable. And yet her body still craved the pain. She choked on a breath. "I'm sick inside and I can't make it stop."

"Is it sick that I enjoyed it as much as you did? You weren't the only one there." Reaching for her, he let his hand wilt to his side when she recoiled from his touch. His jaw firmed. "Everyone's needs are different, Andrea. I can give you that. You need me."

"I *do not* need it." Rage exploded from somewhere deep inside her, a dam bursting. She scooped a glass paperweight off her desk and launched it at his head. "And I don't need you! I don't need anyone."

Lightning reflexes had his hand snapping out to catch the projectile midair. What killed her was the understanding that softened his expression. "Anger won't make it—or me—go away. You have to accept this part of yourself."

She shook her head so wildly the short strands of her hair whipped into her eyes. "Stop. Just stop. I don't want to talk about this. It's disgusting."

"Andrea, please. It's not—"

She didn't listen, she turned on a heel and raced for the door. Tears streaked down her cheeks and more filled her eyes so fast she could barely see through the blur of moisture.

Shooting out into the hall, she slammed into a broad chest. She skittered back to see Antonio. He looked at her and then over her shoulder at her room where Miguel was clearly outlined in the open door.

Swiping at the tears on her face, she tried to sidle past him. "Excuse me. I'm sorry."

"Andrea."

She stopped dead, unable to resist the command in his tone, to disobey her leader. Some habits were just too ingrained to ignore. "Yes, sir?"

He winced and gestured her toward the stairs. "Don't speak to me the way you would Father."

"You have the power he did. Why would I assume that you would wish to be treated differently than him?" Stomping on the emotional upheaval of her conversation with Miguel, she scrambled to maintain the calm she'd worked so hard to present to her family so far. She wasn't the rebellious teenager she'd been when she left, but she didn't know who she was now in terms of Panther society. And everything that was going on with Miguel had the power to make her unravel. She had to hold tight or she'd lose sight of herself.

Antonio rested his hand between her shoulder blades as they walked down the stairs and into his study. "Why would you think I'm different? Solana, for one. Do you think I could mate with her and not understand how poorly Father treated her? That his inability to accept her as she was left her a teenager on the streets with no protection?"

She stared at the floor for a moment, uncomfortable under his probing gaze. "She's no longer a non-shifter."

"I'd already claimed her as my mate by the time we discovered she could shift. I suspected, but in the end it didn't matter.

She was mine and I was hers. It was that simple." He walked around the big wooden desk that dominated the room, leaning his palms on the polished surface.

"And that complicated." She met his eyes, her shoulder lifting in a shrug.

"Indeed. Plus, you know I never got along with Father. I find it . . . sad . . . that you think coming into power of my own would turn me into him." He plopped into the chair that used to belong to her father. Her muscles locked as the familiar tension of being called onto the carpet in this room settled over her body.

Exhaustion rolled over her in an overwhelming wave. Everything that had happened with Miguel and now the ghosts of the past were just too much for her to deal with. If she had to stay here until Antonio's child was born, and if there was no way to convince her brother to let her leave after, then she's have to learn to co-exist with Miguel until his tenure as Second ended and he went back to South America.

With their different outlook and needs in the bedroom, she couldn't imagine them ever deciding to mark each other and lock themselves into a mating with one person who couldn't fulfill them. Because there was no way she could ever let him spank her again, let alone do anything else he might come up with. She refused to let herself think of what that might be. Remembering the closed look on his face when she told him not to hit her made guilt of another kind stab through her. He deserved an explanation of her past, of why she was so opposed to pain in the bedroom. It might help keep the peace between them, which she needed right now.

She swallowed and straightened her shoulders to face her brother, hoping to get this over with so she could crawl into bed and not awaken for a year. A sad smile curved her lips. Maybe it would all have gone away by then.

* * *

Miguel sat in his office when Andrea knocked on the door. It was her, he knew it was her. He could smell the sweetness of her. His hand tightened on the silver pen he was using until the metal groaned. He hadn't gone more that a few moments at a time without thinking about her, wanting her.

Could he handle her right now? His control hung by a tenuous thread. That she regretted what had happened between them made a bitter taste flood his mouth. It also made him angry that something so precious to him would repulse her. She wasn't the first woman not to share his tastes in the bedroom, but she was the first in a long time. He usually judged his bedmates better than that. That his mate was a woman who would recoil from him was a harsh kick to the gut.

But he didn't believe her protests. She knew she shared his desires—she simply didn't *want* to share them. Something had scared her and he wanted to know what. Protectiveness swamped him. No one had ever gotten under his skin so fast. He wanted to soothe her fears, assure her she was safe—if for no other reason than that he'd move mountains to make it so.

Women and children should be protected at all costs. It was a man's duty to take care of what was his, and he didn't give a damn if it was a Neanderthal attitude to have. It wasn't that he thought women incapable of looking after themselves, just that they should be cherished. He knew firsthand what could happen when a man disregarded his responsibilities to those under his care. His father's inattention had cost his older sister her life.

His father was the younger son in the ruling family in the South American Pride. He'd been charming and carefree, pampered all his life, and expected others to do for him. Miguel's mother had worshipped him to distraction, but that hadn't left much attention for either of their children.

Miguel had sensed for weeks that something was wrong

with Nina. Something building, some powerful magic about to burst forward. Perhaps he was more sensitive than most, he'd never know, but when he'd told his father, it had been brushed off.

When Nina disappeared from the Pride's vacation retreat in Peru one summer morning, his father had left it to others to worry. She was fine, she'd return soon. Miguel had been unconvinced and had set out alone to find her. They were close in age, only a year and a half apart, and had learned to depend on each other in the face of their parents' neglect. Neither of them was old enough to shift forms—that part of Panther magic only unleashed with the hormonal influx of adolescence.

And his sister had shifted for the first time that day. It took hours for Miguel to track her into the rainforest surrounding the hacienda—something a full-grown Panther could have managed in a fraction of the time. When he'd found her, it was already too late. Hunters had shot her and left her for dead. She'd barely clung to life—her breathing had the hollow rattle of death. He'd curled his human body around the silky black fur of her young Panther form and held her until the life slipped from her, and her ragged breath stopped altogether, sobbing until he'd been hoarse with it, until there were no more tears left.

He'd never spoken to either of his parents again. They hadn't protected Nina, looked after her, as they should have. Miguel had been determined from that moment on to never be that way, to be trustworthy, to work for what he got, to take his responsibilities to the Prides seriously and help safeguard all Panthers.

He'd found a way to channel that intense need to protect in his sexual preferences. Protecting a woman while she was at her most vulnerable, while she explored her need to submit both aroused and fulfilled him. And that Andrea would be disgusted by that shook him. It also challenged him because her reactions had been so intense that he knew she had the same needs he did in bed. He just didn't know why she would run from it.

Her knock came again, this time softer and more tentative. She knew he was in here, and he didn't have the heart to turn her away. He sighed. "Come in, Andrea."

The door opened and she edged in, the knob clutched tightly in her hand. "Miguel."

A long beat of silence passed while they stared at each other. God, she was so beautiful. The light played over the angles of her cheekbones, caressed the curve of her jaw. Her great dark eyes were hooded, shadowed with secrets she kept from him. He hated that. He wanted nothing between them. "Did you need something?"

"I wanted . . ." She swallowed and looked away, her gaze moving around the room. "It's very different in here than when I lived with the Pride. I noticed it when I took that call in here yesterday. The Second then liked a more . . . old-world ambiance. Leather and carved wood. Like an old gentlemen's club."

He blinked at the light topic, so at odds with the white-knuckled grip she had on the door handle, the complete lack of expression on her face. She was nervous. But, why?

Another secret, another dead end. Too many questions and no answers. It fascinated as much as it frustrated him. He sat back in his chair, forcing himself to relax into the unassuming second in command that most Pride members were comfortable with. "Yes, I redecorated when I got here. Though there were a few Seconds between him and me, I'm guessing no one changed anything because it looked exactly as you described. I prefer a modern flair."

He flicked his fingers to indicate the metal and glass furniture that dominated the room. Interspersed were pieces he'd brought with him from Rio de Janeiro, carvings, painted gourds, glossy ceramic vases and bowls. Touches of color so that it wasn't sterile and uninviting. The previous decorations had made the room feel like a dark cave closing in on him.

"It suits you." Her hands fell away from the doorknob, clasping and unclasping in front of her.

He wished he knew what troubled her, what he could do to help, but her face remained closed. He rubbed a hand over his forehead. "Come in. Sit."

"I—I don't want to interrupt." A giggle burst from her lips, the slight hysteria at odds with her composed expression. "But I already have, haven't I? I'm sorry. I'll go."

"*Stay,*" he barked the order, and she jolted. He took a deep breath, again relaxing his muscles into his desk chair. He smiled. "I'd like you to stay. Please, come in and sit down. You obviously have something on your mind. If you care to tell me, I'd like to hear it."

"I . . . I just . . . okay." She pulled in a deep breath and stepped forward, closing the door behind her. "I'm just going to get right to the point. I want to explain about why I freaked out earlier . . . why I don't want anyone to s-spank me in bed."

He nodded, but when she didn't continue, he decided to make sure they were talking about the same kind of sexual desires. There was a lot she could be misinformed about when it came to dominance and submission during sex. "You know that a submissive has the ultimate control, right? What happened between us—what I hope will happen again—doesn't make you powerless. You can say no. You can stop anything that's happening. It's an exchange of power, Andrea. Not a taking."

She looked down at her lap, a bitter smile twisting her lips. "That's not always true. Sometimes—sometimes they don't stop."

Those few words told him so much about why she'd been terrified to give in to her needs. Rage boiled high and hot within him. That his mate would have been abused, that any man would dare to hurt her, made the feral side of his nature want to claw free, hunt the man down, and rip his throat out. His teeth ground together for a moment before he could form a coherent sentence. "You tried to explore this side of yourself and some asshole pushed you over your limits. Who was he?"

"His name doesn't matter. He was my father's Second."

"Shit," he breathed. His hands actually shook with the need to damage this man. The look on Andrea's face—he never wanted to see that kind of betrayed pain from his mate again. His belly knotted and it took all his willpower not to reach for her. He sensed she needed to purge this more than she needed his comfort. He doubted she'd ever told anyone about this before. Whether she realized it or not, she was trusting him with something she'd locked away for a long, long time.

Her shoulder lifted in a shrug. "Father went through Seconds like toilet paper. It meant they never gained much influence here. He had all the power. But his Second made me realize men don't want me for me. They want to toy with me because of who my family is, they want meaningless sex, or more than I can willingly give. After that—after that I chose to remove myself as a player in my family's politics and . . . I chose the meaningless sex. I was in control. I gave only what I was willing to part with."

He moved around the desk to kneel before her. His hands covered hers, her fingers icy cold against his. He looked up, meeting her troubled gaze. "I am so sorry."

"Me, too." Again, her shoulder jerked in the semblance of a nonchalant shrug and she glanced away. "But it was an important lesson to learn. I never looked back after that."

"I'll kill him for you." His voice went flat, deadly serious. He didn't even try to temper his response in this area. The man deserved to die for damaging a young girl's trust to the point that she ran away from her family . . . and herself.

She huffed out a soft laugh and her fingers curled around his. "He's already dead. I looked into it when Antonio asked me to come back the first time. I had to know."

"I understand." He lifted one hand to cup her jaw and stroke his thumb over her high cheekbone.

"Do you?" Her gaze locked with his, searching his face. For what, he didn't know. "Do you understand why I can't let myself do that again? I can't go there with a man."

He tilted his head from side to side. "I understand why you might not want to try. But know that I would never hurt you, I would always protect you, and you *can* trust me. I'll wait as long as you need, but I hope you learn that I'm telling you the truth when I say I can fulfill all of your needs."

She shuddered, that caged wildness he'd seen in her flashing through her gaze. The moment heated, became purely sexual. She reached out and ran the tips of her fingers over his lips. His cock went rigid at just that light contact, and he was aching for the wetness of her soft pussy. He could smell how ready she was, the scent of her a heady aphrodisiac. It did little to encourage his control, so he made himself let go of her hand and sat back on his haunches.

"It doesn't matter what you can or can't fulfill." Her fingers brushed her hair away from her face. "When I leave here—"

"Andrea, whatever uncertainty there is about our future, you have to know that your brothers will never let you leave again. It would be the stupidest thing Antonio could ever do unless you decided to join another Pride. Just being born a Cruz was enough to make you a player in this game. Having you live among humans turns you into a political wild card and it's just not possible. You know that."

Her jaw took on an obstinate tilt. "You never know. I might be able to talk Antonio into it. Especially if we don't mate with each other."

"Andrea, you could drive a saint to madness." He let his head fall back and it thunked against the side of his desk.

"I'm glad I'm not the only one who recognizes how insane this is. We just won't work out, and I'm not meant to live with other Panthers. I do fine on my own."

His head came up and he glared at her. "*This* is not insane. This is mating. Your stubbornness borders on irrational."

"You can't force me to mate with you. I'm leaving after the loyalty ceremony is done." She nodded for emphasis.

A low growl rumbled his chest. He'd never met a single person who could so quickly drive him to the edge of his tolerance. He was a calm man, always in control of himself. Damn it. "Your brother won't allow it. *I* won't allow it."

"How do you intend to stop me?"

"Tying you up sounds like a viable option," he muttered.

"Tie me up forever?" She folded her arms across her chest, pursing her lips comically. He had to struggle not to laugh, loving this charming side of her even as it made him want to throttle her. "Viable, perhaps, but not a *practical* option."

He sighed, leaned forward to bracket her chin with his hand, and tilted her face toward his. "Your brother won't let you run away from this. He is the Pride leader."

"Even he can't stop me. If I want to leave, I will." Her brows lowered, but she didn't try to pull her chin from his grip. "I spend a great deal of time in Japan and Australia—do you honestly think one of those two Pride leaders wouldn't let me join them? If for no other reason than to spite Antonio? Felines are notoriously fickle—and they'd see it as a great prank."

"Coward."

Her eyes flared wide in shock, and then narrowed to dangerous slits. She shoved a finger into his chest. "Be careful, Miguel. You may be his Second, but until his child is born, *I* am Antonio's heir."

"I'm glad to see you remember that." He arched a brow at

her, enjoying the chance to goad her a bit. He loved the way she always reacted for him. It made him grin.

She hissed at him. "I don't want to be a Pride leader. I'm glad Antonio was born first, but I know my place here. My father never let me forget it."

Firstborn shall rule. That was the way of the Prides. Until three hundred years ago, a female who was firstborn would bow out of ruling in favor of a younger male relative. Only in extreme circumstances would a woman rule, such as an only child or the last in a line. Even then, if the woman had a son, she was expected to abdicate when he came of age.

Spain had had the first female Pride leader who refused to let her brother rule. She had been a revolutionary in so many ways, a leader who inspired her people. Since her reign, no woman had stepped down simply because she was female.

He had a feeling if Andrea had been born first, she would have followed in that tradition of great female rulers. She had the fire and the drive . . . and she definitely had the charisma. She'd channeled her energies in other directions, but she would have been a credit to all Panthers if circumstances had been different. Too bad her father had spoiled that.

Miguel only hoped he could convince her that leaving the Pride—and him—was not something she wanted to do. It was true he couldn't force her, but he was very, very good at persuading people to do what he wanted. He doubted she would be easy to sway, but then, what fun would that be for him. He liked a challenge as much as the next man.

He was no young boy—he knew how precious a mate was and he knew how to work for what he wanted. With time and patience, she would be his.

4

Andrea stepped naked from the bathroom into her suite and stretched, her skin heating as the magic inside her lit. Fangs erupted from her gums and she hissed. Black furr rippled up her arms and down her legs until her body stooped and she shifted into Panther form. She flexed her claws against the carpet and walked forward to jump onto the window seat tucked into the wide bay window. Her tail flicked in rhythmic swishes as she glanced around the room. Anything to distract herself, to not think about the conversation she'd had with Miguel the day before. His words ran around and around inside her head.

I can fulfill all of your needs.

Her eyes pinched closed and she shuddered. God, she wanted that. Turning herself over completely, letting herself be wild and uncontrolled, knowing the man she was with craved her complete abandon as much as she did.

No. She forced her eyes open. It was stupid to think that just because Miguel connected with her on a level she'd never experienced before meant he was any different than any other man. It was the mating instinct. Nothing more. If some part of her knew it was a lie, she ignored it. She'd been wrong about a man before. It didn't inspire much confidence in her own judgment.

And yet. And yet, she wanted to know, truly know, what it was like to let go. If she didn't do it with a man crafted just for her by destiny, would she ever? She doubted it. A week ago, she wouldn't even have considered this. So much had changed in so short an amount of time. It made her stomach knot, but she couldn't deny she liked being with her family, her kind. Her biggest secret was one she shared with everyone here.

While she still couldn't imagine remaining, she might need to talk to Antonio about visiting more often. It would be difficult to convince him to let her leave at all, so she didn't relish the discussion. She'd let herself put it off, but Solana would give birth within the month.

Would Antonio cast out his only sister? Andrea didn't know. He was far more open than their father had ever been. She wished he had been Pride leader when she was younger. She might never have left if he had been. The protective way he treated every member of the Pride made her doubt that he would have thought her a liar when she told him she'd been hurt by a man. Likely, he'd have reacted with the killing rage that Miguel had shown.

It shouldn't warm her that Miguel would kill for her, but it did. Some basic facet of her soul trusted him, but her experience made her wary. Miguel. It all circled back to him.

"Oh, *yes*. Damn, baby."

Jolting, she jerked her head to the side to look out her window at the rear garden, and then did a double take at what she saw.

Diego straddled one end of a cement bench in the middle of copse of bushes. A woman in a short dress knelt on the bench, sliding her mouth up and down his cock while Ric pushed her dress up to her waist and stood at the other end of the bench, fucking her from behind. Diego's fingers buried in the woman's blond hair and when he threw back his head to roar out an orgasm, Andrea could see his long fangs protruding from his mouth and that his eyes had gone gold.

She blinked for a moment, and then jerked her gaze away and unfurled to jump away from the window seat. Well, then. Her brothers had turned out as pervy as she had imagined. They always were adventurous. Too much so sometimes. Their wild habits had worried her when they were younger. She'd feared it was some kind of self-destructive bent, but they seemed to have turned out well enough. It had been so hard leaving them behind, but if she hadn't cut all ties, she knew her father would have used her communication with the twins as a way to get her back, to manipulate her.

She could see that ruthless streak in her brothers as well. In Miguel.

She'd even exhibited it a time or two herself. But that was for business. What would she do if it was personal? Would Miguel be as relentless as her father? Would he grind her under until there was nothing left of Andrea Cruz except Miguel Montoya's mate?

It would be so easy to give in, to submit. To please. The question came down to trust. Did she trust the bond developing between them enough to take him up on his promise and let him fulfill *all* of her needs?

Sighing, she shifted back into human form to head for her closet. It was time to dress for dinner. She'd been vacillating back and forth on the Miguel issue so much she was starting to annoy herself. She liked making decisions and sticking to them. Damn the man for making her question herself.

Fifteen minutes later she was seated across from him at the dining room table. Diego and Ric stumbled in fighting laughter. They still stank of sex. She rolled her eyes when Diego smirked at her. "Enjoy the show, Peeping Tom?"

"Get a room." She wrinkled her nose. "I just threw up in my mouth a little."

"Now *that* is nasty." Ric nudged her shoulder as he sank into the chair next to her.

She flapped her napkin at him to wave away the pheromones oozing from his pores. "Speaking of nasty, you could have at least bathed."

"Knock it off, children." Antonio helped Solana to her seat, lifting his hand when Diego opened his mouth. "I don't even want to know."

Ric coughed into his fist. "Just to let you know, we're planning on heading to Santa Cruz for some surfing this weekend."

Pulling out his own chair to sit, Antonio nodded. "Have fun. Don't get in any trouble."

Silence reigned for a few blissful moments while the twins began packing away more food than an entire professional football team could manage. At least they used the right fork while they did it because they'd been through the same anal training process as their older siblings.

Miguel met her gaze over the table and her breath caught. A private smile that made her chest ache softened his face. In that endless moment, every instinct inside her stilled and her mind and heart settled into a final decision. She was going to do it. Just one more time, she'd try. The breath she'd been holding slid past her lips.

Her hand shook when she reached for her wine. His gaze lingered on her mouth as she took a sip, heated as he moved down to caress her breasts. Wildfire exploded in her veins, made her pulse pound. Her nipples tightened, jutting against the thin fabric of her silk top. She suddenly regretted not wearing a bra, but she didn't need one so she usually went without. Swallowing hard, she almost choked on the wine.

He broke the connection and glanced away, taking the opportunity to speak. "Antonio?"

The Pride leader lifted his eyebrows and leaned forward to look his Second in the eye. "Yes?"

He braced his forearm on the table and also leaned in. "It seems Africa has a new Pride leader. Cesar Benhassi has stepped forward in Casablanca."

"Huh." Antonio sat back in his chair, his brow furrowed in thought. "Does he have a legitimate claim to the Moroccan seat of power?"

"The last Pride leader's great aunt's grandson."

Andrea knew a lot of the reason why everyone feared her being a political wild card was because of what had happened in the African Pride. The last Pride leader had gathered all power for himself, strategically killing off anyone who challenged his authority, including his family. Because he'd died without children or siblings, it had left a power vacuum behind. When several distant relatives stepped up to take control, the Pride devolved into civil war, slaughtering most of the Panthers in Africa and sending the rest scrambling for sanctuary with other leaders. With it being so recent a reminder of how Pride politics could go horribly wrong, it had made the Panther world terrified of any kind of political anomalies. Like her.

Solana piped up, one hand rubbing her stomach absently. "Benhassi's claim seems tenuous at best."

Nodding, Miguel lifted his palm and shrugged. "I've not been able to find a record of any Panther still living who might have a better one."

"What about those with claims just as good?" She poked at her food with her fork. "Those would cause as much chaos if they also came forward."

"True, but Benhassi has made allies of those with similar claims and they form the nucleus of the new Pride." His gaze flicked between Antonio and Solana. Andrea narrowed her gaze at him, trying to decide if he had an opinion on the matter or if he was just reporting facts. His face had gone blank, so it was difficult to tell.

Antonio stroked his fingers over his chin thoughtfully. "It

would seem there are two options here. Wait to see who might try to form alliances with them . . . or be the first to do so."

"You have his contact information?" Diego rubbed a hand over the back of his neck while Ric remained still, staring down at his plate.

Lifting a glass of water to his mouth, Miguel paused to answer. "Of course."

A small smile pulled at Antonio's lips. "Of course. One day you're going to tell me how you know everything long before anyone else has the information."

"Doubtful, sir." Miguel sipped the water and set it down again.

Ric finally spoke, glancing up to meet Antonio's gaze. "If they remain stable, it would put you in an excellent position to be first to contact him and give him some legitimacy."

"If Africa once again falls, then we would be allied to a Pride at war with itself." Diego's face fell into what Andrea was coming to recognize as his serious lawyer expression. "Granting that kind of leader any legitimacy could be dangerous for us and for the balance of power in all the Prides."

Antonio crossed his arms over his chest, nodding. "All good points. What do all of you think? Should we be progressive or conservative in our approach to this new development?"

Their father would never have asked. When their mother was alive, he would have consulted her—and probably done what she suggested—but that was all. After her death, he made decisions alone and expected everyone to fall into step behind his leadership.

Ric tapped his finger against the table. "If he's to have any hope of success, he'll need a show of support from other Pride leaders."

"I agree." Diego nodded.

Solana grinned. "Me, too."

Miguel just nodded his approval and said nothing more.

Turning to look at Andrea, Antonio arched an eyebrow. "Andrea?"

She lifted her hands in mock surrender. "I've only been back in the Pride for a week, brother. My opinion can hardly help."

"I'd like to hear it anyway."

"I believe that if something doesn't work once, it's unfair to everyone not to try again. Everyone deserves that second chance." She watched Miguel still as he took in the dual meaning of what she said. She forced her gaze to leave her mate and focused on her elder brother. "Call him."

His chin dipped in a decisive nod. "Give the number to my secretary so she can set up a conference call for nightfall tomorrow in Morocco."

"Yes, sir." Miguel picked up his fork and knife to resume his meal and everyone else followed suit, but he glanced up to look at Andrea, wicked promise in his gaze. A shiver rippled over her flesh and she bit her lip. A kaleidoscope of carnal memories spun through her mind. The limo, her bedroom, his hands on her skin, his taste in her mouth. She squeezed her thighs together, but it only increased the ache there.

"Aren't you enjoying your meal? Should I send for something else?" Solana's voice jolted Andrea out of her sensual stupor. She managed a smile for her sister-in-law and began eating, but she didn't taste a thing. It could have been cardboard for all she knew, and the rest of dinner passed in a blur.

When everyone stood to leave, she rose half a beat behind. God, she was out of it. Shaking herself, she waved off an offer of after-dinner drinks and pleaded work obligations. She doubted she fooled anyone when she left the dining room with Miguel on her heels. Her legs shook with each step up the staircase and she feared they might collapse under her at any moment. When she reached the top, Miguel's hand settled at the small of her back and directed her toward the Second's suite.

A small shiver went up her spine as they approached the

door. This was the room her nightmare had taken place in. But she needed to confront this—if she wanted to explore this part of her sexuality, then this was the man to do it with, and this was the place to do it in.

He held open the door for her and she pulled in a steadying breath before she stepped over the threshold. The suite was as changed as the Second's office had been with modern furniture and South American art pieces. And it smelled of Miguel, hot and masculine. Her shoulders relaxed a bit while the muscles in her belly tensed and her pussy dampened, readying her for sex.

Sweet scents filled her nose, flowers and sugar. It drew her gaze to the bedside table where a tray of assorted fruit with slender serving forks sat on ice. A bouquet of long stemmed roses stood in a vase beside it. She blinked. "What's all this?"

"Dessert." The way his gaze moved over her body told her what he intended to have for dessert. And it wasn't fruit and whipped cream.

"When did you have time to do this?" She swallowed and watched his nimble fingers flick open the buttons on his dress shirt. The heavy muscles of his chest came into view, dark tanned skin and a light trail of hair disappeared beneath the waist of his trousers. Fingers trembling, she followed his lead and undressed. Within a few moments they were both naked. The jut of his hard cock curved upward toward the muscles in his flat stomach. God, he was gorgeous.

He just smiled and winked at her. "I made time. Other than that, it's my secret."

Trepidation fluttered in her belly, but she squelched it. *Just do it, Andrea.* She closed her eyes and turned away. It wasn't as if she was going to live forever. She'd only have a few years more than the average human; her Panther magic ensured her amazing good health, not immortality. She couldn't live her life always afraid, always wondering. Someday the curiosity would get the better of her, so it was best to get it over with and have her eyes open for what she was getting into. Good or bad, she was ready.

What would Miguel do now that he had her permission? She'd unleashed the beast. He wanted it this way. Her body demanded it, so this was how it was going to be. Resignation slid through her, and she braced herself for whatever came next. Now that she'd agreed to this, she wasn't so sure. And there was no way she could back out. Hot and cold chills ran over her skin, and the slow burn of anticipation pushed through the reservations and fear.

"Andrea?" His fingers brushed up her spine to curl lightly around the back of her neck.

He could use what happened here to force her to bend to his will. To break her the way so many men had tried. From lovers to her father. Only Miguel might actually be able to accomplish it. Self-disgust rolled through her that she would let him hurt her, that she would put herself in any man's hands this way again. Hadn't she learned how wrong this was the first time? Tears welled up in her eyes and she pressed her trembling lips together. She wanted him so much it made her heart ache. "I am so fucking weak."

"No." His lips feathered against her temple, and the heat of his skin burned into her back. "It takes as much strength to follow as it does to lead. Perhaps more."

A sound that was half laugh, half sob escaped her. "Right. Sure."

The palm of his hand slid down her spine, turning her to face him. Her heart pounded in her ears, her breath sounding harsh. Sheer, terrifying lust wound through her and she tensed.

Here it came.

What if he pushed too hard? What if he didn't stop?

His fingertips brushed down her arm, and a tremor ran through her at the automatic reaction her body always had to him. He wrapped his fingers around her elbow and drew her into his embrace. She resisted for a half-second before she collapsed against his chest.

A soft purr soughed from his throat as he slid his hand up and down her back. It relaxed her and she shuddered, wrapping her arms around him. He brushed his fingers through her short hair, pushing it away from her face. "Trust me. I would never betray that."

"Don't hurt me." She pulled back a little to look him in the eyes.

Understanding shone on his face, a sympathy that softened his normally implacable expression. Some part of her knew that he *did* understand what she meant, that the faith she put in him was far more important than the physical act their bodies would perform.

"I won't. You can trust me, but if you're not ready, I don't want to force it." His thumb smoothed over her cheek. "You don't have to do this, Andrea."

"Yes, I do. I need to know." She let the desire show in her gaze, the Panther within her would shimmer the edges of her irises to pure gold. "I'm ready."

"Are you sure?"

"Yes. I trust you for this." If there was more emphasis on the last two words than she intended, she hoped he didn't notice.

He searched her face, looking for what, she didn't know, but he seemed satisfied with what he found because he nodded. "The rules of the game are simple, if you want me to stop, say red light. If you need me to slow down, say yellow light. If I check in with you and you're fine—"

"Green light. I think I've got it." She smiled, but it fell away quickly. "I have a few rules of my own."

Arching a brow, he continued to run his hands over her arms and back. "Oh?"

She licked her lips and his gaze followed the movement. She swallowed and forced herself to continue. "This stays in the bedroom. Nothing changes outside of what we do in bed. You don't own me, you don't tell me what to do."

"Fine. Turn around." His tone was an unmistakable order and she smirked at him, but obeyed. She couldn't help the tension that ran through her body. Her gaze hit the carpet, waiting . . . waiting . . .

Would he bend her over and spank her? Her sex contracted at the mere thought. Wetness slicked the lips of her pussy. Heat wound through her, made her heart pound and her breathing speed until she panted. Her nipples beaded so tightly they ached. Her body was more than ready for whatever he had in mind.

Something soft and cool dropped over her eyes. "Wha—"

"Shh." His breath fluttered the hair at the nape of her neck and he kissed her there. The blindfold tightened around the back of her head, blocking out all light.

She shuddered, sucking a deep breath through her nose. All her other senses seemed to heighten. The scent of Miguel overwhelmed her, the feel of her hair curling under her jaw to tickle her throat, and an excitement that twisted tighter and tighter inside her. What was happening to her?

The smell of strawberries intensified until the slight rasp of one stroked across her bottom lip. Her mouth opened and she bit into the fleshy pulp. The taste of it burst over her tongue and she moaned. The experience was so sensual it almost became sexual. She smiled. Anything with Miguel could be sexual.

"Sometimes, it's not about the pain." The rough satin of his voice stroked over her skin like a caress. "The whole experience should be enjoyed."

It was about the sensation. Every imaginable sensation. Pleasure, pain, and everything in between. Her muscles loosened as her body relaxed to wait for what he had next, turning herself over to the experience. There was excitement, but also a strange calm. The eye of the storm.

"Miguel, I—"

"Shh." A long length of silky fabric wrapped around her wrists. It seemed wider at one end than it was at the other. A necktie? He wound it around and around until she was bound from wrist to elbow, her arms locking into straight lines behind her back. It arched her chest forward, made her hyperaware of her body and the way breathing lifted her breasts.

She hadn't been bound since that night long ago. It startled her, and how much she liked it scared her. She shuddered as her emotions tripped and tangled over each other. "Yellow light."

He froze against her, his hands rising to cup her biceps. "Do you need me to take off the tie?"

"No. Just . . . give me a moment." It soothed her that he had so readily stopped and some small part of the barrier inside her crumbled. She tested the bindings, flexing her arms. Her Panther strength could easily rip free of the silk . . . but she didn't want to. She clasped her hands together to make the position more comfortable. Her head dropped forward until her chin rested on her chest, and her breath sighed out. "Okay, go ahead."

His tongue flicked against her shoulder blade, his mouth opening to suck on her flesh. She swayed back toward him, shivering when his fangs scored her skin lightly. The heat of his big body left her as he stepped away and she felt strangely bereft as though he'd been her anchor when the darkness stole her bearings.

She felt a tiny prick against her arm, the slow drag of cool metal over her flesh. Goose bumps shivered down her limbs. The serving fork. He slid it around her ribs to draw it over her tight nipple. She jerked under the sensation, moaning low in her throat. The scrape didn't hurt, but it was like nothing she'd ever felt before. He chuckled, the sound a low rumble to her ears.

"Then again, sometimes a little pain heightens the experience, doesn't it?" The fork raked hard over the soft underside of her breast and she hissed at the hot sting. Her fangs erupted from her gums, and she leaned into him, her neck lying on his broad shoulder, her arms trapped between them.

"Yes." Her body bowed, arching into the slight sting of the fork tines. More. Pain and pleasure blended, became fluid. Like time in the darkness behind her mask. They could have been here for moments or hours and she wouldn't know. She was lost to the sensation, enslaved by her need for it.

His free hand slipped over her stomach until he dipped between her legs. The scent of her wetness reached her nose as he parted the slick lips of her pussy. Her skin was on fire, the feeling heightening as he continued to drag lazy circles on her torso with the fork. His knuckle rubbed over her clit and an arc of pure ecstasy shot through her. She cried out, pushing her pelvis forward to make him stroke her harder, deeper.

"Do you want more, Andrea?"

"Yes!" Her hips twisted, but he lightened the pressure until he was barely touching her. "Yes, I want more."

She felt him smile as his lips brushed over the skin under her ear. "Say please."

Her eyes popped wide, but she was still blinded by the mask. She wriggled against the bindings, resisting his command. He flicked her clitoris hard and withdrew again. Her breath caught, passion making her muscles quake with need so great it consumed her. She had to have more of him, of this. Desperate longing pounded in her veins and she could feel the sweat gathering to slide down her skin. "P-please. More. Now."

"Such a good girl." His chest vibrated with suppressed laughter, and she hissed at him, but the sound cut off as his fingers plunged between her lips. Two of his long digits worked into her channel, stroking hard and fast.

Her pussy flexed around his fingers, her hips snapping forward to take him as deep as she could. She turned her head toward him, rotating her torso in a way that strained her bound arms. "Miguel. Oh, my God. I need to come. Right now. Please, please, pl—"

Catching her lips with his, he filled her mouth with his tongue. She sucked on it, biting down lightly. He grunted, flicking a nail over her clit in response. She jolted, her sex fisting tight, but it wasn't enough to push her into orgasm. A whimper bubbled up in her throat. Their mouths went wild on each other in a dance of lips, teeth, and tongue. His taste was so hot, it intoxicated her. Their panting breaths mingled, his scent filling her nostrils.

The fork now circled her belly button, each pass over her belly taking it lower and lower until it scraped over the tops of her thighs. The pointed tines drew swirling patterns on the insides of her legs, sometimes soft and tickling, sometimes hard and painful. His fingers still thrust into her pussy, his thumb rubbing in quick strokes over her hard clit.

She didn't know what to expect, she couldn't predict what he would do next. It was too much. Far too much for her to handle. His fingertips angled in until they hit her in just the right spot. Her mouth broke from his and a low cry tore from her. *"Miguel."*

"Come for me, Andrea."

Every muscle in her body locked in a rigid line, her mouth opening in a silent scream as an orgasm slammed into her. It pulled her under like a riptide, tumbling her over and over. His hands kept moving, the sensations drawing out her pleasure. When it finally ended, it left her sagging against him.

His hard cock brushed against her clasped fingers and she relaxed them so she could cup his dick in her palms, stroke her fingertips over the long, hot silken length of him. She wanted his cock inside her pussy. Her mouth watered with the need to suck him. She wanted more. Again.

He closed his hands over her shoulders, removed himself from her touch, and pulled her around so she faced him. She wished she could see his expression through the blindfold so she would know if she'd pleased him. His voice came out a rough order. "On your knees."

She sank down, the carpet rasping against her shins. It was just one more sensation piling on top of the others. It was too good. She felt drugged, hazy. Somehow she knew this is what she'd been looking for the first time. Miguel knew what she needed . . . and she knew he'd give it to her. A whimper slid from her mouth.

Seeking him blindly, her forehead rested against the soft hair that covered his muscular thigh. "I want to suck you. Please, let me."

She heard his breath stop and the little fork clatter to the floor beside her, felt a shudder run through his big body. His fingers brushed against her jaw. "Then do it."

The head of his dick brushed her cheek and she turned her face until it pressed against her lips. She flicked her tongue against the broad crest, catching the salty moisture that beaded there. The lingering sweetness of strawberries mingled with his darker, more carnal flavor. The combination was erotic.

Opening her mouth to take him in, she suckled the head for a moment before she sank down on his cock. Her tongue laved the underside of his dick, her teeth scraping his flesh oh so lightly.

His groan told her how much he enjoyed what she was doing. It made pleasure zing through her chest. Her hips pumped as desire so hot it burned her rolled through her system. Her pussy clenched on nothingness and it didn't matter. She quivered right on the edge of orgasm as she sucked his cock so deep her throat contracted.

"Yes. Harder." His hands cradled her face as she moved in quick back and forth motions.

Excitement twisted inside her and her whole world came down to this. The taste of him, the knowledge that she was exactly where she wanted to be, doing what she wanted to be doing. With him. Her mate.

Something inside her snapped and she lost herself to the moment. It was a rush she'd never experienced before, sexual and yet . . . not.

"Enough." He pushed her away and she sat back on her heels. She squeaked in surprise when he scooped her into his arms and tossed her on the bed. She bounced against the mattress, her bound wrists making her back arch. His hands curved under her thighs, rolling her onto her shoulders to take the weight off her arms. Her legs draped over his muscular shoulders. The head of his cock probed her wet entrance.

"*Dios.*" This. This was what she'd been longing for. This final connection.

He stretched her wide when he pushed into her pussy. The position she was in made the penetration just . . . perfect. He started a slow, deep rhythm that drove her mad with frustration. "Faster, Miguel."

"No. We'll go as fast or as slow as I want to. And you'll enjoy every moment of it." One arm slid under her ass to lift her into his thrusts while the other hand moved up her ribs to tweak her nipples. He rolled them between his fingers one at a time, raking his claws over the hard tips.

She swallowed. Hell, yes, she was enjoying every moment of this. She still wanted more. Clamping her pussy tight around his dick each time he withdrew, she heard him groan. The sound made her smile. She loved how much she pleased him, it fed needs in her that ran deeper than she'd ever guessed.

He drew his claws down her stomach, moving until each hand held her legs against his shoulders. His thrusts quickened until he pounded inside her at a punishing speed. She loved it. It was exactly what she craved. His claws dug into her thighs, his grip tightening to the point of pain. Her hips arched to get closer, to move faster.

Sweet agony whipped through her, and tears slid from the corners of her eyes to soak into the blindfold. Her breath choked on soft sobs. Her skin felt too hot, too tight. Any moment she was going to disintegrate into a million little pieces.

"Andrea," he groaned. His hips froze for a moment and a great shudder wracked his body. Then he slammed his pelvis forward once, twice, three more times, rotating to grind against her clit. "I want more from you. Come for me now."

That was all the encouragement she needed. Her sex clenched around his cock, the tight feel only adding to her pleasure. Tingles raced over her flesh and she twisted in his arms. Every ounce of control left her and she was nothing more than the explosive sensations that rocketed through her system, pushing her further than she'd ever been before. A low, desperate keen slid from her mouth as it went on and on.

"That's it. Just like that." He lifted her and cuddled her close as she broke into harsh sobs. Loosening the tie, he freed her from the restraint, and then pulled away the blindfold. "Shh. Shh. You were so wonderful, so perfect."

"Miguel." She wrapped her arms around his neck, burying her face against his throat. The pulse point there still hammered and his chest rose and fell in pants.

He slid his hand over her hair, rocking her from side to side, soothing her with gentle care. It made her cry all the harder. Never in her life had she felt this close to another person. Her fingers balled in his long silken hair.

Their heartbeats slowed and a strange lethargy sapped at her will to move. She wanted nothing more than to stay in his arms forever. A tiny warning went off in the back of her mind at that thought, but she hadn't the energy to let it surface. She closed her eyes, relaxed and pliant in his embrace.

He lay back against the pillows, letting her legs straddle his hips as he held her tight. "Sleep now."

She obeyed without question, without thinking. At that moment, she was completely his. Consciousness slid away and dreams took her.

5

"Ooh, look!"

Miguel turned to glance at Andrea, blinking as she dragged him into a well-appointed jewelry store and over to a display case. The feel of her slim fingers tightening around his was too sweet. It was something he hadn't experienced with her yet.

He tried to remind himself to enjoy it and tamped down on the frustration that had been boiling inside him for over a week now. Since the first night she'd let him tie her up. He'd only seen her in the bedroom since then, and as delightful as it was to have her at his mercy every night, he could see now that she was using their arrangement to avoid any other intimacies with him.

The wariness he saw in her gaze outside the bedroom angered him. He'd done nothing to deserve it. Try as he might to understand that her past experiences made her unwilling to trust, it still made a hollow ache fill his chest. She was his mate and he wanted to *be* her mate. He doubted very much that she felt the same. Damn it.

The only reason he was seeing her now was that Solana had

had an intense craving for saltwater taffy from some God-awful tourist trap of a shop down by Pier 39, and she'd volunteered both of them for the job of fetching the candy. He'd picked up the taffy and dropped it off at the limo, but insisted that Andrea have dinner with him. He could tell she wanted to protest, but the driver wasn't going anywhere without Miguel's say-so and she knew it. Smart woman.

The fading rays of sunlight caught on the necklace she pointed out. It was a fire opal hanging from the slimmest chain he'd ever seen. It almost looked as though the gem were floating. She smiled. "Isn't it lovely?"

"Not as lovely as you." She blinked, flushed, and glanced away. So many facets. At once shy and bold. It fascinated him. She was like the stone, cool and composed at first glance, but a closer look revealed the fire that flashed beneath the surface.

The saleswoman bustled over. "Is there anything I can help you with?"

Andrea's grin returned. "Oh, no. We're just look—"

"We'll take that one, please." He tapped the glass over the fire opal.

She flipped open the case and pulled out the small stand that held the necklace. Andrea stroked a finger over the gem, an avid gleam shining in her eyes. Then she fisted her hand, let her arm drop, and shook her head at him. "You can't buy this. It's extravagant."

"But you want it and you won't get it for yourself, will you?" He tugged his wallet out of his slacks and dropped a credit card on the counter. He winked at her. "Besides . . . I can buy anything I want to."

"Of course he can." The tiny saleswoman whisked his card away to ring up his purchase.

He plucked up the thin chain, motioning for Andrea to turn around. She spun, glancing over her shoulder at him. "It's too much."

"You're worth it." He lifted the chain up and over her head to fasten it. He took the opportunity to press a kiss to the nape of her neck and then looped his arms around her waist. Possession wound through him, and he found he liked the idea of her wearing something he gave her, something that marked her as his. "Never take it off."

She stiffened, her shoulders bowing away from him as she shimmied from his embrace. "You don't get to tell me what to do outside the bedroom. I'll wear what I want, when I want."

A muscle began ticking in his jaw when he clenched his teeth. It was the tenth reminder he'd had from her of their rules, and it was starting to wear his patience thin. She used it as a way to never have to trust him any further than she already had, to keep him at arm's length. As if he could ever betray her—he held on to his temper by the tips of his Panther claws and forced himself to smile. "Hasn't anyone ever told you to accept a gift graciously?"

Vulnerability flashed in her gaze as she covered the opal with her palm. "I've never had a gift with no strings attached."

He closed his eyes and sighed, suddenly weary. Their sales clerk returned his card to him and he pocketed the receipt. Taking Andrea's arm, he escorted her out of the shop. "Let's go eat."

A few moments later, they were seated in a small seafood restaurant he'd discovered his first week in the city. She leaned forward and fiddled with the salt shaker in the middle of the round, glass table. "Will you return to Rio de Janeiro to become leader the way Antonio did?"

"Ah . . . no." He blinked. In the time he'd known her, she'd avoided almost all personal conversations with him. "I'm not the Pride leader's heir. I'll remain here for as long as your brother wishes me to."

She met his gaze for a moment. Her fingers lifted to the necklace again and she offered up a tentative smile. "It's unusual to have a non-heir or someone not directly in line for the leadership as Second. How did that happen?"

"It's complicated." He sat back in his chair, enjoying the rare opportunity to have her to himself for a meal. Patience. As good as he was at remaining patient in most circumstances, he found it difficult with her. He wanted her too much to want to wait. "I am the Pride leader's grandson, and my Uncle Pedro wasn't interested in being a Second again as he'd just returned from Spain when Esteban died and Antonio had to leave. Antonio suggested—and my family agreed—that I go in my uncle's place."

The conversation paused while they gave their orders to the waiter. Andrea took a sip of her water. "How likely is it you'll ever lead the South American Pride?"

"My Uncle Pedro, his son and daughter, and his daughter's two children . . . *and* my father would all have to die. Very unlikely."

He watched her cross her long legs through the glass table. Her short skirt rode up to expose her slim thigh. "Do you miss Brazil?"

"I do, but I enjoy San Francisco a great deal. More so every passing moment." His eyes slid down her body possessively. Damn, she was so beautiful.

She sucked her bottom lip between her teeth, the briefest shimmer of gold sparkling through her midnight irises. The tank top that she wore did little to hide her hardening nipples. Her voice emerged in a breathless rush. "I don't want to be locked in San Francisco forever. I would miss traveling."

Enjoying the byplay between them, he reached for her hand when she set down her water glass. "You liked constantly moving around?"

"At first it was exciting, forbidden." Her fingers twined with his as she looked down at the table. "I never expected to be allowed to go anywhere that wasn't another Pride den. Then it became routine, and I liked that I looked at a new skyline every few days or weeks."

His gaze narrowed on her face. He wished she would accept that she couldn't leave after Solana gave birth. It could be hazardous not only for the Pride, but also for Andrea. What would happen if someone decided to use her against her brother? She would be alone, defenseless. The very idea of her in danger made Miguel's grip tighten on her hand. He made his voice soft, cajoling. "Your brother would still allow you to travel, though not as much as now. And you'd be forced to obey the customs of the Prides, asking for permission to enter a continent controlled by another leader."

She sighed and looked away. "I know what my duties are. Esteban never allowed me to forget them or who I was in the Panther world."

"It's not a bad thing to know your place in the world." He lifted her palm and kissed the center of it.

A shiver ran through her slender body, and he smiled. He loved that she always reacted to his touch. It gave him hope that they had a future together. The corners of her mouth turned down. "It is a bad thing when that's all you're ever allowed to be."

"True. We always have a choice. You made yours." He released her hand when their food arrived and sat back so the waiter could set his plate in front of him. He nodded to the young man. "Thank you."

"Of course." He cocked a hip and propped his hand on it. "Is there anything else I can get you two?"

"No, we're good." Andrea gave him a smile that was both friendly and dismissive. She turned back to Miguel when they were alone again. "I won't give up my career for the Pride. If anything, I can be more helpful as a cash cow. Solana kept her bar, I can keep my design company."

Picking up his fork, he skewered a piece of shrimp in his seafood jambalaya. "I doubt Antonio would have a problem with that."

"Would you?"

He stilled, his gaze jerking up to meet hers. Wariness slid over him and he kept his tone carefully neutral. "Does it matter to you what I think?"

"Maybe." She shrugged and focused on her meal. "Answer the question."

Since he had no way to avoid whatever conversational trap she'd set for him, he answered honestly. "I think if your career fulfills you, then you shouldn't be denied that. I love my work, and I like that you love yours as well."

"Thank you." She nodded, but didn't look up again and they ate in silence. He sighed, the frustration he'd been battling with coming back in a rush. It was always this way with her. One step forward, three steps back. Every time he caught a glimpse of her through the wall she'd built around herself, she covered the opening. He'd never get through to her. It tore at him to even think of the possibility. She mattered more to him every day and he had no idea what she was feeling.

"Are you almost done?" Her question drew his attention away from his morose thoughts.

"Yes. Why?" He glanced up to watch heat fill her gaze. The way her eyes lingered on his lips before dropping to his groin made his jaw clench as his cock hardened to a painful degree. The way he was feeling right now did not lend itself to any kind of civility in bed. "You don't want to toy with me, Andrea."

"No, I just want you."

The fork bent in his hand, the thick silver handle snapping in half. He set it aside, hiding the pieces with his napkin. He stood and fished out his wallet. Enough bills to cover the cost of the meal and the broken silverware landed on the table, but his gaze never left her. "Get up."

"Don't make me wait long. I need you." The soft yielding in her gaze as she rose to her feet made him want to bend her over the table and take her here and now. She was his woman, his mate, and he wanted to claim her publicly. But if all she wanted to give him was sex, he'd be damned if he wouldn't take it. His inability to resist her made him want to kick himself, but he didn't think his reaction to her would ever go away. He couldn't even say that he wanted it to.

He took her elbow in his hand, leading her out to the waiting limo. Opening the door, he thrust her inside, slid in after her and slammed the door behind him. She shoved her silky hair out of her face, kneeling on the floor in front of him. Her pupils dilated, the edges of her irises shimmering with flecks of gold. He loved when she went wild for him. She fit him so well, so perfectly.

"Home," he ordered the driver and pressed the button to close the privacy window between them and the front seat. His fingers snapped out to catch her arm and he flipped her neatly over his lap. He pushed her skirt up until the sweet curves of her ass were bared to his view. She wore the tiniest scrap of a thong. He slipped his fingers under the lace to find the slickness of her soft pussy.

Anticipation coiled like a spring inside him, waiting to snap as his palm cupped her backside. She lifted into his touch, her muscles flexing in invitation. "Miguel."

His anger burned away until he focused on this moment with her. The only way to have her was to get her past all her fears and teach her she could trust him implicitly. Wary of garnering the same reaction as the last time he'd spanked her, he brought his palm down on her ass. It was little more than a series of quick pats. She wriggled, glancing over her shoulder at him. "Are you kidding me? You have a willing half-naked woman draped over your lap and that's all you've got?"

"Oh, *really?*" He barely suppressed a laugh. "Let's see how willing you are, then."

She bucked and squealed under the next round of hard swats. The feel of her soft hip rubbing up against his cock made him grit his teeth and pant for breath as if he'd sprinted ten miles. Her skin heated under his hand, a deep flush showing under her light tan. That she trusted him enough to let herself go, to let herself enjoy this made emotion band tight around his chest.

The sound of his palm slapping against her soft skin filled the enclosed space. Never had spanking a woman turned him on so much. Everything with Andrea was deeper, sweeter. Better than he could ever have imagined.

If he didn't have her soon, he might go insane. But it would be worth it to make her wait. To tease her without mercy. *Yes.* A grin pulled at his lips as the scent of her wetness filled his nose. He slid his hand inward and found her pussy slick with juices. She moaned when he touched her. A harsh shudder wracked his body, heat fisting in his gut.

Her breath caught when he drew back his hand and smacked her between the legs. It wasn't very hard, but it would make her pussy swell. Her thighs clenched tight, and he could feel the delicate muscles flex as she moved on his lap.

"Please," she whimpered. "I need more."

"In good time." He slid his fingertips in circles over her reddened skin, occasionally scoring her with his nails. "I want to savor you, my mate."

When the car rolled to a stop, he snatched up the bag of candy they'd retrieved for Solana and pulled Andrea out of the limo behind him. Without pausing, he scooped her up and flipped her over his shoulder to carry her into the mansion.

Her arms wrapped around his waist from behind. "Hurry, Miguel."

As soon as he cleared the doorway, he saw several Panthers gathered in the foyer, including the Cruz family. Every last one of them froze and gaped at them as he walked by. He tossed the bag of taffy to Diego. "Give this to Solana. Don't eat any of it, and don't bother us for the rest of the night. We're busy."

"Uh, sure thing, Miguel."

He jogged up the stairs, careful not to jolt Andrea too much, and kicked his bedroom door shut behind him. He dropped her on the bed and had her stripped bare in under thirty seconds. He didn't let himself pause to savor her soft curves; he set her on the floor on her knees. "Stay there. Don't move."

After a week, he didn't have to make sure she obeyed him. He knew she would. Flicking open his closet door, he went to a chest that held a collection of toys for just this kind of sexual play. Tucking a short black crop under his arm, he reached in and pulled out one made up of steel bars that formed an X. On the end of each bar was a thick leather cuff.

He watched her eyes widen when she saw the heavy-duty piece of equipment. Unlike the soft bindings he'd used on her so far, she wouldn't be able to easily escape even with her Panther strength. She would be at his mercy. He set the crop aside and knelt behind her. Her breath caught when he strapped her ankles and wrists into the cuffs. The metal rattled and groaned when she tested its strength, but the crossbar held.

He liked the way the diagonal bars framed the rosy cheeks of her ass, the center point of the X right under the lower curve. Scooping up the crop, he stood and ran the soft leather slapper down one of her arms and across her lower back. "Are you ready?"

Her back arched and she lifted her backside into the tip of the whip. "I can take whatever you can dish out. Make it hurt."

He wanted to laugh, but he refused to let her goad a reaction out of him. Instead, he continued to stroke her skin lightly with the crop. She wriggled in the restraints, making the cuffs jangle. He flicked her with a short pop, knowing it would sting. She squeaked in response.

The next strike landed on the outside of her thigh. It left a slight red spot, and he loved seeing that he'd left a mark on her. It called up every possessive instinct inside of him, and he fought a groan. His cock was so hard, it throbbed painfully. His skin was on fire, he wanted her more than he'd ever wanted a woman before. It killed him to wait to fuck her, but he would. He wanted to draw this out as long as possible.

Sweat gleamed on her smooth skin, rolling down her neck and between her breasts in slow beads. Her soft moans kissed his ears, and as much as she resisted, he knew she was yielding with the way her body undulated toward the whip. The energy flowing back and forth between them was intense, give and take, ebb and flow . . . there was nothing more powerful in his experience than this.

He moved around her, laying a quick series of smacks on the tops of her legs. The bars kept her spread open for him, so even when her thigh muscles flexed, she was helpless to close herself to him. He knelt to lay the crop across the insides of her legs, and the skin flushed.

Her eyes had a soft, glazed look, her breath short and shallow. He paused with the whip mid-swing and let his arm relax to his side, reaching out with his free hand to stroke her shoulder. "Andrea?"

"Mmm?" Her voice was dreamy, distant.

"*Andrea.*" Concern flooded him at her detached response. He moved back a bit so that he wasn't touching her and squatted down to look at her. "Are you—"

Her eyes snapped wide, desperate heat reflecting in their dark depths. "*Green light.* If you don't fuck me hard and make me come right now, I'm going to die. The light, Miguel, has never been so green."

A low laugh rumbled from his chest. God, he loved this woman. The emotion threatened to overwhelm him and made his hands shake with the power of it. He dropped the crop, and leaned forward to speak softly in her ear. "Do you know what I love about seeing a woman bound?"

"No." Her voice emerged a breathless whisper.

"That I can do anything I want to her." His fingers brushed between her legs while his other hand cupped her breast, pinching her nipple hard. "That she's helpless to stop me from taking her. The possibilities are endless. Should I be slow and tease her? Should I be fast and rough?"

She moaned. Her hips moved in quick snaps to take his fingers deeper. His cock throbbed as he watched her work herself faster and faster on his hand. Sweat slid down his face to sting his eyes. Her breathing sped to rapid pants, her lovely face flushing with need. Yes, he loved seeing her this way. Not cool and beautiful, but stripped of composure and completely wanton. The little noises she was making told him just how close she was to orgasm, and he was damn near ready to come in his pants he was so turned on.

He jerked his hand away.

"*No*. I can't wait. Please, *please*, Miguel." Her head fell back and tears leaked from the corners of her eyes. "Please."

He found he could wait no longer either. Rising to his feet, he toed off his shoes and socks while he unbuttoned his shirt halfway and yanked it over his head. The buttons caught on his hair tie, ripping it loose and making his hair stream into his face. He tossed it over his shoulder and had his belt and slacks off so fast he was surprised he didn't give himself a rug burn.

Rug burn. He eyed the carpet Andrea was kneeling on, wondering how the rough texture of it would feel against her chafed backside. Wickedness twisted inside him and he grinned.

"Let me suck you." Her gaze glued to his cock, and he groaned at the avid gleam in her eyes.

He hooked his hair behind his ears. "No."

A low sob sounded from her throat. "Please, I want you. I need *more*. Between my legs, in my mouth, I don't care. Just . . . *now*. I'm dying."

Unbuckling the cuffs, he rubbed her arms and legs to make sure blood circulated through her limbs. He tossed the crossbar aside and turned back to her. Her fingers buried in the long strands of his hair, using her inhuman strength to force his mouth down to hers. She bit his lip hard enough to draw blood and thrust her tongue in to mate with his.

He groaned, sliding his hands down to cup her ass and pull her body against his. Her nipples rubbed his chest and he could feel the heat of her pussy against his swollen cock. He lifted her up and she wrapped her legs around his hips, her feet tucking under his buttocks.

Leaning forward, he laid her out across the carpet and came over her. He braced his hands on either side of her shoulders. Her claws dug into his back, her hips rising in blatant invitation. It was one he couldn't refuse.

Taking his cock in his hand, he rubbed the tip over her hot, wet lips. He had to clench his jaw it felt so amazing. He couldn't wait any longer. He was done teasing. He plunged his dick inside her to the hilt, her creamy depth wrapping around his heated flesh. The musky scent of her called to him, and his instinct dared him to claim her as his mate. His fangs slid forward and a Panther's snarl ripped out. Her eyes went pure gold, and her slim thighs clamped around his waist, already moving herself on his cock.

A rusty chuckle slid out of his mouth and he pinned her to the carpet with his weight. Her eyes widened when he thrust hard inside her and it moved them across the floor. Unless he missed his guess, the rug was chafing her sore ass. Excellent. He purred and shoved into her again and again. His wits fled and soon there wasn't a single thought left in his mind except the drive toward orgasm.

"Miguel, I'm coming." Her body bowed so hard, she lifted him with her. He braced his knees on the floor and hammered into her with hard thrusts, riding her through her orgasm. Her pussy flexed on his cock, and it was so damn good. He shuddered, moving faster and faster. She slid her fingers into his hair, her claws scraping against his scalp as she pulled him down. Her mouth fused with his in a kiss that was animalistic in its intensity.

I love you. The words rang in his head, wrapped around his heart until he couldn't breathe, and the power of it shoved him into orgasm. His pelvis slammed against her, and her tight pussy hugged his cock like a glove. The rhythmic clenching of her sex milked him and he exploded inside her. His arms shook with the effort of holding himself over her, so he pulled from her sweet depths with a reluctant groan and let her roll out from under him.

She curled on her side away from him and the gesture gutted him. Would she ever turn *to* him? He wasn't sure anymore. It felt like ice water being splashed in his face after the intimacies they'd just shared. God help him. Was there a worse fate for a man? To love a woman—a *mate*—and have her feel nothing in return? If there was he'd yet to find it. The pain of her constant rejection burned like the fires of Hell.

What would he do if she never changed her mind, if she never learned to trust him and believe in their future?

6

Andrea hadn't slept. Miguel hadn't let her rest for a single moment. He'd been relentless. No sleeping meant no healing, and she didn't know what drove him to such carnal depths, but her ass still smarted the next night when she crawled out of his bed to start her work. Now she sat with her sister-in-law in the study, keeping her company while Antonio went out to run an errand. She squirmed on her seat, the movement making heat swell between her legs. Running her hand through her hair, she looked for something to distract her and her gaze landed on Solana's burgeoning middle. "I still can't believe you didn't shift until you were in your thirties."

"Yep, and look where it got me." She chuckled and smoothed a palm over her stomach. "Your brother knocked me up."

Andrea laughed. "In some ways, it's unfortunate we can't have children as easily as humans."

"But imagine what things would be like if we could. We'd probably edge into overpopulation rather than under." Shifting uncomfortably, her belly rippled under her hand. "You know there are two non-shifters who live here now, right?"

"Wh-what?" That dragged Andrea's full attention away from contemplating her marathon sex with Miguel. Non-shifters were incredibly rare, which was probably for the best considering how most of the Panther world treated them. She hadn't noticed anything out of the ordinary about any Panther she'd run into here, but non-shifters looked and smelled like other Panthers in their human shape. They just couldn't assume animal form. Now she wondered which of the Pride members they were.

"After Antonio mated with me we were contacted by a male who'd been cast out. When we accepted him the other came forward as well to join us." Solana grinned and wrinkled her nose. "So we have all the non-shifters—and former non-shifters—on the planet in our Pride."

"Wow." That was a courageous step forward for her brother. If anything could prove to her that her brother would never be like her father, it was this. It warmed her to know all her brothers had turned out well and that the Pride was in good hands. She sniffed the air, but didn't scent either of the twins or Miguel. As far as she knew only Antonio had gone out. "Where is everyone?"

"At the airport. The guys decided to make a showing together." Her sister-in-law yawned, her foot bouncing restlessly against the hardwood floor. "Carmen is flying in today with her mate."

"Carmen left the Pride?" Her eyebrows arched. She never would have guessed that Carmen might leave North America unless she mated to someone in a ruling family from another Pride and had no choice. Carmen was the type to cling tightly to her roots, not seek out adventure ... they'd known each other all their lives, but they'd never been close because Andrea was mouthy and rebellious and it had shocked Carmen to her traditionalist soul. She'd never have spoken to her Pride leader the way Andrea had.

Solana rolled her head against the plush leather chair she sat in until she looked Andrea in the eyes. "She didn't have a choice. Her mate was a human."

"Holy shit." That would mean he couldn't change forms and most Prides would treat Carmen no better than a non-shifter. A human mate meant no children for Carmen. Poor girl. She'd always been about hearth and home—or as much as any oversexed Panther could be. Thinking of sex made her think of Miguel. She sighed, leaning back and wincing a little when her sore skin slid against leather.

"Antonio didn't make her an outcast."

"Good." It made sense that if he'd take in non-shifters, he'd let a Panther mated to a human stay in the Pride.

"She needs to take the loyalty oath to the new heir as well." Solana patted her belly and crooned gently to the child inside her. "Isn't that right?"

Andrea grinned at the unexpected softness on her sister-in-law's face. "Are you hoping for a boy or a girl? And don't say 'either as long as it's healthy'."

"Either as long as it's healthy." Solana pulled a face. "Though I'm rooting for a girl just because we need more estrogen in this family. The twins, Antonio, and Miguel are a ton of combined testosterone. I need backup."

Andrea laughed. "So, you don't assume I'm staying when the baby is born?"

"I try not to assume anything. I leave that up to the political strategists. I'm just a businesswoman."

"And a successful one at that." She stretched her arms over her head, enjoying the sweet twinge in her muscles. As much as she'd resisted, she was starting to assume she'd stay as well. It was still too new, too terrifying to talk about it with anyone—especially not Miguel. What if she couldn't do it? She wasn't cruel enough get his hopes up. And if she stayed there would be definite pressure for her to mate with him. She wasn't ready for that, not to bind herself to any man *forever.*

"You're not doing so bad yourself. I love your clothes. Though I can't fit into any of them just now." Solana poked at her stomach, a look of exaggerated sorrow on her face.

Andrea blinked and narrowed her gaze on her sister-in-law. She'd never even considered a maternity line. And wouldn't that be an entertaining fashion show—pregnant models. A wicked grin crossed her face. Maybe Solana would strut down the runway for her. The need to sketch raced through her. Her fingers twitched as images flashed through her head, different ways to highlight the beauty of the female form during pregnancy flashing through her mind.

It would be an interesting branching out for her company. She'd done women's and men's wear. Why not maternity? It would certainly be controversial in high fashion. And she did like to take a risk every now and then, just to shake things up a bit. She tilted her head, considering.

A hand waved in front of her face, making her jolt and sit up. "What?"

"Earth to Andrea." Solana smiled. "Did I lose you?"

"I'm here. Sorry. Just had an idea for a new Pantheras line."

She tilted her head to the side. "You'll have to show me when you sketch it. Sorry it has to wait. Antonio expects us to be here for Carmen's arrival. And frankly, I think having women around might scare her human less—especially women who've spent a great deal of time with humans."

The image of four large, muscled Panther males greeting a terrified human made Andrea laugh. "Poor guy."

"Seriously." Her sister-in-law dissolved into giggles with her.

Andrea wiped tears of mirth from her eyes, trying to regain her composure. "Does he know?"

"If he does—"

She nodded. "He shouldn't. Yeah, we have rules about it . . . but could you keep it from your mate? I mean, really keep it from your *mate?*"

"No." A worried frown creased Solana's forehead. Security was a constant issue for Panthers. No one could ever know about their kind. They'd be hunted to extinction or turned into lab rats. Andrea shuddered at the possibility.

She pulled in a deep breath and tried to ignore the serious breach Carmen had potentially caused. "So he knows."

"I'm guessing yes . . . or else she wouldn't be bringing him with her, would she?"

"Good point."

Solana shrugged, a wry grin pulling at her mouth. "Then again, would I go that long without my mate? The bed would get *really* lonely."

"I don't want to know."

She laughed. "Oh, please. Your brothers are more open about their sex lives than any three men I have ever met. And that includes the drunk ones who patronize my bar."

"Damn." Andrea rolled her eyes. "Yeah, Antonio was always pretty out of the closet with his stuff. And the twins were already doing things men twice their age shouldn't when I left. Bad boys."

"They'd take that as a compliment."

"I'm so surprised," she replied, sotto voce.

Solana burst into laughter, her chocolate eyes twinkling. "Exactly. They aren't very subtle."

"Except about the fact that they're smart." Andrea crossed her legs, the insides of her thighs stinging from Miguel's whipping. The reminder made her sex throb with want. Would she ever get enough of him? She didn't think so, and it terrified her to think of being so dependent on anyone. What if he turned on her the way other men had in her life? She tried to reassure herself that Miguel wasn't like that—he was her *mate*—but reason and fear didn't often match up.

Solana drew her attention back to the here and now. "Yeah,

the twins weren't a threat to your father if they were stupid . . . until they were suddenly useful behind the scenes. Either way, they never challenged his authority."

"Unlike Antonio and me." Andrea grinned. It was too true. She and Antonio had been very public about their disagreements with their father. In many ways, it was why they'd been unable to stay. Their father had shipped Antonio off to be Second in South America for almost ten years longer than was considered acceptable by Panther standards . . . and Andrea had just left the Panther world completely. She wasn't sure if the twins' strategy hadn't been smarter.

"Yeah. All of you have your own strengths."

"And weaknesses."

The front door opened and the sound of male voices and laughter trickled in to the study. Andrea rose to her feet and reached for Solana when she struggled. Concern swamped her that her sister-in-law seemed to be having a difficult pregnancy. Then again, what did she know about pregnancy? The modeling world was dominated by bony, flat-chested teenagers. She hadn't exactly paid attention to the normal course of Panther pregnancies when she was a bony, flat-chested teen herself. Of course, she was still on the skinny side.

A tall, wiry man walked in with Antonio and Miguel flanking him. Human, by the smell of him. This had to be Carmen's mate. The three men were in animated conversation, gesturing widely. Carmen followed a few steps behind with a half-panicked, half-dumbfounded look on her face. Not that Andrea blamed her for the terror at returning to the Pride. She'd done enough freaking out when she'd had to come back, and Carmen's reception was much less certain than her own.

Carmen's mate pushed a hand through his hair, still addressing Antonio. "The thing is, sir, you have a top of the line security system, but it was designed to keep out unwanted *humans*. A Panther can move a hell of a lot faster than a normal person.

You'll need to modify the whole system for your specific needs."

"Hard to explain those needs to a human security contractor." Miguel quirked a brow up.

Antonio smacked a hand on the human's shoulder. "Excellent, let's discuss how you're going to handle it for us."

The man blinked and then flashed a brilliant smile. "Okay, then."

"I love it when he talks all nerdy. It gets me hot." Carmen gave her a surreptitious wink as she sidled up to stand beside Andrea. She gave Solana a quick nod.

Andrea snorted on a laugh. "With the legion of 'all brawn no brains' boys you shagged . . . I love that you ended up with a geekly one."

"Your brothers have brains and brawn." Carmen arched a brow and smirked.

"I was going on your entire track record. At least the part I know about. And, please, who hasn't had one or *two* of my brothers?"

"Or all three. I think I might be one of the few who can claim that."

"That's probably for the best." Especially considering the twins' predilection for tag teaming women, it could happen all in one setting. Solana was right about them being very, very open about their sexuality. Then again, it wasn't as if she was shy about her own past. It was just Miguel who wanted to push her further than she was comfortable going. Now. If he had been her father's Second back then, things would have turned out so differently. Her whole life wouldn't have happened. It was an unsettling thought.

"Not that it matters now. I have Landon. And as hot as the Cruzes are . . . they can't compare to a mate."

"Even a human?"

Carmen's shoulder lifted in a delicate shrug. "It's a magic connection, Andrea. It's not about species."

"I wouldn't know."

"Antonio mentioned that you and Miguel—"

"Yeah."

"You don't seem happy." She slid her hands into her jacket pockets.

"All you wanted was to stay in the Pride. All I wanted was to stay out."

She rocked her hand back and forth through the air. "That's what I thought I wanted. Obviously, I changed my mind. Though I do miss the Pride a great deal."

"I don't think Antonio's going to let you leave any more than he'll let me." Andrea sighed. "He's got non-shifters here . . . why not a human mated to a Panther?"

"He's very different from your father. Your mother had a lot of influence there."

"True." She wasn't old enough to remember much about her mother's political influence on the Pride, but she knew things had changed drastically after her death. Their father had gone from doting husband to rigid Pride leader with no room for his growing children. Meeting Miguel made her realize just how . . . lost . . . her father must have been when his mate died. An unwelcome pang of empathy went through her.

There was so much he had said and done that she couldn't forgive. So much damage he had done to her and her brothers. So much intolerance he had encouraged to flourish in their Pride. But . . . they had all survived. Whether the experience had left them stronger was yet to be seen, but the reality of having a mate and the depth of connection she felt for him without marking him or being marked by him shook her. What would it be like to bite him, to mark him, be mated to him for decades and just lose him? Alone for the rest of her life. It made her father more sympathetic to consider how it must have affected him.

She was also grateful it hadn't driven him completely insane. Though rare, such a thing wasn't unheard of in the Prides. As much as she despised some of his choices, his actions, she had a new respect for the strength he had had in simply surviving.

A sigh slid past her throat. Everything was so jumbled up. When she'd arrived here she'd known exactly who she was and where her life was going. Now? She was just working to keep her head above water in the sea of change her life had become. And she was pretty sure she was swimming against the tide.

She jerked when her cell phone rang in her pocket. She tugged it out and read the main office line for Pantheras Designs on the display. Cocking her wrist, she checked her watch. It was well after midnight in New York. While everyone knew she kept late hours, it was unusual for anyone to call this late. Why were they even still in the office?

She frowned and glanced up to see everyone had returned to the room and they all stared at her questioningly. Carmen raced forward to embrace her mate, contentment shining on her face. Miguel's expression was a mixture of expectation, disappointment, and sadness. It was a look that was all too familiar. She gave a weak smile. "I have to take this. Work. Excuse me."

Turning on her heel, she fled the room. If she was relieved to take the call and not have to hear Carmen coo over Landon or regale Miguel with the wonders of mating, it was no one's business but hers.

His grandfather had died in his sleep the night before. Miguel crossed his arms over his chest, reclined against the mantle of the big fireplace in Antonio's study and closed his eyes. A voice-mail had been waiting for him in his office when he and Andrea had hauled themselves out of the bed they'd done everything but sleep in.

A bittersweet pang hit him. His grandfather had lived a long, full life. One any Panther would be proud of. But it meant

Miguel had to leave to take the loyalty oath to his Uncle Pedro, the new South American Pride leader.

With Carmen and her mate's arrival, he'd put off telling the Cruzes—Andrea—as long as possible, but he was running out of time.

The truth was he didn't want to leave. He wanted to remain, but as a member of the ruling family of South America, he could never stay here without it causing a political problem for Antonio. And yet . . . his uncle and cousins would rule now that his grandfather passed away. Andrea outranked him in her Pride . . . if she lived here after her brother's heir was born *and* if they mated, he could remain forever. The solution was so simple and too complicated for words.

He opened his mouth to tell them, when Andrea came back into the room and said the same sentence that had been on the tip of his tongue.

"I have to go." Her words fell like an anvil over the crowd gathered in Antonio's study. Miguel straightened from his position against the mantle.

He arched a brow, instantly concerned by the worry on her face. "Go where?"

"To New York. There's a problem with the new line and I have to take care of it."

"Can't someone else do it?" Ric set his hands on his hips. "Or why can't they e-mail the information to you like they've been doing for the last few weeks?"

"Look, some things I have to take care of in person. I have clients to make nice with. They pay a lot of money to meet with the CEO, not some stand-in. *I have to leave.* I've already booked myself a seat on the red-eye out of SFO tonight, and I'll be back as soon as I can."

Ric shoved a hand through his shaggy dark hair and turned to Miguel. "Solana could pop any day now and she has to be here. You can't let her leave, man."

"I won't." If there was a touch of irony to his voice, he doubted the younger man heard it. He honestly thought Miguel could snap his fingers and Andrea would obey. Right. Of course. That had worked so well for every other man who'd known her, he was sure.

Andrea's mouth fell open, her face paled, and a look of betrayal flashed through her ebony eyes. "What makes you think you have any say in where I go or what I do?"

"I was teasing." Shit. Of all the times for her not to hear his sarcasm. He lifted his hands in supplication. "Don't you think you're overreacting?"

She snarled, spun on her heel, and stomped out. Antonio, Diego, Ric, and even the human Landon favored him with looks of sympathetic pity. Solana made a scornful noise. "As long as I've known you, I've considered you a pretty smart man. That, my friend, was a really *stupid* thing to say."

His eyes met hers and then moved to his best friend. "My grandfather is dead. I leave for Rio de Janeiro in the morning. Forgive me if I was tactless."

"I-I'm sorry." Solana stepped forward and hugged him. He had to lean over her stomach to return her embrace. She whispered in his ear, "I don't want you to go."

"But I have to." Yes, he did. Andrea's reaction was one more reminder that she would never really give in and belong to him. Her body? Yes. Her heart and soul . . . her love? No. She'd been honest with him from the very first. She gave no more than she was willing to part with. He was the fool who craved her like a drug. Something painful broke inside him, and his hope fled. He was so tired . . . he couldn't even think anymore. He just . . . hurt in a way he'd never imagined possible.

He stepped back and let himself be caught in a bear hug by Diego and then Ric. Last was Antonio. What could he say to a man who'd been his best friend and closest ally for the better part of two decades? There was no real way to say good-bye. So he didn't.

Offering a hand, he clasped Antonio's forearm. The other man hauled him forward into an embrace. If there were tears in their eyes when they pulled away, they'd never admit it. Antonio cleared his throat and clapped Miguel on the shoulder. "Don't be a stranger. You're a part of this family and you are *always* welcome here."

"I know. Brother." But neither of them had any way of knowing if they'd ever see each other again. Miguel was at the mercy of his Pride leader's whims. He went where he was needed and served as he was told. "I have to say good-bye to Andrea."

Antonio nodded. "With any luck, she'll come around . . . soon."

"Don't hold your breath. She's at least as stubborn as you." Miguel glanced away. "I think it really is good-bye. I wish things were different, but they aren't."

He climbed the stairs, each footstep echoing in his head like a death knell. He just wanted this over with. Having her in his arms and being no closer to having her as his mate than the first moment he'd seen her was more than he could bear. It was time.

Not bothering to knock, he walked into Andrea's room. She met his gaze briefly from where she was stuffing clothes in a suitcase and sighed. "Look, you're not talking me out of this. And don't tell me I overreacted. You know how—"

Sudden anger whip-lashed through him. All of his frustrations over the last weeks came boiling out. "You're still waiting for me to betray you. Every second of every day, Andrea."

Her eyes went wide and she paused in her packing. "I'm not."

"You are." He shoved a hand through his hair, ripping it loose from the tie. "You're treating me as though I were *them.*

Your father. His Second. I have never broken a promise to you, never hurt you."

"We only just met." She looked everywhere but him, her fingers fidgeting with a silky shirt.

He shook his head, his anger vanishing as quickly as it had come. If anything, he felt more drained. Grit burned his eyes, pain and loss and too many other emotions for him to sort out ricocheted through his heart. "You don't even see me."

"I see you." She dropped the garment and stepped toward him, some new fear shining in her gaze. "I see what most of the Pride doesn't."

"Yes, but is that all?" He lifted his hands and let them drop. "You don't see that it would kill me to hurt you, but you expect it of me anyway. Always waiting for that other shoe to drop, never trusting me. Or maybe you just don't want to see. It doesn't really matter anymore."

Tears misted her beautiful dark eyes as she walked toward him with her hand outstretched. "Miguel, please. Don't do this to us."

"Is there an us, Andrea?" As much as he wanted to hold her, to comfort her, he forced himself to move back toward the door. "Just because we're mates doesn't mean we'll ever *be* mated. And I'm beginning to believe that maybe that's for the best."

Her hands covered her mouth, smothering a sob. He flinched. It ripped his heart out to leave her, but if she couldn't give them the chance of a future together, then it was torment to both of them if he continued to beat his head against the brick wall that surrounded her heart. Whipping around, he made himself walk away from the only woman he could ever love.

What had just happened? Andrea staggered under the emotional blows that just kept coming. Her breathing was ragged as she tried to force the tears back. He didn't want her anymore.

Oh, God. Wrapping her arms around her waist, she followed him into his room. It couldn't be over. It couldn't end this way.

"Is it because I'm going to New York without you?" Her words sounded stupid and childish to her own ears, but her mind spun in confused circles. "Is it because I didn't ask you first?"

"Your business affairs are your own concern. I told you I wouldn't interfere with that and I haven't. If you wanted to invest some actual emotion and commitment into a relationship, it would be a good idea to talk to him before you make big decisions. Who knows, he might be able to help. I'm sure you'll remember that for the next man." His voice held bitter sarcasm, but his eyes were hollow, his face blank. None of the understanding she'd come to rely on was left. He huffed out an impatient breath, turning to walk into his closet and pull out several trunks and a large duffel bag. "It will always be a test for you, won't it? You'll never actually trust me."

"I—I trust you. Look what I let you do to me." Hadn't she trusted him enough to let him tie her up and spank her? To give in to the fierce sexual needs that she'd denied for so long? Without him to push her, it might never have happened.

"Because you want it as much as I do. And that's only in the bedroom. When I agreed to that, I didn't mean that our whole relationship began and ended at the door. But you never trusted me beyond that."

"That's a lot of trust." Tears blinded her and she swiped at her eyes. Desperate fear flooded her mouth. She watched him walk back and forth across the suite collecting his belongings. God, he was *leaving* her. Her breathing hitched so hard it hurt. "It's more trust than I've ever given anyone else."

"It's not enough. I want more. I want it all. I'm not going to settle for less than everything you have to give." His tone was so distant, so cold it made her shiver.

To let him in. To let him all the way in as a part of every aspect of her life was to lose part of the independence she'd worked so hard for. It was something she'd avoided all her life. "I—I can't—"

"I know." He dropped a stack of folded shirts into a trunk.

"Where will you go?" She hated the weak quaver in her voice, but she couldn't stop it. She felt like she was crumbling.

He didn't look at her. "Back to Brazil."

"Will you be back?"

There was a long pause. "I don't know. My grandfather passed away last night. Things will be reshuffling in the South American Pride. I may not be able to come back."

"Not . . . coming back?" She swayed on her feet, feeling all the blood rushing out of her face. If he left, there was no chance of them being together. Ever. She had to stay with her family until after Antonio's heir was born. And Miguel had to leave. "I—I see. Then I'll . . . let you get back to your packing."

He nodded, his movement stiff. "I hope everything works out for you."

"Thank you." Awkwardness crept over her. How could something that had been so wonderful come crashing down around her so soon? She wanted to scream at him that this was worse than anything her father had ever done. Her father hadn't changed her whole world and then *left her.* Alone.

She heard him swallow, saw the way a muscle ticked in his jaw. "In New York, I mean. Good luck smoothing out the problems in New York."

"I . . ." But what could she say? There was nothing. No way to fix this, no way to stop the political machine from grinding them both under. No way to make herself someone else, someone who could love and trust easily. "Good-bye, Miguel."

Spinning on a heel, she fled and didn't let herself look back. Just as she cleared the doorway, she heard his quiet answer. "Good-bye, my mate."

7

Miguel dropped the shirt he was holding in his hand and strode out of his suite to follow Andrea. Frustration and desperate anger mixed with impending loss and more desire than he could ever have imagined feeling for one woman.

He caught the door just as she swung it closed and pushed inside. She turned to look at him and he saw in her eyes what he couldn't put into words. Damning himself and her for everything they'd never be, he knew he'd take her, touch her, one last time.

Tears shimmered in her eyes, but her soft mouth set in a firm line. Her hand reached out, fisted in his shirt, and hauled him around so that his back slammed against the closed door. "No more talking. Just fuck me now."

"This doesn't change anything." He caught her hand in his and pried it off his shirt.

She pressed her body to his, her breasts crushed against his chest, and her tongue slid up his neck before she whispered in his ear. "I know."

A groan jerked from his throat. He couldn't wait. The woman was a detriment to his control. He turned to lift her against the smooth wooden surface of the door. If someone walked by they'd know exactly what was going on in here and he didn't give a damn.

She wrapped her legs around his waist, already writhing in the rhythm of sex. Her pupils dilated, the edges of her irises shimmering with flecks of gold. He loved her this way, wild and unrestrained in his arms.

He reached between them to unzip his pants, his knuckles brushing against her smoothly waxed pussy. Her dampness clung to his fingers as his fly opened. He kept his hand there, stroking her slick lips until she whimpered and twisted to get closer.

His cock ached with the need to be inside her, and he didn't hesitate. They both groaned when he thrust deep and hard. They moved together without speaking. All the words they didn't dare say closed in around them. His body tightened as he pushed into her soft wet sex again and again. When her pussy fisted around him, her back arched, and her mouth opened in a silent scream, he couldn't hold on any longer.

God help him, he loved her so much.

Jolting awake, Miguel groaned as his body bowed in orgasm. Fire shot through him and he came in long jets, his hips rising under the bedcovers. His fists balled in the sheets until they shredded in his hands, and his claws extended until they sliced into his palms. The pain was a welcome distraction from the too-real dream. The same dream he'd had every day for a week. He jerked upright, rolled to the side of the bed, and pressed his thumbs into his eyes. His body shook with the aftershocks of orgasm, the sweat drying on his skin.

It hadn't happened. He hadn't gone after Andrea. She'd left for New York and he for Brazil. His mind insisted on playing out the fantasy for him every night. He couldn't escape it.

Shoving to his feet, he walked through his rooms to the bathroom and washed the smears of blood off his palms. A quick nap would heal it for him, but he didn't think he could handle the mind-fuck he was playing on himself again. He dug into one of his trunks and pulled out a clean set of clothing. He hadn't been able to bring himself to unpack since his return to Rio de Janeiro. Perhaps he would do that after he ate breakfast.

There was nothing for him to do here. He felt at loose ends, unraveling at the seams. It was time to have a discussion with his Uncle Pedro about how he could be of use to the Pride here. He needed to accept that he was never going back to San Francisco. A pang hit his chest at the thought, but he ruthlessly subdued it. There was nothing he could do to change the reality of his life. It was time to get on with it.

As he walked through the kitchen of the hacienda, a babble of English and Spanish—the two languages all Panthers spoke— as well as the local Portuguese reached his ears. One of the women working in the kitchen set a cup of coffee, a plate of toast, and bowl of papaya in front of a chair at the table.

"*Muito obrigado.*"

The Panther female nodded in reply to his thanks and bustled away to stir a pot that boiled on the stove. Sighing he sat and ate in silence, missing with a fierceness that he couldn't contain the easy banter at meals in North America.

"Miguel."

He turned to see his cousin's daughter, Marisol, hovering in the doorway to the kitchen. "My *avô* is looking for you. He's in his office."

"Tell your grandfather I'll be in there in a moment."

"Okay!" A smile wreathed her little face and she spun on her toes to skip away.

Children. Something else he wouldn't have. Not without being mated. He sighed and shook his head. It wouldn't help to dwell on this. Taking a last sip of coffee, he pushed to his feet and carried his dishes to the sink.

A heavy frown marred his uncle's face when Miguel knocked and entered the office. "You wanted to see me, sir?"

Sitting back in his chair, Pedro stabbed a finger at a piece of paper sitting on his desk. "That Cruz boy has humans in his Pride now. As though the non-shifters weren't bad enough. *Humans.* Did you know about this?"

"It's just the one human, and he's mated to a Panther." Folding his hands behind his back, Miguel kept his expression smooth.

"This goes against the order of things. Humans *cannot* know about us." Pedro thumped his fist on his desk. "This is unacceptable."

As if his uncle had any say in how Antonio ran his Pride. But that wasn't a wise thing to say to a man he had sworn loyalty to. He pulled in a deep breath. "I find myself at loose ends now that I am no longer the North American Pride Second. So, how may I serve you, *tio?*"

"Ha! We have everything we need. Your cousin is a fine heir, courting his new mate in Asia."

"Congratulations." As always, there was little use for him here that he didn't take on himself. He'd kept his contacts in the Pride alive while he'd been gone—he had a few in every Pride. Friends he'd made and kept when he'd toured the Prides at thirty. After his grandfather decided he should find out if there was a mate for him in another Pride. A bitter smile curved his lips. There hadn't been. Not then.

Not now, either. And with the impasse he found himself in with Andrea, not ever.

Pedro sat back and laced his fingers over his flat belly. "We contacted Antonio today, Miguel."

"About the human?" Miguel kept his face carefully blank, always the best approach when dealing with his uncle.

"No. We've demanded that your mate join you here. Didn't think I knew about her, did you?" He winked. "I let them know that you wished it, because mates should be together. The two of you will work through whatever problems ail you when she gets here."

Miguel's jaw clenched tight, and he felt some of the blood drain out of his face. Resignation gripped his belly. Andrea would certainly believe the worst of him—that he would try and control her through someone more powerful than either of them. Would Antonio force her to come? What would he do if she did come?

A deep craving crawled through him. To see her. To touch her again. He needed her more than his next breath. He swallowed, pinning his gaze to the floor. "I wish you hadn't done that, *tio.*"

"Ah, my nephew." Pedro sighed and flashed an indulgent smile. "Always the quiet one. She just needs to know—"

Miguel jerked his chin to the side. "She won't come. Not of her own will."

"She'll come if she knows what's best for her Pride. Antonio isn't so foolish as that. This will only solidify his alliance with us—a good-faith move toward my leadership."

Shit. Making this a political maneuver to force Andrea into moving to South America was . . . ingenious. The perfect way to get a young breeding couple to add to his Pride, and the highest-ranking family in his Pride. It was a winning combination. For his uncle, his family, his Pride, but not for Miguel. Not for Andrea.

She would never forgive him for this.

He should have seen it coming. He was usually good at reading people, situations, Panther politics. It was his gift, Antonio said. To always know things first. Andrea would never believe he hadn't had a hand in this. In cornering her.

Some tiny piece of his soul had hoped that she might come to see that they were truly meant for each other, that he could be trusted never to hurt her. He clenched his fists. Now, that hope was dead. And he had a very angry mate coming with claws bared. His uncle was as conservative as her father had been. She wouldn't adjust well to being contained, controlled, used.

Heaving a sigh, he nodded to his uncle. "I understand you've done what's best for the Pride. Excuse me and I'll see that rooms are prepared for her."

"No need."

"Your mate has taken care of it?"

A booming laugh was his answer. "No, my boy. She'll be sleeping in your suite." He waggled his eyebrows. "You can't tell me you haven't sampled her yet. She is a model, a very beautiful woman—the humans love her face."

"She's also an intelligent businesswoman. She hasn't modeled in years." Now his fists balled for another reason. The kind of comments Pedro was making made it clear how much respect Andrea would get here. He felt as though he were riding on a runaway train with no recourse but to watch a collision happen.

Pedro continued to chuckle, good humor and triumph shining on his face. Yes, his uncle was a Panther who'd maneuvered circumstances to get exactly what he wanted. Apparently, it was a family trait Miguel had never known he inherited. "Money, babies—I'm sure she has many great talents. Fate has gifted our Pride with a wonderful new addition, yes?"

"Of course." Miguel blinked down at his uncle, wondering if the man had ever known him. If he'd ever want to. He thought Miguel quiet and shy, needing help in bringing his mate to heel. He wasn't sure if he wanted to laugh or punch the older man, so he did neither. He turned and left the room, shutting the door silently behind him.

More than three decades in this house and he felt less at home here than he had after only two years in San Francisco. He wondered what the twins were up to—they hadn't an ounce of caution between them. How long would it be before Solana had her baby?

Andrea. How was she doing? The question nagged at him. He hoped she was well. A sigh slipped passed his throat. Damn, he missed her.

*   *   *

Andrea flew to New York and worked like a fiend for days on end, but it was never enough to exhaust her into sleep. Never enough to distract her from the way her chest felt as though a huge gaping hole had been left in it.

It was for the best. They would never have made it. Her inability to trust, to connect, made her a poor candidate for a mate. Miguel was better off without her. She told that to herself over and over again, every time she thought of him, which was only every other minute. A million times she reached for her cell phone, intending to call his office and tell him about something that happened during her work, only to remember that he wasn't there any more.

He wasn't coming back.

The irony of her situation didn't escape her. When she'd arrived in San Francisco, she'd just wanted to co-exist with Miguel until he returned to his own Pride in Brazil . . . or to ride out the storm and then run away again. She'd gotten exactly what she wanted. They co-existed. He'd left. She was as alone as she'd always imagined herself.

But it was worse now. Worse than when she'd left her family the first time. The pain didn't fade, the loneliness ate her alive. Nothing could make it stop. It was the first time she'd ever been unable to lose herself in her work.

God, she missed him. It weighed down on her every moment of every day. She couldn't escape it, couldn't rest. Her instincts screamed and clawed like a wild thing inside her . . . urging her to go to her mate.

It had to get better soon. It *had* to or she would go insane.

She walked around in a daze of pain and exhaustion. A week rolled by and she had no idea where the time went. Grit burned her eyes until they blurred, but she couldn't sleep. Her work finished, she flew back to California. She closed her eyes and forced her body to rest on the car ride from the airport to the mansion. Or perhaps it was to shut out the sight of the limo where she'd first made love with Miguel.

Either way, her mind wouldn't shut down. It buzzed around from one thought to another like a gnat on crack.

The door popped open as soon as the limo slowed to a stop and Ric reached in to haul her out. He lifted her up into a tight hug. She squeezed him back with a desperation that wasn't feigned. She'd missed him and the rest of her family. And she had a feeling clinging to her connection to them might be her only way to survive this.

"Welcome home."

"Thank you." It did feel like home now. It had taken being away to realize just how much. She loved this place and these people. Antonio was as diametrically opposed to her father as a man could be. She believed he could do everything he wanted to in the Panther community. She was proud of him, respected him as a leader.

Miguel had given this to her. He'd given her back her family. Would she ever have unbent enough to get to know them again without him? Probably not. One way or another she would have left after the loyalty ceremony was over.

The moment she stepped in the door, she found a welcoming party waiting for her. Carmen and her mate hugged her and passed her to a dozen other Pride members. Tears smarted in her eyes and she squeezed them all tightly. Her people. Then she was scooped up and twirled around by Diego before Antonio pulled her out of the younger man's arms. "Please, give her space to breathe."

She laughed, the first time in seven days. Antonio ran a hand over the back of her head and rocked her from side to side. "Good to see you again."

"You, too." She pulled back to smile up at him. "Where's Solana?"

"Sleeping." His broad shoulder lifted in a shrug. "She's at

that point where moving is something she has to think about for half an hour before she decides if it's worth the work."

"Poor baby."

A grin lit up his face. "Don't say that to her or she might kill you. She's not big on pity—or even sympathy that might have once come into contact with pity."

"Noted." When the front door slammed, she turned to see the twins lugging her huge suitcases toward the stairs. "Well, then. I'm going to go unpack, knock the travel grime off of me, and be back down for dinner."

"See you in a bit. I have a call I put on hold when you pulled up. I have to get back to it."

She and Antonio parted, she for her room and he for his office. Jogging up the wide staircase, she met the twins on the landing. "Thanks for hauling in my bags."

Ric smiled, paused to smack a kiss on her cheek, and took the steps down two at a time. "No prob, sis. Got work to do. Bye."

"I better keep him from going anal retentive workaholic on me. He's such a fucking *lawyer*." Diego ruffled her hair and hustled after his twin.

Chuckling, she shook her head as she walked into her suite. She took a deep breath, but couldn't even catch a whiff of Miguel's scent. She spun in a slow circle, something twisting and crumpling inside her. He wasn't here. He'd never be here again. It was as if she'd imagined the whole thing. She almost wished she had, but she couldn't make herself believe it. Having him had been worth the pain of losing him.

She huffed out a sad laugh. "Now isn't that a bitch?"

Her voice seemed to echo in her room, and she found herself standing there staring at her bed. The one Miguel had bent her over that first night. A shudder ran through her. God, the things that man had done to her body.

Sucking in a breath, she whipped around, walked into the

bathroom, and stripped off her clothes as she went. This was madness; she had to stop thinking about him. Twisting the knob to turn on the shower, she stepped under the heated spray of water, tried to shut her mind off and focus on all the things she needed to do. She had a new line to develop, a spring fashion show to prepare for, arrangements to make with the European Pride so that she could travel to Paris and Milan for meetings.

The water rolled in hot beads down her body, and she shivered at the sensation. It felt like fingers moving over her skin. And that dragged her back to Miguel. Her sex clenched at the thought of him. She wished she could smile at her Pavlovian reaction, but her body ached with suppressed want. The idea that it might be this way for the rest of her life made her want to scream or break something. But it wouldn't change anything, wouldn't make things better or make it hurt less.

Miguel.

If he were here he'd have her up against the shower wall in under ten seconds. Or on her knees with her mouth on his cock. Or . . . hell, there was no telling what he'd do. The man had a mind full of naughty and a body made for sin. And he used both of them to her advantage. Her nipples tightened as she imagined Miguel's hands on them, lifting and squeezing them.

Heat rolled through her body, and the muscles in her thighs shook. Steam wrapped her in its sensual embrace, sweat and water mixing to slick every inch of her flesh. "Jesus."

She couldn't take it. Her instincts reared their ugly head, clamoring again for her mate. They twisted and screeched inside her, made her body flame with white-hot need for Miguel. Only Miguel. His hands, his mouth, his cock. On her, in her. It didn't matter as long as he made her come.

A moan tore from her throat, agony shredding her soul, desire heating her blood to a boiling point. Her hands shook when she finally gave in. She had to do something to ease the dark longings that tangled inside her. Her fingers cupped her breasts, pinching and tugging at her tight nipples. A whimper slid free when she let her palm glide down her torso until it reached her pussy.

She circled her clit with one fingertip, toying with the swollen flesh. Water pelted her body, but the heat of it was nothing to the molten lava bubbling up inside her. Her legs shook with the effort to keep herself upright. She plunged her fingers deep into her soaking pussy. Her hips undulated, moving to the carnal rhythm her hands set. She needed to come so badly, needed some relief from the endless want that haunted her.

Her heart rate sped, her blood rushing through her veins. Fire licked at her skin, made it feel too hot and too tight for her body. She was going to explode. Moving her hand faster, she worked her fingers over her clit in rough strokes. Her breath hissed between her teeth . . . her fangs sliding out to scrape her lip. The tang of blood flooded her tongue, and it made the feral side of her rip loose. Her sex clenched around her fingers, and orgasm hit her in a blinding rush.

"Miguel," she sobbed. Tears she hadn't let herself cry since he left slid down her cheeks to mingle with the shower spray. She pressed her forehead to the slick tile, bracing herself with her hands. But her legs gave out and she folded to the floor, crying as though her soul had been ripped in two. If it had, she knew she had no one to blame but herself. This was the way she'd wanted it, wasn't it?

The tears slowed, her breath evening out. She dropped her forehead to her knees and sighed. Please, let the pain and loneliness stop. Please. She couldn't live like this. Finally, she reached up to turn off the shower and hauled herself to her feet.

A knock sounded on her bedroom door. Antonio by the smell of it. "One second!"

Shrugging into a robe she'd left behind when she went to New York, she hurried out of the bathroom to open the door for her brother. A concerned look made creases in his forehead. Fear jolted through her. Was something wrong with Solana? With Miguel? Oh, God.

She stepped back to let Antonio in, her fingers twisting in the belt of her robe. Anxiety knotted in her belly. "What's wrong?"

"What makes you think anything is wrong?" He thrust his hands into his jeans pockets and didn't look at her.

She snorted. "Please. I may not have been around for a long time, but I knew you before you got a growth spurt and I was taller than you. I can tell when something's bothering you."

"Just because you were a giraffe at nine—"

"Stop stalling." She put herself directly in front of him so he couldn't avoid her gaze. "Just tell me."

He sighed. "You're not going to be happy."

She lifted her hands, releasing an exasperated breath. "Then get it over with and let me deal with being pissed."

"I got a call from the South American Pride."

Her heart stumbled. God, it was Miguel. Something had happened. Something terrible. She—

"They've demanded you join Miguel there and mate with him immediately."

"*What?*" He wouldn't do that. If there was one thing she knew about Miguel it was that he wanted her willing or not at all. He would never use underhanded methods to get what he wanted from her.

Realization jerked through her, and a laugh that sounded closer to a sob escaped her throat. How had she missed this? When she hadn't been looking, Miguel had actually earned her trust. All of it. Not just in the bedroom. She knew, without a shadow of a doubt, that he would never hurt her the way other men had. He'd probably take someone apart limb by limb for daring to dream of it.

Her heart pounded so hard she could hear it, her stomach

flipping over. God, she needed him. She *loved* him, and she was *such an idiot.* Would he ever forgive her for putting him through so much shit before she got it? She hoped so. What would she do without him? She'd been dying inside for the last week.

Antonio's hand closed over her shoulder. "We have no idea if Miguel had anything to do with this. Don't be—"

"Have one of the twins book me on the next flight out to Rio." Hope and abject terror pressed in on her chest until she couldn't breathe. What would she do if he decided she wasn't worth the emotional risk? She'd shut him down so many times and she knew it had to have caused him pain. She drew in a shaky breath.

"What?" Her brother gave her the kind of look reserved for escapees from the insane asylum.

She gave him a smile that she was sure bordered on maniacal. *She was going to see Miguel again.* The realization was so sweet it hurt. She had to fight to keep tears from welling up in her eyes. "Whether Miguel had any say in it or not, if I don't go, it's going to mess things up for the Pride. So, I'm going. I'll handle it."

Antonio blinked and stared down at her for a long moment before he shook himself. "Okay . . . Then, I'll let you get ready to go. I'll drive you to the airport."

"Fine."

And then he was gone and she was stuffing herself into the first set of clothes on top of her still-packed suitcase and zipping it closed again. At least she was already packed. That simplified things.

Her hands shook with nerves and she had to sit on her bed and stick her head between her knees for a moment. She might throw up. What if he didn't want her anymore? He'd left. He'd said it was best they didn't mate with each other. And Miguel always meant what he said. Cold tingles spread over her skin. Oh, God. Oh, God.

No. She forced herself to sit up and pull in a deep breath. If he didn't want her, she would change his mind. He had changed hers, changed her whole world.

And he'd promised her that he would fulfill *all* of her needs. Well, now she needed him. Forever.

The black hair on his forelegs allowed Miguel to fade into the night as he sprinted across the lush hacienda grounds, pushing his Panther body as hard as possible. His tail whipped behind him as he wound through the trees. Faster. Perhaps he could escape the impending blowup with his mate. Faster. How much longer did he have left? The humid air wrapped around him, filling his lungs with heated moisture. He panted, his lungs straining to suck in enough oxygen. And still he ran, faster, faster, knowing there was no avoiding his fate.

Exhaustion sapped at his strength, but he had no desire to rest, to sleep. It would only bring dreams of Andrea. A cruel reminder of what would never be his. His hammering heart gave a painful lurch, and he forced himself to slow to a stop. His head sagged between his front paws, his muscles shaking.

He sighed and turned back to the huge house. Even with his acute vision, he couldn't see it yet through the foliage, but he could smell it and he followed the scent of many Panthers concentrated in one area until the hacienda came in sight. Entering through a door designed for Panthers in cat form, he ghosted up the rear stairs to his suite.

When he stepped into his rooms, he found his cell phone vibrating on the nightstand. It rattled until it clattered to the floor. Shifting back to human form it a quick flash of heat and magic, he scooped up the phone and saw an American number. One from inside the North American den. His fingers shook a bit when he pressed the answer key. "Andrea?"

"No, it's Solana. I'm sorry, Miguel."

A slow sigh escaped, but the smile that came to his lips was genuine. "Not at all. What did you need? Is . . . everyone all right?"

"Andrea just got on a plane." He could hear the worry in her voice, and it made his stomach clench. "Antonio dropped her off at the airport. She's . . . not happy."

He rubbed a hand over his forehead and dropped down to sit on the edge of his bed. "I had nothing to do with it."

"I know. She didn't say anything to anyone before she left. Not even Diego could get a word out of her. She just booked a flight and left. I'm hoping Antonio got her to talk on the way to SFO, but I won't know until he gets back." She sighed. "For what it's worth, I'm sorry for the shit storm that's probably about to rain down on you."

He barked out a laugh. "You have a way with words. How is everyone else?"

"Everyone's fine. I'm fat." A rustling sounded through the phone line and he could imagine her shifting it against her ear. "My feet are puffy and I can't bend down to tie my shoes."

"Have one of the many men who wait on you hand and foot do it for you."

"The twins would kick your ass for saying so."

"The truth is painful at times." He grinned at the disdainful looks he'd earn from the younger men, but they'd do whatever Solana wanted and everyone knew it.

Her chuckle filtered through the phone. "I miss you. Everyone does. I wish you were here."

"Me, too. I'm sorry I'll miss being there for the baby being born." God, he missed North America. Especially since his uncle was *not* there and he wouldn't have to watch the man try to bring Andrea under his thumb. Damn it.

A breathy gust of air came through the line. "I have to go. Antonio has the twins watching me like a hawk. As if talking on the phone is a strain."

He squeezed the phone so tight the plastic squeaked. "Take care of yourself."

"Ha. You're as bad as them."

"Worse." He chuckled and decided to needle her a bit. What could he say—he was a sadist at heart. "You'd never have gotten near a phone to call if I was there."

"Tyrant," she grouched.

He grinned even though she couldn't see it. "Good-bye, Solana."

"Bye, Miguel. Good luck with Andrea."

"Thanks for the warning." He pushed the button to turn off the phone and collapsed back against the bed. How many hours did he have until she got here? Not enough to keep the dread at bay. He *did not* want to deal with this. But he would. "Shit."

Now that he was lying down, the exhaustion he'd been beating away for hours sapped his strength. He flung an arm over his eyes and sighed. Why did it have to be so fucking hard?

It was his last thought before sleep dragged him under. Sheer feline lethargy made his muscles relax into the soft mattress, and he was out before he had a chance to fight it.

"Miguel."

Someone called his name. Was it real or a dream? He couldn't tell. His mind was fogging, his eyes refusing to open. Something poked his shoulder and he snapped awake in an instant. Jerking his head to the side, he saw Marisol's little face peeking up over the edge of the mattress. It wasn't usual for him to sleep so deeply. No one ever snuck up on him, let alone a small child.

Then he realized he was still naked from the night before when he'd shifted from his Panther form. He reached for a pillow and plopped it on his lap as he sat up. "What's wrong, Marisol?"

"*She's* here. In *avô's* office. You should go see her, she's very beautiful."

Andrea. Shit, how had he slept so long? "When did she arrive?"

"Just now. I saw her come in the door and *avô* took her into his office. I came to get you. He didn't tell me to. Is that wrong?" Sudden worry crinkled her small features, made her dark eyes go wide.

He cupped a hand over the back of her head, dropping a quick kiss on he forehead. "No, you did the right thing. Thank you. Go play so I can get dressed."

"Okay." Her usual smile was back in full force, and she spun to dart out of his room, closing the door behind her.

Erupting into action, he flung the pillow aside and pulled on a pair of slacks and a polo shirt. He didn't bother with shoes, just rushed out of his room and down the stairs. He hooked his loose hair behind his ears and gave a perfunctory knock on Pedro's office door before he stepped inside.

"Come in, come in!" His uncle waved him in and motioned to a chair opposite the one Andrea sat in.

His legs almost collapsed out from under him at the first sight of her in so many days. She was so beautiful. *Mate.* His instincts sang in the same recognition they had the first time he'd seen her. He dragged her sweet scent into his lungs. His heart seized when her midnight eyes met his. Some emotion passed through her gaze, but it was gone so quickly he had no idea what message it conveyed. She held her long, lithe body in a rigid line.

Was she angry? Sad? Upset? He couldn't tell.

The smile Pedro aimed at Andrea was both benevolent and predatory. "We look forward to you joining our family."

"As do I." She pulled her gaze from Miguel, the polite, professional mask of a model settling over her features. For once, he was grateful she was so good at hiding her feelings.

His uncle continued as if he didn't sense the tense undercurrents running through the room. And maybe he didn't. "The Pride will be so pleased to have you. You must tell us more about this business interest of yours. Clothing design, isn't it?"

"Yes, it is." Her courteous smile turned regretful. "I'm afraid that as overjoyed as I am at the prospect of being a part of Miguel's loving family, I won't be joining the South American Pride. It's just not possible."

"Excuse me?" Pedro arched an incredulous brow.

"As you know, I am the North American Pride leader's heir." Her smile didn't falter, and Miguel had to bite the inside of his cheek to keep himself from grinning. He had a feeling he knew where this conversation was going. His uncle, sadly, hadn't a clue.

Pedro laughed heartily, shaking his head. "He is about to have a child of his own, yes?"

"Of course. I'm very happy about the future birth of my niece or nephew, but the child is not yet born. Should something happen to my brother's mate now, he would have no other children. No heirs." She tilted her head to the side, the picture of feminine guile. "I'm sure a man as discerning as you can understand why I can't in good conscience join another Pride."

The smile had fallen from his uncle's face, but Andrea pushed on. "Is it not also customary in the Prides for mates not in the same Pride to join the higher-ranking mate's Pride? As close as you might be to Miguel, I clearly outrank him in North America. I'm afraid he will simply have to join my brother's Pride." Her eyes widened, sweet and angelic.

"I disagree." No mirth shone from Pedro's eyes. Something ruthless flashed in those depths, feline calculation. "We fostered your brother so long, surely he can see that—"

She lifted a slim hand, cutting him off. "But I've spoken to my brother, and he understands that this will rob you of a beloved nephew and a possible breeding pair. He's not unsympathetic to a new Pride leader's duties, so he wishes to strengthen the bond between our Prides and show a deep faith in your leadership. Therefore, he'd like to ask that your son and heir serve as his Second for the next year."

Pedro's mouth flapped open. Losing a breeding couple would be bad, but an open show of faith from another Pride leader was important to cementing the transition between leaders. And having a member of his family mated into the ruling North American family could only be seen as a good thing. His mouth snapped shut and his nostrils flared as he drew a deep breath. A smile stretched his lips. "I'm honored by Antonio's show of faith. I return his regard and wish you much happiness in your mating to my nephew. May you have many sons."

"And daughters. My parents had a large number of children for Panthers. I can only hope to follow their example . . . in that regard, at least." The gracious, businesslike smile curved Andrea's lips once more. "I'm certain your leadership here will be long and prosperous. I trust that with much compromise and understanding of each other's flaws, my mate and I will find happiness together."

Her eyes met Miguel's as she spoke the last sentence. So many things they hadn't yet said flashing between them. He allowed no expression to cross his face—his uncle had no right to be privy to their private problems. He could only be grateful that she and Antonio had found a way to get them out of the tangled political mess they'd been in without leaving Andrea stranded in South America. Whether he and his mate worked things out between them when they returned to North America and he pledged loyalty to Antonio was not his uncle's concern. She stood and Miguel and Pedro hastened to stand with her.

"If you'll both forgive me, I've traveled very far today and I'm exhausted." She swallowed. "Miguel, would you be so kind as to show me to our room?"

He nodded, still silent. He saw that despite her cool exterior, her hands shook, and she balled them into fists at her sides. He caught one in his, uncurling her fingers to twine with his, careful to exude the kind of self-confidence that would keep his uncle from suspecting things weren't as wonderful as he might expect with two people who were soon to be mated.

Clenching his jaw to keep from ripping her clothes off, jerking her against his body, and fucking her until all the pain and longing and frustration burned away, he led her out into the hall and up the sweeping staircase.

What would she think of this place where he'd grown up? The South American Pride den was beautiful, all polished tiles and smooth wood. But it wasn't home. He'd never felt a connection to the place or people the way he had in San Francisco. He sighed as he set his hand on the small of her back and urged her toward the door to his room.

She glanced back at him, uncertainty in her dark eyes. "You're not coming with me?"

"I haven't eaten today, and I doubt you have either." He looked away for a moment, not wanting her to read the turmoil inside him on his face. "I'll be back shortly with food."

Her mouth opened, closed, and her lips twisted. She nodded and stepped into his suite.

Turning, he jogged down the back staircase to the kitchen and gathered a tray of food. He wasn't hungry, he was just distracting himself from a painful conversation with his mate. They'd already said good-bye—now they had to work out how to live in the same Pride without being true mates. Out of the political frying pan and into the emotional fire.

He shook his head and walked back up the steps, passing several Pride members along the way. They smiled at him and he felt the weight of their expectations. A new mating was something Panthers celebrated. He wished he could share their felicity, but it wasn't to be.

He balanced the heavy tray on one hand, opened the door with the other, walked inside and set the food on a side table just to his left. His mouth dried when he turned to see his mate standing in the middle of the room. She sank to her knees before him, naked except for the necklace he'd given her. The fire opal sparkled in the lamplight, and just the sight of her bare flesh made his cock harden painfully. "Miguel, I—"

He jerked his chin to the side. "Don't."

"I have to." The look in her eyes was one he'd craved from the moment he met her. Open, soft, loving. Bitterness twisted in his heart. Was she doing this because she wanted to, or because she now felt she had to? God save him; he couldn't endure this and remain sane.

He forced his gaze away and his voice came out sharper than he intended. "It's a little late for that, isn't it?"

"Is it?" Her expression gentled to naked vulnerability. "I thought . . . it could never be too late between mates."

"You don't want to be my mate."

Tears filmed her eyes, and the sight made his heart wrench. He cursed himself for always reacting to her, always needing to protect her from pain. Her lips trembled as she spoke. "I *am* your mate whether I want it or not. And I want it. Even if . . . even if I'd had a choice, I'd still choose you, Miguel."

It was everything he'd wanted her to say and more. It was too good to be true. He sucked in a sharp breath, closing his eyes. "Stop."

"I can't." She laughed, the sound emerging as a sob. When he opened his eyes, he saw the tears had begun to fall, sliding down her beautiful face. "I didn't trust myself with men anymore, not really, not fully. It was one thing to give them my body, but to trust them with anything else? I couldn't do it. I couldn't let go. Not even with you."

"I should have—"

"You did everything right. I'm here, aren't I?" She gestured to her nude body, to her position on the floor. His cock was harder than steel at this point, his erection never faltering from the moment he'd seen her bare curves. He pulled a slow, steady breath in, reaching for calm. She brushed a palm over her naked hip. "I'm yours. I'll always be yours. Every second of every day for the rest of my life. Even if you decide we should never mark each other . . . I'd still be yours. There's no one else for me. I love you."

He swallowed. Having her there, on her knees in quiet submission was mind-blowing. He wanted to believe what she was saying, needed it to be real.

Her palms lifted in supplication. "I love *you,* Miguel. I see you, understand you, in a way that no one else can. Not even Antonio."

A rusty chuckle slid from his throat. "There are sides of me your brother knows about, but will never see. I think it's best considering we're not close like *that.*"

"Thank God." A tentative smile curled the corners of her mouth. "I'd hate to have to kill my brother."

He shook his head. "Andrea—"

"Mark me."

His breath stopped, shock reverberating down his spine. Of all the things she could have said, that was one he hadn't expected. "What?"

"That first time, that first day, you told me to ask you to mark me. I'm asking. Mark me, Miguel. Make me yours in a way no one can ever deny. Not even us."

"Don't say it unless you mean it." God help him if she didn't mean it. This was no political move to smooth the bumps between them. This was undeniable, real. His hands shook with need, fire arching through his body to make his cock ache at the mere thought of sinking his fangs deep into her soft flesh.

"When I lived with my father, he caged me, and then when I left, I told myself I would never be caged again. But it wasn't true. I locked a part of myself away, even from myself." Her gaze met his, steady, open, and sure, a direct contrast to the tears that still clung to her long lashes. "With you, I'm free. I'm just . . . me. No excuses, no lies, no barriers."

And he believed her. His breath escaped in a slow rush, his heart hammering. Warmth banded around his chest, and the feeling had nothing to do with the desire raging through his system. "I love you so much."

"Show me." Her hands reached for him, but she stayed where she was, kneeling on the carpet. "Take me to that place I can only go with you. Take me."

"Yes." He could no more deny her—or himself—than he could keep the moon from rising. He didn't want to. He wanted her forever, undeniably his, just as she'd said. Pulling his shirt over his head, he dropped it on the floor beside him. He made quick work of his pants and soon he was as naked as she. "Stand up."

She rose, her gaze never leaving his. The irises began to turn gold at the edges. He saw her nipples had tightened to peaks and her breathing sped to an excited rush. Even from here he could smell her moist readiness for him to claim her. "Do you want me bent over? Tied up?"

"No." That wasn't how he wanted their mated life to begin. Plenty of time for that later, to push her boundaries to the limits now that he knew he could. A deep shudder ran through him. This time was for enjoying the closeness between them, the love. His jaw locked as the reality of it coursed through him. She loved him, had given herself to him and only him forever. Yes. Oh, yes. That was perfect.

"No?" Curiosity sparked in her eyes, which had gone to full gold now. Her tongue flicked over elongated fangs as she ran her gaze over his body to settle on his long erection.

He wanted to pounce, but relaxed himself into a loose-limbed walk as he approached her. Her palms lifted to press against his chest, and then she was in his arms as they held each other tight. He buried his nose in her hair to inhale her sweet scent. Only then did he realize how she was shaking. His hands stroked in soothing circles over her back.

How much courage had it taken her to come to him and

offer herself the way she had? But it was what they'd both needed, that final proof that they weren't just mates, but could *be mated* and grow together through their problems. He pulled her closer. "I love you."

"I'm so glad I came." Her voice caught and her arms squeezed him with inhuman strength. "I love you so, so much."

He moved until his lips brushed over the sensitive spot where her neck met her shoulder. She shivered and sighed, tilting her head to give him freer access. He placed a soft kiss there, the moment reverent.

Her hands cupped his jaw, moving to press her lips to his. His tongue swept out to sample the flavor of her mouth. She opened beneath him and their mouths moved together in a sensual dance of lips and tongues, their movements mimicking the carnal act they would perform together soon. Soon. He groaned, curving his palms around her backside to pull her soft body tighter against his. She whimpered, wriggling to get closer still, her soft skin moving against the hard length of his cock. His breath hissed out and he lifted her against him, turning them so he could lay her on his bed.

Settling on top of her, he watched the same satisfaction cross her face that he felt. This was right where he was supposed to be. With her. The golden shimmer of her irises caught the light the same way the stone in her necklace had. Her legs wound around his waist, her body arching in offering.

Sweat beaded on their skin in the hot Brazilian night, sealed the front of their bodies together as it rolled down his back in rivulets. He drank in the sight of her body spread beneath him, waiting for him to mark her. It was something he'd never truly expected to happen, not after he'd left San Francisco. He had to taste her. He bent to suck her nipples into his mouth one at a time. Her fingers slid into his hair, and he could feel the light scrape of her claws against his scalp.

Sliding down her body, he ran his tongue around her navel

and farther still until he was level with her pussy. Her thighs tightened around his shoulders, but he curled his hands around her slim legs and forced them wide so he could see the slick lips before him. He blew on the hot flesh, and she moaned. "Miguel, please."

"You're so hot and wet for me." He glanced up at her, watched a flush race up her high cheekbones.

She nodded, her short hair brushing against the pillow. "For you. *Please.*"

Dipping two of his fingers into her channel, he spun them inside of her. His tongue flicked out to swirl around her hard clit. He bit and sucked at the little nub of flesh. The hot, carnal taste of her burst over his tongue, the sweetness of it almost enough to make him come. He added a third finger to her pussy, stretching her as he thrust fast and hard. Her hips writhed, her hands pulling at his hair in sharp tugs of need. His scalp tingled at the pain, his cock jerking against the sheets as his own body's needs demanded to be assuaged.

A low keen sounded from her. The way her sex pulsed around his fingers told him just how close she was to orgasm. He pushed her higher and higher until he knew she was on the very edge. Then he moved back, sank his fangs into the inside of her leg, and marked her. She screamed, high and thin, and he felt her sex convulse around his stroking fingers, wetness slipping from her as she arched hard against his hand. Her body twisted on the sheets. "Miguel! Miguel, I need you."

He bolted up the bed, her shaking hands reaching for him. He sank his cock deep inside her heated pussy, the slickness of her easing his way. Her hips lifted to take him deeper still.

"I love you." She wrapped her arms around his shoulders, pulling him down to her. "Never leave me alone again."

"Never. You're mine." He pressed his face to her neck, nipping and sucking at the soft, sweat-dampened skin. His body rocked against hers, his hard cock plunging into her pussy again and again until he lost track of space and time and anything that wasn't Andrea. He felt her mouth open on his shoulder, her tongue flicking over his skin. The soft prick of her fangs registered, but she didn't bite him, just tasted him until he thought he'd go mad needing her to mark him. His muscles shook at the prospect. Yes. Mates. *Yes.*

Orgasm built inside him, tightened like a spring in his gut. Not yet, not yet. He wanted it to last as long as possible. To take her as much as he was taken by her. Fire ran through his veins, his chest rising in bellowing breaths. He caught her knee in his hands, pulled her leg tighter around him.

The silk of her skin moving against his hip made a harsh groan rip from his throat. "Andrea, I love—"

Her fangs pierced his shoulder, the bonds snapping between them. Magic and heat. Panther and human. Mates. He threw back his head and roared, his hips pumping hard against hers. Her claws raked down his back, her body moving with his as they came together. The tight sheath of her sex fisted around him in rhythmic waves and he could no longer deny his release. He froze, his body locking in a hard line before he jetted inside her.

It was so good, so perfect. Nothing had ever been this deep. Not even with Andrea. This was the connection he'd craved from the beginning, this unbreakable bond. He loved her so much, he couldn't live without her now.

He belonged to her—body, heart, and soul. Just as she belonged to him. Nothing and no one could ever take that away from them. Their love was free to be as wild and untamed as they were. Always.

Need Me

I
_____

"Your name?"

Isabel jolted as the small silver box mounted on a pole beside the driveway blared with noise. Her heart pounded and she glanced around guiltily. Then she straightened her shoulders. No one knew she was here. They couldn't have found her so soon. If she reassured herself enough times, she might believe it. Clearing her throat, she pressed the button to speak into the box. "Isabel Rivera. I'm here to see the Pride leader's mate, Solana Perez . . . Cruz."

A brief pause followed her words before the gates swung open. "You've been cleared to enter. Please proceed, Ms. Rivera."

"Thank you." She clenched her fingers around the rental car's steering wheel to still their shaking as she drove through and parked. Her claws slid forward to scrabble against the leather covering the wheel and she shivered, concentrating on retracting them so she looked like a normal human instead of what she was—a Panther, one of a rare race of shape-shifters. On so many levels, she wished she _were_ normal. She wouldn't be in this mess if she were. If she were human, Enrique would never have known her, noticed her, hurt her.

Terror whipped through her again, and she suppressed the awful memory. Her stomach knotted tightly. Flicking her tongue forward, she pressed it against the points of her fangs. A glance at the rearview mirror confirmed that her eyes had begun to shimmer from their normal pale brown to pure gold. *Mierda.*

"Get a hold of yourself, Isabel." Sucking in a deep breath, she closed her eyes and reached for calm. Acting like an irrational freak wasn't going to help her make her case with Solana. When she looked back in the mirror, her eyes were brown again.

Forcing herself to breathe deeply, she stepped from the car to face the mansion that housed the North American Panther Pride.

Would Solana be able to help her? They hadn't seen each other in almost twenty years—since they were both children in the European Pride—but she was Isabel's last chance. Her heart slammed in her chest as she approached the massive double doors. She shivered, huddling in her coat. San Francisco was so much colder than Barcelona at this time of year—but Spain was the last place she wanted to be now. One of the doors swung open just as she mounted the step to the porch.

"Ms. Rivera." A man with long dark hair tied back stood on the threshold. Everything about him said *contained*. He looked her over before he stepped back to let her inside.

Though he hadn't posed it as a question, she answered anyway as she entered the mansion. "Yes, I'm Isabel Rivera."

"Miguel Montoya. I'm mated to Andrea Cruz." That would be Solana's sister-in-law, the former model turned clothing designer. He offered her a hand to shake. His palm was surprisingly strong and warm. He moved around behind her to take her coat and said nothing more.

His quiet demeanor made her jump into nervous speech, her hand smoothing down her skirt. "I'm, um, here to see Solana. I left a message for her yesterday, and she returned my call, only I was on the plane so I couldn't pick up because I had to turn my cell phone off, but she agreed to see me. So . . . here I am."

"She's in her office with her new baby." He motioned to a hallway off the main foyer and Isabel fell into step beside him.

She swallowed. "I don't mean to intrude. I know she only gave birth a few weeks ago."

"Two, actually." He smiled, and while she sensed he was still in absolute control of the situation, she also found that steadiness comforting, and she relaxed. It didn't hurt that he was mated and therefore would have no interest in her. He swept a hand toward a closed door. "She's a Panther though, she healed quickly, and Antonio is having trouble keeping her resting. Any distraction is a good one."

"That's nice to know. Thank you." Right. Solana was a shifter now, which was the only way she would have been able to conceive. A shape-shifter had to be born, they couldn't be made, no matter what Hollywood said. And the only way to make a Panther child was to be mated and to breed in cat form. Solana had once been a Panther unable to change forms, a non-shifter— persona non grata in most Prides. It was the reason Solana and her father had fled the European Pride and settled in North America.

As far as Isabel knew, Antonio's father Esteban had cast Solana out. It wasn't until Antonio had returned to take over the Pride after his father's death that Solana had mated with the new leader and rejoined the Panther population. There were many rumors bouncing around about how a non-shifter had become a shifter. Much had changed for the woman Isabel used to know. Now she ruled a Pride alongside Antonio Cruz. A fresh wave of panic rolled through her as she realized just how high ranking the people were that she was asking to see. Oh, God . . . what was she doing here? Miguel opened the door for her and ushered her in.

"Isabel." Solana's easy smile was so different from the cynical teenager Isabel remembered that she almost turned around and fled. Coming to another Pride for help could be the biggest mistake she'd ever made. She would have been better off on her own, on the run.

Stepping into the room, she placed her hand over her heart and bowed her head slightly, as befitted Pride leaders or their mates. "Solana. It's good to see you again."

"And you. Please, sit down." A small squeak erupted from a bassinet in the corner. Solana hopped up from her desk to scoop a tiny baby from the deep fuchsia bed. She laid the infant against her shoulder, bouncing a little until the crying quieted. "Shh, Oriana. That's a good girl."

"I'll have some refreshments sent in from the kitchen." Miguel stood with the doorknob in his hand; he gave Solana a look of mock severity. "Don't overdo it, or I'll send Antonio in to tie you down."

Solana smoothed a hand over the back of the dark-haired baby's head and stuck her tongue out at Miguel. "Whatever. Go pick on your own mate."

"I will, ma'am. Thank you for the invitation." He winked at her and closed the door behind him.

When they'd settled into a pair of comfortable chairs by the window and Isabel had a cup of hot coffee in her hands to warm her, Solana spoke again. "What brings you here? This isn't a social call, and if you were sanctioned to come, your Pride leader would have contacted Antonio."

Isabel nodded and took a deep breath. There were two options open to her at this point, breezily laugh and leave as quickly as possible, or explain the entire situation. She chose the second option. What more did she have to lose? "I would prefer that the Garcia family not know where I am."

"Why?" Solana's gaze was open and frank. She cuddled her daughter close to her chest.

Just do it. This was the moment. Isabel's throat closed, her mouth drying. She took a sip of coffee. "I wish to ask your mate for asylum."

That earned a raised eyebrow. "Oh?"

"I—I escaped Barcelona against my Pride leader's wishes." Her hands were shaking so badly, she had to set her coffee cup down on the table.

"Tell me what happened."

She swallowed, clenching her hands together in her lap. "Fernando Garcia's heir—Enrique—has decided he's my mate."

A short laugh answered that and Solana's eyes sparkled with irony. "No one decides who their mate is. Trust me on this."

"Enrique is obsessed. He insists that it's true, that I'm his. He's convinced his father that I'm just playing at resistance to draw out our courtship, that I'm lying about him not being my mate. But it's true, Solana." Isabel leaned forward, needing the other woman to believe her, needing *someone* to believe her. "I swear to God, it's true. I sense nothing when he's near me . . . he *is not* my mate."

"I see."

Her lips shook and tears welled in her eyes. She sucked in a deep breath, struggling for control. "I can't convince anyone in Spain that I'm not lying. He's so . . . convincing. So certain. And he has so much more influence and power than I do." It was hopeless. She sounded insane even to her own ears. Placing her hands on the arms of her chair, she pushed to her feet. "I'm so sorry for coming to you like this. This isn't your problem. I should never—"

"I'll do what I can to help you."

Isabel froze, still halfway out of her chair. Her legs gave out from under her, and she collapsed back into her seat and stared at Solana. "What?"

She gave a sympathetic smile. "I'll speak to my mate and his family. I'm certain they'll agree with me."

Blinking, Isabel's mouth opened and closed. Shock rolled through her. It couldn't be this easy. After all these months of terror in Barcelona, it couldn't end with so simple a solution. "You are?"

"Yes." Solana stood and set her daughter in Isabel's arms. "Here, hold Oriana for a moment."

Startled, she spread her fingers to support the newborn infant. She weighed next to nothing. It was odd to think that as Antonio's firstborn, this tiny girl, would grow up to be one of the most power people in the Panther world. Isabel could only hope her parents gave her siblings one day. The Cruz family was exceptionally large—most Panther couples had one or two children, if they were lucky enough to conceive at all. Solana and Isabel were both only children, but Antonio had *three* siblings. What would it be like to have had someone close to her in the past year? To have family to reach out to when things had spiraled out of control? A brother or sister would have been wonderful. Isabel lifted Oriana until they were eye level with each other. She had great dark eyes, a little rosebud of a mouth, and tufts of downy black hair. Some of the tightness eased in Isabel's chest just holding the child. "She's so beautiful."

"She is, isn't she? I think she looks like Antonio." A soft smile curved Solana's face as she reached for the phone, punching in a series of numbers. "Send one of the twins in here, please. Thank you."

Solana returned and gathered her daughter back up. "There's something comforting about holding a baby, isn't there?"

Allowing herself a grin, Isabel nodded. "Thank you. For everything."

A short knock sounded on the door before it swung open. A large man stepped inside. He was well over six feet tall with shaggy black hair that brushed his collar, high cheekbones, midnight eyes, and a full mouth she could only describe as sensuous. He was beautiful . . . but far too young for her.

She offered him a quiet smile, hoping to go unnoticed. His gaze swept over her, and she had a feeling she'd been assessed in that one penetrating glance. She wondered what conclusions he'd come to about her.

Solana leaned forward. "Isabel, this is Ricardo, Antonio's younger brother. Ric, this is Isabel Rivera—an old friend of mine who needs some help."

She'd heard of him. Everyone in the Panther world knew of the wild Cruz twins. They liked extreme sports and had done some insane things to risk their lives in the name of fun. The things she'd heard about what they did to women *at the same time* was wicked even for the sensual Panther people.

They were playboys, both of them. So, no matter how attractive this man was, he was too young and immature for her. She'd had enough of men in leading Panther families . . . there was nothing she needed more right now than to fly under the radar.

His hand reached out to shake hers. A jolt of shock went through her when they touched, her body and instincts lighting up like a Christmas tree. Mate. This man was her *mate.* Her sex clenched, dampened with want. A breath caught in her throat, strangling her. Her nipples beaded tight, and heat exploded within her.

A connection snapped tight between them, and lust so deep she couldn't contain it made her legs shake. His eyes widened and she knew he sensed it, too. His fingers tightened around hers, the rasp of calluses stroking over her palm. Her breath shuddered out.

Oh, God. This couldn't be happening now. Not with another man in one of the ruling families—spoiled and with more power than he knew what to do with, but no real claim to any kind of responsibility. No. A thousand times no.

Her luck couldn't possibly be this bad.

"Isabel." The sound of his deep voice was enough to make goose bumps break over her flesh. Her name was like a lover's promise on his lips.

She stared at those lips, wanting them on hers, his big hands on her body. All of her instincts were crying out in agreement. Yes. She wanted this man. Here. Now. It was all she could do not to grab his silk tie and use it to drag him to the floor and rip his suit off. A wave of heat rolled through her body—she didn't think her pussy had ever been this wet in her entire life. He still hadn't let go of her, and his other hand had lifted to stroke the racing pulse point in her wrist. She wanted those clever fingers between her legs, caressing her where she needed it the most.

"Yes." His gaze slid over her face, the edges of his irises flickering from black to gold. The color of a Panther's eyes when they unleashed the animal within them.

For a moment, she was confused. Had she actually spoken out loud? Then she realized he was now looking at Solana. The other woman had been explaining the basics of her situation to Ric while Isabel had been wrapped up in her sexual fantasies. She flushed, wishing her embarrassment would rid her of the longing that twisted inside her. It didn't.

"Antonio's going to want to speak to her," Solana went on as though she couldn't feel the sexual tension in the room when any Panther could sense the physical reaction Ric and Isabel were having toward each other. The pheromones were so thick in the air, she could cut them with a knife. "Ric, why don't you take her to his office? He should be out of his meeting in about ten minutes."

Ric stepped closer to Isabel and all the oxygen seemed to suck out of the room. She tilted her head back to look him in the eyes. Her heart raced, her nipples beading so hard they chafed against her bra. Her clothing felt too tight and restrictive. She wanted them off, wanted nothing between this man and her except naked flesh and time to do something about all this desire that was exploding in her belly.

How had this happened so fast? She didn't have time to think about it because her mind shut down the moment he reached for her.

Yes. She wanted him to touch her so badly she ached. It was her last coherent thought.

Yes.

Isabel. Her name rolled through Ric's mind like distant thunder. A storm approaching. He had a feeling it was the kind of wild tempest that would sweep across the landscape and leave everything changed when it passed.

Because she was his *mate.* With the way he and his twin had come to love playing with the same woman at the same time, Ric had doubted either of them was destined to have a mate. But he was wrong. The way his instincts thrummed inside him left him with no more doubts. Cold sweat broke out across his forehead. It was a sharp contrast to the fire burning in his veins. His cock was a steel pole in his trousers and had been since the moment he'd seen her. He shifted to the side, trying to adjust for a more comfortable fit.

Her bones felt delicate under his hand as he took her elbow to lead her out of the room. He had to clench his jaw to keep from groaning, savoring the softness of her skin. Her thin black silk shirt was buttoned up to the neck, but did little to hide her full breasts. They looked large enough to overflow his palms . . . and, damn, but he wanted to find out if they did.

She stepped in front of him to precede him out of Solana's office. His gaze was drawn like a magnet to his mate's ass, concealed as it was in a demur knee-length skirt, the luscious curve making his fingers twitch with the need to touch.

And that wasn't the only thing twitching with need. His cock throbbed, and he jerked his gaze away from her body as they passed into the hall. He closed the door behind them, leaving them alone in the hallway that lead to the main foyer. His mind drew a blank for a moment about why he wanted to go to the entryway and not to the back stairs that would lead up to his rooms where he could get his hands on Isabel's lush form. Oh, right. He was supposed to take her to Antonio's office. A growl of frustration vibrated Ric's vocal cords.

She glanced at him. "You're way too young for me."

"I'm twenty-seven." He arched a brow. That wasn't something he'd expected her to say, and he was usually pretty good at reading people. As a lawyer for the Pride, it was his job to assess any situation and spin it to his people's advantage. He and Diego made a good team that way. Diego was the charming, gregarious one who put the people they negotiated with at ease and convinced them he wasn't a threat . . . and no one noticed Ric until it was too late.

"I'm thirty-two."

"Oh." He'd certainly been with women who were significantly older than that, but it didn't seem the right thing to say to his mate. He doubted she wanted a laundry list of his affairs, and those women didn't matter. There had never been an emotional connection, for them or for him. They wanted him physically . . . usually both him and his twin together. He smiled. It wouldn't be sporting not to give a woman what she wanted. But now there was Isabel, and nothing would ever be the same again. No more fucking women with his twin . . . a mate meant a relationship, something to be cherished.

Even between mates, there was no guarantee of a happy future. It was something a couple had to work on. If there was one thing he was good at, it was work. Diego always claimed without him, Ric would have become a workaholic a long time ago. He winced. It didn't help that his twin was right.

They passed a large side table, so he fell back to let Isabel go ahead of him. She stopped and turned to look back at him, her mouth opened to speak. But he'd already stepped forward, so he collided with her. Off balance, she stumbled, and his hands snapped out to catch her before she fell. Her long, dark gold hair slapped against his face, the sweet scent of it filling his nose. His arms tightened around her, and she slammed back against him, her ass fitting itself against his cock. A groan escaped him, the fire within him raging out of his control. *Dios,* he wanted her. Now.

"Ric." His name was a breathy sigh on her lips, and her head leaned back to rest on his shoulder. The rich, whiskey-brown eyes flickered with golden fire. Her hand slid into his hair, twisting in the strands, and she pulled his head down to her. Their mouths met and heat exploded between them. She bit his lip, and their tongues twined, stroking against each other with a desperation born of pure, sweet need. He could smell how wet she was for him, and the scent intoxicated him. It was an invitation he couldn't resist.

This was insane. And between him and his twin, he'd done some crazy shit in his life. A shudder ripped through him at the feel of her soft body against his. He jerked his mouth away from hers. A quick glance around revealed a closet. He tightened his arm around her waist and steered her toward it. Snapping open the door, he thrust her inside and shut the door behind them. The darkness closed around them, but his extra senses kicked in and he could see just as well in the dark as he could any other time.

God, he couldn't fuck his mate for the first time in a cramped closet, but her hands were on his chest, her lips on his neck, and there was no way in hell he could deny her. But if he didn't get control of this situation now, he was going to come in his pants before he ever got the chance to fuck her. Nothing had ever gotten him this hot, this fast in his entire life.

Spinning her, he braced her hands against the wall. Her skin was pale, her bones fragile compared to his. "Don't move."

A whimper escaped her, and she arched back into him. "But—"

Jesus, he could smell how damp she was for him. Closed in the closet like they were, the scent surrounded them, taunting him with its sweet fragrance. He sucked in a deep breath, hoping for a calm he didn't find. "Do you want me to fuck you until you scream?"

"*Yes.*"

"Then don't. Move." He leaned his weight on his hands, pressing hers flat to the wall. Sliding his knee between hers, he nudged her legs apart. The hem of her skirt caught on his thigh, and he moved his hand down to tug it up around her waist.

He buried his nose in her hair while his fingers made quick work of his belt and zipper. His cock sprang free of its restraint, hot and eager to get inside her. He usually had more control than this. What the hell was wrong with him?

She pushed back against him, the soft curve of her ass rubbing against his hard cock. "What are you waiting for?"

His sanity to return. It didn't happen. He moved both hands to let his fingers trail down her arms, her skin like warm satin. She gasped when he cupped her breasts, the weight of them heavy in his hands. He was right. They did overflow his palms. She had generous curves, his mate.

His mate. The snap of his instincts made him clench his jaw as heat whipped through him. Her nipples jutted against his palms, and he flicked his nails over the hard tips through her shirt.

He slipped one hand down over the silk of her shirt and the bunched fabric of her skirt until he reached her lacy panties. Hooking his finger in the inset, he pulled them to the side. He couldn't even take the time to get rid of them. Desperation fisted in his belly, urging him to fuck her hard and fast. Taking his cock in his hand, he rubbed the head against her slick lips.

"Please." She choked, her hips moving back sharply to try and take him in.

Anticipation harsher than any he'd ever known had him in its grip. His cock pressed against her damp pussy and he thrust in hard and deep. They both groaned. God, she was tight, and the angle made it almost painful. Not that that would stop him.

She shoved back against him, rocking her hips into his thrusts. They moved together, his lower belly slapping against her backside. His breath bellowed out, making her hair flutter against her cheek. The fingers holding her panties out of the way slid forward to press hard against her little clit. Each thrust moved his fingers on her flesh, and she gasped with every stroke of his hips.

The feel of her wetness closing tight around his cock again and again made him clench his teeth. He was so damn close to coming, he had to close his eyes and try to review some tort law in his head to try to bring himself back under control. No way in hell was he coming before she did. He rolled his fingers over her clit, moving hard and fast. Her back bowed, and he could feel her muscles fist around his dick.

She moaned, her head falling back onto his shoulder. He opened his mouth on the exposed skin below her ear and sucked lightly. Low cries kissed his ears, and he could feel her moisture increase. She twisted in his arms. "Ric, I'm going to—"

"Come for me." He slammed his cock deep, pistoning his hips forward in short, rough thrusts.

A sob burst from her, tangling with a sharp scream. She rocked back against him, her body shuddering. "Yes. I'm coming, I'm *coming.*"

"Isabel." He moved his hands to her hips, gripped them tight, and his fingers dug in to her soft flesh. He let his control slip loose of its reins and hammered his cock into her slick, wet sheath. One, two, three hard thrusts and he jetted deep inside her. It went on and on, his heart pounding, fire flowing through his body.

"Oh, my God. *Ric.*"

He loved his name on her lips, the soft Spanish accent rolling the "R" into a caress. He flicked his fingers over her clit while her muscles milked his cock as she came. God, it was so good. Better than he'd ever had before. Better than he'd ever imagined it could be—even with a mate. For once, the rumors weren't exaggerated. It was damn near perfect with a mate.

"You know, I just realized something. Two somethings, actually."

The suppressed laughter in her voice made him smile. He kissed the top of her head. "Oh, really?"

"First, I'm suddenly seeing the benefits of having an energetic younger man."

He laughed outright at that and it made his cock slide free of her body, which made him laugh harder. He had to brace his hand against the wall in front of her to keep from falling on his ass. After a few long moments, he managed to get his mirth under control with only the occasional chuckle escaping. "Okay, now I have to hear the second something."

"This isn't Antonio's office." She giggled, pushing her skirt down. "I think we were supposed to be there about fifteen minutes ago."

Antonio. Brother. A shudder ran through him, and reality returned with a snap. How the hell was he going to explain to his twin brother Diego that in the blink of an eye, everything had changed for him? Which meant it had changed for both of them?

2

Diego watched his twin stumble into their office, a stunned look on his face. Concern whipped through him. Ric was the calm, collected one of the two of them. Now, he looked . . . panic-stricken. Diego closed his laptop, pushed away from his desk, and loped around to grab his twin by the shoulders. "Ric? What's wrong, man? You look like your snowboard kicked back and hit you in the face."

"I . . . met my mate." Ric shoved a hand through his hair, gripping the strands.

Shock to match his brother's rolled through Diego, left him gaping. They'd sampled every available woman in the Pride, and the scent of sex and female coming off of his twin was one he'd never smelled before, so Ric's mate was either a human or . . . "The friend who came to visit Solana."

"Isabel Rivera."

Steering his brother over to the nearest chair, he shoved him into it and clapped his hand on Ric's shoulder. "Cheer up, bro. This is good news."

He shook his head, the dumbfounded expression never leaving his face. "She's . . . I've never . . ."

"Knocked you speechless, huh? She must be one hell of a woman." A chuckle pulled from Diego's throat. He didn't think it sounded too forced. While he was ecstatic for his brother, a tiny part of him twisted into knots. For so many years, it had just been he and Ric putting their heads down and sticking it out through their father's leadership. While Antonio had been shipped off to serve as Second to the South American Pride leader for fifteen years because he'd challenged Esteban's conservative rigidity one too many times, and Andrea had run away at eighteen to model, Ric and Diego had been left to *survive*.

Inseparable, that was them. Diego and Ric. Ric and Diego. The Cruz twins. Now that was ending. What would they be if they weren't in on everything together? He felt like a complete ass for not being 100 percent happy for his brother, but . . . he wasn't. He'd never kept a secret from Ric, but this wasn't something Diego could share. Ever. He cleared his throat and mussed his twin's hair. "Get yourself together and I'll go meet her."

Now the panicked look was leveled at him, and Ric lifted his hands. "D. Be nice, man. She's having a bad time of it. She came to Solana seeking asylum." He sketched out some of the details and Diego's eyebrow arched. Ric's mate had certainly landed herself in a world of trouble . . . and Ric looked ready to hunt Enrique down and rip him to shreds with his bare hands. Diego would have to help, of course. It was a twin's job to serve as backup. Then Ric zoomed right back to looking freaked out. "So, take it easy with her. I know how you can—"

"Relax, bro. I promise not scare her, and I'm sure you'll work out how to help her. The family will get in on it, and everything will be fine." Diego fought to keep from rolling his eyes. His twin was older by four minutes and sometimes he acted like it was four years. Just because Diego liked to enjoy his life and had to drag his twin out of the office so he didn't turn into an old man before his time didn't mean he had no brains at all. He'd passed the California Bar Exam the same way Ric had, damn it. Did it really matter that law school was Ric's idea because he wanted Esteban to value them, to think they were worth something? Their father hadn't given a damn about them any more than he had their older siblings. They'd have been just as well off staying at the Pride's property up in the Sierra Nevada Mountains and becoming ski instructors.

Diego shoved his hands in his pockets, curling them into fists. If his twin didn't want him around for this mating thing he had going on, it might be time to make an exit up to the ski slopes. Ric was more than capable of handling all the legal paperwork for the Pride—Diego doubted anyone would miss him. A grin pulled at his lips. There were always a few choice human women willing to spend some time out of the snow and in his bed. Or, hell, *in* the snow would be fun, too. Made warming up afterward that much more entertaining.

Ric scrubbed a hand over his face and then stared off into space for a moment. "And she's, like, a *woman*, you know? She's older than me, and she's not someone you just fuck around with."

"Dude, she's your mate." Diego made his voice light, and some part of him *was* amused to see his unflappable brother in a tailspin over a woman. "No one's going to fuck around with her ever again. Except you."

"Holy shit."

"You said it."

"So, what did you do for the European Pride?" Antonio sat back in his chair, the leather creaking when his big body moved. Sharp intelligence shone in his midnight gaze and she found herself categorizing the similarities between Ric and Antonio.

The Pride leader was broader, more muscular . . . and that was saying something because Ric was a very large man, but he was also taller than his older brother. He had an intensity that rolled off him in waves, barely leashed. They had the same eyes, same cheekbones, same coloring, but Antonio was more regal, contained.

If it wasn't for the open brotherly affection on his face when Ric had shown her into this room, Isabel might have found Antonio terrifying. Except for a brief, very pointed glance between her and Ric, Antonio had not indicated that they reeked of sex. Her mate had retreated and left her with the Pride leader, and she was grateful Ric hadn't mentioned their newfound discovery. Under normal circumstances, such things were considered private for Panthers because there was so much societal pressure to mate and produce children. She didn't want to deal with any kind of public scrutiny right now. Or ever again.

Antonio motioned her into a chair opposite his desk and began discussing Pride matters, asking no questions about what had obviously happened between her and Ric. Gratitude spun through her at his tact. That, combined with the charisma he had oozing from his pores, and she completely understood why people said his Pride adored him. He had the kind of charm one might have associated with John F. Kennedy, only he was a Panther, and much, much better looking.

When his eyebrows rose, she realized that she not only hadn't answered his question, but she was staring at him. A flush heated her cheeks, and she cleared her throat. "I . . . wasn't anything special. I served as an administrative assistant to the leader's heir most recently. Before that, I was one of the chefs for a while and was fairly good at it—I have some culinary training in the human world."

In fact, she'd attended a culinary school in Paris. She'd been a pastry chef for the European Pride before Enrique had taken an interest in her and had her transferred to keep her closer.

There wasn't a day that went by that she didn't wonder how her life might be different now if she hadn't been in the kitchen that day. She'd taken on a double shift for two weeks while one of the other chefs had been on his honeymoon. That was when Enrique had come in and torn apart the existence she'd managed to piece together after her parents lost their lives in a sudden squall that overturned the boat they'd been sailing on. Her only family.

They'd been so close, their family loving and . . . everything a person could ask for from parents. Her heart ached now just remembering them. She missed them so much. Her only consolation was that they'd gone together. Neither of them would have coped well without the other, and she knew it. But, it hurt to be so bereft, so *alone*.

She hadn't been able to stand remaining in the Pride after that; everything had reminded her of them, of that connection she'd lost. So, she'd gotten permission to attend school in Paris . . . she'd needed some time to come to grips with the sudden tragedy, with the understanding that it was no one's fault; she had no one to blame but fate and nature for stealing the people she'd loved the most. A smile twisted her lips. It hadn't hurt her case for leaving that Fernando Garcia had a sweet tooth. The idea of having a professionally trained pastry chef in their den had appealed to him.

Antonio's chair squeaked as he leaned forward, breaking into her reverie. "We typically rotate tasks here unless someone has a particular talent or desire to remain in one area."

"That was how we did it in Spain, too. I preferred the chef's duties, but I'm willing to do just about anything . . . including being an administrative assistant again." That came out sounding a bit more desperate than she'd intended, but then, she *was* desperate, and anyone with a brain would be able to tell. This man certainly had a brain.

His brows contracted, and he thrummed his fingers against

the blotter on top of his huge wooden desk. "I don't really need an assistant, but we could always use more help in the kitchen. If you have training, we can put you to work there."

Some tightness eased from her muscles. "You mean, I can stay?"

"Since you obviously didn't have permission to be here, I had Miguel look into your background last night." He smiled when her eyebrows rose. Somehow it didn't surprise her that this man would be able to get his hands on any information he wanted. Especially with Miguel's help. The two of them were ... intimidating. Antonio rubbed a hand over the back of his neck. "As far as I can tell, you've had a fairly uneventful life. No criminal history, not even a hint of scandal, a good family who'd been with the European Pride for almost a century. That, and what my mate told me while you and Ric were ... ah, while you were busy." He coughed into his fist, his eyes twinkling. "Plus, Solana's vouched for your character, so that will get you a place here, if you're willing to pledge loyalty to—"

"I am. I will." Her hands dropped to the arms of her chair, gripping them tightly. Please let them allow her to stay. The need had sharpened with the realization that her mate was here. Twice in as many days, her life had been shaken up and tossed out like dice in a board game. It was too much ... and she needed something to hold on to. Something still and calm. A home.

Antonio stood, offering her a hand over the desk. She rose and shook it. He smiled. "Welcome to the North American Panther Pride."

"Thank you, sir." Shouldn't she feel more ... relieved? She had somewhere to stay, a Pride to call her own again. It hadn't even been as difficult as she'd imagined. But, no. The terror that had ridden her for months was still there. She didn't yet know if she was safe here. These people didn't know her. There was no telling if they would turn on her the way the members of her last Pride had. None of them had believed her when it really counted. If people who had known her her whole life didn't trust her, then why would the North American Pride members? The moment Enrique or his father got wind of her location and demanded she return to Spain, it was likely she'd be turned out without a second thought. A regular Pride member wasn't worth the kind of political trouble she could cause for them.

Maybe she should run—try to disappear into the human world. The idea of being away from Panthers terrified her. Except for her time in Paris, she'd never been away from her own kind. As much as she'd needed the distance then, it had stifled an integral part of her to be separated from other Panthers and only able to shift into cat form in her darkened apartment with the curtains drawn. But every Panther knew the consequences of slipping up and revealing their true nature to humans. Death. Simple, clean death. The end of a political threat to everyone. She understood that. The one thing all Panthers had to protect was their people. Without the code of secrecy they all lived with, they'd be hunted to extinction or used as lab rats. Either way, their way of life would end.

Could she pass for a human for the rest of her life? She didn't know. If she failed . . . she would die, and she could take her entire race down with her. No, she'd take her chances here first. If they turned on her . . . well, she knew what her real options were. They were few, and they sucked.

And then, there was the not-so-small problem of her mate. Ric. His scent still mixed with hers on her body, and the thought made her flash hot. She wanted him again. Nothing and no one had ever made her throw caution to the wind that way. It was disconcerting. And dangerously attractive.

The door opened, and she and Antonio both turned to see Ric step inside. A more carefree smile crossed his face than she'd seen so far.

His dark eyes met hers, and the same soul-deep recognition she'd felt in that first moment echoed in them. "Hello."

Closing the distance between them, he continued to stare at her as though he'd never seen her before. He smelled different, but she couldn't put her finger on what the change was. It was slight. Perhaps he'd showered, because he didn't smell like sex anymore, and a new cologne muddied his scent. The feeling was the same, her instincts screaming that he was her mate. Surprise flashed across his face when she stepped into his personal space and lowered her voice. "Ric, we need to talk."

They did need to talk, needed to decide how this thing between them was going to proceed, how much they would tell his family and the rest of the Pride. She was new here, and she wanted to fit in as smoothly as possible.

"I'm Diego."

She blinked and jerked back. "What?"

He grasped her elbows, keeping her from escaping. "I'm not Ric; I'm Diego. His twin."

"*I'm* Ric." An identical man stepped through the door, and her senses screeched with recognition. Of both of them.

She shook her head so hard her hair flew in a cloud around her face. Shock reverberated through her system. "No. It's not possible."

"What isn't?" Ric's gaze sharpened, flicking from her to Diego and back again. She felt pinned by its intensity, but his face smoothed and he slid his hands into his pockets, arching a dark brow.

Diego answered for her, his tone as disbelieving as she felt. "I think . . . we're *both* her mates."

"Don't even say it." Panic whipped through her when he put into words what her instincts had told her, and she wrenched herself free of his arms. Why couldn't anything make sense anymore? Anger followed on the heels of her panic. She was so fucking tired of not understanding anything. One man insisted they were mates when she felt nothing. Now *two* men set her instincts screeching? She clenched her jaw. "This. Is. Not. Possible. No one has two mates. Not ever. Not even if one dies."

He arched a brow identical to his twin's and folded his arms. "Well, I'm sensing it, and Ric sensed it, and clearly you've sensed it with both of us or you wouldn't be freaking out."

"I do not *freak out.*" She growled, rounding on him to blast him with the brunt of her anger. She knew it wasn't fair, and right now she didn't care. All of this was wrong. "Everyone knows the two of you are the spoiled babies of your family who think nothing of throwing yourselves into dangerous situations, so how do I know this isn't some new stunt? Just . . . just mess with the woman who has no power to stop you because you *can?*" *Oh, God.* Tears began welling in her eyes and she spun to face the window, frantically wiping her cheeks.

"Maybe Enrique did that to you, but don't put us in the same category. Anything we've ever done to a woman is something she was willing to participate in. We're not assholes. Jesus." Ric stepped up behind her to set his hands on her shoulders. His touch was gentle, the heat of his skin warming her through her shirt. She could smell herself on his hands.

A flush heated her cheeks at the reminder of what she'd done with him. What her body was more than willing to do again no matter how her mind argued against it. Lust curled in her belly, more insistent than any she'd ever experienced before. Senses singing with recognition of the two younger men, her muscles softened with the need to lean into him and seek deeper contact. No. She didn't know how it was possible to create such a muddying of the instincts, but she knew there was no such thing as a mated three-way. Somehow they were managing to toy with her.

She stiffened her knees and bit out, "Everyone knows you like to tag team women. So, what is this? Your attempt at making it permanent? It isn't funny. Go jump out of a plane or something if you want some thrills."

"Isabel." Solana's voice sounded from the doorway. How had Isabel missed the other woman's approach? She pulled away from Ric and turned from the window to face the rest of the room. Longing sliced through her when Solana tucked herself against Antonio's side—the adoration on their faces was an enviable thing. "What Ric and Diego don't like to let out of the bag is that they're the legal counsel for our Pride. They're only spoiled on weekends. The rest of the time they work their asses off."

"Work hard, play harder." Diego stepped closer, stroked her hair away from her face, and smoothed it over her shoulder. The same powerful reaction gripped her when he touched her. She closed her eyes and swallowed as fire licked through her system. Her sex heated, pulsing with want. His dark masculine scent caressed her nostrils, made her sway toward him. Her thighs locked, squeezing together to still the rising flames.

The twins closed in on either side of her, and it was all she could do not to moan. She shouldn't let them near her. She wanted to drag them somewhere private so she could do something about the need clawing through her. The intensity of her response scared her, confused her.

So much had happened to her in the last year, she couldn't take it all in. She felt storm tossed, swept under by forces she couldn't control. She didn't like it one bit. There was no way both of these men could be her mate. It wasn't possible. It was one more powerful man jerking her around. She wanted no part of it. Being a normal Pride member was just fine for her—she didn't want to be a part of politics in her world. She liked things quiet. Once upon a time she might have liked bad boys, but then she learned how bad a boy could be. No more of that for her. She was done. Peaceful calm sounded great right now.

"What is *that*?"

Shock made her stomach clench as she realized what Diego was asking about, his gaze pinned on her neck. With the chaos of her day, she'd almost managed to forget about it. Her eyes closed as shame washed over her, and her hand clamped over the collar of her shirt, drawing the edges together. The top button must have come undone when she was having sex with Ric *in a closet*. Jesus. "It's nothing. Don't worry about it."

Diego reached out a single finger and edged it along her collar until she had to let go or wrestle with him over her clothing. She swallowed and eased her grip. Her humiliation was complete. He made a small choked sound in the back of his throat. "This isn't nothing."

She couldn't meet his gaze, didn't want to see the look on his face when he saw what Enrique had done to her. "He bit me. Enrique Garcia. Tried to mark me as his mate. That's when I ran—I knew there'd be no reasoning with someone that convinced of himself."

The raw puncture wounds from his fangs still sported dried blood, and her skin was swollen and bruised around the bite. She snatched her shirt from Diego's hand to hastily button it up. Her stomach executed a slow pitch and roll, and she stomped down on the memories of Enrique trapping her against his desk, tearing at her clothes, sinking his fangs into her flesh. Even her superhuman strength was nothing compared to a full-grown Panther male's. It wasn't until he ripped her pants open that she'd managed to wriggle back over the top of the desk, slamming her heel into his nose when he grabbed for her again. The sickening crunch of his cartilage giving way still echoed in her mind, but it hadn't stopped her when he howled in agony, crimson blood gushing down his white shirt. She'd sprinted for her room, jerked on the first outfit she found, thrown everything she could get her hands on in suitcase, and slipped out the back of the Pride den. She could sense the activity at the front of the mansion as Enrique's wails drew the attention of every Panther in the vicinity. It was all the opportunity she'd needed, and she'd made a run for it.

"Panthers heal when they sleep, Isabel. This should be gone."
Ric's fingers brushed over the silk that concealed the wound.

She swallowed and looked away. Exhaustion at the emotional roller coaster she'd been on swamped her. "I haven't . . . I haven't been able to sleep since then."

"When you do, it will heal as though it never were." Diego lifted her chin, forcing her to look at him. "You can put this behind you."

The only mark that would ever stay on her skin was a mate bite—it left a scar that anyone could see. Sleep awakened the magic within her blood and healed her of any sickness, injury, or blemish. If only memories were as easy to erase.

Diego's thumb brushed over her jaw. "You're safe here."

Safe? When was the last time she'd felt truly *safe?* Not since her parents died. Then she'd found that no matter how old she was, she could still feel like an orphaned child. Part of the Pride, yes, but belonging to no one. The Pride didn't need her. It was a status symbol to have many Panthers in a Pride, but she, Isabel, wasn't needed for anything. What had happened with Enrique showed exactly what could happen to a Panther alone. Her parents would have stood beside her, guarded her as best they could. But they were gone, she reminded herself with as much brutality as she could manage. Nothing with Ric and Diego was certain; she still had to find a place for herself in this Pride, and she had to accept that the only person she could trust enough to rely on was herself. She was alone, unprotected . . . unsafe.

3

Diego felt the tension running through Isabel's body as they walked up the stairs just before dawn. Panthers were naturally nocturnal, so the sun rising was their cue to head for bed. He glanced down at his mate. Those amber eyes of hers were . . . haunted. Fear and wariness warred with the exhaustion in her gaze. He clenched his fists. No one should have to go through what she had—especially not a woman. She looked both ways when they reached the top of the steps, confusion puckering her forehead. "I forgot to ask Solana where I'm supposed to sleep tonight."

"With us." He slid his hands into his pockets and waited for her reaction to that. "You don't have to be alone tonight. You're safe here with us, Isabel."

Instead of protesting the sleeping arrangements, she looked even more terrified. Her arms hugged around her waist. He wanted to pull her into his arms, but he doubted she'd welcome his touch just now. She blinked fast to get rid of the tears that momentarily sheened her eyes. "What if he followed me? What if he comes when I'm asleep and I'm so tired I don't sense him?"

"No one enters this Pride's den without someone knowing." He couldn't hold himself back, reaching out to set his hands on her shoulders and cup the delicate joints. "We have guards at the entrance at all times. You had to get passed them to get to the mansion, remember?"

Her throat worked when she swallowed and nodded. Ric stepped up behind her and rubbed his palm up and down her back. She glanced over at him and then back at Diego. "I know that, but—"

"But, also, we're here." He caught her gaze with his, willing her to believe him, if only on this one issue. He stroked his fingers down her arms, the silk of her shirt giving way to the satin softness of her skin. "Even if he makes it passed the guards and security systems and all the other Panthers in this den, he still has to get through both of us to get to you."

Moisture welled in her eyes again and she sucked in a shuddering breath. She tried to smile, but it wavered as a tear tracked down her cheek. "You're not what I expected."

"We get that a lot." Ric's hand cupped the back of her neck.

Diego shrugged and smiled, trying to turn the conversation to something lighter. "As I said, work hard, play harder. When was the last time you played, my mate?"

A short laugh burst from her, the shadows in her eyes fleeing for a moment to be replaced with a shimmer of heat. "I won't let you bait me. You can't both be my mate. This is part of your *playing* hard. Mating isn't a game."

"It is if you're playing for keeps." He leaned in until his mouth was a hairsbreadth from her lips, locking his gaze with hers so she could see he was dead serious.

Her breath caught, and he saw the edges of her amber eyes give way to gold. Her gaze latched on to his lips, and she licked hers. "Touché."

He barely held back a groan, watching that little pink tongue of hers dart out to moisten her lips. Didn't she realize what that sensual motion could do to a man? His cock went rigid. The protectiveness he felt for her twined together with hot lust. "I know you don't necessarily believe the two mates thing, but at least trust that we wouldn't let anything happen to any member of our Pride. That includes you now."

He saw the keen desire in her eyes. To believe him. To trust. She wanted to reach out, he could tell. Her soft mouth twisted, and her chin dipped in the slightest of nods.

"Are you ready?" He proffered his hand.

She lifted her hand toward his, her fingers hesitating for the briefest moment before they settled in his. "Yes."

He and Ric each put a hand on her waist and steered her into the sitting room of their suite. She paused to collect herself before stepping into the room. Arching her eyebrows, she gave a pointed look to where her suitcase had already been unloaded from her car and placed beside the door. "Did I really have a choice?"

"Always." Ric slid his hands in his pockets and leaned against the door after he'd shut it behind them. A smile kicked up the corner of his mouth. "That doesn't mean we won't try to influence your decisions. They affect us, too."

Diego wandered over to a chair and plopped down, hooking a leg over the arm. He gave her a slow, easy smile, letting his gaze slide over the full curves of her body. A flush washed up her cheeks, and a shy smile curved her lips. Fascinating. Bold and sweet at the same time.

He wondered what time would reveal about the depths of her. It would be interesting to see how she reacted to the sports the twins loved, and he was curious to see if she'd be willing to participate. There was nothing that could strip away the layers of a person like an extreme situation. She had courage—just walking away from Spain and coming here proved that, but he'd like to see more of her. He'd like to see all of her, the feral Panther beneath the very human woman.

"I'm ... um ... just going to take a shower." She scooped up her bag and scurried toward the open bathroom door, but she paused and turned back before she entered. "Do you two share the same bedroom?"

"We're grown men, so ... not usually." He didn't say that they only shared the same bed if a woman shared it with them, but considering her earlier statements about their reputation, he doubted she needed him to elaborate. It wasn't as though their reputation hadn't been well earned. Then again, it looked like they might be sleeping with the same woman for the rest of their lives, so the legend continued. He nodded toward the two closed doors that led off the sitting room. "The one on the left is mine. The one on the right is Ric's."

"Oh." A flush raced up her pale gold skin. Her fingers fidgeted with the handle of her suitcase. "I didn't mean to make it sound like you couldn't sleep by yourselves—"

"It's fine. You don't know us." He let a beat pass before he spoke again. "Yet."

Running a hand through her hair, she closed her eyes, and huffed out a soft laugh. "Right. Of course."

The second she entered the bathroom, Ric turned on him. "This is completely insane. You know that, right? I mean, shagging one chick at the same time is one thing ... but to have the same mate? How the hell does *that* happen?"

"Fate." Diego shrugged, watching his twin pace the length of their suite. "It seems kind of appropriate considering we are who we are and we do what we do to women."

"Since when are you the calm Ghandi-like one?" Ric flipped open the door to his room, shooting an irritated look over his shoulder.

"I'm sure it'll pass. Don't freak out, bro."

He scrubbed a hand over his hair. "I'm not unhappy; I just never expected any of this."

"I know. We both never really thought there'd be any mates for us. But it's not a bad thing."

"Yeah." He sighed and walked through his bedroom door, but left it standing open. "We'll use my room tonight. Bring her in when she's done."

"No problem."

Diego sat up when the bathroom door swung open and Isabel stepped out wrapped in a fluffy purple bathrobe. Even its bulk didn't disguise her curves. He doubted anything really could. Thank God. His gaze traveled from the tips of her toes curling into the carpet, over the swells and dips of her body. Damn, she was hot.

When he reached her face, he sobered. She looked exhausted, barely holding together. Solana and Andrea had both had that haunted look in their eyes when they returned to the Pride, though for different reasons. Still, every protective instinct lit up inside him.

His fists clenched at his sides. Enrique Garcia better pray they never met. Especially not in a dark alley away from the prying eyes of humans. Diego almost smiled, running his tongue down a canine tooth that had elongated into a fang in the last few seconds. On the other hand, it would be healthier to get rid of the rage bubbling up inside him, so maybe he should arrange a meeting.

That anyone would dare put his hands on a woman in anger made him want to hit something. That the woman in question was his mate made too many emotions run through him. He didn't bother to put a check on his anger . . . he had Ric to consider things rationally. One of them had to shake things up a bit, and that was Diego's job.

He rolled to his feet and strolled over to the bathroom door.

She tilted her head to the side, but didn't step back as he drew closer. He leaned in until he could feel the heat of her flesh, the tips of her breasts a hairsbreadth away from his chest. A spark of heat simmered in her gaze, calling him like a siren's song.

Clenching his jaw, he refused to let himself grab for her. There was time for that later. At the moment, she needed rest more than she needed sex. She licked her lips, staring at his mouth. His cock went rock hard. Christ. "Don't start something you can't finish."

She glanced away, a little smile curling her lips. "I won't."

When she looked back up at him, he saw the fire in her gaze, saw the way her amber eyes flickered to gold and back again. Stepping forward, she pressed her body to his. He groaned, his arms rising to snap around her waist and haul her closer. Damn, but he wanted a taste. And he'd never been one to deny himself what he wanted, especially if he had a willing woman nearby.

He brushed his mouth over hers, letting her flavor roll over his tongue when he flicked the tip of it over the seam of her lips. She opened for him. He delved into the hot recesses of her mouth, taunting and teasing her tongue into dueling with his. The soft sounds she made in her throat only spurred him on. Heat roared inside him, the Panther inside him recognizing its mate and wanting to claim. Her robe fell back when she lifted her leg to wrap it around his thigh, her hips pushing closer. God, the scent of her intoxicated him. She was dangerous, addicting. There was nothing that could have attracted him more. He tilted his head to slant his mouth over hers at a different angle, nipping at her lower lip.

Cupping his hand around her knee, he hitched her leg higher on his hip before he stroked his fingers up the soft skin of her thigh. He expected to meet the resistance of clothing, but found her naked instead. He groaned, tearing his mouth from hers. "No pajamas."

"I didn't manage to grab any when I left Spain."

"Thank God." His dick was so hard it almost hurt. He was so hot for her, he was afraid he'd come in his pants before he could get inside her. Even as a randy teenager, he'd never been this desperate for a woman.

Twining her arms around his neck, she let her head fall back. "This is insane."

"Then go crazy for me." He pressed a line of kisses up her jaw until he reached her ear, sucking the lobe into his mouth.

A gasp erupted from her throat as she arched closer. "I don't know how."

"Let me show you." His hand lifted to the collar of her robe, shoving it out of his way.

She cried out, her fingers tightening on his hair hard enough to make him still. He pulled back to look at her, and her amber eyes had lost the sparks of gold. Pain shone there, and he saw that he'd accidentally touched the wound on her collarbone. It brought him crashing back to reality. Enrique. Why she'd come to San Francisco in the first place. Damn. He drew away, straightened her robe, and tamped down his own need.

He scooped her into his arms and cradled her against his chest. She sighed, wrapped her arms around his neck, and rested her cheek on his shoulder. "I'm sorry."

"Don't be." He kissed the top of her head. "None of this is your fault."

Stepping into Ric's room, Diego nudged the door closed with his foot. The light was already out, and when his eyes adjusted to the dark, he saw that his twin had already fallen asleep. He set Isabel on the bed, tugging the covers up to allow her to scoot into the middle of the mattress.

Vulnerability flickered in her gaze as she stared up at him, but she resolutely closed her eyes. She rolled to her side and faced away from him, but the tension was back in her muscles. He crawled in behind her, curving his arm around her waist. "If you're going to close your eyes, then really sleep. Nothing and no one will touch you unless you want. Not while we're here. You're safe."

"I'm safe," she whispered the words, but he doubted she believed them. He stroked his hand through her damp hair and down her side, petting her anywhere he could reach. A low purr rumbled from her throat, and her body softened under his touch. Within a few minutes, her chest lifted and fell with the slow, steady rhythm of sleep.

He kept sliding his hands over her, partly to make sure she stayed asleep and partly because he wanted to savor the opportunity to touch her. Something inside him loosened at the knowledge that as much as his world had changed today with her stumbling into it, she wasn't going to be a catalyst to drive a wedge between Ric and him. The more things changed, the more they stayed the same. A permanent woman that they both developed a relationship with was something new, but he welcomed the challenge the way he would any other.

Things were going to get very, very interesting. He couldn't wait. A smile lifted the corners of his lips. Curling himself around her, he let himself slide over into slumber, his mate's sweet scent teasing his nose and haunting his dreams.

Light filtered through her eyelids when Isabel awoke the next day. She took a deep breath and smelled no one in the room except Diego and Ric. The heat from their big bodies surrounded her, embraced her without touching. She opened her eyes and found the sunset playing over Diego's features. He was already awake and watching her. She smiled. "Hi."

"Hey, there." His palm cupped her shoulder. "Feel better?"

Did she? She felt . . . wonderful. Comfortable. Relaxed. Safe. It was disturbing that just sleeping in a bed with them could cause such a change in her mindset, but she pushed that away. She could deal with it later. She tucked her hair behind her ear and nodded at Diego. "I feel rested. Thank you."

"Anytime." His shoulder hunched in a shrug, and his hand moved to tug the collar of her robe to the side.

She realized she didn't feel the nagging ache of Enrique's bite anymore. "It's gone now."

"Yeah, not a scratch on you." He bent forward to press a kiss to the healed flesh. Her breath caught, and she tilted her chin to the side to allow him greater access. Heat spun inside her, and her pussy clenched in want. His tongue flicked out, drawing a damp path down her collarbone until he reached the base of her throat. There he opened his mouth over her neck and sucked lightly on the skin.

Pleasure arced through her system. She whimpered and wriggled closer, lifting her leg to curl it over his lean hip. Her robe fell back, and his nimble fingers loosened the belt to spread the terry cloth open. He grasped her thigh, pulling her tight to his body. Her naked flesh rubbed against the clothing he'd slept in. His dress shirt felt rough against her beaded nipples, and she rubbed her breasts over his chest to increase the friction.

"I can feel how hot you are, Isabel." His pelvis rotated, the muscles in his ass flexing beneath her leg as he rubbed his hard cock against her. The fabric of his slacks stimulated her clit, made her want to scream. His breath whispered over her ear, his low voice an erotic litany. "I want to slide in so deep, start fucking you slowly and moving faster and faster until we can't take it anymore."

A cry burst from her throat, liquid fire pulsing in her veins. She needed it just like he described it. Her pussy clenched each time he arched his hips into hers. She tightened her leg around him, twisting to get closer. "Please, please. Oh, my God. Please."

"Shh." His arms wrapped tight around her, stilling her movements. His cock pressed to her pussy, but she couldn't get enough friction to make herself come.

Her claws slid out to rake down his chest and slice through

his shirt, ripping it open. The pads of her fingers brushed over one of his flat nipples. "But, I need—"

"I know. I'll give it to you, baby." His hand slid to her hip and then around to her pussy. She gasped, widening herself for his touch. His fingertips brushed over the lips of her sex, not pressing in, just teasing her.

She moaned, wrapping her fingers around his wrist to try and force him deeper. He resisted, still moving in those light strokes. "*Please*, Diego."

He twisted his wrist in her grasp until he caught her hand in his. Pushing both of their fingers in her wet sex, he demanded, "Show me how you like it."

"Yes." Fire raced through her body as she cupped her palm over his hand, masturbating herself with his fingers. His skin was rougher than hers, the friction better than when she touched herself.

"Isabel." He groaned, letting her direct the movement of their hands. She pushed one of his long fingers inside her soaking channel, sliding one of her fingers in with his. They stroked her pussy together. His head dropped forward, his tongue licking a path down the length of her neck. "I love the feel of you. So hot and wet."

"Diego." Fisting the fingers of her free hand in his hair, she pulled his mouth up so she could kiss him. Her teeth scraped his lip, and their kiss became rough, brutal. She tasted the coppery tang of his blood as his lip split, but the flavor turned her on even more. Every sensation just added to those that already threatened to overwhelm her.

She broke her mouth away from his and kissed her way down the smooth muscles of his chest until she reached the edge of his slacks. Tugging open his belt and zipper, she moved so she could kneel over him and eased his pants down. He lifted his hips to help her. The hard length of his cock filled her palms as she fondled him. He was so hot, the flesh stretching taut over the flared crest. He groaned. "Stroke me, Isabel. I want you to pump my cock through your fingers, and then suck me hard."

"Oh, God. The things you say." They made her hotter, made her blush so hard her skin burned. But she wanted to do exactly what he said. She slid the fingers of one hand up and down his dick, while the other cupped the soft sacs beneath.

His breath hissed out and she glanced up at him. His irises had gone pure gold, and he leaned up on his elbows to watch her touch his cock. Then his gaze moved to something over her shoulder. "Enjoying the show, bro?"

"What?" She stiffened in surprise, trying to turn and follow his gaze, but his fingers slid into her hair to hold her in place. He pulled her down until his cock brushed against her lips. His pre-cum smeared over her mouth, and she flicked her tongue out to taste it. Him. The salty flavor of his come burst over her taste buds. She sucked him deep into her mouth. His hips arched, and he groaned.

"Good morning, Isabel." Ric's hand curved around her hip from behind. His other hand balled in the back of her open robe, pulling it off her body and leaving her naked. The cool air in the room made her nipples pucker tighter. His fingers stroked up her bare legs until he reached the crux of her thighs. He rubbed her swollen lips, parting her so he could flick his nail over her throbbing clit. She whimpered around Diego's cock, her body burning hotter than it ever had in her life. She'd never had two men at once, and the feel of four rough male hands on her was startlingly erotic.

Her breath seized when Ric's mouth replaced his fingers. He lapped at her wet sex, sucking her plump lips between his teeth. His palm stroked over her ass, moving to the small of her back to arch her toward him. Her muscles shook with need, her pussy fisting on emptiness. He bit at her clitoris, stabbing it with the tip of his tongue. Her fingers curled into the sheets beneath her, her knees digging into the mattress as she pushed harder against those talented lips.

"Do you like that, Isabel? Does it feel good when he eats your pussy?" Diego's black magic voice purred above her. She choked on a shuddering breath, squealing when his palm slapped her backside. She'd never felt so feral, so uncontrolled, and everything inside craved more of this. Of them.

Ric's mouth left her and she moaned a protest, but whimpered when his cock slid over her swollen lips. He plunged into her with one hard stroke. She hissed on Diego's cock at the harsh stretch, but it felt so damn good. She was so wet from the teasing earlier that Ric slid in smoothly, his hard belly spanking against her ass with each deep thrust.

His thumb and forefinger slid along her vaginal lips, stretching her so each thrust of his cock was so tight it was almost painful. She rolled her tongue over the head of the cock in her mouth, working it with the feverish intensity that burned through her. His hand moved up to tease her anus, drawing her slick moisture up to lubricate her ass. She jolted in surprise. God, she loved anal. It was her naughty pleasure. A flush burned her face, but she couldn't keep from shoving her ass back into his stroking fingers to push them deeper.

She sucked Diego's cock in so deep, her throat contracted around him. His fingers tightened in her hair. "Oh, shit, Isabel. That's amazing. I want to see your cheeks hollow from sucking me so hard."

Cream flooded her sex at his words, making a liquid slapping noise on Ric's next thrust. It was so forbidden, so naughty to have them do this to her. She didn't want it to ever end. She pulled Diego in deep enough that her eyes teared up, but she loved that she could make him so uncontrolled he groaned with every movement of her mouth, tugging on her hair in his desperate need for orgasm. It made her feel powerful, wanton, and sexy to have both of these men want her so much.

He hissed, his hand sliding over the naked skin of her back. His claws raked her flesh lightly and made her shiver. "Yeah, just like that. Now, use your tongue and slide it down the bottom. That's how I like it."

God, the two of them made her burn. They were very different men. Diego said the filthiest things to her, made her shiver with the naughty images his words painted for her. But Ric preferred to let her know what he liked with actions. He didn't say much, just pushed her to new heights with his mouth, fingers, and cock.

Diego's hand tightened on her hair, his thrusts coming faster and hard between her lips. She licked his salty flesh, suckling his long cock. His harsh breath ended on a hiss when his lean hips froze, his dick pulsing in her mouth. His come flooded her tongue, and she swallowed it, drawing on his cock until it softened against her lips. He shuddered and pulled away from her, rolling to lie beside her. His long fingers massaged the hinge of her jaw. The muscles there burned from his harsh thrusts, so she sighed in pleasure.

She couldn't relax though. Ric wasn't done with her, and the need for orgasm still raged through her system. He plunged his finger into her ass, rubbing the head of his cock through the thin membrane that separated the two. The walls of her pussy fisted around him, which only accentuated the dual penetration. Her breath sobbed out, and she dropped lower, pressing her cheek to the mattress. She could smell their three scents mixing with that of musky sex, and it drove her wild. Her hips undulated against him, taking him as deep as possible. Ecstasy wound tighter and tighter in her belly.

Diego slid his hand under her, cupping her breast to tweak her nipple. He pinched and rolled it between his fingers. Fire blasted through her. It was too much, one too many sensations lashing through her at once. She screamed, her sex convulsing around Ric's cock. He pumped into her hard, three powerful strokes before he froze, his cock buried deep, and came in long, hot spurts inside her. He continued to thrust his finger into her ass, drawing out her orgasm as long as possible while Diego fondled her breasts. Her body shook in rough shivers, and she closed her eyes to focus on the pleasure that seemed endless.

All the while her instincts sang in recognition. Mate, mate, *mate*. Both of them. Hers. Undeniably hers. Collapsing, the twins again curled around her on the bed. Diego murmured sweet things in her ear while Ric ran his big hands over her body until her heart stopped hammering and her breathing slowed to normal. She'd never felt so cherished by any lover before, let alone two of them.

She had no idea what the future held for her, what she would do if Enrique tracked her down, but for the moment her present looked amazing. If she focused on that, maybe everything would work out for the best. She knew it was irresponsible not to be prepared for the Garcia family interfering in her new life here, but the feline lassitude that pulled at her thoughts urged her to enjoy the now and worry about the future when it came. Wrapping an arm around each of the men, she sighed, shut off all her very human worries, and let the Panther within her take over to drag her down into a catnap with her mates.

4

Ric watched Isabel over the next week to make sure she adjusted to the Pride . . . and to her two mates. Since that first night, she hadn't mentioned not believing they weren't both her mates, but she didn't tend to say much. She was quiet, like him. At times, he worried that she was almost too withdrawn, too cautious. He didn't think her reticence was as natural to her as his was to him, though she didn't seem as gregarious as Diego.

It was unusual for Ric to spend so much time thinking about one woman, to wonder what she thought, what she felt. It was Diego who got people to open up, to laugh and talk. Ric preferred the solitary nature of his work. Unless he was in a meeting, he buried himself in the minutiae of the law. With his twin as company, he'd never needed anything or anyone else.

Until now.

He found himself looking forward to the end of his workday, to the time he and Diego spent with Isabel. Like now. He folded his hands behind his head and leaned against the back of the couch in their sitting room, propping his feet on an ottoman. The news played on the flat-screen television they'd mounted to the wall like a painting. Leaning forward, he snagged a folder containing a trade contract they were currently negotiating with a South African company Antonio wanted to buy into. Investing in companies inside the territory of another Pride was always a delicate situation. Each Pride ruled a continent, but the African Pride had special circumstances to consider. Until recently, the Pride had been defunct because of a civil war that sent surviving members fleeing to safer continents. Cesar Benhassi, a distant relation to the last Pride leader, had just stepped forward to re-form the African Panthers. Antonio had been the first leader to offer an alliance to Benhassi, which put the North American Pride in a good position for negotiating. Aside from the convoluted history of Panther politics, Ric's job was to research the stability of the company under consideration.

Spreading the African file across his lap to read, he waited for Isabel and Diego to join him. His twin had gotten stuck in a meeting Antonio, Miguel, and Solana were having with their security expert Landon. He was a human mated to Carmen, one of their Pride members. It had been more than a little controversial when Antonio let a human join the Pride. Until now, no human was allowed to know about their kind. Ever. If Panthers had the misfortune to be destined to mate with humans, they were cast out of the Prides and were forbidden to reveal their true nature to their mate. Only time would tell how this affected the Panther world as a whole.

Ric had been more than willing to miss that meeting because Miguel had been a bear lately. Andrea was introducing a new line of clothing for her design company at some fashion show in Tokyo, and he hadn't been able to go with her because he was needed here for some tricky political meetings they were having with delegates from the Australian Pride. Miguel was, hands down, their best political advisor, but mates didn't do well when separated, and the older man was showing the strain.

The entire family had been ecstatic when Antonio's longtime

friend from South America had been their sister's mate. The two had had a rough courtship, but they seemed happy now, and Ric was glad for them.

His head came up and turned toward the door when he caught Isabel's scent. A moment later, the door to their suite swung open, and she stepped inside. She shut the door behind her, leaned back against it, closed her eyes, and sighed. She looked tired . . . and sad. He had a moment's panic when he realized he was alone with her, and this meant he'd have to deal with whatever was bothering her by himself. Soothing people was Diego's area. Political debates, family discussions, extreme sports, and the law were the only topics Ric could hold up his end with, but he was willing to try for Isabel.

"You look upset. What's wrong?" He winced at the bald question. *Smooth, Cruz. Very smooth.* Just what every woman wanted to hear, that she looked like hell. Her head came up and she gave him a flinty stare.

Swallowing, he gave up on talking and patted the couch next to him. He tossed the file on his lap aside and punched a button on the remote to turn off the television. Isabel sighed, straightened, and walked over to sit beside him. He pulled her closer, curved his arm around her, and ran his hands up and down her back. She rested her cheek against his chest, relaxing by degrees.

He kissed her forehead. "Are you all right?"

"Yeah." She kicked off her shoes and curled against his side. The way her arms went around him and held on tight had a desperate edge to it, but her voice remained calm. "It was a long day. The head chef, Benita, has a granddaughter turning seven tomorrow. We made a huge cake."

When she didn't say more, he stifled a curse. She couldn't just tell him what was going on? He was just as likely to make it worse as he was to make it better if he had to pry it out of her. "What else happened?"

There. That couldn't possibly get him into trouble, could it? A simple, straightforward request for information.

She sniffled, and a downward rush of horror twisted through him when he realized she was crying. Her tears soaked through his shirt to dampen his skin. Oh. Holy. Christ. Where was Diego when he needed him? Ric patted her back, his mind racing for something to say to help. Feeling completely useless was something he'd tried to avoid his entire life, and here he was, flummoxed by a crying woman.

"It's so s-stupid." She tried to pull away, swiping at her cheeks.

He didn't let her go, pulling her into his lap until she straddled his hips. "What is? Did someone do something to you? Tell me who, and I'll fix it."

Instead of fighting him, she dove into his embrace and the tears fell faster. His arms tightened around her as he waited for the storm to pass. She clung to him. "N-no one did anything. It just made me think of my p-parents the way Benita was so excited about doing something for her family. My mom used to do things like that for me all the time, even after I grew up. She was just so amazing. Both of my parents were." She buried her face in his shoulder as her breathing began to slow to normal. "I told you it was stupid."

"Missing people you love isn't stupid." But that was about as much as he could relate to her pain. He'd never lost anyone he loved deeply. His mother had passed away when he was too young to have known her as a person, though he knew her death profoundly affected Antonio, Andrea, and their father, Esteban.

When their mother had lived, the Pride was a happier place, but that was about as much as Ric remembered. Everything had changed when she died. The balancing influence she'd had on Esteban had gone with her, and he'd become less of a leader and more of a tyrant. He'd banished Antonio to the South American Pride, and driven Andrea away from the Panther world completely. That was the Pride that the twins had grown up in, had lived with until the day Esteban died. It was only since Antonio returned to take over—and managed to get Andrea to come back—that Ric had seen how good things could be again. He and Diego did their level best to make sure Antonio had whatever he needed to make sure they never went back to the way it was with their father.

It was difficult to imagine a life with parents who adored their children. In that way, Oriana's life would be very different from her parents' and uncles' and aunt's. He was glad that his niece might have the kind of nurturing experience that Isabel grew up with . . . and have fond memories of them when they were gone. But, as normal as they would make Oriana's childhood, there were certain realities she couldn't escape no matter how much they loved her. As a member of a ruling family, her actions would always be more scrutinized than anyone else's. It was part of the reason both Ric and Diego found it so necessary to cut loose and do wild things, like free climb to the top of mountains only to paraglide down once they reached the summit.

"I do miss them. Every day." She sighed, and her breath whispered over his flesh. He gritted his teeth against the automatic reaction his body had to her. The way her breasts pressed to his chest didn't help, but she didn't need him grabbing at her right now. And, as he'd told her that first day, he wasn't an asshole. Most of the time. She curled her fingers around his biceps. "I was doing better before everything happened with Enrique, but it just brought back how *alone* I was without them. There was no one else in the Pride that I was really close to, so they believed him and not me about us not being mates."

"You're not alone now. You have us." When she looked up at him, her gaze wide and soft, he couldn't help but kiss her. He didn't have the words to tell her that no matter what had brought her to him, he was glad she was here now. Her breath caught when their lips met. It never failed to make him hard that she was so responsive, and tonight was no exception. His cock went rigid in his pants, chafing against his zipper. Still, he kept the contact light and gentle. Her tongue flicked out to tease him, and she tilted her head to deepen the contact. His hands dropped to cup her ass, pulling her closer. Her hips rolled, and he rocked his pelvis into hers. Her little moans told him she liked what they were doing as much as he did. If he didn't get inside her soon, he was . . . no, that wasn't the right thought to have. She'd been crying a few minutes before, and now he was trying to inhale her tonsils. Shit.

She nibbled on his bottom lip, making him groan. He broke the kiss, his fingers biting into her soft flesh, already sweating and breathing hard. Jesus, no one had ever gotten to him so fast. She chuckled. "Well, that wasn't what I was expecting when I came in here."

Wincing, he tried to sink his hips into the couch to lessen the friction against his aching cock. He forced his hands away from her backside. "Diego would have done this better. He could have talked you through it."

She gave a watery chuckle and cupped his jaw. He leaned into her touch. "I don't know. I think you did just fine. Sometimes all a girl needs is a hug and someone to listen."

"That I can do. And then some."

A short laugh burst from her. He smiled at the sweet sound, and she gave him a crooked little grin in return. It warmed something deep within him to hear her merriment, and he dropped a quick, hard kiss on her lips. She hummed in the back of her throat before she levered herself out of his lap and curled up against his side. Sighing, she rested her head on his shoulder. A peaceful calm settled over the room, and the energy of it flowed between them. He closed his eyes and let himself savor the quiet time with her. Diego was louder and more talkative than both of them, so Ric was glad he could offer her something she seemed to crave as much as he did. He rarely let himself relax this way, but if she liked it, he was more than willing to make a habit of it for her. It felt . . . right to have her here with him.

They each startled when the door to their suite opened to admit Diego, and he fell back against it to shut it, groaning loudly. Then his gaze snapped to Ric. "Bro, you leave me alone with Miguel again before Andrea comes back and I will kick your ass. Don't think I'm kidding either. My foot, your ass. Believe it."

By the look in his eyes, Ric had no doubt his twin was dead serious. He sighed, knowing he wouldn't be getting out of any other meetings. Isabel glanced back and forth between them, sucking in her cheeks to keep from giggling. Her eyes sparkled with suppressed laughter, and he winked at her.

Diego sniffed the air and gave them a look of mock severity. "You leave me hanging with Miguel, and then you start without me. Where's the brotherly love?"

"Sorry, D." Though Ric didn't bother to inject much regret into his voice.

"Were you watching anything before I came in?" Diego nodded to the television, hauled himself away from the door, and plopped down on an armchair next to the couch.

"The news." Isabel and Diego issued moans of pain. Ric snagged the remote control and lifted it for them to see. "Hey, there is no ganging up on the man with the remote. I have the power."

"He has the power." Diego slanted her a sly glance, and some silent communication passed between them. It made Ric suspicious and he watched them with a narrowed gaze, waiting for whatever game they were playing.

She turned wide eyes to him, gave him a coy grin, set her hand on his knee, and began drawing patterns up his thigh with her fingernails. "May I have the remote, Ric?"

"What are you going to give me for it?" Folding his arms to

prevent himself from grabbing her, he did his level best not to pant. The second she'd touched him, his cock had risen to chafe against his zipper.

"Offer him a blow job. Guys like those." Diego tossed out the suggestion, giving a sage nod.

Ric cleared his throat and tried to hold on to the thread of the conversation. Isabel's hand had moved higher and higher on his thigh as every second passed. Jesus, the woman got to him like no other. "I like anal more. She can offer me that."

Huffing, she pulled her hand away and tossed her tawny hair over her shoulder. She gave him a glare. "How about if you don't give me the remote, neither of you is getting laid tonight. No oral, anal, or vaginal. That would be *D) None of the above* as the correct answer, Bob."

"You've been watching too many game shows. That stuff will rot your brain." He couldn't hold back a chuckle at their banter. The two of them constantly made him laugh. That, and their love of bad reality shows, made them an entertaining match. They understood each other's sense of humor, no matter how warped it was. Isabel had almost appeared . . . surprised the first few days every time Diego made her giggle. Ric had the feeling that she hadn't laughed in a long time. By the way she'd described what had happened in Spain, he doubted she'd had much to laugh about since her parents died. It was good that they'd been able to change that for her.

Horrified desperation flooded Diego's face, and he turned on Ric. "Give the woman the remote, bro. Don't be a cock-blocker—I want to get some tonight."

Isabel whooped with laughter and buried her face in Ric's shoulder. After a long moment, she sat up and wiped tears of mirth from her eyes. "*Madres,* the two of you kill me. I never expect what comes out of either of your mouths. Ric looks so quiet and reserved. He doesn't say a lot, so it's always shocking when he says things like *I like anal better than blow jobs.* And then Diego just goes beyond outrageous every single time. I love it—I so needed this after the kind of day I had."

Dimples curved into her cheeks, and the shadows that always seemed to be in her eyes lightened. She looked younger for a moment, less burdened. He wished there was a way he could help her to hold on to that. He'd have to see what Diego thought about it. Between the two of them, they should be able to come up with something.

Isabel had the next day off, so she slept late and dark had fallen before she rolled out of bed. Her toes curled into the thick carpet as she sat on the edge of the mattress. A huge yawn threatened to crack her jaw. She closed her eyes, stretched her arms over her head, and bowed her back. "Mmm."

Rising to her feet, she wandered into the closet. She'd split her clothes between the two bedrooms because she never knew which bed they'd end up sleeping in, and it annoyed her to have to figure out where to find something to wear. This way, she could get dressed in either room. She tugged on a lacy bra and a polo shirt before she rifled through one of the built-in drawers for a pair of socks. Sliding them on, she reached out to pluck a pair of khaki pants off of a hanger. She stepped into them and fastened the front. She didn't always bother with underwear, but she hadn't been able to go without a bra since she hit puberty. That hormone rush had not only given her more curves than she was happy with, but it was also when Panthers gained the ability to change forms. Maybe she'd shift and laze around outside in the moonlight. She purred. That sounded like the perfect way to spend her day off.

"Oh, good. You're awake."

She turned her head to see Diego standing in the doorway of the closet dressed in some kind of odd, shiny jumpsuit. Her eyebrows drew together. In the week or so she'd been here, she hadn't seen either of the twins wear anything except jeans or business suits. And they really seemed to hate the business suits. "What's with the outfit?"

He brushed a hand down the jumpsuit, and the fabric crinkled. "We're going skydiving. The wind is perfect today."

"At night?" People jumped out of airplanes when it was pitch black out? She didn't really know much about skydiving other than what Hollywood put in movies, and most didn't feature nighttime jumps.

His broad shoulder lifted in a casual shrug. "It's not that unusual for experienced divers. Plus, it's not like we can't see in the dark."

The man had a point there. Hollywood also didn't portray shape-shifters with any kind of accuracy, so it shouldn't surprise her they messed up skydiving as well. She didn't understand the two men's proclivity for dangerous sports, but except for a few days where they'd gone surfing together, she had yet to see them do anything truly unsafe. Maybe the rumors about them weren't true either. Then again, Diego had just said they were leaping from an airplane. Didn't parachutes fail sometimes? Worry twisted in her belly. Why would anyone take such a risk? She gave him what she hoped was a grin rather than a grimace. "Right. Well . . . have a good time."

"Come with us." The smile he gave her was brilliant and charming. It was enough to make her wary. If Diego was here and Ric wasn't, she'd already discovered that usually meant they were trying to get away with something.

She narrowed her eyes at him and shook her head. "No, thank you."

Now the grin turned cajoling. "Have you ever been?"

"Of course not." She crossed her arms, arching an eyebrow in a way that told him exactly how sane she considered the very idea.

"You have no idea what you're missing out on."

Subtly obviously didn't work with this man. She huffed a

breath and turned away from him to shove her feet into a pair of tennis shoes. "Flinging myself out of an airplane is hardly what I call a good time."

Diego crowded her up against the built-in drawers, his fingers tracing a line up her arm. "You know, your accent thickens when you get . . . passionate about something."

She fought a shiver and lost, goose bumps breaking down her flesh. "I have no idea what you're talking about. I've been speaking English *and* Spanish since I was born just like every other Panther. My accent is hardly noticeable."

"Let us take you." He bent forward to nudge her shirt out of the way with his nose. His lips closed over her collarbone, sucking a trail of biting kisses to her neck. Her nipples hardened, and her breathing sped. Her fingers lifted to thread through the silky hair at the nape of his neck, pulling him closer. His knee slid between her legs, his hands dropping to her hips to work her over the hard muscles of his thigh. "Let us take you, Isabel. You always love what we do to you, don't you?"

A hum slid from her throat, and her thoughts went fuzzy around the edges. His hand moved to cup her breast, his claws extending to flick over the nipple. She shuddered, the fire she wasn't sure she'd ever get used to roaring high inside her. "Yes. Take me."

When the muscles in his leg flexed to stimulate her clit, she purred in pleasure. Her fingers fisted in his hair. His big hands stilled her hips, and she blinked up at him. Why was he stopping? He smiled, took her hand, and pulled her out of the closet. "Okay, let's go."

"W-what are you doing?" Confusion swamped her when he walked right passed the bed. Desire burned through her veins. They could wait to find somewhere exotic for sex when they had a perfectly good mattress beckoning. Or the floor. Or the wall. In fact, there wasn't a thing wrong with the closet they'd just left.

Diego glanced back at her with a grin. "You said to take you, so we are. Ric's waiting for us in the Jeep."

It took a moment for the fog of lust to clear long enough for her to understand why he was dragging her out of the bedroom and down the main staircase. She dug in her heels, jerked her hand out of his, and propped them both on her hips. "That was *not* for jumping out of a plane and you know it."

"Oh, but there's one last thing I didn't tell you about sky-diving." The wicked lilt in his voice drew her in, as he'd intended, damn him.

Desire still fizzed in her blood. She narrowed her gaze at him, knowing she shouldn't ask. "What?"

"The rush." He stepped closer, bending until his lips brushed her ear. She shivered when his deep voice tempted her. "The adrenaline from your first jump gets you so high it's right next door to orgasm. And if you come with us, Ric and I will make sure it *is* orgasm. Again and again."

"And again." Ric's warm tone sounded from behind her as the two fenced her in. When had he come inside? "Come with us. Come *for* us."

She closed her eyes as their scents surrounded her. It wasn't fair. She was outnumbered here. Diego's breath whispered against her neck. "Live a little, *querida*. You aren't going to let Enrique turn you into a hermit afraid of her own shadow, are you?"

"I am not afraid." Jerking back, she glared at him. "Just because I don't want to take the chance of smashing headfirst into the ground doesn't make me scared. It makes me sane."

He grinned, holding his hand out to her. "Take a chance anyway. You're safe with us. We'd never let anything happen to you."

There was a challenge in his gaze, but also a quiet need for trust. For her trust. She sighed. She didn't have the heart to deny him. Being near the two of them had already turned her into a complete wanton, and she found she wanted nothing more than to please them and be pleased by them. She wanted to trust them, to trust someone again. Her pulse sped until it raced. Oh, God. She was going to leap out of a plane. Equal parts excitement and terror whipped through her. When Ric's hand slid down her back to cup her hip, excitement won out. She reached out to twine her fingers with Diego's and offered him a grin. "I expect you to make this good for me."

"We will," they chorused.

What had she gotten herself into?

She was still asking herself the same question two hours later while she stared down at the ground from the open door of an airplane. Buckles and straps attached her to Ric's chest, and Diego balanced on the balls of his feet on the other side of the door. The engine made the floor rumble beneath her feet while the wind roared in her ears. She reached up to adjust her goggles and helmet for what had to be the tenth time. Diego gave her a reassuring smile, and Ric patted her shoulder. It was odd that they noticed so much about her. All the time. As someone used to being ignored, invisible to everyone but her parents, she found it a bit . . . disconcerting. And endearing. It was a heady thing to have the attention of two such virile men. She smiled back at Diego, lifting her gloved fingers to squeeze Ric's. She could only hope the smile didn't hold the edge of hysteria that bubbled inside her as Ric eased them closer to the gaping maw of the door.

What *the hell* had she gotten herself into?

It was the last thing that went through her mind before he flung them out into the starlit sky. Her heart pounded so loudly, it was the only thing she could hear. Adrenaline screamed through her veins as she spread her arms and legs the way Ric had told her to. Cold wind whistled passed her cheeks, smashing her face flat.

A dark shape rushed by them, then seemed to slow and draw even with them. She glanced over to meet Diego's gaze. Even with the wind contorting his handsome face, she could tell he wore a huge grin. He moved his arms and legs, swayed back and forth midair, and showed off with flips and spins. She just focused on not closing her eyes and giving him more ammunition for calling her a coward. For a moment, she almost wished she were human so she couldn't see in the dark.

The wind stole the sound of her scream as the ground rushed up to meet them. Oh. God. OhGodOhGodOhGod.

Diego's tricks carried him in a broad sweep underneath her. Then he flipped over, seeming to hover closer and closer until his big body sandwiched her between him and Ric. Shocked desire rolled through her. She never would have dreamed she could get horny while falling from thousands of feet up. The rigid line of Ric's cock pressed to her ass, the corded muscles of his chest burning into her back through their jumpsuits. Diego's gloved hands ran down the sides of her breasts, over her ribs, and between her spread legs. Trying to wriggle away from the terrifying lust that slammed through her, she found herself wedged too tightly between them. The wind trapped her as surely as their large bodies. A whimper burst from her when the tips of Diego's fingers ran over her vaginal lips, flicking her clit through her suit. Over and over again, he stroked her flesh. She dampened, shuddering. Heat flamed in her pussy, rolling out until her entire body shuddered with need. She screamed again when he pressed down on her clit hard.

Then her body snapped back as Ric pulled the cord to open the parachute. She watched Diego continue his freefall, still executing tricks on the way down. The desire cleared from her mind, and for a moment, her heart stopped. He was too low. Why wasn't he opening his parachute? Had it malfunctioned? She reached for him, as though she could save him from this far away. Tears welled in her eyes, and a blade of pain sliced through her. It was too soon to lose either one of them. She wasn't ready. She hadn't had enough time.

Relief exploded inside her when his parachute bloomed from his back. She watched him maneuver through the air the same way Ric directed their descent to the ground. Her heart hammered, blood rushing through her veins. Diego landed neatly in the middle of a large grassy area, gathering his parachute before the wind could billow and use it to drag him away. Ric circled them through the air until they landed in the meadow as well. Diego jogged over to take care of their parachute for them.

Adrenaline, relief, and a powerful, triumphant joy burst inside her. She'd done it. She'd actually jumped out of an airplane and survived the fall. A giddy laugh slid from her throat. Glancing around, she felt a bit dazed. Ric disengaged the buckles that attached them, and she stumbled as she broke free. She reached up to fumble with the chinstrap on her helmet, tugging it and her goggles off to drop them on the ground. The wind cooled the sweat on her skin, ruffling her damp hair. She closed her eyes and let her head drop back, reveling for a moment in being alive and the hot, wild blood that pumped through her.

Big hands closed over her breasts, and she gasped, her eyes snapping open to see a naked Ric kneeling before her, his fingers lifted to stroke her curves. His cock curved in a hard arc to just under his bellybutton. Desire again bloomed within her, and the sensual cat inside her writhed. She could feel how wet she was, so ready for anything they had in mind for her. Diego pressed against her from behind, his arms closing around her. He was nude as well, and she could feel him hard and hot against her ass.

They stripped her in under five seconds, and the cold night air rushed over her bare skin. Adrenaline still streaked through her, and she wanted nothing more than to have them fuck her hard. Nothing mattered but the drive to come as her muscles in her vaginal walls rippled and flexed. "Now. I need—"

Ric's tongue delved into her pussy, lapping at the juices there. She screamed, fisting her fingers in his hair so he couldn't get away. He sucked and bit at her hard clit. Tingles raced over her skin, and she panted for air. Her thighs locked as an orgasm rushed toward her with the same terrifying speed as the ground had in her freefall. Diego's fingers stroked over her pussy, trailing the moisture to her anus and pushing inside.

"You have the tightest ass, Isabel. It's so hot. I can't wait to slide in here. I've been thinking about it since I saw you bending over to put on your shoes *hours* ago. That's a long time to wait. I shouldn't have to wait anymore." Excitement bubbled in her veins when his fingers stretched her muscles, working her own wetness into her ass. She moaned, and then screamed when his cock replaced his finger. Her body jolted under the hard push. "I love to hear you scream. It makes me so hard."

"You were already hard." She shuddered with each movement. He was so big it stung to have him inside her, and she lifted on to her tiptoes to get away, but he fitted his hands to her hips and pressed fully into her. She moaned, arching to get closer. It felt so good, she loved it. Sensations ran through her, pleasure and pain, until she didn't know where one stopped and the next began. It didn't matter. She just wanted more, and gasped when he started to withdraw and push back in slowly.

Ric drew away, pressing his thumb to her clit as he continued to toy with her. Diego's thrusts only rolled her faster and harder over Ric's finger. Both men moved faster and faster until she could only scream and give herself over to the intense rush of ecstasy. That was the way of the twins. Powerful and untamed, they were a storm that pulled her in and twisted her around. Thunder and lightning.

Diego slammed deep, rotating his hips against her. Something inside her broke, crumbled. Orgasm hit her then, and her empty sex contracted. Flames licked at her flesh, and she sobbed for breath as her ass fisted around Diego's cock. Her ears rang when he roared, and she felt the hot pulse of his come fill her. His claws raked down the outsides of her thighs, and the burn made her pussy flex.

She screamed as she came, but Ric dragged her down to the ground, rolling her under him. She barely had time to moan as Diego's cock slid out of her before Ric shoved into her pussy hard and fast. He braced his hands on either side of her shoulders, and she could see his dark eyes melt into pure, incandescent gold. Again and again, his dick forged into her, stretched her. Jesus, they were big men, but longing ripped through her again. She wrapped her legs around his trim hips, lifting herself into each of his demanding thrusts. Sweat slid down her face to sting her eyes, and Ric's hair ruffled in the wind that cooled her skin. His muscular thighs slapped against the insides of her legs, and she moaned each time he filled her. She could hear how wet she was, could smell it and him and Diego on her skin. The combination was beyond carnal.

Her back arched, her fingers curled into his shoulders, and her claws extended to bite into his flesh. He changed angles as he slammed into her, and it was so good. She wanted it to last forever, but the adrenaline coursing through her catapulted her up and over the edge into orgasm again. It caught her by surprise, but she couldn't stop it, didn't want to, and the heat ripped through her system. Her pussy milked his cock, and she shuddered at the incredible feel of him. His cock pounded inside her twice more before he froze, his back bowed, and he jetted into her wet sex.

Her muscles shook when he slumped over her. She wrapped her arms around him. His big body shuddered, and he dropped his face into her throat to nuzzle her neck. Tender sweetness filled her, warring with the way her heart thudded in her chest. She closed her eyes and sighed. It would be too easy to get used to this, and she tried not to let the worry nag at her. She should savor what time she had here and not think about the fact that she still had the specter of Enrique looming over her. He still wasn't gone, and she knew from experience how unwilling he was to hear the word *no*. Especially from her. Her leaving would present a challenge no male Panther would resist. Now that she'd calmed down from her mad rush from Spain, she could see that her time here was limited. Sooner or later, her only real option was going to be living among humans.

She could only hope it was later.

5

American Panthers were so different from their European counterparts. The atmosphere of the Pride den was more relaxed and had a younger energy to it. Isabel liked it, but it was an adjustment for her. A grin curved her lips. It was good to be back in a kitchen with an adoring audience for her food. She'd received more compliments on her pastries in the three weeks she'd been here than she had in the two years in Europe after she'd returned from Paris.

She got along well with Benita, the head chef for the Pride. Her mates had managed to not throw themselves off a building lately. Life was . . . good.

And it scared her to death.

She was terrified to grow accustomed to it, to need it too much, to get too close. It could all be snatched away the way her last home had been, the way her parents had been. Safety *now* didn't mean safety *forever*. But the ebb and flow of this Pride around her threatened to lull her into a sense of security and trust. Diego and Ric were hardly helping her with that.

It was a vicious cycle. She wanted to trust but knew she

shouldn't, she wanted to belong but knew she couldn't, she needed to stay but was certain she wouldn't. When Enrique tracked her down, it would all be over.

Unless she let the twins mark her. That would change everything. The thought turned her on, but she knew by now she could never forgive herself if she put them or anyone else in this Pride in danger. And Enrique was dangerous. The irony didn't escape her that she'd so quickly gone from wanting to stay for her own protection to wanting to leave for everyone else's, but she shut down that hopeless line of thinking. She'd gone over her situation so often that it felt like an endless loop in her mind. When Enrique tracked her down, she'd leave. It was that simple. Until then, she'd enjoy her mates as much as possible.

Passion sluiced through her body, loosening some muscles, tightening others, making her ready for sex. She'd get off work soon, and maybe she could convince the twins to get her off in an entirely different way. As oversexed as their reputation painted them, she'd found herself eager and willing to keep up with them. She bit her lip to fight a naughty smile.

Plating the last dessert for the day, she brushed her hands off.

"Isabel?"

The way Benita said her name made it clear the other woman had been trying to get her attention for some time. She flushed and wrinkled her nose. "Yes?"

Benita lifted her eyebrows. "You're done for the day . . . ten minutes ago, actually."

"Well." Isabel smiled and tugged off her white chef's hat and jacket to tuck them into a small closet off the kitchen. "I'll be going then."

"The twins are in their office."

She glanced back and hunched her shoulders guiltily. Had it been that obvious that she intended to go jump her mates? "I didn't say I was going to see—"

"They asked for some of your scones and coffee. I thought you could drop off a tray on your way out."

"Oh."

Benita cracked up as a hot blush washed up Isabel's cheeks. The twins had made a habit of asking for her pastries on a daily basis. She wasn't sure how they stayed so trim inhaling as much food as they did, but she certainly appreciated the hard muscled bodies she was sandwiched between every night.

Scooping up the tray Benita had set out, she exited the kitchen with what little dignity she could claim. The sound of the older woman's laughter trailed behind her. She slowed to a stop outside of the twins' office door, shifting the heavy tray to one hand, her Panther strength taking the burden with ease. Her other hand rose to knock on the door when it snapped open suddenly.

"Isabel." Diego leaned his shoulder against the door frame and gave her a once-over. He looked tense and tired, but his eyes crinkled at the corners. "You look good enough to eat."

Proffering the tray, she gave a coquettish smile. "You ordered coffee and scones, sir?"

He blinked, and his brows drew together. "Don't ever call me that."

She jerked back. Diego was usually the outgoing, good-natured twin, so she flushed at being ordered around by him. She'd heard the dictatorial tone from leading family members so often in her life that she reacted automatically. Her gaze dropped to the floor in subservience and she pushed the tray into his hands.

"Well, that puts me in my place, doesn't it?" Anger followed on the heels of her ingrained response. Her jaw clenched and she turned away to stomp down the hall. "Please, excuse me, sir."

"Isabel, wait!" The rattle of porcelain against the silver tray rang out before a crash of dishes sounded behind her. "Damn it. Ric, take care of this."

Rounding the corner, she skirted the rear staircase and kept going right out the back door. She didn't want to be in a suite that smelled like him. Turning right, she walked toward one of the many gardens that surrounded the mansion. This one looked like a maze with high hedges that gave some shielding from the house. Before she reached it, Diego's hand closed over her shoulder and spun her around. "I told you to—"

"You don't get to tell me what to do. You aren't the Pride leader, and I didn't take a loyalty oath to you." Her finger poked him in the chest. "You are just like *him.*"

She didn't have to specify who she was talking about. Diego's ebony eyes went wide, and then narrowed to furious slits. "That's not fair."

"*I'm* not being fair?" She huffed out a breath. Whether she was being unfair or not was beside the point. He didn't get to talk to her the way he had—she wasn't under his thumb or anyone else's. She had the right to choose what she did and where she went. She poked his chest harder. "I'm not the one who got nasty. *I* was just doing my job."

"I know." He sighed and slid his hands through his hair. "I'm sorry."

"Fine." With the wind sucked out of her sails, her anger crumpled along with his, and she ran her hands down the slacks she was wearing. "I'm sure you have better things to do than follow me around."

She turned away and walked into the gardens. The high shrubs would shield her from the prying eyes of any curious Panthers who happened to be looking out the windows. Attention was not something she wanted, and it wouldn't have been that difficult to overhear her spat with Diego.

Her lips pressed together as she tried not to cry. It hurt to fight with him, with either of them. She didn't like it ... it smacked of dependency, of them being indispensably important to her, and she couldn't have that. Slowing to a stop, she covered her face with her hands and worked to steady her breathing.

Diego's arms curled around her and pulled her back into his embrace. He kissed the back of her neck. "I'm sorry, Isabel. I'm having a crappy day, and I took it out on you. I'm an ass."

Her shoulders curved in, and she clamped her hand tight over her mouth. Having him comfort her almost made it worse. It was too easy to lean on him, to let him soothe her. Spinning in his embrace, she tried to step back. He pulled her forward and pressed her face to his chest, hugging her tight. Her breasts were plastered to the hard muscles of his chest. Emotional and physical craving tangled inside her so fast it left her gasping for air.

Please, God, don't let her cry. Diego didn't think he could handle it. Guilt whipped through him again when he recalled the stunned look on her face after he'd snapped at her. A hellaciously bad day of negotiating with the Asian Pride had made him react instinctively when someone had called him by the title Esteban had insisted even his children use for him. Diego hated it—so he'd acted the same way his father would have when displeased. Shit.

He buried his face in her neck, hugging her tight. "I'm so sorry, Isabel."

Shoving her hands in his thick hair, she lifted his head and latched on to his mouth. A shocked punch of lust went through him. He groaned and dropped his hands to her ass to haul her closer until his erection rubbed against her belly. The friction felt incredible, but he wanted the connection of being inside her slick, hot sheath. He burned inside, his cock straining against his fly.

Wrapping her arms around his neck, she hitched herself higher and twined her legs around his waist. Ah, yes. Now he was rubbing her right where he needed it. Too many clothes, though. He could smell how her pussy was soaked with juices. His mouth fed on hers, nipping and sucking at her full lower lip. She twisted to get closer, and he damn near exploded right then.

He unhooked her legs from around his hips and set her down. She whimpered, her eyes burning to gold. "Please."

"You have five seconds to strip or I'm ripping your clothes off." His muscles shook, his voice rougher than he'd intended.

Her hands dropped to the waist of her pants, and they raced to undress. He pulled her to the ground, but he didn't trust himself to be civilized enough to not hammer inside her until he came, so he rolled to put her on top. Her legs parted to fall on either side of his hips, and his cock brushed against her creamy pussy. He clamped his fingers over her slim thighs. "Ride me."

She reached between them to grasp his cock, guiding him to her opening. Lifting herself, she sank down on him. He clenched his teeth at the feel of her liquid heat closing around his cock and felt his fangs pierce the tip of his tongue. He ignored the coppery taste of blood in his mouth. His palms moved to cup her breasts, flicking his nails over her nipples. "You're so beautiful. There's this look on your face every time I get inside you that makes it damn hard not to come. It's so hot. There's nothing better than seeing you all flushed and pretty and ready to fuck."

Her head fell back, and she rolled her hips in undulating waves. "Diego."

"And then there's the *feel* of your pussy all hot and tight around my cock. The fit is so fucking perfect." He lifted his ass to meet her on her next downward push. "Can you feel how tight you are?"

She whimpered. "Yes."

Sitting up, he pulled the tips of her breasts into his mouth one at a time. He glanced up at her, watching her watch him suckle her pretty pink nipples. He pressed a kiss into the valley of her cleavage. "Do you know what it does to a man when you're always wet for him, Isabel?"

Her back bowed, and she rocked her pelvis against his faster. She smiled down at him, her eyes sparking with laughter. "Do you know what it does to a woman when you're always hard for her, Diego?"

Her grin turned wicked when she tightened her walls around him. Planting her hands on his chest, she shoved him flat on his back. Damn, but he loved that about her. She was more challenging than the most difficult stunt he'd ever done, better than any adrenaline rush he'd ever had. She moved faster and faster until her ass slapped against his balls, she took him so deep. He groaned and gripped her hips, working his dick inside her. He could never get enough of her. Isabel.

She threw her head back and screamed as her inner muscles clamped down on his cock. He had no choice but to come with her. His belly tightened, jerking him almost upright as he spurted inside her. "Jesus Christ, Isabel."

Panting, she rested her palms on his chest. A lazy grin pulled at her full lips. "Well, that was fun."

"Understatement of the century." A laugh slipped out of him. He loosened his grip on her hips and stroked her soft, soft skin. She was so lovely it killed him sometimes.

"Diego. Isabel." Antonio's voice sounded from the other side of the hedge next to them. "I need to speak to you. While I'm not shy at all, I thought I'd give you a chance to get dressed."

Her eyes widened, and she slapped a hand over her mouth. A flush reddened her smooth cheeks, and she went from warm and wanton to embarrassed and upset in a split second. He snarled a curse and considered dismantling his brother limb by limb.

A furious whisper spilled from her, "Oh, my God. Your brother just heard me scream like a cat in heat. The *Pride leader.*"

Laughter boiled out of him. He knew it wasn't smart to

chuckle right now, but the look on her face was just priceless. The idea that his brother would give a damn about a little screaming was too much. Antonio and Solana could bring the house down when they wanted to—Diego had harassed them about it a time or two just because he could. Another chuckle rolled out. His cock slipped out of Isabel and it made him groan.

She hissed at him, shoved herself into a standing position, and punched his shoulder on her way to their pile of hastily discarded clothing. She threw his shirt in his face. "Jerk."

"I've called him much worse things." Antonio's tone was mild, but there was something in the sound that sobered Diego. He pulled his shirt away from his head. Something had happened. Something bad or Antonio wouldn't have come to get them. He certainly wouldn't have interrupted Diego during a lovemaking session with his mate. Antonio seemed to think mating was going to get the twins to settle down. Diego tried not to smirk. Isabel seemed to like skydiving well enough— with time, they might just make her as wild as they were.

The scent of Ric and Oriana lined a soft gust of wind that came from the house. The baby's happy gurgle made him smile, but didn't quite manage to assuage the dread that suddenly weighed on his chest. His twin's voice came from the same place Antonio's just had. "Solana had to run down to the Mission District, so she said it was your turn with Oriana. Actually, what she said was 'tag, you're it'."

Hauling himself to his feet, Diego tugged on his pants and zipped them up just as Ric came around the corner of the hedge. The look on his face told Diego he was right. Whatever had happened was bad. His fingers fisted in the shirt in his hand, but he gave Isabel a reassuring smile. Ric reached out and helped her fasten the top buttons of her blouse. Diego forked a hand through his hair. "All right, Antonio. We're decent. Tell us what's going on."

His older brother stepped around the bushes, his daughter

pressed to his shoulder. He had the perpetually exhausted look of a new parent stamped on his face as he glanced from Isabel to Ric to Diego before he spoke. "There's no kind way to say this, so I'll just get it over with. I received a call from Europe today. The Garcia family is demanding the return of their heir's mate."

All the blood rushed out of Isabel's face, and she swayed on her feet. Diego and Ric reached out to steady her. She turned her face into Diego's shoulder, and he could feel the hot puffs of breath exploding from her mouth. "I knew it was too good to—"

He squeezed her tight, cutting off her soft words. Rage pumped hot and hard through his veins. His hands trembled with the force of it, and his need to comfort his mate warred with his need to track Enrique Garcia down, rip his arms off, and beat him to death with the bloody stumps. The visual was a satisfying one, but he got a grip on his temper as best he could. "I'm afraid their heir's mate isn't here. There must be some mistake."

Laughter that sounded like a low sob erupted from Isabel. "A mistake. You know, that's what I said the first time, too. Maybe the mistake was trying to remain in Panther society. I can't stay here."

"What?" The word echoed from all three men. Oriana jolted and started to fuss, so Antonio rubbed his daughter's back while he spoke to Isabel. His dark brows drew together in a deep frown. "You're not going anywhere. How can the Pride protect you if you leave?"

Plucking at the wrinkles in her shirt, she didn't meet his gaze. "The Pride isn't going to want the kind of trouble I'll cause just by being here."

"You'd be surprised what the Pride members will do. They didn't want to like or accept Solana—or the non-shifters, or the human mate I've let join us, but they did. Hell, they didn't want to like *me*, but we do well enough now. If push came to shove, they'd be much more likely to stand by you than they would by someone who's never been here or sworn loyalty to our Pride."

She looked up. "Politically, it—"

"Let me handle the politics. It's my job. Yours is to be a chef . . . and my brothers' mate. That alone would earn my protection, even without the loyalty oath." He gave a decisive nod, looking every inch the ruler he was. "You are *not* leaving."

Diego watched Isabel swallow, the torment of a trapped animal in her gaze. "I can't stay. He'll come for me. If he knows where I am, someday I'll slip up, someday I'll leave the mansion to shop or just to take a walk and that'll be it. He's unbalanced. No Panther would insist this much, would claim someone who was *not* their mate, unless they were seriously off."

"Then we'll go with you." He tightened his arm around her.

Her eyes flared wide, her gaze snapping up to meet his. "What?"

He glanced over at his twin, and Ric nodded his agreement before he answered her. "You aren't facing this on your own. You're our mate. If you go, we go."

"Don't be ridiculous." She tried to wriggle away from them, but they both held her firmly. She glared at them and stopped struggling. "We aren't mated. You belong with your family."

"And you belong with us, so you'll have to stay, too." Diego gave her the kind of look that usually let people know he wasn't dicking around. He doubted it would have the desired effect on her, but it didn't hurt to try. "This isn't negotiable. You stay, we stay. You go, we go with you."

Ric slid a hand down her tangled hair. "Don't try to run either. With our instincts and political connections, we could track you anywhere. It wouldn't matter if you did leave the Panther world. Don't even think about it. It won't work out for you."

The stubborn tilt to her jaw relaxed, and her shoulders bowed with defeat. A tear streaked down her cheek. She swiped it away impatiently and sniffed. Shrugging out of their embrace, she tucked her hair behind her ears. "Fine. For now. If the Pride freaks about it when they find out, I'm leaving. I don't care what any of you say."

Diego leaned forward to speak in her ear. "If we have to hunt you down, sweetheart, we're going chain you down and spank you for making us go through the trouble."

The hitch in her breath was almost inaudible, and he might have missed it if he hadn't been watching her so closely. He watched a slight shudder run through her body, and he caught the scent of their recent lovemaking on her skin. He'd give a lot to see the ecstasy on her face again and have this problem go away.

Her expression went blank for a moment, and then some of the haunted look that had faded from her gaze in that last few weeks returned. She drew herself up and gave him a wan smile before turning to Antonio. "I know you're busy, so I can put Oriana down for her nap if you'd like."

His brother stroked the baby's downy black hair, kissed her forehead, and handed her over. She fussed for a moment, but Isabel crooned to her softly, and the baby quieted. She looked *right* with a child in her arms. The thought hit him with a pang. She couldn't conceive until they'd marked each other as mates. Once they did, it was their duty to produce children as often as possible. Breeding was one duty he looked forward to. And until they'd marked each other, she could hold on to her argument that they should be separated.

No. He didn't want her to leave. Having her here was good for all of them. He couldn't put his finger on what the subtle shift inside him was, but he now craved this woman with more than the instinct of mating. Not a mate in general, but Isabel specifically. It was profound and emotional, this connection. She couldn't leave. They'd do whatever they had to to keep her, to convince her this was the best place for her. That *they*—Diego and Ric—were the best option for her. They wouldn't let Enrique hurt her ever again.

Diego pivoted on his heel to return to his office, jerking on his shirt along the way. There was work he and Ric needed to get done before they could spend the evening with Isabel. They'd have to trust Antonio to deal with the Garcia family. His older brother knew what he was doing—and what he didn't know, Miguel did. Everything would be fine.

The platitude did little to assuage the need to vent his anger, and it ate at him. If he couldn't kill Enrique, he wanted to sky-dive or bungee jump or do something that would give the energy vibrating his body some outlet for release. He felt like he was going to explode out of his skin. He felt helpless, useless in a situation that affected his mate. It reminded him too much of his life when his father was alive—when he *was* useless, dispensable, easily replaced according to everyone except Ric. He clenched his jaw and shoved his hands in his pockets, turning away and trying to focus on doing the right thing for Isabel. Tension ran through his muscles, drawing his shoulders in a tight line. He fought the urge to pace. Containing himself wasn't something he cared for.

6

At dinner that night, Ric kept a close watch on Isabel to see if she intended to stick by her promise to stay. For now, she'd said. Forever, if he had his way. He had no doubt that his twin agreed with him on this. She'd already become too important to lose. The tension that ran through her body, that held her in a rigid line, disturbed him. He hoped she didn't try to run again. Diego and he would track her down, but the very idea that Enrique might find her first knotted Ric's gut. They needed to mark her, but she'd never seemed open to the idea. At first, he hadn't pushed because she thought they were useless play-boys and was obviously shaken by her experience in Spain. She'd needed time to adjust to them. With today's phone call from the Garcias, it was a waiting game to see what she would do—and he knew how to outwait just about any opponent, but he didn't relish using the tactic in his love life.

She motioned in a few Panthers carrying trays and set the dishes on the long table where all of his family sat. Andrea had finally returned from her trip to Japan the day before, and she and Miguel sat arm in arm. Ric's gaze swung back to his own mate, watching the way her shirt and slacks hugged her curves when she leaned forward to set a plate down. Casting a critical eye over their work, she nodded when everything met her approval. The teenage boys who'd been roped into serving for the evening smiled and jogged out of the dining room.

She turned to follow them, and Ric opened his mouth to call her back when Antonio's voice stopped her in her tracks. "Isabel."

"Yes, sir?" She pivoted to face the head of the table, balancing on the balls of her feet, obviously fighting the desire to run for the door. The attention of anyone who outranked her always seemed to disturb her, and Ric could understand why she'd feel that way, but she'd been here long enough to know Antonio wasn't like most Pride leaders.

Antonio's jaw tilted as he considered her. "You know, I think it's time you started eating with the family. We all know that you're Diego and Ric's mate. We don't have to pretend otherwise."

"Oh, I couldn't intrude, sir." She gave him a bright smile and edged toward the door. "I'm happy eating with the rest of the Panthers on kitchen duty."

He waved her into a seat next to Ric. "Sit. And call me Antonio, please. It makes me think of my father when you say *sir.* No one in the family does it except Miguel, and usually just to annoy me."

Instead of glancing at Miguel, her gaze shot to Diego, whose eyes had gone blank. Ric's eyebrows rose. So that's what had set his twin off this afternoon. She'd called him sir. Ric winced. Barking at their mate wasn't a good plan, but none of them wanted to be associated with a man who'd done a great deal of damage to them all. They didn't want a reminder of him. Especially Ric and Diego. Isabel's mouth formed a small moue, and she stepped forward to smooth her hand over his hair. *I'm sorry,* she mouthed.

Diego caught her fingers and kissed them. "Have dinner with us."

Standing, Ric offered her his chair and moved one seat down so she'd be positioned between them. Where she was meant to be. It was good to have her here. She'd insisted on skipping family meals so far because she wasn't mated to them yet. Antonio had effectively cut that argument out from under her, and Ric was grateful. Any extra tie they could form to keep her here was an excellent thing. He cleared his throat in the awkward silence that fell over the room and looked at his older brother, trying to get back to the topic they'd started before the servers had come in. Politics—something he could actually converse about well. "As I was saying, Miguel, Diego, and I tracked down an orphan child in Australia. The Pride leader there is willing to let Carmen and Landon adopt her for a few political concessions from us."

Carmen's mate was a human, which meant she'd never be able to conceive. Panthers could only breed if both mates were in cat form, and Landon couldn't shift. Ric knew that Isabel wholeheartedly approved of them helping the couple to have a child to call their own. This was one more way to remind her that this was a good place for her to remain. She liked them; they were an accepting Pride who treated all their members well. He doubted Fernando Garcia would have done the same or that Enrique would even consider it after he took over in Europe.

Antonio sat back in his chair. "I'll call Australia tomorrow night and work out the details. I'll need the three of you there to advise me, so clear your schedules."

Miguel, Diego, and Ric nodded. He made a mental note to organize his day so that he finished at the same time his mate's shift in the kitchen ended. Best not to let her spend too much time alone or she might decide that her decision to stay was the wrong one.

Clearing her throat, Andrea leaned in. "You can have him tomorrow, big brother, but after that Miguel's mine for two whole weeks."

Solana arched a brow and gave her sister-in-law a teasing smile. "Are you sure you can pry yourself away from your fashion designing that long?"

"For weeks with Miguel on a nudist beach?" Andrea fingered the jewel on a necklace her mate had given her and turned to smile at him. "Hell, yes."

Isabel choked on the sip of wine she'd taken. Diego patted her back. "She's kidding. They aren't going to a nudie beach."

The look on his sister's face was pure innocence. Even the sole female Cruz couldn't pull it off. They didn't have an ounce of innocence left between them. "What? There's a beach; we'll be naked. I think it should count."

Antonio scoffed. "It does not."

Diego and Ric nodded their agreement. He leaned back in his chair and waited for the inevitable fun of a ridiculous family debate. They didn't disappoint, and his sister-in-law opened with the first volley.

"If she wants it to count, it counts." Solana waved a fork loaded with green beans at her mate.

Heaving an exaggerated shrug, Miguel weighed in. "A smart man doesn't disagree with Solana and Andrea. As long as I'm getting laid, I say it doesn't really matter if we're naked on a beach or anywhere else. The naked part is what counts."

"Ha!" Solana stuck her tongue out at Antonio.

He smirked, leaned back in his chair, laced his fingers together over his flat belly, and gave her the kind of glittering look that told them all what he'd be doing to her right now if they weren't in a public setting. "You're just agreeing with her to be contrary."

"Nuh-uh. The women in this family have to stick together. We're outnumbered." She threw her napkin at him. "And quit looking at me like that. You're not getting any until after I've had one of the peach tarts Isabel made for dessert."

An expression of wounded dignity crossed his face. "Thrown

aside for pastries. And they said being Pride leader meant I'd never do without."

The rest of the table hooted with laughter at that. Even Isabel giggled, her shoulders relaxing as she watched the banter between his family members. It hadn't always been this jovial at family dinners, so Ric savored the experience. He smiled and dropped his hand to twine his fingers with hers. She turned her amber gaze on him, a quiet smile on her face.

Antonio looked over at her. "Well, we have a fifty-fifty split. Isabel, you're our tie-breaker. Does it count?"

All the blood fled her face when the entire table quieted to pin her with their gazes. Ric sighed as she stiffened again. She swallowed and opened her mouth, but only a squeak emerged. "I—um . . . I think if Miguel and Andrea agree, then who are we to judge what they want to call it? I hope you two have fun being all naked at the beach. It's better in your hotel room anyway . . . you can't imagine how much it sucks to dig sand out of your—never mind."

Andrea's laughter rose and fell like a music scale. "Oh, I have dug sand out of my *never mind* many times. I couldn't agree with you more."

Her mate's dark brows snapped together as he turned on her. "And just who have you been—"

"For photo shoots, Miguel." She tilted her head, and her short sweep of black hair brushed against her cheek. "I was a model, remember? The pictures of me dancing around in the waves in bathing suits? Yeah, that was a real beach with real sand that got in really hard to reach places."

His expression relaxed to be replaced with a look of pure sin. "Oh, well . . . I bet I could make sand fun for you."

They all groaned and rolled their eyes. If it was possible, the two of them were worse than Solana and Antonio with their flirtation.

Andrea's eyes lit with interest, and her voice lowered to a silky purr. "I know you can fulfill all of my needs."

The way her mate's body stiffened, Ric was betting his sister had her hand on Miguel's leg—and maybe in a bit more central location—under the crisp white tablecloth. Miguel narrowed his eyes. "Don't push me."

She just smiled and waited for a long, long moment before her hand returned to the table and she resumed her meal.

Solana glanced over at Isabel, a little grin playing over her features. She shoved her long brown hair back over her shoulder. "Forgive us, Isabel. The Cruz family has *no* shame."

"And we tend to mate with people who don't either." Antonio tugged one of her curls forward to let it slide between his fingers. "Isn't that nice?"

Her chocolate-brown eyes crinkled at the corners when she laughed. A chuckle went around the table, but Isabel didn't join in this time, just hurried to finish her meal. Ric brought her fingers up to his lips and kissed them. She glanced at him, and he saw the same draining fear there that he'd hoped was gone. They could and would protect her from Enrique. No one would touch her except her mates ever again. He ruthlessly contained the anger that pumped through his system that anyone would terrorize a woman who'd come to mean so much to him in such a short amount of time. Life had changed as much as he'd suspected it would, but for the better. Even he and his twin were closer if it was possible. Having Isabel drew everything into a perfect circle for them. It was good to have her. He wasn't willing to give that up, and he'd work like hell to keep it. Her.

7

_____

Okay, so it wasn't really that high, was it? After skydiving this should be a piece of cake.

The piece of cake she'd had with the picnic they'd brought to the beach felt like a lump in her stomach. It was early for her, just after dusk. So what the hell was she doing standing on top of an enormous boulder about to leap into the freezing waves of the Pacific Ocean?

After they'd eaten, the twins decided they should swim out to a huge rock in the middle of the small inlet they'd pulled off the highway to explore. She wasn't even sure it was quite legal to be there, but she was staring out over the open sea, her back to the shore.

It had been two weeks since Enrique had contacted the North American Pride, and Isabel still hadn't managed to find a way to escape. The twins watched her like a hawk. And when they weren't watching her, Solana, Antonio, or any number of people in the Pride were. Benita kept an especially sharp eye on her. Isabel never had a moment alone. It was as endearing as it was maddening. She wanted to stay, but she couldn't. Didn't these people know what Enrique would do to them if they got in his way? He was obsessed and dangerous. She rubbed the area on her collarbone where he'd bitten her in his attempt to mate with her. Revulsion crawled through her belly. She needed to come up with a plan, a way to slip away unnoticed. A pain so great it was almost physical wrenched her heart. Tears misted her vision, and she blinked fast to clear them. She would miss her mates so much. It was why she'd agreed to come out here today. She wanted just a little more time with them. She knew it was foolish to linger, but . . . she'd fallen for them so fast she hadn't been able to avoid it. She loved them.

"Come on in, Isabel. The water's great." Diego pulled her attention back to the present, flashed a naughty little boy's grin up at her, and shoved his wet hair out of his face.

He and Ric had already taken the huge plunge off the boulder to splash into the water. She stood alone in her bikini and stared down at her mates, not sure she had the courage to jump. It reminded her too much that her parents had died at sea . . . and that life had recently taught her the value of caution no matter how much the twins wanted her to shed the armor she'd grown.

Plus, it was a *long* way down.

Butterflies took flight in her belly. Jumping out of the airplane had almost been easier than this. Once she'd agreed to it, they'd strapped her in and leaped . . . taking her with them for the fall. This she had to do by herself.

Both men kept themselves afloat easily, their arms cutting through the water below her. Ric gave her a quiet smile and lifted the small two-way radio they were using to be heard over the crashing waves. It hung from a lanyard around his neck, and its counterpart lay on the boulder near her feet. It fuzzed with static before his voice came through. "We'll wait as long as you need. Don't be scared."

"Do I have to jump?" she called back. She swallowed, shivering in the wind that sheared the top of the boulder.

"Oh, yeah." Diego cupped his hands around his mouth to shout, kicked back in the water so he floated, and let his muscular body ride the waves. She could see his erection tenting the front of his swim trunks. "But you know we'll make it worth it for you. All you have to do is jump."

The wicked promise in his gaze made her shudder. Her nipples beaded tight against the triangles of her top, and it had nothing to do with the chilly sea breeze. Her heart began to pound, adrenaline pumping through her veins. God, she wanted him. Them. Again. Hell, *always*. There hadn't been a single moment since she'd met them that she wasn't horny.

Well, there was only one way to get what she wanted right now.

Sucking in a deep breath, she felt her muscles bunch and stretch as she leaped straight out from the boulder. Her stomach lurched as she hung for a moment midair before dropping like a stone. Her legs slapped hard against the water as the cold waves swallowed her whole.

A strong hand closed around her waist, propelling her up to the surface. When she broke through, she threw her head back and sucked in a breath, wrapping her arms and legs around the twin who'd grabbed her. She opened her eyes to see Ric. Her heart still thumped hard in her breast, and she smiled hugely. She'd done it. Flung herself off a mountain of a boulder into swollen waves. She tightened her limbs around Ric. His hair was sleeked against his skull, and it only made his sharp cheekbones stand out . . . and emphasized the hard glitter of lust in his gaze. He shoved the two-way radio over his shoulder so it floated behind him and pulled her closer.

His cock prodded the lower curve of her belly, and heat ran over her skin despite the chill of the water around her. She gave him the kind of slow grin that should have all his blood rushing southward. "I want you."

"Good," he grunted.

Twisting in the water, he kicked through the waves to take her into a hollowed alcove in the boulder. She hadn't been able to see it from the top. Diego lounged with his elbows braced behind him on a short outcropping of rock, waiting for them to join him. Excitement knifed through her, a sweet slice of unstoppable need.

Anyone could see them from a passing boat, and instead of turning her off, the realization made the heat boiling through her intensify. She'd never considered herself an exhibitionist, but she'd found the twins could talk her into sex just about anywhere.

Diego lunged forward when they approached, and the twins closed in on either side of her. She kicked her feet to stay afloat, but they seemed to have solid footing. She looked down. "How—"

"There's a rock shelf we can stand on." Ric's hand closed around her arm, turning her in the water until her back pressed firmly to his front. His arm around her waist anchored her in place. "I doubt you could reach even if you stood on your tiptoes."

He nudged her chin to the side and slid his hot tongue up her neck. She shuddered, her hand clamping over his forearm. Diego's fingers slipped down her rib cage until he reached the edge of her bikini bottom. He rubbed her through the fabric, honing in on her clitoris. Her thighs jerked, and she spread them wide so he could reach anything he wanted. She craved his touch.

"But you don't need to stand, do you? We'll hold you up. Together. First, Ric's going to stretch that sweet little ass of yours. You like it when we do that, don't you?" His hands worked the bottom of her swimsuit off, and she couldn't hold back a little whimper. He was right, she loved it when one of them fucked her ass. She loved it even more when it meant they'd penetrate her together. Diego tossed the wet bathing suit on to the outcropping he'd leaned against. "And when he's so deep inside you, you don't think you can take anymore, I'm going to slide my cock in your pussy. You're hot and creamy for me, aren't you, Isabel?"

"Oh, my God. Yes." She moaned, his words painting a hot image in her mind. She reached over her shoulder to grip Ric's hair. He opened his mouth against her neck, sucking hard on her skin. Goose bumps broke out over her entire body, and her nipples tightened in reflexive response.

Her other hand dropped to her breast, toying with her nipple. Diego caught her fingers and moved them away from her body. "That's my job. Ric, untie her."

The string behind her neck loosened, and soon the top of her bathing suit floated in the water, only the tie around her ribs kept it from swirling away. Diego's palms closed over her breasts, his hot skin contrasting with her cooler flesh. His mouth closed over her nipple, and her body bowed in response. He nipped at the hard tip, worrying it between his teeth.

Ric probed her anus, pushing in a finger to stretch her muscles. He added a second finger and began to thrust them inside her, widening her ass. She groaned, shoving back to take him deep. It burned, but she loved it. She loved everything they did to her, every time they touched her the sensations were beyond incredible. When he withdrew, excited anticipation screeched inside her. Here it came. Yes. Oh, God, *yes.* His fingers dug into her hips as he seated her on his cock. She sucked in a sharp breath at the sting on his penetration, but as soon as he dug in as deep as he could, Diego straightened, giving her nipple one last lick. She choked when he jerked her thighs wide, and the blunt tip of his dick pressed into her pussy. Leaning forward to bury her face in his neck, she felt her fangs slide out as the sweet pain of having them both inside her at once ricocheted through her.

She opened her mouth on Diego's throat, tasting the dark musk of his flesh mixed with salty seawater. The urge to bite down, to mark him as hers was almost too much, but she couldn't and she knew it. She contained the feral cat inside herself with harsh effort and focused on the very human cocks working inside her. They picked up a slow rhythm. One of them entering her as the other pulled out.

The waves rocked her forward and back, intensifying the depth of their thrusts. A tear streaked unchecked down her cheek. She couldn't help it. Her feelings for them made everything with them more powerful. Better. She didn't want it to end, but she knew something so good couldn't last.

"You like it when we tag team you, don't you, Isabel? It makes you hot to take us both." Diego rolled his finger over her clit as he withdrew from her pussy and Ric powered into her ass.

"You know it does." Heat burned her from the inside out, and the feel of both men moving in her and the water swirling around her was just too much. Her hips bucked, shoving against each of her mates faster and faster until time blurred and became elastic. There wasn't a moment when she wasn't filled with the hard length of a cock. Their scents mixed with that of saltwater, their hands slid over her body, their breath panted against her skin. Her muscles tightened, clenching with each movement of her hips. She was so close to orgasm she could taste its sweetness. Throwing her head back against Ric's shoulder, she sobbed. "Please. More. I need more."

"Yes," they both hissed out, and slammed into her at the same time. She exploded, coming so hard stars burst behind her eyelids in tiny pinpricks of light. The walls of her sex flexed, and her anus closed tight around Ric's cock. He groaned, the muscles in his big body jerked, and she felt his heated come flood her ass. Diego continued to thrust in short, hard jabs against her cervix. Something desperate and wild shone in his eyes. She wrapped her arms around him and held on for the ride.

Her orgasm went on and on, each time he entered her set off another wave of contractions that made her pussy fist in rhythmic pulses. She moved her hands to cup his cheeks, forcing him to meet her gaze. "I want you to come inside me, Diego. It's so good, I—"

"Fuck, yes." His hips snapped in quick thrusts before he froze against her. His chest crushed her breasts flat, his rougher skin chafing her sensitized nipples. He jetted into her with long, hot spurts of come. He shuddered, and it shook both her and Ric. Sucking in a breath, he dropped his forehead to her shoulder. She stroked his hair back, pressing her lips to his temple. Her body softened around them, her heart slowing as they slid from her body. She shivered at the empty sensation, but let herself float in the circle of their arms and enjoyed this quiet moment with them.

They finally hauled themselves out of the water before they became too waterlogged. Isabel fastened her bikini top and had to wrestle with a laughing Diego for her the bottom half of her bathing suit. She splashed water in his face in retribution, and he pinned her to the rock outcropping to kiss her senseless.

Once she was decently attired, she and the twins dove off the boulder several more times. After the first jump, she found it easy to go again. Shoving her sopping hair out of her face, she grinned at Ric from where he stood behind her, getting ready to make a running leap into the water with her.

The little two-way radio around his neck fuzzed, and then Diego's voice emerged. "Hey, guys! Check this out."

She turned to see him waving from on top of the insanely high cliff that formed the north edge of the cove. Huge waves slammed up against the rugged cliff face before the water sucked away to reveal jagged rocks underneath. Her heart all but stopped beating. "What is he doing?"

"Looks like he's going to make a wicked cliff dive." He cued the COMM on the radio. "Dude, make sure you do a blind entry."

"Blind entry?" Her hands and feet went numb, her face tingling with shock. It was surreal. This couldn't be happening.

"Yeah. He'll land feet first so he can't see the water below him when he goes in."

"He's not going to look to see if there's even water *underneath him* when he lands? No way in hell. That's too dangerous."

"It'll be a sweet trick." Ric grinned, slanting her a look that said he thought she was blowing this out of proportion.

Anger roared through her, terror on its heels. She rounded on him. "It's not a trick! This isn't some kind of magic. He could get himself killed. There are things even Panthers can't bounce back from. Being crushed against rocks would be one of them."

"He knows what he's doing."

"Does he? Or does he just not care if it goes wrong?"

Ric didn't answer.

She jerked the radio out of his hand, snapping the thin lanyard, and pressed the button. "Diego, come back down. Please. Please don't do this. It's not funny."

"I am coming down. Be back over there in just a sec."

"No!"

But it was too late. He jumped, a triumphant shout echoing over the inlet as he executed quick flips and twists on the way down.

For a moment, it looked like he would make it. And then she watched it all go horribly wrong. The wave that came in was larger than the ones before it, higher and faster. He'd leaped far enough for those, but this one slammed his big body into the rocks.

Shock rolled over her like the wave that just dragged Diego under. She was vaguely aware of Ric diving off the boulder they stood on and into the water. She swayed on her feet. Her hands clamped over her mouth in horror and she stood frozen, her gaze glued to the water where Diego had gone under, praying harder than she ever had before that he would resurface. It was too cruel that the ocean would take another of her loved ones. Oh, God. Oh, God, he couldn't die. She couldn't lose one of them so soon after she'd found them. It was one thing for her to walk away because she had to, it was another for either of them to die.

There. Was that his dark head breaking the surface? Her stomach flipped, and she strained her eyes to see. Only the fact that she had extra Panther senses gave her the ability to make out the details. It was him! Her heart squeezed tight as rage and relief exploded inside her with dizzying force.

Ric reached his twin, caught him around the chest and started swimming for shore. She tightened her grip on the radio and jumped into the water to meet them there. Her muscles shook with the emotions roiling inside her, but she shoved them away to focus on reaching the beach. The cold water buffeted her and stole her breath away, the waves heaving her up, trying to push her away from shore. She dove under the surface and kicked through the water hard. Drawing on her inhuman strength, she powered through and came up in time to have a wave roll her toward the sand. But a riptide tried to suck her feet out from under her. The tide was shifting and the water was getting dangerous.

By the time she reached the twins, Diego was sitting up on the beach, a cocky smile on his face. His jaw sported a nasty bruise and small cuts oozed blood all over his body. Other than that he looked fine. "Hey, Isabel!"

The white-hot rage returned in a flash, burning away her concern. He acted as though nothing was wrong. As though he hadn't almost died because of some stupid *stunt*. Her hand drew back, and she launched the radio at his head. If he hadn't had cat reflexes, it would have nailed him in the temple. As it was, he ducked the projectile. "What the *fuck*, Isabel?"

"That should be my question! What the hell were you think-ing, throwing yourself off a cliff?" Her hands fisted at her side as she fought the urge to scratch his eyes out with her claws. She'd never been so angry in her entire life. Not even at Enrique. She hissed at Diego. "I asked you not to jump, Diego. I begged. Why didn't you listen? Look at you. You're all bloody and—"

"Dude, I'm just scratched up a bit. I'm fine." He had the utter gall to look offended.

"Fine? Is that what you call this? You're not *fine.*" Tears streamed out of her eyes as her anger dissolved. All the bottled terror from the last several minutes caught up with her, and when she opened her mouth to speak, a sob came out.

Ric rose to his feet, his palms raised in supplication. "Isabel, please. You're overreact—"

"Don't you tell me I'm overreacting! Just because he didn't die doesn't mean he couldn't have. And you encouraged him. You're just as much to blame as he is. What is wrong with the two of you?"

Diego heaved himself to his feet. "A catnap in the car on the ride home and I'll be fine."

"Did you even hear what I just said?"

"Isabel—"

"Don't use that patronizing tone of voice with me." She gave them the kind of glare that should have frozen their blood, though she doubted it had much effect on two such hardheaded men. She doubted they cared that she was so upset. It didn't seem to matter when she asked them to stop their antics. But that was *her* problem, wasn't it? She loved them and they loved the challenge and adrenaline rush she presented to them. It must be even more intense with a mate than all the other women they'd played with. What would she do when the thrill got old and they decided to find a new playmate? They hadn't marked her as their mate, hadn't tried once in all the times they'd made love—they hadn't even mentioned wanting to. They could move on from her the way they had everyone else. And she would be alone again. No more of Ric's quiet intensity, no more wild laughter with Diego. Nothing. Despite their assurances that they would come with her if she left, this was a better indicator of their true feelings. They didn't have any for her, not really. There was nothing left to keep her here.

The tears flowed faster now as depression crashed the adrenaline her terror and rage had caused. Her shoulders bowed, and she turned to walk away. She climbed into the Jeep in silence. There really wasn't anything left to say. It hurt that they didn't want her, didn't listen to her. And it made her angry all over again . . . because they'd kicked down the protective walls around her, made her care, made her love again, and it was just because they *could*. They lived for the challenge, pitting themselves against the law and nature. It was one of the things she loved about them—and one of the things she hated with a passion.

She didn't speak the entire ride home, tried to keep her sobs as quiet as possible, but she couldn't seem to stop crying. Ric and Diego were smart enough not to say a word. She might have killed them herself if they had.

The car was still rocking to a stop when she unsnapped her seat belt and jumped out. She raced for the house, wanting nothing more than to lock herself away until she could find a way to deal with the terror streaking through her. Diego's close call still replayed in her mind on an endless loop that made her stomach heave.

She hurried into the house, flinging the door shut with more force than any human could manage. It didn't give the resounding slam she was hoping for, and she spun to see Ric had caught it in his hand. The twins followed her in, wariness stamped on their faces. "Isabel—"

"*No.*" She sliced her hand through the air, her chest heaved with every tortured breath, and tears still streaked down her cheeks. She didn't bother wiping them away. "This is too much. It's not safe for me to stay here with Enrique hunting me down and causing problems, and you said you would protect me, but how can I trust either of you for that if you're willing to take these insane risks with *your* lives? This is the last straw. If the two of you want to kill yourselves, I obviously can't stop you. You don't give a damn about yourselves so why would you care if you terrify me? So, you know what? Go ahead. But don't expect me to stay around and watch. Or worse yet, have to clean up the mess when you splatter yourselves across some mountainside. I have already lost everyone and everything that ever mattered to me. I know exactly how it feels, and I won't do it again. Not even for my mates."

With that, she spun on her heel and narrowly missed colliding with Antonio. He looked furious. Oh, God, she couldn't deal with explaining why she'd made a scene. She just couldn't handle any more today. He could yell at her later—if he caught her before she finished packing and leaving. She twisted away from his reaching hand and bolted up the stairs as fast as her legs would carry her, passing more than one curious Panther along the way until she slammed into the suite.

She locked every door. The twins could sleep in their office for all she cared. Stripping off her bathing suit, she threw it in a heap on the floor and curled into the middle of the bed that still smelled of the three of them. She tucked her knees to her chin and quit fighting the tears that wouldn't stop. She would pack in the morning and be gone. This was the end of her little fairy tale. Two princes and no happily ever after for her. She sobbed, her heart breaking into a million pieces. Her body shook with each ragged breath, and she cried until sleep claimed her, tears still wet on her cheeks.

His father was right about him. Diego felt sick. He was as useless and stupid as Esteban had always claimed. The adventurous escape from his problems that Diego had used for more than half of his life was what cost him his mate. Not time, or some faceless enemy, but *him*. His need to blow off steam with dangerous pastimes had driven her away.

She was leaving.

The realization hit him like a punch to the gut. It hurt so bad he almost doubled over and howled. His twin was never going to forgive him for this. It was all his fault, and they were both going to suffer for it. Somewhere in the back of his mind, he always knew he'd blow it. She was just too good, too sweet. Too amazingly perfect for them. It had been too easy to have one mate when they preferred women that way.

He loved her. That was the damnable part. He was so freaked out to lose her because she ran from Enrique—and them in the process—that he'd needed a rush to burn off the fear. So he'd taken a crazy cliff dive, knowing it was dangerous, but needing the danger anyway. Now Isabel was going to run from them all. Guilt corroded his insides like acid. Maybe she would let Ric go with her. Diego knew he didn't even deserve to have a second chance with her—the way he'd terrified her sickened him. He'd seen that horrified look on her face when she talked about Spain, but to have it directed at him . . . His eyes slid closed for a moment, and he swallowed, trying not to vomit.

"Ric. Diego. I want you both in my office." Antonio jerked his chin toward the door, looking more like their father than he ever had before. *"Now."*

By the way his older brother's nostril flared and the veins throbbed in his neck, Diego had no doubt the Pride leader was beyond pissed.

Shit.

He followed the other men into the office and closed the door behind them. Straightening to attention, he faced Antonio over his desk.

Anger made the older man vibrate, and his fists clenched as he set his fists against the polished wooden surface. "Does someone want to explain to me what the hell happened today and why your mate is in hysterics?"

"She's not in—"

He hissed, and Diego shut his mouth.

"Can you deny that she's crying and upset about your antics today? *Dios mio,* you two. I thought when you found your mate you would settle down a bit, slow down with some of this reckless behavior."

"We are who we are, Antonio." The words came out of Diego by rote. Numbness crawled through him. It didn't matter what his older brother might say about him or what he'd done today. None of it mattered. He'd already fucked up the best thing that had ever happened to Ric and him. What adrenaline rush could compare to Isabel? In a way, he'd betrayed the two most important people in his life just by being himself.

Antonio kept speaking, obviously struggling to get his temper under control, and Diego just let the words roll over him. "I'm not saying you have to give up the skydiving and snowboarding and all the other shit you do, but you act like your lives are easily replaced, like you're disposable."

Diego met Ric's gaze, and the history they shared was there. Which one of them was going to tell the ugly truth? Talking was always Diego's specialty, so he opened his mouth. "We are disposable."

"What?"

Ric swallowed. "We *are* disposable. Father made it very clear from the time we were thirteen and Andrea left that he had no problem getting rid of us the way he had his older children. We were useless to the Pride, and we'd never amount to anything. Wastes of space."

"Not worth the air we breathed." Grim satisfaction slid through Diego as he said it. Who knew his father would be so right about his youngest son? He'd fought so long and so hard to prove he didn't give a damn what Esteban thought—and in the end, it didn't matter what he thought, it mattered what he himself did. He'd fulfilled that little prophecy, hadn't he? He choked back a bitter laugh.

His twin ran a hand through his hair. "Definitely not worth the time and energy we took up."

"So we stayed away as much as possible." Shrugging, Diego tried not to wince as the bruises and cuts on his body burned. No way had he caught a catnap in the Jeep with Isabel sobbing in the backseat. Each heaving breath had made him ache and want to reach for her, but he wasn't worthy to touch her. He was a total asshole. Focusing on Antonio, he made himself finish the story. "We started surfing and snowboarding. The first woman we . . . Well, she liked that there were two of us, and she liked walking on the wild side. She got us into it, and that's when we stopped trying to please him."

"But we also went to law school and suddenly we were useful. It was good to be . . . worth something." But even Ric didn't sound so certain. Some of the regret burning through Diego was reflected in his twin's expression. "We knew that he could always replace us. There are other Panthers who could do what we do. Father knew that . . . it was always clear to us as well."

"*Dios.*" The look on Antonio's face was nothing less than stunned. He choked and sank down in his chair.

Diego focused on his older brother, knowing how ugly this discussion was for him, how badly he'd take it. Antonio felt responsible for everyone, which is why the twins had never gone into detail about how their lives had been before he'd returned from the South American Pride. Now that it was out, Diego decided giving him the bald truth was kinder than trying to pretty it up. Reality was what it was. "We are disposable. It's not something anyone likes to hear, but that is reality. We aren't needed."

Antonio scrubbed his hands over his face, and for a moment Diego thought that there might be tears in his brother's eyes. "I should have found a way to stay . . . or I should have come back sooner, challenged Father for the leadership. I failed you both. Andrea, too, when it comes down to it."

"You were a kid when he sent you away, too." Ric reached over the desk and squeezed Antonio's shoulder.

He shook the comforting hand away and jerked to his feet. "I was twenty. Old enough to lead."

"He would have torn you apart. Not now, but then? Yeah." Diego stepped back as his brother rounded the desk toward them. They stood maybe half a head taller than him, but he was a huge man, built wide and powerfully. He didn't look like a king now, just a man in pain. Diego wasn't sure how much more grief he could cause the people he loved today without shredding inside. "At twenty, you were still dealing with Mom dying. So was Esteban. It would have been ugly for everyone. Maybe even civil war. But you know all this."

Yeah, they all know that civil war was a very real possibility in a Panther Pride. Each continent had a Pride of it's own, but until a few months before, Africa's Pride had been embroiled in a civil war that ripped it to pieces. The very idea that the same thing could have happened here was a horror he couldn't even contemplate after the emotional blows of today. He rubbed a hand over the hollow ache in his chest.

Antonio stepped in front of them, met each of their gazes in turn. "You are *not* disposable. Not to me. I can get new lawyers if you don't want to do that anymore. I can't get new brothers. You don't have to prove you're useful to me for me to keep you around. I love you both. And I can't stand that you've kept this from me for almost two years."

How could they have told him? It wasn't something to be proud of, that their father, who should have loved them the way Isabel's parents had loved her, had believed them worthless. They were extra children he didn't need. Most Panthers would kill to have four children. Hell, Carmen and Landon would kill to have just one. Panther cubs were rare and precious. What did it say about them that their father didn't think so and felt the need to tell them repeatedly for the last fifteen years of his life? On the one hand, he'd needed someone to take out his frustration and grief on with the loss of his mate and the scattering of most of his family. On the other, no man should do that to his children. Either way, this wasn't something the twins wanted to ever discuss with anyone. Especially not their recently returned siblings.

Antonio laid a hand on each of their shoulders, looking at Ric. "You don't have to work yourself into an early grave." He turned his gaze on Diego. "And *you* don't have to be so crazy that you end up getting yourself killed to prove you don't care if people think you're useless playboys." He shook them lightly. "Father is dead. Let him go."

Let him go. Was it really as simple as that? They were who they were, Diego had always said. But what if he wanted to change who he was? What if he wanted to be a man worthy of the respect that his brother offered, of the mate that fate had been kind enough to bless him with? He loved her; he wanted her forever. Why couldn't he learn to be good enough for her? It wasn't that he wouldn't be *himself* anymore, just that he didn't have to be the Diego that was constantly reacting to his father's opinion of him.

It was freeing to hear Antonio say the words. Diego had needed to hear them. He didn't *have* to be what his father had accused him of being. And he wasn't. He was loved, valued, *needed* for something more than his skills as a lawyer. Just because he was a member of this Pride, a Panther, and a brother to two good men. He suspected his father found it easier to push all of the people he loved away in order to avoid dealing with his mate's death.

As much as Diego could now sympathize with how the love for a woman could bring a man to his knees, he couldn't excuse what Esteban had done to all of his children. Antonio was right—their father was dead, and it was time to let him go and move on with life. Only a boy would hold out for the love of a father who wasn't the man he should have been. It was too late for Esteban to have a better relationship with his sons, even if he'd wanted one. But Diego was a man now, and he had a life of his own. A destiny that had looked very promising until a few hours ago. He had to find a way to get that back. Running a hand over the back of his neck, he pulled in a breath.

If he managed to keep Isabel happy and laughing the rest of her life, maybe she wouldn't notice that she might have been better off on her own. She filled up a hole inside of him that he hadn't even realized was there until she arrived. He thought everything was perfect with Ric and him shagging every woman they could get their hands on, but *perfect* was the quiet moments when Isabel sat between them, talking about her day. When they stripped her naked and made her scream. That was what he wanted for the rest of his life. If only he could convince her to give him a second chance. He didn't deserve it—or her—but he wanted it anyway. Even if she was better off without him, she'd never find anyone who loved her as much.

But first, he had to apologize and hope she would listen, forgive him, and let him explain why he'd acted the way he had. And believe him when he said he'd dial it down a notch so he wouldn't scare her. He never wanted to see that look on her face again—let alone be the one to put it there.

8

Ric watched Isabel's eyelashes flutter as she slowly awakened. They curled around her in their Panther forms. Diego's head lay on her shoulder with the end of his tail wrapping and un-wrapping around her calf. Ric let his tail fall over the side of the bed and rested his chin on her bare thigh. Neither he nor Deigo were inclined to wake her. Both of them had a great deal to think about.

Regret sliced through him like a blade. They'd scared her today and needed to make it up to her. There'd been several times he and Diego had gone over the line with their stunts, es-pecially Diego, but they'd gone through everything together, and Ric knew why his twin pushed himself so hard. The same way Diego knew why Ric pushed himself to the limit.

Perhaps they'd gotten too used to that, to no one trying to curb them or draw them back into the reality of what the right kind of behavior should be. Everyone who knew them knew they worked hard and played even harder. But Isabel hadn't known them for years—she came to them with an outsider's perspective. It was a perspective he'd learned to appreciate, and today had only reinforced that.

They'd been fighting their demons too long. Antonio was right about that. So long, in fact, that after the demon had died they went on fighting. He closed his eyes. Reality had returned with a rude awakening, but one they'd needed. One *he* had needed. The shell he'd been locked in for so long crumbled away. Who was he now? Still a lawyer, still one of the Cruz twins, but one who no longer needed to fight for his place in the Pride, to fight the stigma of useless throwaway his father had left him with. He was a man blessed with a wonderful mate, a family who liked him just as he was.

He was loved. And he loved in return. His family, his twin . . . and his mate. In the short amount of time he'd known her, she'd come to mean the world to him. He respected her, cherished her, but why hadn't he seen that he *loved* her? The depth of his need for her shook him. He'd never needed any woman in his entire life. He and his twin had always been two against the world—not really needed by anyone and needing no one but each other.

Isabel had changed all that. She'd broken down the barrier between them and the rest of their Pride and family. Made them all see how much they'd let the specter of their father haunt them. And yet, she let her own past haunt her as well. Something they'd have to deal with. Soon. For now, they needed to reconnect after the scare they'd given her.

A quick indrawn breath told him that she'd surfaced from sleep. "Wha—"

He broke into a rough purr, laying a paw on her leg to let her know he was there.

Laying her hands on each of their backs, she curled her fingers into their black fur. "I thought I locked the door."

His twin huffed out a breath that sounded almost like a laugh. As though they didn't have a key to their own suite. Just because they never locked the door didn't mean they couldn't get in. Hell, even if they didn't have a key . . . locks had never posed a problem for them.

Nothing was going to keep him away from his mate. He flexed his paw against her thigh, his claws digging into her soft flesh. She gasped, her gaze shooting to him just as Diego dragged his tongue down her shoulder until he licked her nipple. A shudder wracked her body, and he watched gooseflesh ripple over her limbs. He knew from experience how a Panther's cat tongue could rasp against the skin. The delicate scent of her dampening pussy reached his nose, and he couldn't help the quiet purr that soughed from his throat.

Her fingers clenched in their fur hard enough to make them both freeze. "Stop. I want you both in human form. We need to talk."

In a quick flash of heat and magic, he shifted into a man as his twin did the same. He sat up to face her, his cock already hard and aching with need, but he squelched the feeling and focused on her. She was right, they had to talk about what happened.

She looped her arms around her knees as she drew them up to conceal her ample breasts. What a shame. He struggled to hide a smile and met her gaze. The expression on her face made him sober abruptly. He stroked his fingers down the side of her calf and curled them around her ankle.

Diego sat up and swung his feet over the side of the bed. He scrubbed his hands over his face for a moment before he sighed and looked back at them. "I'm sorry, Isabel. I was a complete and total ass. I've spent the last fifteen years or so trying to prove that my father's poor opinion of me didn't mean anything. And you know what? The good opinion of you and Ric and the rest of the family is more important than anything Dad might have thought. Hell, my opinion of *myself* is more important."

Trying to keep the surprise off his face, Ric didn't bother hiding the smile this time. He reached over to clap his twin on the shoulder. "Glad you figured that out, bro."

Isabel leaned against Diego's back. She curled her fingers around his bicep and he laid his hand over hers. He glanced over to meet Ric's gaze for a moment before he looked back at their mate. "Being so insane that it scares the shit out of everyone I love isn't the kind of man I want to be. I'm not going to give up my hobbies, but even as extreme as they are, I can still be safe while I do them. What happened today—I will never do that to you again. I swear."

As much as he'd been willing to let his twin do whatever he needed to do, there were times Diego's antics had even scared Ric. He was glad to see that bottled anger—no matter how charmingly it was disguised to everyone else—dissipating. It was a relief.

He squeezed his twin's shoulder and his mate's ankle. "I'm sorry as well. I let things go too far in work and in play. It was easier to be a workaholic than it was to just admit my father was the one who was really fucked up. Because I could control *me*, but not his opinion of me." He pulled in a deep breath. "We've both tried so hard to prove we're not as useless as our father thought we were that we lost sight of the kind of men we should be. The kind of mates we should be to you. Forgive us?"

Tears shone in her honey-colored eyes, and she shook her head. For a second panic flashed through his belly. They'd said something wrong. She couldn't forgive them. He swallowed, pain ripping through him. What if she decided to run again? Could they really stop her? He doubted it. What would he do without her now? His heart contracted, and his eyes closed tight for a moment. They snapped open again when her hands cupped his jaw.

"Don't scare me like that again." Her lips twisted, the expression on her face more honest and vulnerable than he'd ever seen before. "My parents—it reminded me too much of that. Don't leave me alone. Not ever."

"We won't." Diego spoke for both of them, and Ric nodded his agreement. Relief unlike any he had ever known whipped through him.

She sat up and reached for him. He slid her away from his twin to kiss her, using the hand he still had on Diego's shoulder to pull him back and flatten him against the bed. He chuckled, knowing what was coming next, even if Isabel didn't. Ric lifted her slightly and swung her so that she straddled Diego's face.

His hands closed over her thighs, pulling her legs wide and lowering her until his mouth touched her pussy. She squeaked and tried to jerk away, but his fingers tightened to still her movements. After a moment, she moaned. Ric slid his arms around her torso until he cupped her breasts. She whimpered when he flicked his nails over the taut nipples and rolled the tips between his fingers. He pulled one hand back to push her hair out of the way so he could press his lips to the back of her neck. He opened his mouth, sucking on the tender flesh. His fangs slid forward and pricked her flesh. He wanted to mark her so badly it burned.

"Yes, Ric." Her voice was little more than a soft breath of air. He froze for a moment, certain he'd misheard her. He scored his fangs deeper into her skin, a silent question. She shivered. "Oh, my God, Ric. *Yes.*"

His instincts screeched in agreement, clawing at him to claim her, mark her, make her his forever. Heat flowed through his body, and his cock was steel hard. He couldn't hold back any longer and sank his fangs deep into the nape of her neck, flicking his tongue over the sweet flesh. She screamed, her body twisting in his arms. He felt her muscles quake in rhythmic spasms. The aroma of her increased moisture reached his nose, and he dragged the scent deep into his lungs.

When he released her, she moaned and tried to move away,

but Diego held fast, still sucking and lapping at her sex. She whimpered. "Diego, please."

He grunted, but didn't pause for a moment. Ric chuckled and stroked his fingers over her breasts to stimulate her, plucking and pulling at the tight nipples. Her breath caught, her body beginning to writhe again in the carnal rhythm of sex. A grin tugged at his lips. Time to expand her horizons a bit, just to make this game more interesting.

Keeping one hand moving over her full breasts, he ran his other palm down her back until he squeezed her buttocks. She had one of the prettiest asses he'd ever seen, lush and soft. He rolled his hand inward until his fingers reached her anus. She gasped when he sank two fingers in, groaned when he added a third. Oh, he wasn't even close to finished with her.

He began stroking inside her, widening her with each hard thrust. The muscles of her ass gripped him tight, but she pressed back into him to give him more access. The heat of her pulsed around his hand as he withdrew and slid back in with slow, measured plunges. He could hear every sob of her breath, every whimper and moan. The scent of sex and *her* permeated the air. He didn't think his dick had ever been this stiff in his entire life, but right now was about her . . . about pushing her past all her limits.

Planting a hand between her shoulders, he bent her forward so he could get a better angle and continued to shove his fingers deep into her ass. Her hands hit the mattress on either side of Diego's hip. He still suckled and nipped at her wet pussy. She hissed, the sound of a feral animal pushed too far. Her head turned to the side, and he watched her fangs extend. Then she sank them into the flesh that made up the lowest part of Diego's abdomen. Right beside his hard cock. His entire body went rigid, and then bucked beneath her. The sound he made was like a volcano erupting.

Ric scooped her up and off his twin to deposit her on the

floor on her knees. Holding her upper arms, he jerked his head at his brother. "Get behind her. Fuck her."

"You don't have to tell me twice." Diego was on his knees in less than a second. He jerked Isabel's thighs apart and thrust deep with one jolting push. She moaned, shoving back against him. Ric let go of her arms, and her back arched like a cat in heat as her body rocked to the rhythm his twin set.

"Suck me," he growled. She peeked up at him through her lashes, sparks of gold flashing in her eyes. A coy grin curved her lips. He loved that. She was two parts bold to one part shy. He couldn't get enough of her. And she was *his.* He'd marked her, mated with her.

Her fingers wrapped around his hard cock, stroking up and down the shaft. Her tongue flicked out to taste the head, and he slipped his hands into her silky hair. The hot wetness of her mouth closed around his dick, and she sucked him deep inside. He rolled his hips, thrusting in as her tongue worked over the length of his cock.

Her hands lifted to hold his hips, then slid around to clench into his ass. She pulled him forward so that he pushed deeper into her mouth. His teeth ground together when he felt the back of her throat contract around the head of his cock. "Oh, *fuck.* Isabel."

Christ, she was good at this. He felt her chuckle, and it vibrated up the length of his cock. Only by concentrating hard did he manage not to come then and there. He wanted this to last. He choked on a breath when her fingers parted his ass cheeks to swirl around his anus.

A hiss slid from his mouth as fire licked at his flesh when she pushed a finger inside him. Excitement ripped through his system, and his skin felt too hot and too tight. Her slim finger pumped into his ass to the same tempo that his cock pumped between her soft, full lips. He groaned, his fingers gripping her hair tightly as he held her in place. Watching his cock disappear into her mouth was the hottest thing he'd ever seen.

Pulling back a bit, she sucked just the head of his cock. Her head tilted as she let him slide free of her mouth and ran her tongue down the underside of his dick. His only warning was the momentary flash of her eyes burning to brilliant gold before her head whipped to the side and her fangs sank into his lower belly. At the same time her fingers pressed inward to stroke over his prostate. A Panther's scream ripped from his throat as he had no choice but to come. It boiled forth to shoot from his balls, and fire fisted in his gut. His cock jerked in the air as he came all over her face and breasts.

His chest heaved with every tortured breath, and another wave of orgasm shuddered through him as he looked down at the mark she'd left on him. He blinked for a moment, then chuckled. The little witch had bitten him in the same place she'd marked Diego, only upside down. He doubted anyone would really be able to tell the difference once they healed. It looked like they'd still be identical twins. Unlike most injuries, a mate mark left a scar on a Panther—their magic didn't allow it to disappear or fade. They would wear her marks just as she would wear theirs. Forever. The thought made him purr. She undeniably belonged to them, and it was so damn good.

She whimpered, drawing his attention. Diego's eyes went gold before he pressed his forehead to her back. He pistoned in and out of her from behind, his tongue trailing up her spine, and his mouth closed over the point of her shoulder blade.

Ric dropped to his knees and pulled her hair out of his brother's way, fisting his hand in the long blond strands. He jerked her head up, shoving his tongue into her mouth. She moaned, her lips molding to his as they shared a fierce kiss. They nipped and bit at each other, and the tang of blood flooded his tongue. His or hers, he didn't know and didn't care, but it called to the deep, feral Panther within him.

His claws extended, and he raked them up the inside of her thighs. Her muscles tensed beneath him and she shuddered, whimpering in his mouth. He slid a finger inward to roll over the hard nub of her clit. Diego's hammering thrusts moved her on Ric's finger.

Her cries vibrated against his lips, gaining in intensity. He felt her body jolt when Diego bit her shoulder blade. They both groaned as they came. The scent of her wetness filled Ric's nostrils, and she broke away from his mouth, screaming. Her body arched, writhing as her pussy contracted.

Ragged breathing filled the room. Tears slid down her cheeks, and he let go of her hair to wipe them away with his thumb. "Diego . . . Ric . . ."

"Shh. Shh." He gathered her into his embrace, burying his face in her neck. He whispered in her ear, "I love you."

He had to say it—the words wouldn't stay contained. Her arms wound around his neck, hugging him tight as she shuddered and cried. The wetness of her tears dampened his skin and he stroked her soft hair and rocked her from side to side. Diego rubbed his hand up and down her back, crooning softly to their mate.

Mate. God, the word gripped Ric tight and wouldn't let go. He was mated. Emotion exploded inside him and he closed his eyes, pulling her even closer. Her sobs quieted, and her breathing slowed. He felt her eyelashes flutter against his skin, and her body went soft and pliant in his arms. "Sleep. We have you. We love you."

He'd never spoken any truer words in his life. It was so good, so perfect. Contentment shimmered through him, a quiet peace he'd never experienced before settling over him. He squeezed his eyes closed tight and let himself savor the feeling. This. *This* was what he'd always wanted. Belonging. The kind of deep, unshakeable belonging that he hadn't even been sure existed. Until now. With Isabel. He and Diego had been born belonging to each other, and their life experiences had only cemented that for them.

But with Isabel, it was something else. An inner balance that he and his twin had never managed alone. Gratitude twisted together with the love and contentment that flooded his soul. Thank God she'd come when she had. Thank God they had her now. No matter what horror had brought her here, he was grateful for it. He couldn't live without her ever again.

9

_____

The look on Antonio's face could chill the blood. When all that charisma fell away and the fangs came out, he was a terrifying sight to behold. Isabel didn't know how his mate handled that, but she was glad she only had the twins to contend with. She'd left her new mates sleeping in bed and come down to the kitchen for a cup of coffee. She'd been sitting at the stainless-steel-topped island, enjoying the rare moment at the end the workday when the kitchens were empty, when the Pride leader came storming in to tell her the Garcias had called again. They'd offered veiled threats to the North American Pride if she wasn't returned immediately, which explained Antonio's foul mood. She could only be grateful they weren't yet foolish enough to enter another Pride's territory without permission. That was coming, she knew.

And she didn't intend to let it happen.

She met his gaze and dredged up as much calm courage as she could. "We have to deal with Enrique. The twins and I are mated—this can't go on. I'm not going to run from him anymore, especially if it means dragging my mates along until he finds me and things end violently."

"Good. One of the twins would have no problem handling him—he's pretty much fucked if he has to face both of them after he's threatened their mate." He sniffed, a reluctant smile parting his lips as his fangs retracted. "It might be fun to watch, though."

"I hope I don't have to, but you're right." A shiver of dread ran through her. "Enrique is a pathetic excuse of a man, especially compared to my mates."

"True." Folding his arms, he pulled in a deep breath, a contemplative look on his face. "There seems to be a rash of activity in the Panther world today. I got another phone call just before the lovely one from your instinctually handicapped admirer."

She snorted, for the first time able to find something to laugh at about the entire situation with the Garcias. Standing, she poured Antonio a cup of coffee and motioned him onto a stool across from hers.

Sipping the steaming coffee, he heaved an appreciative sigh. "Cesar Benhassi has called a meeting of the Prides to officially recognize his leadership. Pride leaders or their official representatives need to convene in Africa at the end of the week. Normally, I'd send Miguel . . . he has a gift for political strategy."

Even though she knew she was stating the obvious, she spoke up anyway. "He's on his honeymoon."

He nodded. "I'll just have to go myself. Though I've toured all the other Prides, I haven't been to Africa."

"Don't be ridiculous. You have an eight-week-old baby . . . you can't leave your mate now." Diego stepped into the room, his bare feet padded against the tile floor, and he shook his head at his brother. "No, the three of us will go."

"The *three* of us?" Isabel's eyebrows arched. The idea of

representing a Pride was more than a little intimidating, but since she was mated to members of a ruling family, it was something she knew she'd have to get used to. Better to start now and avoid dragging it out for herself, right?

Ric followed on his twin's heels and met her gaze. "Enrique will probably come with his father or in his father's place."

A colder and more calculating smile than she had ever seen before crossed Diego's face. "Let him come."

"You *want* him to be there." Her heart sank, and her stomach twisted into tiny knots. She tried to hold on to her calm, tried not to panic. She wasn't alone anymore—she had mates who loved her. Their marks had remained on her flesh even after she'd slept, so no one could deny what that meant, even if it was unheard of to have two mates. Would she ever be free to love them in return, to be worthy of that love, if she didn't confront her demons the way they had theirs? For her? She closed her eyes and tried not to vomit. God help her, she wasn't sure she could. Sucking in a deep breath, she opened her eyes and faced her mates. They had the kind of understanding in their gazes that she'd never imagined finding in one man, let alone two. They knew exactly what this meant to her, how much it scared her, and they were going to be at her side when she did what she had to do.

"Fine. We can handle whatever comes up. Let's go." She took a sip of her coffee and kept her gaze glued to the countertop.

No more running. She'd been on the run since her parents died. First to Paris to escape the grief of losing her family, and then from Enrique to escape his unwanted advances. She'd gotten so used to running away from her problems that she'd almost forgotten what it was like to face them head on. It embarrassed her how terrified she was to do so, but if she wanted a normal life with her mates—or as normal as a woman with two adventurous Panther males in her life could have—then this was the only way to get it. Confront Enrique openly if he tried to continue his claims.

Despite her earlier brave words, her stomach roiled as they prepared for the official recognition ceremony in Casablanca three days later. She hadn't slept, had barely eaten. She knew her mates noticed, but wisely neither of them had commented. Shaking herself, she forced her attention back to the task at hand. Getting dressed for the meeting of the most powerful people in the Panther world. Her stomach executed another quick flip at the thought.

The dress she wore looked very conservative from the front and was fitted to the knees before it flared out like a mermaid's tail to the floor. The black satin cut straight across her collarbone to cling to the very edge of each of her shoulders. Then it dove into a daring vee all the way to the small of her back. The gown made her feel sexy. She piled her hair high on her head and left a few loose curls hanging down her bare back and over her shoulder.

Slipping on a pair of black pearl stud earrings that used to belong to her mother, she felt a pang when she thought about her lost family. She pulled in a shaky breath, bittersweet emotions winding through her. What would her mother think of all of this? What she'd been through and done in the past year? Enrique and then her *two* mates? Her mother would have liked the twins, she was sure. It was too bad they would never meet, but she could appreciate even more now that it was best her parents died together. She hoped they were at peace, and she accepted that she would always miss them, but she needed to focus on the future. A future with her mates.

She smoothed her hands over the slippery satin that covered her hips, checking her reflection one last time. A smile curved her lips when Ric stepped up behind her, and she saw him in the mirror, his dark hair combed back neatly, his big body encased in a black tuxedo. He looked delicious. Her wild mates cleaned up well. A rush of emotion raced through her . . . she adored them so much, she didn't know how she could handle all the feelings they seemed determined to drag out of her.

Spreading her hands, she arched a brow at Ric. "Andrea sent it when she got back from her honeymoon yesterday. Do you like it?"

"Oh, yeah." He stroked his fingertips down her bare spine, heat sparking in his gaze.

Diego stepped out of the bathroom fastening a bowtie around his neck. He winced and tugged at it as though it were strangling him, and she laughed up at him. He bent forward to press a quick kiss to the side of her neck. "You look amazing."

"You two look pretty damn amazing, too." She turned back to the mirror to take a last look, and paused to admire the reflection of the two of them flanking her. "When this is over I can't wait to strip those tuxes off you and make you fuck me until I scream."

Diego groaned and leaned around her to look at Ric. "Remind me again why we *have* to go?"

"Enrique."

His name was like ice water going down her spine. She shivered. The mix of a hundred Panthers' scents filtered through the Africa Pride, and one of them belonged Enrique. She couldn't help the dread that automatically flowed through her at the familiar stench of him. Before she could lose her nerve, she snatched up her evening bag and walked toward the door. "Okay, let's go."

A fist poised to knock drew her up short when she opened the door. She took a few quick steps back and would have tripped over the hem of her dress if Ric hadn't caught her. She glanced back at him, but he smiled a greeting at the large man standing in the doorway.

"Ricardo Cruz. This is my brother, Diego, and our mate, Isabel."

"Welcome." The man offered a quiet smile and a solid handshake to the three of them. He had dark skin and black eyes, and his wild salt-and-pepper hair reminded her of a lion's mane. "Antonio told me to expect you. Congratulations on your Pride's new heir."

Ric nodded. "Thank you."

"Oriana is a beautiful name. I'm so pleased for your family." A tiny woman with smooth chocolate skin that belied the silver streaks in her hair stepped around Benhassi. "I am Nerea Benhassi, Cesar's mate."

She gave them a warm, welcoming grin and pulled each of them into a hug. Her arm looped through Isabel's as she drew them into the hallway. One of the Pride members had escorted them to their suite when they'd arrived so Isabel hadn't had time to explore the large white stucco mansion. She found their rooms had the same creamy plaster walls and carved wooden ceilings as the rest of the Pride's den. It was stunning inside with sculpted plaster moldings, stone columns, and marble floors. But the mosaics through the house were what were most incredible.

On the flight over, the twins had told her that their research showed that Benhassi was a successful businessman in the human world, and this house was an outward showcase of his wealth. She had to admire a man who would give up his independence to serve his people. She wasn't sure it was a choice she'd willingly make. But, then, she hadn't been raised to rule—and there was no telling what a person would do when his family became embroiled in a civil war that led to near genocide and a diaspora that separated them from their homeland. She was glad she hadn't had to live through what these people had.

"My mate tells me you're a chef."

She blinked and focused on the woman beside her. "Yes, I am."

"I am, too. I met Cesar when I was cooking for the Australian Pride. He wanted to offer the chef his compliments while he was visiting relatives that settled there after the war." A musical laugh rippled from the petite woman. "I got a bit more than his compliments."

It surprised Isabel to find Nerea so . . . normal. Logically, she knew that Pride leaders mated with Panthers not in other leading families. Solana used to be a regular Pride member, but until the twins, Isabel had always seen those in ruling families as larger than life somehow, and what had happened with Enrique had only served to reinforce her conception of them. Her interactions with the Cruz family has humanized them for her, but it was good to know that leaders outside of North America were approachable, especially since she'd have to get used to spending time with them. Her life had changed so much over the past weeks—in good ways, she reassured herself. Everything that had happened was for the best. She just had to take care of one last little detail. Right. No problem.

Nerea continued with her stream of quiet conversation. "First mint tea in Cesar's office, and then we'll serve dinner in an hour. I put together a menu of local cuisine. Have you ever tried *kaab el ghzal?*"

Isabel had heard of it, but wracked her brain to remember what the dish consisted of. "It's a dessert pastry, right?"

"Filled with almond paste and topped with sugar. It's a pastry traditionally served at celebrations, like the ceremony tonight for my mate." Nerea's sweet voice took on a stern bite, and Isabel had no doubt that everything would go smoothly . . . or else.

Cesar glanced back and gave her a wink. "*Kaab el ghzal* translates into 'gazelle horns,' though it looks more like a crescent moon. Well, you'll see. Nerea's recipe is the best."

"I can't wait to try it." She offered him a grin and patted Nerea's hand. "Tell me about your children. You have two sons, isn't that right?"

"Oh, yes." Her tone warmed again, and she spent the remainder of the walk to the office chatting easily about her boys and their transition back to the African Pride.

It gave Isabel time to panic again. Enrique's scent came closer and closer as they went, so she knew he awaited them in Cesar's office. Oh. Sweet. God. Her breathing sped until she was almost panting. Beads of sweat gathered on her forehead and under her arms. She swallowed and tried to remind herself the twins were near, and they wouldn't let Enrique touch her ever again. No more running.

Pulling herself up as they reached the door, she drew a deep breath and set her shoulders. She had to do this. And not just for the twins, but for herself. This was a fear she had to face, and it was more powerful than any one man could be. She wouldn't live her life in terror. Not anymore. She smiled at Cesar when he opened the door for her. He held out his arm for Nerea while the twins stepped forward to flank Isabel and set proprietary hands on each of her shoulders as they entered the room. It was full of Panthers, but her gaze went straight to the Spanish contingent. To Enrique.

He was . . . shorter than she remembered. He actually had the gall to step forward and offer his hand with a flourish as though she should come to him. He didn't even spare her mates a glance. Rage, hot and wild, exploded inside her. She'd never felt anything like it—it was terrifying in its ability to burn away the last of her fear of this man. Lifting her lip in a sneer, she gave him a look filled with all of the contempt she had for him.

His face mottled with ugly red spots, and he stepped closer to hiss at her. "It's good of you to come to your senses and join me here, mate."

She lifted her chin. He really was delusional, but that wasn't her fault . . . or her problem. "I'm here with my mates. Neither of them are you. You're quite wrong about me."

"What's going on here?" Cesar appeared at Enrique's side, and Isabel could hear the hushed whispers of the other Panthers in the room as they took notice of the scene unfolding before them. This incident would be all over the Panther world by morning, so she'd better make sure it went well for her Pride.

A sense of confident calm she didn't know she possessed slid over her. She looked Cesar in the eyes and spoke in a clear, carrying voice. "Enrique Garcia has the mistaken impression that I'm his mate. He attacked me when I was under the protection of his family as a member of the European Pride, so I sought asylum in North America. That's were I met my true mates, Diego and Ricardo Cruz."

Enrique hissed a low, dangerous warning. "That's a lie. She's *mine*. I bit her . . . marked her as my mate. You can check for yourself."

She felt the twins close in on her, but she held up a hand to still their approach. She could feel the frustration vibrating through their big bodies, but they obeyed her. If Enrique tried to attack her, she knew nothing would stop them from protecting her, but this was something she had to do for herself. She loved them for understanding that without her having to tell them. They'd probably guessed it before she had. She focused on Enrique.

"We are not mates. All you did was assault me." She jerked the edge of her gown down to reveal her collarbone. "Look. If you were my mate, the mark would still be there—it wouldn't have healed." She spun, pulling the loose curls out of the way to show the back of her neck and shoulder blade. "*These* are mate marks, and they didn't come from you. I swear to God this man is not my mate. Diego and Ric are my mates. I will have no others."

"No one has two mates." A cruel smile crossed his face when she turned back around to face him. "Besides, if you ever had children, you'd never know who the father was."

"Yes, I would. *Both* of my mates will be the father of my children." She arched a brow and gave him a scornful look. Whose children she bore was not his concern, and it was typical for him to sidestep the fact that he had hurt her and driven her from her home.

Ric spoke up behind her. "And our children will be Cruzes. Nothing else matters besides that."

"Keep telling yourself that when people call your child a bastard." Enrique's lips parted as he hissed, deigning for the first time to look at her mates. "She'll be tired of playing and come back to me soon enough."

"This is hardly appropriate, Garcia." Cesar's deep voice cut across the last of Enrique's words. "Anyone can see the mate marks on her."

Diego ignored the Pride leader and addressed Enrique. "Not all mates marry—their children aren't considered bastards and neither will ours be. But it's good that you acknowledge Isabel belongs to us. Only mates can have children."

His eyes bulged with rage as he realized how Diego had trapped him. The whispers in the room rose to a cacophony of voices, which were drowned out by Enrique's scream of rage. Spittle flew from his mouth as his veneer of control fled. It was the same look he'd worn just before he'd attacked her in Barcelona, and Isabel's stomach turned when he began to rave. "She's *mine*. I sensed it. No one else can have her! Mine, mine, *mine*."

He lunged for her, claws and fangs bared, but she was ready for him this time. Not like the last time he'd touched her, pinned her down, bitten her. Her own claws shot out and she raked them down his cheek, leaving streaks of dark crimson.

Ric pulled her out of the way as Diego's fist connected with Enrique's jaw. His head snapped back, and the last thing Isabel saw was shock widening his eyes before they rolled back, and he collapsed to the floor. She clung to Ric's broad shoulder, panting for breath as adrenaline shot through her system. Her heart pounded so loudly in her ears it overwhelmed the shouts from the gathered Panthers for long moments.

Cesar turned to Enrique's father, righteous anger overtaking his previously implacable façade. "Fernando, your heir is clearly insane. And I have no doubt that this woman speaks the truth when she says he's attacked her before. Under *your* roof. Do you honestly think the Prides wouldn't find out he's mad . . . or did you hope to foist him off as a leader among our kind after you died?"

"I . . . I . . ." Fernando's face mottled the same shade of red his son's had as he looked desperately for some support among his peers. None was forthcoming.

The African Pride leader hammered home his point. "If someone tried to force your heir to step down it could have caused a civil war. Haven't *my* people shown exactly what can happen to a Pride with internal struggles for power?"

Resignation slid over the Spaniard's face, making him look decades older as he glanced around again. "You all stand as witness to my words. I formally denounce my son as my heir and give such honors to my second-born child, my daughter, Teresa. I also acknowledge and accept this man, Cesar Benhassi, as the true and rightful leader of the African Panther Pride."

Motioning to a few of his advisors, they picked up the fallen Enrique and left the room. The air seeped out of Isabel's lungs when the door shut behind them. Exhaustion rolled over her in a wave, and she realized how badly she'd been sweating and that Enrique's blood had splattered over her dress and face.

Ric cleared his throat and intoned quietly. "The North American Panther Pride acknowledges and accepts this man, Cesar Benhassi, as the true and rightful leader of the African Panther Pride."

The phrase was echoed around the room until Cesar's place had been recognized by every Pride in the world. Even though he'd called the meeting for just this purpose, he looked stunned for a moment. Nerea stepped forward and placed her hand on his arm. "All this excitement is most . . . unexpected. Why don't we adjourn to the dining room? I find nothing settles me the way good food does."

The couple led the way out of the room, and as they passed, Isabel spoke softly. "I'll need to clean up before I join you."

Nerea nodded to indicate she'd heard, but she remained poised and smiled, pretending as though nothing upsetting had happened. She turned to chat with the Australian Pride leader's delegate, an older woman with solid-white hair.

When everyone was gone, Isabel slipped out and walked back to her room. She was aware that her mates followed her, but her mind spun in dizzying circles. It was over. It was really over. Months and months of terror had ended so quickly. So simply. It was almost anticlimactic. None of the other Pride leaders had disbelieved her; no one had claimed she couldn't possibly have two mates. She dragged in a deep breath as she walked through the door of their rooms. The scent of Enrique's blood curled in her nostrils.

She blinked and looked down, reality returning with a jolt. "My dress is ruined. And it was a gift from your sister. She's going to kill me—it's a *designer gown.*"

Diego snorted as he shut the door. "You know a woman is fine when she starts to worry about her clothes."

"Oh, stop. I'm not obsessed with clothes, but it was a present." She flapped a hand at him, and relief bloomed inside her. By not protesting, the most powerful Panthers in the world had acknowledged her mating as much as they had Cesar's leadership. Everything would be all right. A huge grin split her face until her cheeks ached. Tears welled in her eyes, and she spun around to hurry into the bathroom. She couldn't believe it. Her nightmare was over. She didn't know what to do with the intense joy that exploded inside her. "I'll, um, wash off, and we can get back to the party. Give me just a minute."

Stripping off her gown, she flipped on the spray in the huge mosaic tiled shower. She hopped inside and closed the glass door behind her. The rainbow of colored tiles flecked with gold blurred before her eyes. The shades oddly reflected her mood, and the giggle that bubbled out of her bordered on hysterical. Plucking the pins out of her hair, she let them drop to the floor, turned her face into the spray, and washed the blood off of her body.

"Isabel." Diego's voice rang through the bathroom, and she could sense that both men had entered the room.

She shoved her wet hair out of her eyes. "I'll be out in—"

The glass door opened with a gust of wind that made her shiver. She twisted around and found Ric and Diego crowding into the shower with her. It had seemed so much larger a moment before, but they dwarfed the space. They were naked . . . and hard. Her gaze dropped to their cocks before moving to the mate marks she'd left beside them. Possession flooded her being as passion flooded her body.

"We don't want you to come out, mate. We want to come inside . . . you." Diego's smile was as naughty as his words.

Pressing her palms to her belly, she squeezed her thighs together to try and quench the ache between them. Her breasts felt heavy, the tips tingling. Her voice emerged a breathless whisper. "It looks like we won't be making it back for dinner."

"Too bad." Ric's ebony gaze slid over her curves. She barely held back a whimper of need. She took a step toward him, and his hand snapped out to wrap around her wrist. Her breath caught as his hands moved to cup her breasts. His claws slid forward to rake over her hardened nipples. The water from the shower rolled in slow beads down their bodies, and she shivered at the mix of sensations.

She arched toward his touch. "Kiss me."

"No." Diego's breath brushed over her cheek as he closed in behind her, his hard cock rubbing the cleft of her ass. "We like you like this, ready for us to fuck any time we want to. You're wet. I can smell it."

Every time she thought she'd grown used to the things that came out of Diego's mouth, he surprised her. It never failed to get her hot. She swallowed when his hand slid down her back to cup her ass. "Please."

"Are you begging, Isabel?"

Her teeth clenched when his hand slipped between her legs from behind. His touch made her want to scream. She moved with his fingers, her empty sex clenching on nothingness. Liquid heat dampened her pussy, and she could feel her slick lips seal together. Arching her back, she bent her neck over Diego's shoulder and pushed her breasts toward Ric's stroking palms. She was burning up inside, her fangs slid forth as the feral animal inside her clawed for sexual release. She was going to die if she didn't get some relief soon. Choking on a breath, she twisted her fingers into Ric's hair so he couldn't escape. "I need you."

"Well, that's nice, but it's not what we want to hear from you." Diego chuckled, taunting her with his touch.

He wanted to hear that she loved them. She'd been holding back, afraid to take that final step until she'd confronted Enrique. Until she was worthy, and she knew she had the courage to stop running away. Stupid of her. Love wasn't something a person could be *worthy* to give or receive. It just was.

She opened her mouth to tell them when Ric sucked her nipple between his lips, biting down lightly on the taut crest. A cry ripped from her throat. Her thoughts scattered under the onslaught of sensations. The mist from the shower cooled on her flesh, making her shiver and moan. She felt as though her skin were on fire. Diego's palm closed over her shoulder, pushing her to her knees. He bent down to speak into her ear. "You know what would be really hot right now?"

She whimpered when he paused, drawing out the moment. Whatever he said was going to be wicked, and a million possibilities raced through her mind, each more daring than the last—just as she was sure he intended. "Tell me."

"Touch yourself." They pulled away from her, but Diego kept speaking. "Watching you please yourself would be the sexiest fucking thing I've ever seen. I want you to fondle your creamy lips and play with your hard clit until you're almost ready to come."

"And then stop. Don't come without us." Ric settled against the shower wall in front of her, his muscular arm propped on an upraised knee.

God, he was gorgeous. They both were, and she wanted them. She would do anything for them. She bit her lip and let her hand drop to her midriff, slid her fingertips down until they circled her bellybutton, moved over the lower swell of her stomach, and into the soaked curls between her thighs. Her muscles jerked at the direct contact, and the feel of water slipping down her skin became a sensual pleasure that added to the ecstasy rolling through her. She did exactly as Diego suggested, moved over her slick lips, and flicked her nail over her clit. Her hips swayed, bucking with the quick rhythm her hands set. She was so hot. Her gaze traveled over her mates' bodies. Diego's long fingers grasped his cock. A second later, Ric rolled his palm over the broad head of his dick. Each man lounged on the shower floor before her, gazes hungry as they watched her movements.

The sight of both men fondling themselves was beyond erotic. She moved her fingers into her pussy at the same rhythm as they pumped their cocks. Her knees widened, sliding against the slick tiles. The heat of the shower water was nothing to the inferno building inside her. Her sex clenched around her stroking digits. The waves of pleasure that crashed through her had her hips arching into her hand. Little moans spilled from her throat until it was too much to bear. "I'm going to come."

"Stop," Diego's command snapped out, and she sobbed for breath as she obeyed. Her hands curled into fists and her claws bit into her palms, but she barely noticed the sting. Her body shook with the longing coursing through her veins. He turned to his twin. "Ric, stretch out."

Ric nodded and obeyed, laying flat beneath the pounding spray of the shower. She watched water pool in his bellybutton and slip over the rippling muscles in his chest and abs. Her gaze locked on his cock, flushed deep red and quivering with every panting breath he took. She didn't wait for Diego's next instruction. She crawled forward until she could swing her leg over Ric's thighs and straddle him. His dick prodded at the opening of her pussy, and she sank down on the long shaft. She was beyond coherency; she just wanted to come. Tensing the muscles in her legs, she lifted and lowered herself to ride his thick cock.

Diego's hands closed over her hips, stopping her. She twisted to get away. She needed to *move.* "No!"

"Shh." He urged her forward slightly, his hands sliding down to part her ass cheeks. She shoved herself back into his touch as his cock pressed into her anus. The stretch was painful, and she wasn't ready for him, but she didn't care. The pain almost made it better, more erotic. All she wanted was more of them.

She drove her hips forward to take Ric's cock to the hilt, then rammed back to accept Diego's thrust. They built a steady tempo, their bodies in perfect time with each other. It was incredible. There wasn't a moment she wasn't filled by one of them, and she loved it. Everything inside her screeched for more,

more, *more.* The ecstasy streaked through her again, only this time it was better, more intense. She picked up speed, and they were with her the entire time, responding automatically. Diego's arms came around her from behind to stroke her breasts, chafing her nipples almost roughly. She cried out, then gasped when Ric reached down to caress her clit, flicking his thumb over the hard nub. It was too much. It was just enough to push her over the edge into orgasm. "Ric! Diego!"

Ric's fingers bit into her hips as he pulled her tight against the base of his cock and came hard inside her. Tingles raced over her skin, and pure fire followed in their wake. Her sex contracted tightly again and again, her ass closing tight around Diego's cock. He moved in and out of her anus with punishing speed, his stomach spanking against her ass until he froze and released into her as well. She felt the heated jet of his seed as he filled her ass. It made her pussy fist again in an aftershock of orgasm. Her body shook and tears mingled with the mist on her face as sparks ricocheted through her system. It was so good. It had never been this wonderful for her before, not even with them. "Oh. My. God."

They collapsed in a pile of intertwined limbs. Diego scooted until he had her sandwiched between his body and Ric's. Their bellowing breaths were the only sound to be heard over the hiss of water from the shower.

"Talk about a great end to the evening. That was fucking awesome." Diego folded his hands behind his head. Ric threw an arm over his eyes and groaned a chuckle. He brought his arm back down to watch while Isabel laughed until she had to hold on to her sides.

God, she loved them. No one would ever fulfill her, understand her, *love her,* the way they did. She struggled to catch her breath, needing to tell them. The last of the loneliness she'd known since her family died slipped away like the water running down the shower drain. A huge weight had lifted from her when she'd confronted her fears tonight. One that not even finding her mates could remove. She was *free*. Free to love and be loved, free to live her life.

She sat up and moved her hands to cup each of their strong jaws. "I love you, my mates. I love you both so much. I need you every day of my life."

"We need you, too." Diego's palm covered hers. "I love you."

"I love you, Isabel." Ric turned his head and kissed her fingers.

Diego grinned at her and then at Ric. "We have probably a day or two left of negotiating for trade rights here, but then I say we get permission from Cesar and take a few weeks to honeymoon in Africa. Ever wanted to go on a safari?"

She laughed, sweet contentment winding through her. She hugged them close, knowing that she might have run from the only home she'd ever known, but she'd found where she belonged with these two men. All she'd wanted was calm and normal, but the endless adventure they'd given her was so much more than she ever knew she could hope for. They filled in the missing parts of her, and it might not have been what she'd wanted, but it was what she needed.